Flight of Cranes

Flight of Cranes

by
Christine Brückner

Translated from the German by
Ruth Hein

FROMM INTERNATIONAL PUBLISHING CORPORATION
NEW YORK, NEW YORK

Originally published in 1977 as *Nirgendwo ist Poenichen*
Copyright © 1977, Ullstein Verlag GmbH, Frankfurt/Main—Berlin

Translation Copyright © 1982 by Fromm International Publishing
Corporation, New York, N. Y.

Printed in the United States of America

First U. S. Edition

Library of Congress Cataloging in Publication Data

Brückner, Christine, 1921–
Flight of cranes.

Translation of: Nirgendwo ist Poenichen.   I. Title.
PT2603.R7753N513   1982   833'.914   81-22176
ISBN 0-88064-001-4   AACR2

To my husband,

Otto Heinrich Kühner,

himself a writer,

who for five years shared with me

the life of the Quints,

advising and helping me.

Flight of Cranes

1

Maximiliane Quint was sleeping, flanked by her children, two on each side. She had arrived at her destination. Her sights had never been set too far. This particular goal was called the West. To make room for the children, she had folded her hand under her cheek. She was seven months pregnant.

Never again flights of cranes. Never again wild geese.

She was only one among untold millions who left the eastern territories of Germany ahead of the approaching Soviet troops. Now, in the autumn of 1945, Russian guards allowed batches of three or four thousand each night to cross the border into the British Zone of Occupation. In the dark these pilgrims passed through the woods, clutching their bundles. They hid from all figures in uniform as they crossed the "green frontier" over which the Iron Curtain would soon drop.

Maximiliane was lying on a makeshift cot in the unheated barn of a large estate. A few weeks more, and she would have given birth to her fifth child in a stable and laid it in a manger.

When she was christened in November 1918, old Baron Quindt, Maximiliane's grandfather, celebrated the event by donating a potbellied stove to the village church, of which he was the patron. Even then it was remarked that the baby girl had brought a little warmth to the world; later others were to say that any room grew several degrees warmer when she entered it. The first toast ever drunk to her, at her christening dinner, proclaimed, "Before God and the law, all children are equal." Her grandfather uttered it, with more foresight than he could have suspected—and he suspected a great deal.

That occasion, too, had been overshadowed by war, with Maximiliane's father away at the front, and her mother, young and longing for Berlin, marooned with her husband's parents in the farthest end of Pomerania, on Poenichen estate. Old Quindt, as the baron was universally known, had steadfastly devoted himself to his land, a link in the chain of Quindts who had farmed it for generations before him and who would, he had fully expected, farm it for generations to come. His heir's heir turned out to be a girl—Maximiliane—but this fact in no way lessened Old Quindt's joy and affection.

Perhaps the most memorable moment of the christening dinner came when Vera, the young mother, took the baby from her cradle and placed her in the emptied soup tureen—an unmistakable indication that the child represented her contribution to the survival of the estate. To this day the tureen, part of the valuable Courland service, was known as the christening bowl. Now it was preserved among the many household goods traveling away from Poenichen in the wagon train.

Of Maximiliane's father, Achim von Quindt, little more was preserved than a telegraphed triple "Hurrah, hurrah, hurrah"—his response to the triple set of letters announcing the birth of his first and only child just before he was killed during the final days of the First World War. The telegram was among the treasures in the small box her oldest child, Joachim, pressed close as he slept. In sleep you keep what you love by your

2

side—a child holds a doll; a man, his wife. Maximiliane had gone to sleep with her children at her side.

Details about her mother were almost as scarce. Maximiliane only knew that in 1935, Vera and her second husband, a Jewish physician named Grün, had fled to safer shores.

At the age of five Maximiliane had said to her grandfather in the broad Pomeranian dialect, "Grandpa, I wanna lot of kids." And he had replied, "Later." As it turned out, the event occurred not so very much later. Now, at twenty-seven, she was the mother of four and a half children, three of them by the same father, Viktor Quint. A loyal subject of his Führer, Adolf Hitler, Viktor had died the previous April, though the news had not reached his widow yet.

Joachim, the firstborn, was seven years old. Sometimes she called him Mose, a private pet name in memory of the golden day when the baby had floated on Lake Poenichen in a wicker basket. Nowadays Joachim, who was delicate and affectionate, struggled valiantly against his natural anxiety.

Then there was Golo, fearless and unruly, right now the best-looking of her children, with brown curls and the round, lively eyes of his mother. A Polish lieutenant had mysteriously managed to hand down these "saucer eyes" to what was now the fourth generation. For lack of a gun, Golo kept a stick by his side.

Next came Edda, who owed her Germanic name to the daughter of the former Reich Marshal. Viktor Quint was Edda's father, and though Maximiliane was not her mother, she had accepted and adopted this love child—more properly, a child of love for the Führer. Beside Edda rested a doll that in the course of their wanderings had lost some of its hair and one arm.

Last was Viktoria, three years old. In spite of her triumphant name she was a difficult child, menaced by illness and accident. She was sucking a hand-hemmed batiste diaper that had finally outlived the purpose for which it was intended.

Then there was the "half-child," the result of a rape by a Kirghiz soldier from Lake Balkhash.

Until her flight from Pomerania, Maximiliane had hardly been touched by the war; her husband was absent because of it, but even that was no great hardship. Then, in the final winter of the war, she had had to leave home along with the people on the estate. They set out with horses and wagons, oxen and tractors, children and women, a couple of cats and dogs. At the edge of Poenichen village the cats turned back. Her grandparents, the Old Quindts, and a few others remained behind.

One morning during the journey Maximiliane slept through the departure of the wagon train. Thereafter she continued westward alone, with a handcart and her children, until the advancing front swallowed her, washing her up in the silt of the homeless and dispersed.

She was no longer a Quindt on Poenichen. Her name had been lost along with everything else. She was addressed as "my dear lady."

"You must have saved your children's birth certificates, my dear lady."

"I saved the children," she answered.

The camp chaplain offered spiritual comfort. "Man does not live by bread alone, my dear lady."

And she replied, "But without bread he cannot live at all, Pastor."

"You will have to change your attitude, my dear lady."

"Later, Pastor."

Where she came from, they said *pastor* with the stress on the second syllable.

Pomerania. In the old days the word was cause for hilarity, denoting a region at the back of beyond. Now

4

she learned that she had been living "beyond the Oder-Neisse line," and no one laughed. A cause for compassion. Where did the Neisse flow? Like all the other refugees, Maximiliane Quint was still convinced that she would return. "It'll pass, you'll see," as that archetypal Pomeranian literary character, Bräsig, frequently put it. She had been raised to be the mistress of Poenichen—a nineteen-year-old woman who became a mother before she could become a lover or a wife, used by her husband only as a breeding ground for the children with whom he intended to populate the German East. Over the years she and her children would reappear in the storage bins of statistics as "war widows and orphans,"as "expellees."

Loud commands. They were being awakened. They would have to make room for the refugees who had crossed the border the previous night. A transit camp with a name that for decades would represent the first haven to many: Friedland.

The travelers were putting on their shoes and hastily gathering up their bits of luggage, slinging on their knapsacks and bundles. The children tugged at their mother, but as always it was difficult to wake her. At last Joachim's voice penetrated through her ear to her heart. "Mama! We have to move on!"

Maximiliane tied the scarf under her chin, like all the women from the East; nothing remained to distinguish her from the rest.

In one barracks they were deloused, in another they were given food coupons: 75 grams of meat and 100 grams of shortening for the current week; for expectant and nursing mothers, a liter of milk and 500 grams of grains and cereals—on paper. Instead of money, they were given travel vouchers.

"We're going on the train," Golo shouted in rapture. Their flight seemed at an end—on paper. The Salvation Army was ladling out cocoa. As always, Maxi-

5

miliane and her children went to the end of the line. "She's got her share of patience," the midwife who brought her into the world had been the first to remark. Nevertheless, Maximiliane was not among the last to be served.

The Americans had the most to eat, it was said, but they thought every Youth Squad leader was a dyed-in-the-wool Nazi. The British were no better off than the Germans, but they treated the vanquished decently. Hearsay. The refugees banded together according to their origins: East Prussians, Silesians, Sudeten Germans, Pomeranians—all linked by their dialects. The Pomeranian wagon train had gone from Mecklenburg to Holstein, it was rumored. On to Holstein, then. That meant staying in the British Zone of Occupation—hunger. "What has to be, has to be." A Pomeranian does as he is told.

At the camp exit Joachim stopped to read aloud a sign the British had erected as an admonition. He was a fluent reader, though in all his seven years he had never warmed a school bench. "Entering Lower Saxony. Only persons with valid residency permits will be entitled to housing, food coupons, or welfare support."

He was shaking like a leaf. "Mama!"

His mother was quick to comfort him. "We'll find our wagon train. Martha Riepe has kept it all—our horses and our beds and our coats and our shoes and—"

"Do you promise?"

"No, Mose, I can't promise."

Joachim closed his eyes, struggled for composure, straightened his shoulders, returned to his place in line, and took little Viktoria by the hand.

When the train of refugees left the camp, the five Quints could not keep pace. They were caught up in the stream of new arrivals, pushed back, and given a second ration of cocoa. A flood of cocoa was being poured over starving West Germany. Maximiliane licked the traces of cocoa from Viktoria's lips—the simplest way of cleaning her; a handkerchief would have to be washed. The other children used the backs of their hands.

The cattle cars the English Occupation Forces brought to Friedland railroad station to transport the refugees onward were stormed. Clusters of human beings hung from them like grapes; even the roofs were crowded.

Once again the five Quints were forced to remain behind. Even years later, when Maximiliane found herself on a railroad platform, she would sometimes stare thoughtfully at the new railroad cars—coupled by accordionlike bellows, without running boards, without open platforms, with overhead electrical conductors—and she would think, Nowhere here for crowds in flight . . . .

They set out on foot, moving northward for the first time; until then they had headed west. The weather was still pleasant, and the autumn rains had not yet started. At noon the sun was still strong enough to warm them.

Before long they came to a brook. They stopped to wash. For months now the children had been cleaned only according to necessity and opportunity—the latter being much less frequent than the former. Apples and turnips were made to do duty as toothbrushes.

Maximiliane's nose sniffed Golo's hair. "You reek," she said. "All of us reek of sweat and delousing powder. Get out the soap, Golo."

But Golo had only just acquired the sliver of soap through a clever piece of dealing in the camp. He refused—he needed it as capital in further trading.

"Now what we need is soap," his mother ruled.

Need was the operative word—decisive. "We need

it, we don't need it." Even Golo bowed to her judgments.

Maximiliane knelt at the edge of the brook to wash the children one by one. Viktoria weighed so little that her mother could swish her through the water like a piece of laundry, making the little girl laugh—a rare event. For towels they used diapers hemmed by hand, embroidered with a coronet and the Quindt coat of arms.

"Run," Maximiliane commanded the children. "Run until you're warm again." Then she bathed her own body, already heavy and clumsy with her pregnancy.

On the riverbank less than thirty meters away, half hidden by the shrubbery, a man was sitting in the grass watching. "There's somebody there," Edda shouted. But Maximiliane did not even turn her head; she could not worry about other people and about what they might say or think. Right now the man was saying nothing and thinking a lot. Maximiliane spread the damp diapers to dry over a bush, as women have done for thousands of years.

When she finished, the man rose to his feet, came up to her, and held out his hand. She placed the soap in it. She was a practical woman, not a sensible one, as one might have thought.

The man looked at her, taking off his glasses—gasmask goggles tied around his head with cloth strips. He looked into her eyes, at the same time covering his own, then lowered his hand and looked again into those eyes that had already gained her so much and must gain so much more. Then he said, "Oh." Dropping to the grass, he pulled off his boots, unwrapped the rags, and dipped his feet into the brook. He submerged his arms and splashed handfuls of water into his face, but he did not wipe it off, allowing it to drip inside his padded camouflage jacket.

"Blood and soil," he said, "but more blood. You

can't wash the war away with soap. There isn't enough soap in all the world."

Golo, standing on the other side of the brook, watched. "Hey, you, man. You've got to take off your hat when you wash."

"It's my magic hat, boy. I can't take it off; I got it by magic. A hat is what you wear in peacetime, and now it's peacetime. No more steel helmets and no more forage caps."

He withdrew his feet from the brook and stood up. Still barefoot, he came to attention before Maximiliane and barked orders at himself. "Right! Left! On the double! Division, halt. Forward, march." He carried out every one of his commands before stopping to face Maximiliane. "They started me marching six years ago, and now I've got to find a way to halt. I've been discharged. The war has become useless. But I'm still useful—I just don't know for what." He held up his empty haversack, turned his pants pockets inside out, knocked his hollow-sounding canteen. "That's what six years earned me. A loser at war! But I've got a signed paper. I've been discharged. I can show you proof. I've learned how to entrench myself. I've learned to shoot people. Anyway, I made it to the same rank as our Führer— buck private!"

The children kept their distance, observing in silence. Then Golo leaped from rock to rock across the brook, came up close to the stranger, and asked, "But who are you?"

The man, looking at the child, saw the mother's eyes. Then he squatted down. "I've got nothing, I am nothing, I'm Mister Nobody." He raised one leg and hopped on the other, singing, " 'Ha! Glad am I that no one knew. . . . ' Well, what is my name?"

The children took a step backward. Viktoria started to cry, and Joachim said cautiously, "Rumpelstiltskin."

9

The man laughed, threw his hat up in the air, and caught it.

"Run," Maximiliane said. "See if you can find any blackberries."

She lay down in the grass, shoving one of her bundles under her head. The man dropped to the grass next to her. The children's voices faded. Splashing of water, cawing of birds. Maximiliane closed her eyes and transported herself to the Blue Pond on Poenichen. After a while the man placed his hand on her stomach, feeling the double heartbeat.

"I'm dreaming," he said. "I'm pretending to be dreaming."

An idyll such as can happen only on the edge of catastrophe. Zero hour. Return to Paradise. But Mary was with child. The war was over. They had come through, and as yet no one was asking them to mourn, to come to terms with the past, to build up a new existence and establish new values.

They turned to each other, staring.

Maximiliane understood every word from his lips, even those that never crossed his lips. His question about her origins was answered with a gesture toward the East; the reply to his question about her destination encompassed the whole Western Hemisphere.

A chill set in, dew began to fall. The children came running, shivering, Golo and Edda bringing carrots and apples. They had stolen them from someone's garden, an action that earned their mother's praise. The booty was distributed, the larger apples to the older children, the smaller ones to the younger. "And what are we going to eat tomorrow?" Edda asked, an apple in her hands, a carrot between her teeth.

"We'll worry about that tomorrow," Maximiliane answered. She rummaged in the bundles for the shearling coats Baroness Quindt had woven during the lean years after the First World War. These she put on the children as overcoats. She kept the largest for herself, but she could no longer make it close over her swollen belly. Demonstrating how his camouflage jacket flapped on his emaciated body, the man took it off and handed it to her. She gave him hers. Each coat still held the warmth of the other's body.

Maximiliane straightened her shoulders and prepared to settle down in the jacket that would camouflage her unborn child.

"Now I'm one of you," the man said to the children. Turning to Maximiliane, he asked, "Do these little lambs have a father?"

"Yes."

"Where?"

"Missing."

"You miss him?"

"No." Maximiliane did not hesitate.

Her *no* was enough; he would go with them. He told the children, "You need a house. I will build you a house—one for each of you." He conjured paper and pencil from his pockets and turned to Joachim. "What kind of house do you want?"

"The kind that has pillars in front." Joachim did not need to think it over.

"Fine. You'll have one."

Ten minutes later each of the four children had a house according to personal specifications—Golo, a fortress with flags flying from the buttresses and towers; Edda, an apartment house of eight stories, where everyone had to pay rent. "And a glass house for this little glass girl," the builder decided, handing out the drawings.

Joachim carefully put the paper in his little box. He was the only one who wanted to keep his house.

In the meantime Maximiliane had clumsily put on her boots, army issue, which Golo had taken off a dead

German soldier six months before. The man helped her get to her feet.

"We must march on," he said. " 'Till all about us lies in ruins.' The old songs are the best songs; we'll mend the ruins."

"Most of all we need a hatchery," Maximiliane pointed out. She gathered up the diapers, still damp, from the rose bush.

"You can depend on me," he called—the eternal cry of men.

So a returnee joined the Quints, seeking shelter with the women and children, intent on surviving, tired of being a hero. He picked up Viktoria and put her on his shoulders. Shivering and delighted all at once, the child closed her eyes; it was just like another time long ago, when she had ridden to the Blue Pond on her father's shoulders.

They set out in a new marching order. But these children already knew from experience: men come and men go; only Mother is dependable.

For a while they walked along the road. Every time a vehicle passed, the man waved his hat, until a truck stopped.

"What did I tell you! It's a magic hat," the man shouted, putting it back on his head.

They were allowed to ride on the flatbed of the open truck. The floor was covered with pig manure— a familiar smell, reminiscent of Poenichen. For a few seconds Maximiliane had a vision of the farm, the barns, the manor, the portico with its five white pillars, and her grandparents watching the retreating wagon train of refugees. Again she heard the three fateful shots; she began to tremble. Believing that she needed support in the shaking vehicle, the man placed his arm around her shoulders. She looked up and leaned against him.

The truck picked up speed, and sparks flew from

the pipe. As they rounded a curve, a gust of wind swept the magic hat from the man's head.

He let go of Maximiliane's shoulders, hammered his fists against the driver's compartment, gestured, and called to the driver that he had to get out. When the truck stopped, he jumped down to run after his hat.

But the driver, without waiting for the man to come back, stepped on the gas and drove on. Maximiliane knocked on the window, but the driver indicated by gestures that he could not wait; it would soon be dark, and his headlights were not working properly.

The children sang, "Blow, blow, thou gentle wind, I say, Blow Conrad's little hat away, And make him chase it here and there. . . ."

It would not be long before they forgot the man. But whenever their mother read them the story of Rumpelstiltskin, the imp would wear the face of this returnee, have gas-mask goggles, and hop on one leg along the brook near Friedland, tossing his hat in the air. The children always took fairy tales back to the places where the Brothers Grimm had collected them.

Maximiliane leaned against the driver's compartment, holding on to the fencing with one hand. She pressed little Viktoria to herself with the other and watched as the man waved, growing smaller and smaller until he finally disappeared.

2

The truck came to a stop at the railroad station in Göttingen. The driver lifted little Viktoria from the pig enclosure and helped her mother to get down. The other children jumped off by themselves. He tipped his hat, said, "All right, then," and chugged off. He had no idea of his crucial part in the life of Maximiliane Quint.

Maximiliane rummaged in all her coat pockets, looking for some clue to its previous owner's identity, but all she found was a paper bag. She poured some of its contents into the palm of her hand: flints— hundreds of flints. Golo shouted with joy. He was the only one who immediately understood their value—a six-year-old on field duty. The unknown man's estate would keep them alive for weeks.

The trains were already overcrowded when they pulled into Göttingen station, and they merely reduced speed instead of stopping. Some of the refugees waiting on the platform jumped on the running boards, but there was no way for the Quints to make it.

Under cover of darkness Maximiliane and her children crossed the tracks to a passenger train that was standing on a siding. One of the carriage doors was unlocked. They got in and found a compartment where none of the windowpanes was cracked and the door could be shut. The children clambered into the luggage nets, cuddling up in twos.

A little while later a watchman employed by the railroad police walked through the train, shining his flashlight into every compartment, pulling doors open, slamming them closed again. The beam of his flashlight lit up a soldier who had pulled the hood of his camouflage jacket over his head and propped his boots against the wooden bench. The watchman shook him. "Get out, fellow. The war's over."

His final words were drowned out by the children's screams, first a cacophony, then a chorus—deafening. For as long as they had been on the road, the children had awakened and protected their mother by screaming. The light traveled to the luggage nets, where disturbed young faces bobbed up.

The soldier pushed back his hood and kerchief, revealing a woman's face drawn with exertion. When Maximiliane raised her tired lids, her eyes were bright with tears.

"Get out," the auxiliary policeman ordered, as he always did when he came across anyone in the trains stalled on sidings. But even as he repeated his order, his voice lacked conviction. "My dear lady! Are all of these yours?" The beam of light glided over the children's heads; then he turned off his flashlight and pulled the door closed behind him. "What the hell am I supposed to do with you?"

The National Socialist shibboleths regarding the sanctity of mother and child still worked. Maximiliane would be able to use them to her advantage for several years more. Besides, the policeman's need to talk was greater than his sense of duty. "We just had one," he said. "We thought that was all we could afford. And now we don't have any at all. We lost our boy in Russia. A bridgehead near Braslov. Ever hear of it?"

Maximiliane shook her head.

"It's on the Bug River. Nobody ever heard of it.

Maybe you'll have better luck and get a couple of them through."

"Could you use some flints by any chance?" inquired Golo from his luggage net. But he was making his offer to a nonsmoker.

"Not even one?"

"Well, maybe one, boy. Just one." He turned his flashlight back on, pulled a flat flask from his pocket, and handed it to the woman. "Have a sip, it'll warm you up."

Maximiliane drank. Then she passed the bottle to Joachim, who handed it on to Golo.

"But my dear lady, you're raising them to be drunkards."

"It takes more than that to make a drunkard out of a Pomeranian."

"Pomerania! The places people live! I'm from around here myself. I always worked on the tracks. Now I'm doing police work because I'm not political, and the guys who used to be policemen are working on the tracks. But I'm not made for police work. The people . . ."

Maximiliane heard no more of his opinions about the police. She had fallen asleep again.

The man pocketed his flask, mentioned that the train would leave around six in the morning, and asked the children, "Where do you want to go, anyway?"

"To Holstein. That's where our wagon train is," Joachim answered.

"Then make sure you're out of here in time. This train's going in the opposite direction, south." He turned to go.

"Hey, your flint," Golo called.

"That's all right, kid."

But Golo had already adopted the honor code of the black marketeer. "Business is business," he declared. He pulled a flint from the bag and handed it to the watchman, who took it and left on tiptoe so as not to wake the sleeping woman.

Around six o'clock in the morning the empty train started southward without stopping at the Göttingen railroad station. A shunting device decided the Quints' fate. They were fast asleep and noticed nothing.

When Maximiliane realized that the train was going south rather than north, she decided, "Well, then we'll go to Mount Eyckel. We can go anywhere we want."

"But when are we going to go home?" Edda asked.

"Later."

"But at Great-grandma's in Poenichen—"

"We will not talk about Poenichen now," her mother declared.

Back at the camp the refugees stormed the train. Suitcases and bundles, boxes and children had to be stowed away. Someone asked Maximiliane to take at least one of her children on her lap. She pulled Viktoria between her knees.

"Gawd Almighty," the woman next to her exclaimed. "She's gonna have another one." And she lifted the little girl on her own lap. "Prussian Eylau," she added.

Maximiliane responded with "Poenichen near Dramburg." People never gave their names, always the places they had come from.

As the train traveled on, the children grew hungry. Viktoria complained that her feet hurt; all the children had aching feet because their shoes no longer fit them. Maximiliane brought out the book of fairy tales. Once again she read about cold and hungry fairy-tale children, about Hans in Luck and the Star-Money Girl. And when Golo, who disliked books, slammed the volume shut, she told them about Eyckel Castle, about the dungeon and the sanctuary, about the deep, deep well, the owl Shoohoohoo, and the old lady of the castle, Max-

17

imiliane, after whom she herself was named, and who must be well over eighty by now. Taking a deep breath, she ended her story with the old fairy-tale formula: "And if they haven't died, they're alive to this day."

A woman sitting on her suitcase in the corridor said, "It would have been better if you'd brought some bread. Stories won't fill your children's stomachs."

Maximiliane lowered the book and raised her eyes. "We would have eaten up the bread long ago. A book lasts longer."

"You just wait and see," the woman said.

"I'm not waiting any longer."

"Is she a wicked witch?" Joachim whispered.

"Yes." They were surrounded by enchanted princes and wicked witches; good and evil tidings were prophesied to them, and all came true.

A hundred kilometers by train—a day's journey in those days. Somewhere or other they were made to get off and carry their luggage for a long stretch because the railroad bridge had been destroyed. What hadn't been destroyed by enemy bombers and artillery had been blown up by irrational, enraged party leaders. They blew up the bridges behind themselves to spite a people that "did not deserve to survive," that "did not deserve its Führer," as that leader himself announced to posterity in his last will and testament.

All trains came to a halt in the terminal at Kassel. No more roof over the station halls, soot-blackened walls in ruins, stark iron framework against a bare sky. The sinking sun lit up the remnants of the city and the distant countryside beyond, clearly visible now amid the rubble. Joachim, whose bravery hardly ever lasted through the day, clutched his mother's arm.

"Mama! Why . . . ?"

What was it he had meant to ask? Why had they been on the road so long though every town they passed through was destroyed? Why had they left Poenichen though Grandpa and Great-grandma were there? He summed up all his questions in a single, despairing "Why?"

"Ask your father," said his mother, summing up in her reply her own horror and dismay.

Perhaps this statement was partly to blame for the fact that all his life Joachim would ask about his father and was already condemned to come to terms with the guilt of the fathers. It helped hardly at all that his mother pulled his head to her and added, "Mose," using the secret language she shared only with her firstborn.

The five Quints were sent to the nearby town square, where an emergency refugee camp had been set up—tents for a thousand people, a welfare center for mothers and children, and a first-aid station where Red Cross nurses and aides from the railroad mission were keeping busy.

As soon as the fighting had stopped, the men promptly ended their war. The women did not. While the war lasted, they had driven streetcars through blacked-out cities, put out fires after air raids, worked in munition factories. Words and music had praised the "brave little soldier women." Now they were knocking the mortar from the stones of ruins—rubble women, especially suited to emergency times. They had not gone on strike during the war, and they did not go on strike in peacetime, these great sufferers of old, of whom Maximiliane was one.

Once again there was a mug of cocoa for everyone, and with it a piece of bread white and soft as cotton, a gift of the American Occupation Forces. Golo crumpled it in his hand. "What is it supposed to be?"

"It's good, it's special," Maximiliane explained. "It comes from America."

"But I'm hungry for bologna." Unlike the others, who were simply hungry, he was always hungry for something in particular. So now it was bologna. "Let me give it a try." Carrying his bag of flints, he set off for the railroad station.

The Quints were assigned two beds in an air-raid shelter. An old woman made room for the pregnant Maximiliane and squatted at the foot of the bed, pulling Viktoria onto her lap. "What a little worm," she murmured, rocking the child and winding a strand of Viktoria's fine hair around her finger. "Hair can tell you a lot about a person," she noted, reaching deep into Maximiliane's sturdy curls. "Springy," she remarked. "You can take it. Anybody who tries to wrap you around his little finger is going to have a time of it."

"That's right," answered Maximiliane.

"Flippau." The old woman introduced herself. "Twelve kilometers past Pasewalk."

"Poenichen," Maximiliane returned. "Dramburg County."

"My children stayed behind. They didn't want to leave. But my husband has a brother in Stuttgart, and that's where we're headed. You got somebody in the West too?"

"I hope so."

"If they haven't died," Edda added.

At this, the woman launched into a new line of conversation. "The children! They've already had to go through too much. You've got to give them potato water to drink. From raw potatoes. Potatoes have everything a body needs. We always had potatoes. Not milk, though—that we had to deliver to the gentry. I bet you were one of the gentry."

"Yes," replied Maximiliane.

"It's not your fault," the woman continued. "We had two cows and the goats, and every year we fattened up two pigs. They weighed over three hundred pounds."

Golo returned a half-hour later, triumphantly holding up two cans. "Meat!" he shouted. "Pure meat! For ten flints!"

20

Using the keys soldered to the cans, Maximiliane opened one, handed it to the children, opened the other, and handed it to the woman from Flippau. "You let us have your bed."

Edda flared up. "And what are we supposed to eat tomorrow?"

"Tonight we won't be going to bed hungry, and tomorrow we'll see."

When the cans were empty, Edda washed them out at a faucet and stowed them away in her baggage. Then they settled down to sleep. Maximiliane covered Joachim and Viktoria with the blanket left behind by the soldier from Lake Balkhash. "God preserve us," she said instead of a longer prayer.

"If one could only sleep," the woman from Flippau complained. "If there just weren't all these thoughts."

Maximiliane could sleep.

In the morning the woman shook Maximiliane awake. "They're making up a train going south."

When the Quints stepped out of the tent, it was still dark. With the others they rushed to the station. The hall was already overcrowded with people, all of them waiting, all hoping to get on the announced train. The children, still drowsy and chilled, clung to their mother, who tried to shield herself from the shoving throng by standing up against a remnant of wall. The train had not yet pulled in. The gates were guarded by American military policemen, their white helmets shining in the dawning day.

A bystander poked Maximiliane. Laughing, he pointed to the wall behind her, and she turned to look into the Führer's eyes. For a fraction of a second she felt the burning gaze that had struck her in person at close range one single time, shortly before her husband begat his last child—Viktoria. She stared at this final, torn poster. "Ceaselessly the Führer watches and works only for you. And what do you do?" Someone had chalked an answer: "Shiver in our boots."

"And we're still shivering," the man said.

Maximiliane turned back. "But not with fear now, just with cold."

"It doesn't matter what it is that makes you shiver." Then the man disappeared in the crowd.

When the train pulled in, the anxious mass rushed forward, pushing and shoving. Some fell, crying out.

One of the soldiers, a black man, jumped up on a broken pedestal and shouted, "Get back!" No one paid any attention. The soldier raised his submachine gun. Still more people stumbled and fell; others ran on. The soldier fired a shot over their heads, shouting once more, "Get back!" His attempt to bring order out of chaos failed; the people assumed that he was trying to stop them from boarding.

Golo let go of his mother's hand, jumped over the fallen, stopped by the soldier's pedestal, and shouted in rapture, "A blackamoor! A coal-black-as-a-crow blackamoor!"

The arm holding the submachine gun lowered, the muzzle pointed at the child. Golo had never been in such mortal danger before, but he had a deficient sense of self-preservation. He laughed. He laughed until the colored soldier began to laugh as well, raised the gun again, and shouted, "Get back."

Horrified, Maximiliane was rooted to the spot. Joachim wept loudly. "They're going to shoot some more!" They watched as Golo jumped over a suitcase, fell, and stayed down. One of his feet was at an angle— the same foot he had broken once before.

And once again a train left without the Quint family.

Until now the Quints had been refugees among thousands of refugees, returning evacuees, and displaced persons—the dregs of war, an army of ants who

22

became confused and strayed this way and that. But now Golo's accident drew attention to the crying child, to his brother and his sisters, and to his pregnant mother. Poor little boy, sobbing so it would break your heart! What a good-looking child, with his brown curls, his dimples, and his black-fringed saucer eyes!

An American soldier gave him his first piece of gum. He shoved it in his mouth and chewed, eager to learn.

An ambulance took all five Quints to a onetime field dressing station, where first aid was now dispensed. The orderly who admitted the case asked their name and address.

"My name is von Quindt. We are on our way to the family estate in Franconia." Maximiliane spoke in the same tone of voice she employed to tell the children fairy tales, hoping to draw further attention by mentioning her origins and destination.

The orderly did not even look up. "So? Anyway, you can't have your baby here. We deal only with accidents. We're an infirmary."

Golo's ankle was X-rayed and set. When the old fracture was discovered, his mother was asked about it. For a moment she closed her eyes and saw Golo, who did not want to leave Poenichen, hanging high overhead in the copper beech, clinging to a branch. She wrapped her arms around the file cabinet, pressing her face against it as she had against the tree trunk that day.

"Are you unwell?" they asked, pushing a chair her way.

Since no one knew where to quarter the injured boy's family while he had to be hospitalized, his mother and brother and sisters were allowed to stay in the infirmary. At night they slept in whatever beds happened to be empty. When it rained, they kept to the corridors of the infirmary. Golo, who had been given a walking cast, carried on a lively black-market trade with wounded ex-soldiers. When the weather was fair, Maximiliane took the children to the Karlsaue, a ravaged area where the bomb craters were filled with water and they found bits of wood that could be floated like ships. For the first time the children were playing again. Twice a day all of them were given a bowl of soup.

Golo's broken ankle was one of their strokes of good luck.

At Golo's final visit the doctor on duty looked at the boy's crooked toes and said to the mother, "Apparently his shoes are too small."

"All my children's shoes are too small. We've been on the road since February. Children's feet don't stop growing just because we're in flight."

The doctor looked at Maximiliane, then checked her name on the chart. "In Königsberg I knew someone named von Quindt," he said. "If I'm not mistaken, a Baron Quindt. We were in the castle cellar, at the 'kangaroo court.' He provided us with an excellent white Chablis, along with mussels in a wine sauce. And that was the third year of the war!"

"Uncle Max," Maximiliane explained. "My grandfather's cousin." Her eyes filled with tears.

"A clever man, but a little resistant," the doctor continued. "He made a few remarks that could have proved dangerous to him. But no one wanted to harm the old man." The last sentence was drawled—somehow revealing. "By the way, Sautter, Major Sautter."

Maximiliane saw that his army uniform, complete with the mirror embroidered in silver, protruded above the collar of his white coat.

"You come from Königsberg yourself?" he asked.

"No," Maximiliane answered. "From Pomerania. Dramburg County. Poenichen manor."

"So your husband is an agriculturalist?"

"No." Maximiliane gave the doctor a meaningful

look, which he interpreted as a sign of trust. "My husband was active in the Party administration. Reich Genealogical Office, subordinate only to the Reich Chief SS."

"Very brave of you to admit it so freely. Where was his last assignment?"

"He lost his right arm in Normandy, but at the time he wrote me that he could still serve his Führer with his left arm alone. Ordnance officer in the Führer's headquarters in Berlin."

"There were great men among them," Dr. Sautter said. "There still are."

Maximiliane smiled. "Women, too."

"Marvelous women. We couldn't have done it at all without them. Now we have to stick together. There are still enough loyal people—it's just a matter of tracking them down. We all have to look out for each other now."

"With children's shoes," Maximiliane said.

"Right." The doctor looked at Golo's foot, which was still resting in his lap. "That's where we started. Women certainly have an admirable practical sense for immediate needs. Especially the women from the East show great composure. Firmly determined to return. I'll give you an address." He reached for his prescription pad, managing a tiny smile. "Shoes for the return. An absolutely reliable man. Gudbrod, Marställer Platz, formerly SA Platz. He has plenty of shoes in store, though officially he's bombed out. Don't go at night; it might arouse suspicion. Besides, we have no need to shun the light! You have funds?"

Maximiliane nodded.

"Where do you intend making your temporary home?"

"On my family's ancestral seat in Franconia. In the possession of the Quindts for six hundred years."

Until now the children had been quiet, but suddenly Edda spoke up. "If they haven't died."

The doctor turned his attention to the children. "Children mustn't run wild in these times. They need a strong hand. New blood. There are good people among the nobility—unfortunately not all of them, or the twentieth of July could never have happened."

Maximiliane played her last trump card. "My husband wrote to me at the time—from the hospital, by the way—'If there were even a single Quindt among the traitors, my first bullet would be for him, the second for myself.'"

Joachim was the one who got the new shoes. Golo was given his brother's castoffs, and so on down the line. Viktoria's shoes were left over, and Edda packed them away—"We'll need those for Mirko." The unborn baby was always referred to as Mirko, after the imaginary Polish boy in the stories Maximiliane had invented to accompany their flight through all of Pomerania and Brandenburg.

This Dr. Sautter, former major in the medical corps, not only helped the children to well-fitting shoes, but also spurred their mother to a crucial realization. From that time on, as need arose, she would identify herself as the wife of a Nazi or the daughter of a Jewish stepfather, as a member of the nobility or a woman who had married into the middle class. "Not everyone can afford to have opinions," her grandfather had said on numerous occasions—one of his Quindt-essences, translated into action by his granddaughter.

Before they moved on, Edda dug out one of the empty cans that had held the meat Golo got at the train station for ten flints. She looked at the label and asked her mother, "What does it say, anyway?

Maximiliane picked up the can and read the English words—"For army dogs only." She said, "It's what American dogs eat."

3

The stream of refugees that had been pouring over what was left of Germany since spring was followed by a flood of expellees after the end of summer.

Six months earlier, Stalin had declared that the old Polish provinces of East Prussia, Pomerania, and Silesia must be returned to Poland. This statement made six hundred years of German history null and void—a proposition for history class, hard to understand, hard to memorize, but accepted readily by many for the sake of peace. It could have become a burning issue, but it did not catch fire even in subsequent election campaigns. The Prussian virtues—adaptability, common sense, endurance, and a will to live—combined with the eastern mentality as refugees and expellees tried to adjust and deny their uniqueness.

At about the same time, the British prime minister, Winston Churchill, declared that expulsion was the most satisfactory and permanent method of achieving the stated end since it would avoid the mingling of unrelated populations, which could only lead to continual unrest. Nor could he see, he added, why there should not be room in Germany for the inhabitants of East Prussia and the other ceded territories; after all, the war had killed six or seven million Germans. A brutal calculation, but true. The Germans from the East replaced those eliminated by the war in the West; the

Polish resettlers from the eastern part of Poland, which was assigned to the Soviet Union, replaced the eastern Germans who moved out; and Russians moved into the eastern territories of Poland. The interchangeability of people seemed to have been proved once more. Old Quindt may have been right when, in his speech at the christening of his granddaughter, he said, "The main thing is to be Pomeranian—that's always proved to be the strongest. In the long run the Goths, Slavs, Wends, and Swedes, all of whom settled here at one time or another, turned into good Pomeranians." The proof for his assertion was still outstanding.

"Flood of refugees"—it had the sound of a natural catastrophe, and the inhabitants of what was left of Germany accepted it as such. They tried to protect themselves accordingly. Dams were built to ward off the flood; sluices deflected it to remote, sparsely settled areas. Villages in Holstein and small towns in Bavaria were inundated.

Images of flood and inundation were more aptly chosen than their originators realized at the time. Human dung. How fruitful they were would be shown in the years of reconstruction.

But for the present the flood of refugees was trapped in the empty barracks of the former Reich Labor Service, in air-raid shelters and abandoned schools. Maximiliane always turned firmly away from these havens, since it was easy to get in and hard to get out again.

Once more she was told, "But how do you intend to get on, my dear lady, in your condition? And with so many children?"

"Four," Edda corrected. She liked to be precise. She always counted and counted out and counted over.

The official, a German hired by the Americans to take down particulars for registrations in the American Zone of Occupation, grabbed Maximiliane's thumb and pressed it on an ink pad before applying it to the left-hand corner of a form.

"As if we were all criminals! Fingerprints! I bet they're afraid to take our pictures. They don't want anyone to know what we looked like."

He raised his eyes to Maximiliane. What he saw made him ask, "Surely you don't believe in miracles, my dear lady?"

Maximiliane returned the look. "But I do."

Her faith was a help to her. As it turned out, the official became the agent of a miracle. He arranged for Maximiliane and her children to ride to Nuremberg, this time in a closed truck that transported not pigs but sugar beets. For the length of the trip the Quints fed on them, though they were too hard for Viktoria's little teeth. Not for the first time, Maximiliane nourished her problem child in the manner of birds, mouth to mouth.

Edda spit out some chewed slivers of beet. "Hog swill."

"The prisoners at Poenichen ate beets when they were hungry," Joachim said, forcing down the pap.

"But they were Russians," Edda objected, parroting what she had heard back home. "Little better than animals."

"Russians are human beings too," her mother instructed her. "Now we are as badly off as the Russian prisoners used to be." With this private lesson she made a stab at correcting a vignette from history.

Having abandoned the country roads, the truck now drove along the highway through the mountains of the Rhone, the valley of the Main. Maximiliane was more interested in nature's utility than in its beauty. Of all the leafy trees, beeches were the most important because they supplied beechnuts—fat. Pine stands meant brushwood as well as cones for heating and cooking. Plowed fields promised acres of maize and potatoes, now being gleaned by human beings, no longer by geese and wild boars. Hoarders traveled the roads with empty and filled pockets, with handcarts full of wood.

The Quints came too late; the fields had long since had their second harvest, the pinecones had all been gathered. It was the beginning of December.

Pomerania, Franconia—what a difference! The tiny fields, subdivided over and over according to Roman laws of inheritance, looked to someone from the East more like gardens, the mountains rising abruptly to cut off the view, the valleys steep and rocky. Maximiliane felt hard pressed by the narrow-fronted, multistoried houses in the small towns, most of them undamaged by the war. She clutched her throat, unbuttoning her jacket to get some air.

The last two hundred meters of her flight to safety were as hard for her as the first, when the wagon train had passed along the linden-lined avenue that ended at the manor house. To the east the sky had been red with the glare of the approaching front. Never turn back!

Another thin blanket of snow lay over the land.

And now she stood at the foot of Mount Eyckel, the castle before her eyes. When she was seventeen, she had come here for a family reunion, a Pomeranian acorn on the family tree of the Quindts. Less than ten years had passed, and now five acorns stood at the gate.

"The castle is beginning to show that the waves of a great era have beaten against it." These words, or something like them, had been written by the owner, Maximiliane Hedwig, to her brother in Poenichen, and he had delivered himself of the opinion that Eyckel Castle had managed to withstand a thing or two in its time. For three years the building had served as a hostel to "provide German youth with a concept of Germany's chivalric past," as Viktor Quint, keeping the Thousand-Year Reich firmly in sight, had put it. That summer of 1936, when the Quindts—with and without the *d*, with

30

and without the *von*—met at Eyckel Castle for the family reunion, the flags of the Third Reich were waving in the wind, and under them, standing with upraised arms, they sang the Horst Wessel song in close harmony, though not always in close spiritual accord. Since that time the ranks of the Quindts had thinned.

The great hall and the hunting room, which had been remodeled into dormitories, served after the hostel days to give temporary shelter to bombed-out and evacuated residents of Nuremberg, who used blankets to subdivide them into living quarters, none bigger than nine square meters. By and by the people of Nuremberg returned to their city, making room for the shifts of Quindts arriving from East Prussia, Mecklenburg, Silesia and Lusatia. Once more Eyckel Castle became a sanctuary. The solemn family reunion day would turn into miserable family weeks and months—for the older ones, even years.

The same name, the same fate—how intimately allied these survivors must feel! But already there were distinctions. No matter how closely related people are, their shared horizons still embrace all the directions of the compass, said Nietzsche. To some, the end of the war meant the collapse of the Greater German Reich; to others, it was the day of liberation from dictatorship. A humiliation and a blessing—to some, even both at the same time.

The National Socialist mental powers of old Maximiliane Hedwig von Quindt had blurred with time, preventing her from perceiving the end of the New Era in which she believed so fervently. She had fallen silent and turned to stone, had become senile and incompetent. Sometimes, frighteningly like a castle ghost, she appeared on the stairs leading to the yard, a blanket around her shoulders. Whoever spied her avoided her.

Black stovepipes protruded from windows whose panes were frequently replaced by slats or cardboard.

The garden was parceled out into vegetable plots, the last cabbages carefully watched by their owners; the food rations did not come close to the daily minimum of 1,150 calories established by the Allies. There was no coal allowance for household use during this winter; no more shrubs lined the castle walls, and the trees were bare of branches as high as a man could reach. Everything that could be burned had been burned.

"Work is ennobling" was one of the great slogans of the Third Reich. On Mount Eyckel, it might now have read, "Nobles work," but these first postwar years were short on slogans. Those who had managed to survive the war were not anxious to starve or freeze to death in peacetime. Hunger drove some in search of food, others into meditation. Roswitha von Quindt was one of the latter.

At the time of the family reunion Maximiliane had been joyfully embraced and kissed by old and young Quindts. Now, when she appeared in the forecourt—misshapen, four little children and her miserable bundles in tow—the joy of reunion was mixed with the fear that everyone would be even more crowded and their living space even more limited. Still, a baroness born to the name of Quindt, a Quint by marriage—Maximiliane's claims were doubly secured. No one would dispute her rights.

"Wait," said Roswitha von Quindt, who in February 1945, a refugee from East Prussia, had tarried a week at Poenichen. "I'll let my mother know."

Elisabeth von Quindt, called the General, had grasped the scepter on Mount Eyckel with no justification other than the fact that she and her daughters had been the first refugees to arrive; they had been here since April. She had learned from a reliable source that her husband, a lieutenant general, was a prisoner in Russia. An East Prussian in her bearing and beliefs, she radiated confidence—though Old Quindt would probably have said that only half was confidence, the other half being arrogance. Whenever she opened her mouth, the whole of Germany's order of knighthood rose up behind her, complete with shield and sword. Even in the present situation she expected the inhabitants of Eyckel Castle to resist hunger and cold with proper deportment. She had been able to salvage next to nothing of her possessions, but she had lost none of her convictions in flight. Even in December 1945 she knew what a young person had to do regarding both the past and the future. Now she marched down the broad staircase and strode toward Maximiliane, who was leaning against a wall, holding the chain of children by the hand.

One more destination had been reached. Shelter. The images blurred before Maximiliane's eyes. Why did everything remind her of Ingo Brandes from Bamberg, a young man in his last year of school who had sung into her ear "Quindt and Quint united" at the reunion religious service, who had picked cornflowers for her, who had hooted below her window like a screech owl "when moonlight flooded the valley." Once more she faltered under the onslaught of scenes from the past, and she sought support on her oldest son's shoulder. Joachim made himself strong.

The General's first question concerned Maximiliane's husband. Confusing him momentarily with Ingo, the young and shining boy who had pursued her in 1936, she almost answered that he had died in the crash of his plane—though Viktor had been in the infantry. She had married the one and loved the other, a fighter pilot, lost during a combat mission. Her body took refuge in the anesthesia of memories.

The General made arrangements circumspectly and confidently. The children were sent to the kitchen, and a room in the attic was set up for their living quarters: a bedstead, linens, water bowls, and a lamp.

33

This seems the appropriate moment to cast a backward glance at the so-called Green Rooms on Poenichen, where in 1918 Vera von Quindt, née von Jadow, born and raised in Berlin, gave birth to her daughter, Maximiliane, under "imaginably primitive circumstances," as she put it. Schmaltz the midwife was at hand, as was Dr. Wittkow, the family physician, though he arrived just a little too late. The housekeeper's part consisted of preparing pigeon broth. Though the heir's progenitor was at the front, the elder Quindts waited in the anteroom for the birth of the heir. In time these attendants were joined by a series of Fräuleins and by other servitors—solicitude, spoiling.

Now, in 1945, the Quindt batiste diapers were again ready; a wooden bucket was filled with warm water, the laboring mother was given a heated brick for her cold feet, another woman sat at the edge of Maximiliane's bed and held her hand. "Anna," she said. "Anna Hieronimi. My mother was a Quint. I'm from Giessmannsdorf, near Bunzlau. You can call me Anna."

"Amma," Maximiliane said, brushing damp hair from her forehead. She took a deep breath, and her features relaxed. "Amma," she repeated. In the old days on Poenichen, she had called Anna Riepe "Amma" because a child of the gentry was not allowed to call the housekeeper Mama.

"Don't strain," Anna Hieronimi urged. "Let it come by itself. Children want to live. This one has a lot of time yet."

Without defenses or will, Maximiliane let the birth take its course, just as she had let the rape, which had resulted in the conception, take its course. Her own powers were diminished, but the baby's will to live was all the stronger—the relative from Giessmannsdorf turned out to be a wise woman. She herself had borne three children.

34

Once the General stuck her head in the room. "Everything proceeding satisfactorily?"

At last Anna Hieronimi held the newborn babe, a girl, in her arms. "What a miracle, a child of God. We are not made of sand, and we do not turn to sand. We are made of blood, and we turn into blood."

Anna did what needed to be done, and Maximiliane allowed it all to happen. When the baby was washed, swaddled, and diapered, Anna placed her under the gray blanket with her mother. "Sometimes I think that when we give birth to a child, each one of us becomes a kind of Mary. Because all of us are born children of God—we just keep forgetting it."

Maximiliane stored these words in her memory; they fell on fruitful, plowed soil. For it was only with the birth of this child that she learned the secret of becoming human, which is more than a biological process.

The light of the world that was visible at this moment consisted of two candle stumps. From eight to midnight the electricity was turned off, and the buildings lay in darkness. No more blackout regulations, but no light either. So as not to waste the hot water boiled for the baby's birth, the other children were brought in and bathed. There were five of them now, true to their name—Quint.

The fifth child, though the result of a brief meeting with a Kirghiz soldier, was born on the Quindt family estate—an additional reason for her being entitled to the name of Quint, although a refugee child, although born in the West. But a refugee gives birth to further refugees; they increase in the natural way.

A newborn baby touches the most hardened hearts and opens eyes used to evil. Here was someone even poorer, even more helpless than oneself. The child was brought a few sticks of wood, a bowl of oatmeal, a woolen receiving blanket, a bottle of petroleum. What a dowry for a little girl! "The poor give freely to the poor"—a saying from the primer. No one felt so poor that he did not have a gift to bestow.

The General, too, approached the bedside of the new mother, with empty hands but good advice. "These children must learn from the beginning that they are Quints. That alone gives them a special obligation, even if at present they have no property."

Maximiliane contradicted her, though reluctantly. "They must learn that they are not special, Aunt."

"You seem to have something of your grandfather's spirit."

"I hope so, Aunt."

She was not always as brave as she managed to be during this confrontation.

The other children called the new baby Mirko until they were told that she was a girl. Then they called her Mirka, although the baby bore no resemblance whatever to the real Mirko.

For three days Maximiliane stayed in bed. Then she set out to register the birth with the authorities.

The new mayor, Joost, until recently a plumber, qualified for the office by virtue of not having been a member of the National Socialist party, just as his predecessor's qualifications had consisted in being a member of it. Denouncing, being denounced. The great cleansing process was at work. Where the Führer's picture had hung on the wall behind the desk, there was only a white spot with a dusty edge. The gods had been toppled without sound or fury.

But the Allies could not rely solely on the conquered nation's self-cleansing. Not far from Mount Eyckel, in Nuremberg, the International Military Tribunal had been sitting since November, judging guilt and innocence, deciding on life and death. The German people were divided into five categories: major offenders, offenders, accessories, fellow travelers, and the innocent. Black sheep, white sheep.

No denazification court had yet decided on the proper category for Maximiliane—a leader in the League of German Girls, and the wife of an active Nazi. As yet she was no more than one of the refugees from the East, and as far as Mayor Joost was concerned, all of them were "half Polish." The mention of her maiden name, the title of nobility, and the estate only increased his distaste. He had no idea how close he was to the truth: Maximiliane was a quarter Polish, and a member of the Red Army was the father of the child she had come to register.

First of all Mayor Joost rejected the name Mirka as unsuitable for the locality, handing Maximiliane a list of names common in Franconia. The list had been made up in 1938, and Herr Joost's index finger pointed out such possibilities as Erika, Gerline, and Ingeborg. The four other children, who had come along, broke into their habitual screaming. Maximiliane made no attempt to quiet them. She simply waited until the name Mirka was entered into the records of the Bureau of Vital Statistics. She named her husband, Viktor Quint, as the child's father. Army officer, missing in action, born in Breslau. If ever called upon to do so, she was prepared to swear to this statement. She never felt any obligation to tell the truth to officials. If you consulted only the calendar, it was entirely possible for Viktor to have been the father.

Mirka was now the only one of Maximiliane's children to possess a legal birth certificate issued in the West. She came into the world during a year that was later labeled "scant in births." Born under the sign of Sagittarius, she was—if we can believe the astrologers— generous, just, thoughtful, liberal, beloved, optimistic, independent, adventurous in spirit, self-aware—and furthermore, "with proud, springy step and a longing for distant isles."

But for the present the little Sagittarius child—never weighed or measured—rested in a potato crate fitted out as a bassinet. She provided her mother with extra coupons for nursing mothers and with additional milk and cereals that Maximiliane called nursing food. These were additional rations to those provided by the five cards for infants and children. Any ordinary consumer could not but envy her when she walked down the mountain to the village carrying her milk cans.

4

The first peacetime Christmas. On Christmas Eve the curfew for the conquered and liberated population was extended to two-thirty in the morning. The Americans raided their own supplies to give the people a kilogram of wheat flour and four hundred grams of sugar per head; the sugar, from Cuba, was brown and tasted like sweetened meat extract.

The large old kitchen range in Eyckel Castle was normally used to render drippings from stirred white beans spiced with thyme, to simmer fermented skim-milk curds with false fennel picked at the edge of the road, or to make a kind of pudding out of damp slices of bread so that they would not be gassy. Now, in the days before Christmas, the women spent the afternoons at the range baking cookies, the old amounts and ingredients in their heads. But instead of the eggs the recipes called for, they used milk; instead of regular milk, they used skim milk; when that was gone, they made do with water. In place of honey they used sugar-beet greens, and in place of sugar they added saccharine. A drop of vinegar had the same leavening effect as baking powder. They made cookie cutters out of tin in every conceivable shape—stars and hearts, trees and moons, birds and fishes. There was a substitute for everything. Even the Christmas peace was something like a substitute peace.

The tree was put up in the kitchen. Everyone who was sound of wind and limb took part in the preparations, wove stars out of straw, made candles, dusted pinecones with plaster of Paris. A swastika flag was cut into narrow strips, the strips were tied into bows, and these were used to decorate the tree. In the window recesses they set Hindenburg lamps—candles in a deep dish, designed to illuminate bunkers and shelters.

Deacon Quint assumed responsibility for the spiritual content of the Christmas Eve celebration. His son Anselm, released four weeks earlier from the French prisoner-of-war camp at Kreuznach, filled his hollow cheeks and blew the trombone his mother had salvaged among her refugee bundles. "Break forth, O beauteous heavenly light, And usher in the morning. . . ."

Maximiliane pushed the crate that held her newborn child closer to the hearth. "This child, now weak in fancy, Our confidence and joy shall be." Of course all eyes turned to the baby in the makeshift crib.

Before the deacon could utter a word, even before the first verse from the second chapter of the Gospel according to Saint Luke was spoken, there was some suppressed but contagious weeping, which the General routed with the words, "And though we may have lost everything else, we have not lost our pride."

The deacon did his utmost—he was not a brilliant preacher at the best of times. He forgot what he had rehearsed, spoke from the heart, and did not open the Bible he held in his hands. This was the moment for the revelation.

" 'And I saw the new city, the tabernacle of God among men, and he will dwell with them and they shall be his people, and there shall be no more death, neither sorrow, nor crying, neither shall there be any more pain. And God shall wipe away all tears from men's eyes. . . .' "

The baby had opened her eyes, and Maximiliane

watched her, no longer hearing the words. Her soul needed little nourishment; a few sentences were enough. Why not now? she wondered. Why only in a new city? What is He waiting for? He will wipe the tears from our eyes.

The Quindts with and without the *d* moved closer together. Frau Hieronimi saw to the drinks, pouring a hot, red, sweet liquid into heavy mugs. They sang Christmas carols, sang away their misery. The Christmas cookies were passed on tin plates, and for once no one checked to see how many the others took. The children sat around the large kitchen table, using stars and hearts to make a puzzle. Maximiliane pulled Viktoria onto her lap. For days the little girl had been feverish in anticipation of this event, as she always was before any celebration. Maximiliane harmonized with Anna Hieronimi on "Lo, how a Rose e'er blooming from tender stem hath sprung!"

The ancient aunt, Maximiliane Hedwig, whose armchair had been placed close to the stove, gave forth a sound of woe that resembled the noise of colliding ice floes.

Edda fetched an armful of wood from the shed and piled the logs up in the oven to dry. "What a thoughtful little girl." "You don't have to tell her anything; she does it all by herself." Everyone praised her, at the same time praising her mother. Maximiliane never had to stick up for this lucky child's rights. Even Cuckoo, the nickname Old Quindt had given the foundling, was used less and less often.

Joachim came to stand by his mother. It had been quite a while since the General had reminded the Quindts of their pride, but the boy always needed time to think matters through.

"Do we have pride, too?" he asked.

"No," his mother replied.

"Why is Aunt Elisabeth proud?"

"Because her husband is a general and she has borne and raised two children."

"We have five children."

"Pride isn't important, Mose."

"What is important, Mama?"

Maximiliane took a moment to think. "Courage is important. And patience," she said at last. "And now close your eyes and think of home. What do you see?"

Joachim made an effort, stiffening. "The five columns. And the horse-drawn sled. And Riepe on the coachman's box. And—"

"You see, that's what's important, Mose. To be able to see something even when your eyes are closed."

And then it was time for Joachim to recite his poem. He trembled all over; even his voice was unsteady. But he never faltered, never mispronounced, omitted not a line. A long poem, a high-school favorite transferred from the mother's memory to the memory of the son.

Praise was heaped on Joachim; he was hugged, kissed—"A genuine little Quindt."

A basket of apples circulated, and then everyone brought out a few presents—food saved out of their own portions, things they had whittled, items steeped in love and of no wordly value whatever. But a toboggan was produced as well, nailed together by the village wheelwright, with runners furnished by the smith. Golo pounced on it and let Joachim pull him across the stone floor of the kitchen, swinging his crutch, which he had not yet given up, like a whip. Old Uncle Simon August, from the Baltic, was given a handful of cigarettes, and Frau Hieronimi received Maximiliane's entire month's ration. She lit one immediately, and glancing sidelong at the General, she said, "The German woman smokes again."

The aunts from Mecklenburg distributed round linen doilies with eyelet embroidery, the pattern devised by themselves. It was not until the next day that anyone realized that there were no tables on which such dainty needlework could be laid. The doilies would disappear into the boxes they all shoved under their beds because they had no cupboards.

Frau Hieronimi solemnly presented the two old ladies with an enameled chamber pot decorated for the season with pine twigs and straw stars. The gift occasioned great merriment, for everyone was aware of the aunts' nightly hardship: their room was separated from the nearest lavatory by long, unheated corridors and stairs.

The General steered the conversation back into proper channels, initiating a round robin of Christmas stories.

"At home in Königsberg," she began, "every Christmas Eve at the onset of dusk, around four o'clock, the town band marched through the streets. They got to our house in Regentenstrasse around four-thirty. The children crowded near the window, waiting impatiently. The household staff was also in the salon, at the other window. In front of our house the band played 'O Tannenbaum,' my husband's favorite Christmas carol—in march tempo! When they finished, the cook handed my husband the tray with the homemade marzipan. He had had the mold cast especially for our family. It was based on the Order of the Black Eagle, which his great-grandfather had been awarded by Frederick William the Third—actual size! He picked up one of the marzipan medals and handed it to me. 'The first Order for my dear wife, Elisabeth.' And then he said—"

"*Suum quieque,*" Roswitha interrupted her mother.

"The sow squeaks," her sister Marie-Louise added, and the two of them giggled heartily.

"*Suum cuique,*" the General corrected, raising his voice. " 'To each his own.' As it said on the Order. And then he handed the children their medals, first the oldest, then the youngest, and then the staff as well. Precisely in order of rank, the cook first. Each year it was like an award, and all took it as such. We used up more than ten pounds of almonds to make the marzipan."

The other Quindts responded with a respectful "Oh."

"Anyway, we all celebrated together, like a large family," the General concluded; but her daughter Roswitha added, "And afterward the servants went to their rooms and wept."

Maximiliane, too, allowed her thoughts to travel backward and wondered whether the governesses and the housemaids on Poenichen wept in their rooms after they had been given their gifts. Probably so, she decided.

Frau Hieronimi was next to tell her story. She smoothed her hair, keeping her hands cupped over her ears as if to hold her thoughts captive.

"In the afternoon, even before we went to church, we had fresh, sweet poppy-seed crescents, stiff with currants and strewn thickly with sugar and cinnamon. Every house had a Christmas cone, turned on a lathe and painted. Each one was different. Ours had the date 1797 painted on it. They all held candles, which were lit just outside the church. Then one child from each family carried the cone into the church like a candlestick. Some set theirs into holders in the chancel; other children climbed the stairs to the choir loft and set their cones on the railing. Each cone of light made the church brighter. Last year we still had candles—we had made them ourselves from beeswax. My youngest carried the cone, though at first he didn't want to. He was fifteen years old. Two days later they drafted him into the antiaircraft service. When we got ready to leave home, none of us remembered to bring the cone."

"Cones can be replaced," said the General.

"Yes," Frau Hieronimi replied. "We can replace

44

everything, even a fifteen-year-old boy's leg." She broke into uncontrollable sobbing.

"Everyone here has a cross to bear," the General pointed out with displeasure.

"But not all of us have the strength to bear it," the old Baltic uncle objected, and he made an effort to change the subject. From his coat pocket he produced a bottle. "I happen to have a little sip. Pure corn! A spoonful for each of us."

His hand was steady as he wielded the spoon someone handed to him. "Refined people never have more than one, at the very most two brandies. And we are all extremely refined people—aren't we? And you have to eat something with it. They call it *sakuska* where I come from. And now I'll tell you a story, a funny one. A story should always be funny. Where I come from we tell funny stories, the kind you can repeat when you're back home. It happened on a blustery Christmas night. The roads were sleety, and a snowstorm was brewing, the kind that makes you think you can hear the wolves howling. . . ."

That was as much as Maximiliane heard of that story. The key words were enough. Methodically she chewed all her fingernails to the quick as she envisioned the Christmas day when she and her husband, driving from the railroad station to Poenichen, were caught in a Pomeranian snowstorm that threw him into a rage. Then there was the overcooked carp à la Polonaise, the weeping housekeeper, and finally Viktor's categorical "Come here!"—more an act of vengeance than of procreation, its outcome being Golo, the impetuous child who broke his collarbone even as he was born. Maximiliane could just hear Schmaltz the midwife saying, "Dear God in heaven" as she emerged from her Pomeranian snowstorm with an audible sigh. Now her eyes searched for Golo and discovered him between the knees of the Baltic uncle, his mouth agape so as to swallow all he heard.

". . . and in the end the carp was devoured after all." The story came to an end. The Baltic uncle pulled out one of his new cigarettes. Edda rushed to the range, put a pine sliver into the fire, and carefully carried it over to the old gentleman. He took his time lighting his cigarette from it.

"I thank you all for this wonderful Christmas Eve," he said.

But only the children had been listening. The adults sat quietly and gave themselves over to their own memories. All told their stories more for themselves than for the others.

Instead of telling a Christmas story, a certain Herr Österreich from Breslau, a retired financial councilor who had married a Quint during the war and made a hobby of tracing the family's ancestry, began to tell about the exodus of the first Quinten, the feudal liege of the burgrave of Nuremberg. In the early fifteenth century he had followed in his lord's train on the eastward advance into Brandenburg territory. The burgrave had sold his castle to the town of Nuremberg, but fortunately Eyckel Castle had remained in the possession of a branch of the Quindt family, albeit an illegitimate one.

"And now, the return." He ended his report, and the company again gave itself up to private thoughts.

Golo startled them out of it. He had somehow gotten hold of the trombone, climbed on a chair, and put the instrument to his lips; with his cheeks chubby and red, he blew with all his might, a sturdy baroque angel. He managed a few clear notes, which won him a round of applause.

Maximiliane let Viktoria slide from her lap, picked the infant out of her crib, and withdrew into one of the dark window recesses to nurse the baby. At that moment Viktoria made a lunge for the stove and placed

46

her hand on the red-hot cooking ring. Cries of horror from all sides. The burn was inspected, advice given—"wet soap"; "the fresh inner skin of an egg"; "flour." None of these was available. Rejecting all suggestions, Maximiliane took Viktoria back on her lap, licked the injured hand, and put it in her mouth. She knew what this child needed and what she could obtain no other way—attention, now that all the other children had been admired, even the baby, who was back in her crate sleeping peacefully and hadn't even cried when she was taken from the breast.

The children grew tired. There was a lap for them all, a pair of arms to go around each.

When all the songs had been sung, Anselm Quint turned his radio to the American Forces Network. Bing Crosby was singing "I'm Dreaming of a White Christmas." A message from a distant, rich country, bound to melt hearts even more. Once again the plates of cookies were passed around and praised. "All is calm, all is bright."

When the village bells rang out at midnight, the deacon opened the window. The village, too, had been celebrating Christmas; how, none of the refugees on Mount Eyckel asked.

In later years, when the Quindts who had joined in the first postwar Christmas celebration at Eyckel Castle talked about it, they always mentioned the cookies. "Without anything, and with vinegar," they said while eating lean roast turkey, low in calories. And as they sipped their Riesling they told about the "hot punch" of 1945, which looked chemically red and tasted of artificial sweetener, just as in 1945 they had reminisced about Königsberg marzipan and carp à la Polonaise.

"Is that all you did—eat?" their children asked. And none of them was able to remember anything else about that Christmas celebration.

5

The agreements reached at the Potsdam Conference delayed the final determination of Poland's western boundary until such time as a peace conference should convene. It was not until the summer of 1950 that Pomerania was divided into two administrative districts—Stettin, now called Szczecin, and Köslin, now Koszalin. The county seat of Dramburg became Dravsko.

And what became of Poenichen? *Vae victis!* Woe to the vanquished! The three fatal shots fired by Old Quindt as the wagon train turned into the sleety highway were the last anyone heard of Poenichen.

Old Riepe had carried out his orders, seeing to it that the Baroness and his master and friend, the Baron, were interred in good time. Even Texa, the dachshund, had been buried near them. "A piece of Pomeranian earth, that's worth something," Old Quindt had once said at the bedside of his granddaughter, during one of her confinements. In that short but profound conversation they had discussed life after death.

Riepe had not been able to hide the fresh graves, and it had not started to snow until the following day. But once the looters who attacked the site with their spades uncovered the fresh cadaver of a dog, they stopped digging. Besides, the enemy soldiers were not interested in a dead estate owner. Even the Russian prisoners of war released from the camps and the Poles freed from forced labor felt no need to avenge themselves on the dead. Instead they looted the manor and ransacked the surroundings for buried valuables. For months they found one cache after another, even as Maximiliane—patiently, but with more imagination than accuracy—was making maps and sketches for her relations. Their inquiries always contained an explicit or tacit reproach that the boxes they entrusted to her had not been brought along on the flight.

The few estate workers who had remained behind on Poenichen showed their submission by hanging sheets out the windows; as a precaution, they also stayed in hiding. Only Willem Riepe approached the Soviet tanks and waved the red flag he had been concealing for twelve years. It is possible that in the gray light of dawn it was not clear that the black swastika in the white circle was missing; in any case, Willem was felled by the butt of a gun before he had a chance to show the number burned into his skin in the Oranienburg concentration camp. But later he was given a job as a publicist in a German prisoner-of-war camp near Minsk. His wife and her two youngest children were among those Pomeranians who were compulsorily evacuated in the summer of 1946.

In the hasty flight no one thought to remove from the servants' hall the map of Europe on which Martha Riepe had marked Hitler's invasions with pins and yarn, left in the positions of November 1942. In addition, a newspaper with a headline about the capture of Orlovsky, a suburb of Stalingrad, still hung from a hook. Both fell into the hands of a German-speaking Soviet officer, and as a consequence not only the manor but also the farm cottages and the village huts were put to the torch. Three times they lit the fire at the manor, but the stone walls stood fast. The white columns were blackened by flames, the windowpanes burst, but from a distance the whole continued to give the impression of "Pomeranian classic," as Old Quindt was wont to label the style.

It was rumored that seven inhabitants of Poenichen village were still living in the barn at the Blue Pond and in the half-destroyed inspector's cottage at Lake Poenichen, among them old Riepe, Finke the wheelwright, and the two old Jäckels. In nearby Arnswalde no stone was said to have remained in place. The Russians had gone off by now, and Polish farmers from the Ukraine, also forcibly removed from their homeland, poorer than the others, had arrived with kith and kin.

News from Pomerania penetrated infrequently and in distorted form to the ears of those who believed that they had only been temporarily evacuated and would one day return. The expellees still carried the fear in their bones and their eyes, more so than the refugees: Your house is on fire, your children all gone. There was nothing cheerful to report from Poenichen except that Klara Slewenka, the smith's wife, was said to have remarked after her first rape, "It's been one hell of a long time since any of us had any of that." But even this statement elicited little laughter.

Of the 143 people and eight carriages that had left Poenichen under Martha Riepe's direction, nine people, two horses, one tractor, and three wagons reached the village of Kirchbraken in Holstein. All the other people became stuck somewhere along the road or left the wagon train and scattered to the three winds searching for relatives. Seven people did not survive the rigors of the exodus.

Several things must be said about Martha Riepe. She was a downstairs child, born in the substructure of the manor to Otto and Anna Riepe. Her parents, coachman and housekeeper, were respected by everyone on Poenichen and loved by Maximiliane for as long as they lived their long lives of servitude. Their daughter rose to the confidential position of estate secretary, but she surely had some of her brother Willem's rebellious blood. After the First World War, Willem—obeying the slogan "Peace to the cottages, war on the palaces"—had tried to burn down the manor. A Communist, Willem was given shelter by Old Quindt after his release from Oranienburg camp. As for Martha, no sooner had Viktor Quint first visited Poenichen than she conceived a grand passion for him, Maximiliane's future husband. Her admiration, along with her love for Hitler, survived the collapse of the Third Reich, and now she was administrator of the remaining Quindt property—multiple, contradictory connections.

Who owned what had been salvaged—the original owner or the person who had managed to save it? Questions about ownership could be answered legally and humanely to the extent that they were asked, which Maximiliane did not do.

When she arrived on Mount Eyckel, she found a letter from Martha Riepe, mailed in Kirchbraken and addressed to her, Maximiliane. Instead of postage it had a rubber stamp attesting to the fact that the proper fee had been paid. In addition it bore the remark that its contents—"Check appropriate box"—were composed, not in English, French, or Russian, but in German, the language of the vanquished. Besides a query about Maximiliane's wherebouts it consisted of nothing more than the head count of people and horses from Poenichen and their present address.

The subsequent correspondence between these two very different women was short on words but rich in content; it never for a moment touched on how it could have happened that on the fourth day of the flight Martha Riepe had allowed the wagon train to start out without checking to be sure Maximiliane and her children were on board.

In one of her earliest communications Maximiliane wrote, "Send the christening bowl," adding no explanation of this strange request. Martha Riepe still harbored enough of the servant's mentality to comply at once, filling the bowl with drippings and packing it safely in a box with wheat kernels. She asked no questions but in the accompanying letter mentioned casually that they had been able to rescue Lieutenant Quint's hunting jacket, a statement that translated into an anxious query concerning his whereabouts.

The package with the undamaged bowl from the Courland china service—Royal Prussian Manufacture—did not arrive for two months, which was one of the reasons why the Kirghiz child was never baptized. Maximiliane was not particular about the sacraments; one could no longer count on her keeping to the conventions. Anyway, as a child of God, hadn't the newborn babe in the crate already stood in for the child in the manger? "He will wipe away all tears." Why should the child have wept? So close to her mother, sleeping in the curve of Maximiliane's stomach at night, during the day slung in a wool blanket on Maximiliane's back so that her hands would be free for the milk cans and baskets. This child was seldom any farther from her mother than she had been before birth.

During the months that followed, Martha Riepe consigned to the Quints such foodstuffs from her salvaged stores as she considered suitable. She kept to this habit until the hoard from Poenichen was exhausted.

Every time a letter with the Holstein postmark arrived, Joachim went for his pencil and the list of names he had compiled. As his mother read—"Old Klukas died in Mecklenburg"—he would draw a cross behind the name, using it as a punctuation mark, a symbol of woe. When his mother read something like "Kalinski the foreman and his wife are said to be living in Friedrichshafen, in the French zone," he would put a check mark against the names.

"You yourself heard the three shots." There is a

world of difference between knowing something in your head and reading it with your own eyes. "Get your list, Joachim. Make a cross for Grandfather and Great-grandma."

Joachim turned frightened eyes to his mother.

It is a time-proven remedy for one's own sorrow to have to comfort another. "Think about it, Mose. Would you like Grandfather to be picking up the Americans' discarded cigarette butts? Have you forgotten how much he liked to smoke? Should your old Great-grandma, who felt the cold so much, go gathering wood in the forest?"

"Where are they now?" Joachim wondered.

"At home." Maximiliane left moot whether she was referring to a heavenly or an earthly home. A piece of Pomeranian earth.

"Let's not tell the little children," Joachim suggested. "They wouldn't understand anyway." He folded up his memorial list and carefully put it back in the box he kept under the bed which held three children. Then he came to stand in front of his mother; rising on tiptoe, his arms tight against his body, he trembled. Not until then was Maximiliane aware that her oldest child had passed beyond crying.

It could be assumed that Martha Riepe was acting honestly when she made out a list of salvaged goods. She had traded the tractor to a farmer in exchange for his stabling the horses. Martha Riepe could handle figures, not horses; neither she nor old Frau Görke, with whom she shared a room, was able to perform coachman's services, and Griesemann, the head coachman, had found employment in a dairy. The Courland service had remained intact, as had the rolled-up paintings from the ancestors' gallery, but these were growing moldy because the barn that stored the expellees' possessions was damp. The other items on the list were: 160 white damask table napkins, 100 by 100 centimeters in size;

eight matching tablecloths for twenty-four persons, bearing the crests of the Quindts and the Malos from Königsberg; the rugs from the ladies' parlor and the smoking room; the letter from Bismarck that mentioned the difficulties of being a patriot and referred to the famous Poenichen pâté of wild game—the recipe for which, however, had been lost along with the last housekeeper. The list went on for two pages, and four additional pages enumerated what had had to be abandoned, such as bedding, linens, and clothing.

"We need . . . " Maximiliane wrote each time, and then, after a long interval, the desired items arrived, among them the table silver and the silver goblets. Maximiliane undertook the difficult task of teaching the children manners, particularly how to handle a knife and fork, which she considered essential to their upbringing. In Golo's case her attempts met with failure; as soon as he thought himself unobserved, he drank out of the bottle instead of the cup.

Martha's lists were incomplete only in that they never mentioned that Viktor's letters from the front had been preserved, as had the family tree he had worked out, showing the roots of the Pomeranian Quindts and the Silesian Quints combining into a single trunk, Viktor and Maximiliane, which began to branch out into the future, each of the children being represented as an acorn dangling from one limb.

Martha Riepe's favorite among the children was Edda, who resembled her father more than did the others, and whose mother she had never seen, which allowed her to fantasize that the child was hers. As she had once knitted for Lieutenant Quint, now she never tired of plying her needles for Edda, producing sweaters, skirts, and stockings out of yarn that had been intended in a time of free enterprise for binding up sheaves of maize in the conquered Ukraine. Having

54

been produced in excess, it could now be worked into durable pieces of clothing.

As Maximiliane tried one of these new garments on Edda, she held the child between her knees longer than necessary and examined her searchingly, trying to recall Viktor. She kept on forgetting how he had looked and how his voice had sounded. Like her father, Edda got goose pimples if you stroked her arm. When Maximiliane dreamed of her husband, he was wearing his uniform and still had both his arms; but in contrast to Christian Blaskorken and Ingo Brandes, Viktor had never been the man of her dreams.

At the end of the Quints' first winter on Mount Eyckel a request for information was forwarded to them by the grandmother in Charlottenburg. The inquiry had come from the United States.

"Who is Mrs. Daniel Green?" Joachim wanted to know.

"She's your grandmother," Maximiliane answered.

"How many grandmothers do we have anyway?"

"You can never have enough grandmothers."

Maximiliane then told the children about her mother, who had been a well-known photojournalist and had married a doctor. She tried to explain to them why a doctor whose ancestors had been members of the Jewish race had had to leave Germany. It turned out that the children were not interested in such explanations. A set of grandparents in America was interesting enough.

"Are they rich?"

"Do they live in a skyscraper?"

"Do they drive one of those big cars?"

"Pacific Drive," their mother read, "San Diego, California." The children squatted around her, and she told them about America, about oranges and coconuts, cocoa bushes and figs—stories from Never-Never Land.

"Summer lasts the year round, and the roses bloom forever." She waited for the effect.

"And when can you go sledding?" asked Edda, who tobogganed down to the village every day.

"You can't do that in California, but you can go swimming in the ocean. It's like paradise, the land of milk and honey," Maximiliane explained.

"Are we going there?" Golo asked.

"Later. First we have to write a letter to America."

This letter had to inform her mother, who had never wanted to be a mother, that in the intervening years she had become a grandmother five times over. After considerable reflection, Maximiliane restricted her information to the number, age, sex, and names of the children. She gave their address and added that twenty-six Quindts of all sorts were living together on Mount Eyckel. She listed the names of the living and omitted those of the dead; it was signs of life that were being looked for. "And you?" she wrote at the foot of the letter, penned an overlong dash, and repeated the question—"And you?" Ten lines of her large script were enough to fill a sheet.

Golo, who did not know how to read yet, stood at her side, urging her on. "Did you tell them to send chocolate? And cigarettes? And chewing gum!"

"It's written between the lines," Maximiliane assured him.

Vera, née Jadow, wedded to Maximiliane's father in an early marriage lasting all of five days, was not one of those Americans who made sacrifices in order to help the destitute population of postwar Germany. Her relationship to Germany was permanently disrupted; her emigration had meant the end of her brilliant career as a photojournalist. During the early years she had sustained herself and her husband by photographing teenage brides. After that she had given up photography

56

altogether. When she came across pictures of the destroyed cities of Europe or of the concentration camps, she looked at them only for their technical quality. Her husband, who no longer called himself Grün but Green, had managed to establish a practice and, like so many other psychiatrists of the Viennese school, was just beginning to make a name for himself.

Dr. and Mrs. Daniel Green were living in the lap of luxury compared to Europe in 1946, and Vera occasionally sent off a luxurious package, for the most part luxury items, quite impractical, though she assumed that a twenty-seven-year-old German woman must be in urgent need: silk scarves and a cocktail dress, pleated, pale yellow, with fringe at the neckline and hem. She also included a pair of nylon stockings—though these tore as soon as Maximiliane wore them inside her army boots. Each package was opened to cries of astonishment and disappointment.

The first package also contained a jar of Nescafé. One cup was enough to keep Maximiliane awake in her overcrowded bed—at her back Golo, damp with perspiration, and against her stomach the baby. Unused to insomnia, she did not know how to deal with her restlessness. She rose and left the children.

In her coffee intoxication she walked to the edge of the woods, her quilted jacket over her nightgown, her bare feet in her boots. Stopping to embrace a tree trunk, she rubbed her cheek against the rough bark as if it were a man's jacket. When she returned to the castle, she met old Great-aunt Maximiliane on the upper staircase. Instead of stepping to one side as she usually did, she hugged the old woman, shook her, and for a few seconds roused the dormant mind. An instant of recognition.

"The little Quindt girl from Poenichen!"

"My hat's off to you," Maximiliane replied—an echo of her grandfather.

The old lady slightly more lucid than usual, the young woman slightly crazier.

After the American aid organizations combined to form a central organization, CARE, Mrs. Daniel Green ordered a package a month and thus at long last became the support of her only daughter, whom she had abandoned as a baby. Once more Maximiliane was better off than others. At a time when it counted, she had a mother in California—a land where the cows gave powdered milk and the chickens laid powdered eggs, where they made butter out of peanuts.

America! America!

6

A Quindt commune could have come into existence on Mount Eyckel—surely shared need is as good an impetus as shared conviction. There was enough wood to heat the huge kitchen range; there was not enough to fuel the many potbellied stoves. But instead of cooking for everyone in a large pot, eleven families pushed their small pots and pans around on the stove top every noon. Any delicacy was prepared in secret by using electric hot plates, heaters, or pressing irons, which constantly led to short circuits because the wiring was overloaded. Since these operations continually consumed more than the allotted amount of electricity, the meters had to be set back to the proper number each night, a maneuver requiring a magnet; without illegal activities, you couldn't survive. Nor did the Quindts do a group laundry in the washhouse; each family did its own washing in a bowl stored under the bed. The big cooking buckets of the former youth hostel were used as rain catchers under defective gutters and served as water cisterns to sprinkle the tiniest of garden plots.

Most of the Quindts were willing to work, but not all were able to work. There were no jobs to be had, even if one gave up all expectation of employment suited to one's talents. So they gathered wood in the forest, sawed and split it, so that the wood warmed them even before it burned in the stove. By the same token, a basket of plucked blueberries provided weariness, satisfaction, and a sandwich spread.

Weather permitting, the Baltic uncle, Simon August. sat on a sun-warmed bench in the yard, wearing a discarded frock coat from a clothing donation, stretching his aching back whenever he had chopped wood for too long, and smoking homegrown tobacco in his pipe. "This is how it should be when you get old. It makes the leave-taking easier," he said at times. In spite of such thoughts, each dawn he carried his chamber pot to his tiny plot of ground and carefully emptied it over the tobacco and tomato plants.

New times brought new attitudes. By sacrificing various foodstuffs and some tobacco, the Quints from Lusatia replaced their son's trombone with a jazz trumpet. Anselm Quint continued to listen to the American military station on his old radio; these were new sounds for the German people, who had spent twelve years living in isolation and were now seeking a connection with the new world.

Anselm retired to the attic with his radio and the jazz trumpet, Louis Armstrong his teacher and model. He played by ear, without music—"Sentimental Journey"! No one who lived on Mount Eyckel during those months would ever forget his practice sessions. The General's distaste for everything she considered jazz was reinforced hourly. But if you were practicing with a career in mind, you were allowed to practice until midnight; survival was at stake. "Gonna take my heart back home," every day, a hundred times over. Sometimes Maximiliane and Frau Hieronimi stole up to the attic and danced together to the new beat.

Maximiliane was living on a mountain of women, as she had lived on an island of women at her boarding school, Hermannswerder. Did she or Frau Hieronimi have reason to dance, with their husbands missing, Frau Hieronimi's son still in the hospital?

60

Each morning Roswitha von Quindt, too, retired to the attic; she had been teaching herself Russian for a year. One day she confronted her mother with the *fait accompli.* "I've accepted a temporary position as an interpreter with the military tribunal in Nuremberg."

The General was outraged. "In our family no woman has ever worked for pay."

"Then it's about time," her daughter replied.

"Your father is a captive of the Russians, and you plan to speak the language of his enemies!"

"You should have let me learn it sooner. The border was only a hundred kilometers away."

Viktor's oldest sister, Ruth, at one time a Red Cross nurse, had established a nursery school in an empty barn in the village. First it was attended only by the children of the refugees, but then a few of the village children joined in. Ruth taught them counting-out rhymes and nursery rhymes, played hopscotch with them, sang songs for them. The various dialects mingled. Instead of a salary she was given a bottle of syrup, a bag of green peas, an occasional piece of bacon. In the true sense of the word she earned her daily bread, and she contributed to raising the villagers' opinion of the refugees, especially as she was not a Catholic.

In the little turret, "close to the birds in the sky," lived the so-called white aunts, the unmarried sisters Friederieke and Hildegard, who were related by marriage to the East Prussian Quindts. They were good at fancy needlework and at nothing else. Their refugee baggage contained countless sheets from which their numb and soon arthritic hands indefatigably pulled threads, stitching them back in other places—very laborious and very artful, but also useless. Eyelets and shadow stitches. Frivolities from the white aunts. Fortunately their Heavenly Father sustained them as well. Frau Hieronimi tried to assist Him in this, taking the delicate doilies to market. There was not much call for impractical aesthetic objects, however.

The best room was occupied by the widow of Ferdinand von Quindt, onetime president of the senate, who had not attended the family reunion because he was "unwilling to make common cause" with the middle-class Quints. His widow, having no choice but to make common cause, had to be thankful to have found shelter on Mount Eyckel. "I have to be thankful," noted each of her elegiac letters.

Deacon Quint had found a job as assistant minister in the nearby town of Moos-Kirchbach. With his own food coupons and with American cigarettes contributed by his son, he came into possession of a bicycle—without a light or bell, to be sure, but with bellows and inner tubes and an undamaged coaster brake, essential because of the steep hill. Each morning he left his shelter, returned at night, and brought back the Nuremberg newspaper. The Quindts made themselves cognizant of its most important items, which consisted mainly of public notices. Public notices about cereals, sugar, coal; reduction of the electricity allotment; shortening of the curfew hours: energy was parceled out to the Germans just as scantily as freedom. Death sentences in the Nuremberg trials; major industries decartelized; renewed rumors of impending war. The ashes were not quite cold yet. But for the moment it was more important to know which coupon would get you how many grams of shortening.

Klaus von Quindt, the General's brother-in-law, sent a card from his Russian prisoner-of-war camp containing the prescribed number of words. For several years Eyckel Castle did service as the central post office for all the Quindts.

Mathilde von Ansatz-Zinzenich, one of the General's sisters-in-law, was said to have saved nothing but the Almanach de Gotha, that venerable listing of the nobility. She wrote daily letters, using the Almanach like an address book. She wrote to the de Quintes in Strassburg—now, after a four-year interval, spelled Strasbourg again; she wrote to Adolf von Quindt in Friedberg; to Louisa Larsson, née von Quindt, in Sweden; and to the Zinzenichs in Xanten. But she received few answers, and even fewer of the hoped-for packages. One of her statements became proverbial: "Rich people like us simply don't know what it is not to have money."

One day Mathilde was observed sneaking out of the Baltic Quindts' room, slipping a piece of bread into the folds of her sleeve. Word got around. Old Simon August von Quindt would have chosen to ignore the incident, considering that the accused was a seventy-year-old woman, but the General sat in judgment, making Deacon Quint and one of the white aunts act as associate judges. The old man—a onetime Superior Court judge, a lifetime official, and already the recipient of a pension—went up to the culprit, planning to kiss her hand. He spoke of "mitigating circumstances," but the thief ignored his hand and never forgave him. Her lips grew even more pinched; she had had to swallow too much in her lifetime.

Mathilde's hysterical cough came on her, and she coughed for all the Quindts night after night, thus gaining consideration. So easy to explain yet so hard to put up with, almost as hard as the phrases with which the General opened and closed sentences—"East Prussians like ourselves," "We in the East." Since her own daughters had removed themselves from her tutelage, the General focused her need to exert influence onto new subjects. Maximiliane and her little children were there for the taking.

"You must not allow this boy"—she meant Golo— "to go on drinking from the bottle, Maximiliane. You let the children grow up like little savages. They are Quindts. Show yourself worthy of your task. Even if your name and rank and property have lost their meaning, even if it comes to the total debasement of all values, we must still distinguish and differentiate ourselves by the way we live. We in the East . . . ."

During such one-sided conversations with her aunt, Maximiliane as a rule stood by wordlessly chewing her fingernails, prompting the General to announce to her sister-in-law that this Maximiliane seemed a tiny bit feebleminded—"but that will make it all the easier for me to marry her off again."

What should Maximiliane have replied? It was a fact that she let the children grow up naturally, without constraint. She treated the baby, in her aunt's words, "like a bitch treats her puppies." When she wanted to straighten the sheet under the tiny body, she grabbed the baby's jacket with her teeth, held the infant aloft, then rolled her back and forth like a rump roast, much to her aunt's indignation and the baby's delight.

Though Golo and Edda no longer played "Come, woman" with weapons drawn, they had only switched to "Hello, Fräulein," with Golo as an American soldier in the army of occupation, Edda as a young German girl at whom he had merely to wave and throw some chewing gum for her to start sashaying at his side, wiggling her sturdy rear.

On their weekly bath nights Maximiliane did not wash her children separately by gender; for the sake of efficiency, she dunked them all in the same tub. She explained to the General, who had witnessed this procedure and clearly showed her outrage, "If I wash the boys first and then the girls, the water will get cold and the waiting children will get chilled."

To which the General countered, "It's a matter of morals, not of what is more practical, Maximiliane."

"When you've got nothing to start your children off with, there's nothing you should stop them from, either," Maximiliane did say another time.

64

"Now I lay me down to sleep." She made the children pray as she had been made to pray. With five children there was not much time for prayer, but she never missed a bedtime to say with assurance to each child, "God preserve you." Golo was the only one who turned these prayers into a dialogue, at the end of which he said, "Good night, God," and God answered, "Okay, Golo." Maximiliane did not feel called upon to object to God's form of expression.

One day Golo came back from the village with a handcart. Two of the wheels were missing tires, and the shaft was bent.

"Where did you get the cart?" his mother asked.

"The Wengels have two of them. I took the worse one," Golo replied. Maximiliane considered his answer sufficient to establish rights of possession in the case. For a month's supply of tobacco she acquired some blue paint for the cart. Maximiliane had lost her sense of property, and in questions of child rearing she managed without guidelines.

By now some of the child rearing, at least as far as the three older children were concerned, had been assumed by the village school—or, more precisely, by Herr Fuss and Fräulein Schramm, the teachers. And every morning Viktoria, holding her Aunt Ruth's hand, went to the nursery school—where, alas, she was most unhappy. While all the other children played and roughhoused, she stood in a corner chewing her nails, explaining to her aunt, "I'm bored."

The question of the children's missing father, which for various reasons had rarely been raised, was now discussed more and more openly in the Quindt circle, somewhat along the following lines: whether it was preferable to be the wife of a dead National Socialist or a living one; and whether Viktor Quint had, like his Führer, escaped the might of justice by killing himself or, along with his Führer, had disappeared from the

65

face of the earth—people did say that Argentina had taken in high party officials and military officers. Neither those who feared him nor those who revered him were willing to believe in Hitler's shameful suicide.

Maximiliane never expressed any strong interest in the question of her husband's fate; she was used to his absence. But deep inside her a desire was growing for arms stronger than those of children. Only a single time had she heard the cry of the screech owl at night, jumped up as if she had heard the call of the returning wild geese, and stood yearning at the window. Her ears were still not proof against the sounds of the jazz trumpet; they reminded her of Christian Blaskorken, the object of her first passion, the man at the lake—a man cloaked in mystery—who had blown his signals on an old hunting horn.

Although, statistically speaking, Maximiliane was among the surplus of three million women, you could not talk to her about "the fate of the women." She merely said, "The men are dead. We are alive." She was coolly aware that the future offered her three choices: she could lose herself totally in her children; she could look for fulfillment in a career; or she could make her loneliness more palatable by surrounding herself with beautiful objects. Whatever she chose, she must never lose sight of the commandment, "Thou shalt not covet thy neighbor's husband."

Frau Hieronimi, who absorbed rumors and news like a sponge, reported that she had heard of a woman in Nuremberg, a Frau Vogel or Vogler, who could give you information about a missing husband by dangling your wedding ring from a hair over the picture of the man in question. Depending on the direction the pendulum swung, east or west, you could tell where he was imprisoned. And if the ring did not move at all, then you had a definite answer at last. Two marks for the consultation, though you had to add a whole tobacco card, thirty cigarettes—an entire month's ration. West or east, living or dead. But unlike Frau Hieronimi, Maximiliane had no desire to know whether her husband was still alive. "Time will tell."

Spring was here. Though it came sooner than it did in the east, it arrived more hesitantly, preceded by many harbingers. The swallows returned, along with the soldiers of the occupation army. Anselm Quint was still practicing his jazz trumpet, and by now he had achieved a certain modest skill. Edda collected fresh thistles and new dandelions, and Joachim picked the first primroses.

Maximiliane left later than she had during the winter to get the milk in the village, and she took along two buckets. She had one of them filled with milk and sent the children home with it; then she herself took the empty bucket to a meadow where for days a mare had been grazing with her filly. Both animals could be talked to, especially if you brought a crust of bread or a carrot. The mare willingly shared with Maximiliane, and so Mirka was raised on mare's milk. It was thinner and sweeter than cow's milk, more similar to mother's milk. It was said that babies who were fed on mare's milk would have delicate, dusky skin but would grow up to be wild. Each day Maximiliane placed her arm around the mare's neck, rubbed her forehead against the forehead of the horse, and breathed in the familiar scent. Alas, Falada, hanging there!

By the time she returned with her milk bucket, she would be singing the old sentimental songs of her girlhood—"In the twilight, in the twilight." Jazz rhythms mingled with her voice—"Gonna take my heart back home." Anselm Quint had become proficient enough to play for the Americans; he was no longer playing in church for the honor of God but in American officers' messes in exchange for Nescafé, chewing gum, and Camel cigarettes. Sometimes he brought the children

sweet rolls, whose name they spoke with reverence—
"Doughnuts!" Soon his jazz group was being called the
Anselm Quint Band.

"My son is coming up in the world," his mother
announced proudly, but the General declared, "In our
family we do not come up in the world. We do our
duty."

One day Maximiliane was finally ready to accompany Frau Hieronimi to Nuremberg and consult the
"sibyl." The three older children were in school, Viktoria was in nursery school, the baby had been entrusted
to the white aunts. Her hair freshly washed, Maximiliane wore her only summer dress, the same one old
Frau Görke had made on Poenichen from blue-and-
white-checked sheets. Frau Hieronimi was dressed in
the yellow pleated number Maximiliane's mother had
sent from America.

The two women asked the way to Mittlerer Pirk-
heimer Strasse and then looked for the house. According to the description they had been given, it was a
corner building next to a mound of rubble. They did
not know the house number, and the name "Vogel" or
"Vogler" could be spoken only in whispers.

A rear house, twenty-four tenants, every stone step
on the staircase occupied by waiting women. Halfway
up, the key to the washroom hung from a peg. Smells
of cabbage. Finally Maximiliane, too, sat across from the
old woman. She pulled off her wedding ring and tore
out a hair without being asked, but the woman, half
high priestess, half witch, had evidently changed her
technique. She shuffled a deck of cards and, without
looking up, held it out to Maximiliane. "Pick three cards
toward your heart."

Maximiliane obeyed.

Then the old woman laid out seven cards face up,
placed seven more cards under them, and mumbled,
"One, two, three, four, five, six, seven, could my

mother be in heaven, my wife, my son, my father?" She looked up to say, "My cards do not lie." Starting with the jack of hearts, she counted out every seventh card and placed it on the table. She showed Maximiliane the ace of spades—"Death and horror." Then she held out the nine of clubs—"A small gift, perhaps an inheritance. But small. Here I see much happiness preceded by a lot of black, a lot of death." She repeated, "My cards do not lie," and dropped her hands into her lap. Her head drooped as well. The hour of truth had come to an end. Maximiliane discharged her obligation of two marks and put a slab of bacon into the basket that stood beside the table, half filled with paper bags.

Frau Hieronimi anxiously examined her face, walked past her, and in turn had a glimpse of the future. Five minutes later she caught up with Maximiliane, who had walked ahead to the next street corner. "Seven of hearts," she called out from a distance, "twice in a row." She hooked her arm under Maximiliane's, pressed it to her side, and beamed.

Maximiliane looked at her in surprise. The seven of hearts—a love card! Anna Hieronimi was forty years old!

The two women walked along the springtime streets, untying their kerchiefs; the wind blew through their hair and through the yellow daffodils blooming amid the ruins. A jeep drove past, and an American soldier called out, "Hello, Fräulein." One seven of hearts was sufficient to rejuvenate Anna Hieronimi. She brushed back strands of black hair, and her eyes glowed. Her lightheartedness was infectious. Together the women went to a coffee shop, drank artificial coffee, and ate a piece of cake in exchange for a fifty-gram bread coupon and a five-gram shortening coupon. Then they visited the black market and traded the sheeps' wool they had brought for an inner tube for Frau Hieronimi's bicycle.

In the train on the way back, Maximiliane listened

to two women talking. The first said to the second, "The girl's legs are as bowed as those of a Kirghiz."

That night she bandaged Mirka's legs, tying her knees together with a batiste diaper. She did not own anything more suitable. She kept this up for some time, but after a while she forgot all about it.

From spring to late autumn Maximiliane worked in the fields for Seifried, a farmer. She was a field hand. When it rained, she used a sack to keep her head and back dry. She hoed and pulled beets, she planted and hoed and harvested potatoes, she washed sugar beets in the brook and helped when they were boiled down into syrup. In good weather Mirka remained at the edge of the field, sleeping or crawling, always within sight or shouting range of her mother.

Once again Maximiliane jumed in with both feet. Whenever she was asked to do another job, she said, "Well, I could try." Her salary consisted of five hundredweight of winter potatoes and a bucket of syrup. At night she mixed raw-potato water into the children's milk. Her children looked healthier than the village children; even Viktoria was growing sturdier.

The fruit ripening in the gardens and on the trees that lined the roads was protected by field guards. Three of Maximiliane's children happened to be of climbing age, and she was supposed to keep an eye on them. Instead, she herself scaled the trees, pressing down the branches so that the children could reach the apples. She too was of climbing age.

On one occasion, Joachim, usually so diffident, came running, beaming with joy. "I climbed free today!" His conquest was one of the tallest pear trees far and wide.

As soon as Heiland, the field guard, drew near, Joachim and Edda would run away, but Golo was more apt to rely on his eyes and his dimples. One day the

70

guard caught him, took him by the collar, and dragged him over to his mother, who was sitting on a slope hiding the stolen fruit under her skirt. He called her to task. She only looked at him and said. "Our Pomeranian pears are being eaten by strangers, too."

"Polacks," he said, taking the few pears from Golo.

When Maximiliane munched apples, lines of poetry invariably came to her mind, for ten years earlier she had ingested both together; different varieties of apples called for different poems. Her need for words was greater than her need for calories and vitamins. Accidentally she came across a dog-eared copy of *Gone with the Wind*, and she spent the next few nights sitting on the stairs, the book on her knees, the barn lantern and a little basket of apples at her side. Wrapped in the quilted camouflage jacket, her feet in felt boots, she read, taking a liking to Rhett Butler, gripped by Scarlett's fate, with which her own could easily keep pace. What a war! What a country! America! America!

A country that sent packages now, at regular but widely spaced intervals. Butter from peanuts! Milk powder and egg powder in cans! Coconut flakes! A Never-Never Land.

A clothing collection for refugees yielded jackets and caps and shoes for the little Quints, just as in the old days Lenchen Priebe had received Maximiliane's castoffs. A great shift in roles was taking place, the former givers becoming takers; but now the givers were as joyless as the takers. The "ladies' bower" filled with piles of boxes, and there was no more room under the beds. Several layers of clothing hung from the stags' horns in the great hall. Maximiliane had had no experience in tidying up. Tidiness was, for her, something that maids brought about and that one was not allowed to disturb. Troubled, she saw possessions accumulate. Who was to carry all this stuff when they moved on one day?

She sewed clothes for the children from American sugar sacks imprinted "Oscar Miller." She spread the unstitched sacks out on the floor, and since she had no pattern or tape measure, she laid the children on the fabric one after another and wielded her shears to follow their outlines. The wife of Fuss the teacher lent her a sewing machine with manual controls. Joachim turned the wheel, faster or slower depending on her instructions, and his mother sewed the fine seams she had been taught at boarding school. The result was tunics of primitive originality, equipped with the essentials for any piece of clothing—holes for the head and arms. The Quint children were transformed into little bedouins—an image Maximiliane would read about twenty years later in the French fashion magazine *Madame*.

She tried to make the same sort of tunic for herself, but she foundered on the tucks; and unfortunately sack dresses would not be in vogue for another ten years. She did not own a mirror—but wait: Frau Görke was still living in Kirchbraken. She sent the two flour sacks with the unpicked seams, and four weeks later a package arrived from Holstein, containing among other things a dress for Maximiliane. "Oscar" ran in large letters across the back, but the front was free from print and all the tucks were in the right places. Frau Görke still remembered the measurements of her Pomeranian client.

In addition the package brought garments for all the children. Frau Görke had run up trousers and jackets for the little Quints out of remnants left over from cutting up Wehrmacht uniforms and turning them into civilian clothes; since December 1, the wearing of uniforms or parts thereof had been forbidden. Because many Holstein men had been in the navy, there was a lot of blue cloth along with the field-gray. Now the Quint children looked like little foot soldiers and were the butt of much laughter in the village.

72

Accompanied by the first warm sunshine of March 1947, Maximiliane set out one day with the handcart and all the children to gather wood and pinecones in the forest. They ran into Herr Wengel; it was impossible to avoid him. Seeing his cart, he stopped and flew roughly at Golo, who was holding the shaft. "That's my cart. Hand it over!"

"This beautiful toy cart?" Maximiliane inquired, giving Wengel the same kind of look that had once confounded her teachers.

But Wengel was made of sterner stuff. "Gypsies! Polacks!"

Maximiliane's eyes filled with tears. The children looked anxiously at their mother, waiting for a signal to burst into their wonted screaming. But Maximiliane lifted little Mirka from the cart and pressed her into the farmer's arms. "Hold the child so I can clear out the cart."

She then lifted out Viktoria, who fought back, uttering shrill screams. Spreading the pillows out by the side of the path, she took the baby from the confused man, laid her down, and handed the farmer the shaft. "Take it. The blue paint is free."

"Get out of here and take the damned cart with you," said Farmer Wengel. You could hardly expect more from him in the way of graciousness.

7

More and more frequently Maximiliane clutched her throat, opened the top buttons of her blouse, gasped for air, and breathed deeply. Eyckel Castle was beginning to hem her in.

"How much longer are we going to stay in this pigsty?" Golo asked. "I thought we were going to America."

"Later," his mother replied.

For now, they were still tied to the place, if only by two egg-laying Leghorns. Using wire mesh and boards, the residents of Eyckel Castle had built hutches along the walls where they kept rabbits, pigeons, and chickens. Maximiliane's chickens sublet part of Baron von Sixt's chicken coop—great property owners had become small animal keepers. Cash grew scarcer even as it kept decreasing in value; the creeping inflation could easily turn into a galloping one, just as it had after the First World War.

In the emergency shelters on Mount Eyckel emergency industries arose, turning out straw stars and hand-carved kitchen spoons: regression to the preindustrial era, handwoven materials, hand-thrown pots, hand-knitted goods. The lack of material and machinery for the necessities resulted in the manufacture of many unnecessary articles. In village cottages butter churns and looms reappeared, as did spinning wheels. The wardrobes in farmers' houses filled with rugs and leather satchels, woolen cloth and jewelry. Every morning Maximiliane ran into city dwellers coming to the village for hoarding forays, on errands of beggars and scroungers.

Deacon Quint heard that a woman from Nuremberg, in dire straits, had traded her wedding ring for a bag of potatoes in Moos-Kirchbach. From the pulpit he urged the ring's recipient to return it—that is, to place it surreptitiously in the collection plate. He tried to move hardened hearts, and he spoke of the sacrament of honor.

Maximiliane's money, too, was about to give out, although she spent little and worked a great deal. She was given emoluments by Farmer Seifried, just as the farmhands on Poenichen had been rewarded by the Quindt family. She wrote short letters to her boarding school friends—Isabella von Fredell in Nienburg, Wilma von Reventlow in Münster, Marianne Stumm, the officer's widow, in Bad Schwartau. Containing such sentences as "I'm working like a horse!" and "I'm learning to stoop," they expressed astonishment rather than complaint. Marianne Stumm wrote back that because of her two children, she was learning to do without personal happiness.

In Pomerania the farmhands worked together in rows in the potato and beet fields; here in the west a single worker hoed a field—which Maximiliane called a "bed"—of barely three acres. Her only company at work was little Mirka, who lay and later sat at the edge of the cultivated land. The solitude did her good. She gathered up potatoes with both hands at once, spread out beets with both hands, and hardly ever looked up from her work. She lived like a person who was half blind; she had no eyes for the natural beauties of Franconia, comparing whatever she saw with Pomerania.

The residents of Eyckel Castle were not very popular in the village, where they were still considered something special. For this reason they had to go even hungrier and, in those rooms that were so hard to heat, even colder, especially as they lacked the most important thing—connections. They particularly lacked connections to artisans. As more and more rain seeped through the faulty tile roofs, more and more containers were set in the attics to catch the water. The beds had to be moved away from the damp stone walls. The floorboards became splintery, the stairs crumbly. Nobody wanted the castle, even as a gift; there was general agreement about that. It was barely adequate as a refugee camp.

By and by the more competent and younger Quindts left Mount Eyckel. Marie-Louise, the General's younger daughter, went to Hersbruck to be apprenticed to a potter. She took up temporary residence in his kiln room, the kiln providing occasional heat. Deacon Quint had established temporary quarters for himself and his wife in the sacristy of his church.

Every letter Maximiliane received used the word *temporary*. Martha Riepe and Frau Görke had taken up temporary quarters in a farm cottage abandoned by the bombed-out Hamburg refugees. "What should be done with the horses?" Martha asked. "And the wagons can't stay in the barn forever. I have acquired a knitting machine and do knitting on commission. The people have to bring their own wool. Frau Görke sews the parts together for me. You could also find temporary shelter here, but you have to have an entry permit and a residential permit and a permit for ration coupons."

Frau Hieronimi had also moved out, but only down to the village, where a death had freed up a separate apartment in the house of Kroll, the carpenter. She had set up a temporary shoemaker's shop. Kroll furnished her with wooden soles made to measure, and on these she nailed webbing and leather straps cut from old handbags and school satchels, occasionally even from the leather thongs made for opening and closing train windows. She had still had no news of her husband, but more and more frequently a car parked near her home and remained there for increasingly long periods. Its owner, a certain Herr Geiger from Nuremberg, was said to be bringing materials and orders for shoes. Frau Hieronimi became the subject of gossip.

Sometimes in the evenings Maximiliane went to visit her on the way home and sat with her a while, handing her the metal studs as they talked. "Why do you do it?" she asked.

Frau Hieronimi pounded the wooden sole. "You don't know anything," she said. "You're not a woman, you're just a mother. Fidelity! People don't know what they're talking about. At home, and all through the war, I could stand being alone. But not here, where I'm a stranger. I'm over forty!"

"The seven of hearts, in Nuremberg?" Maximiliane searched, forcing herself to keep her voice cheerful.

"Not an honor card, just a little one," Frau Hieronimi answered. "They ought to lock up women like me, but whatever they do, they can't let us go on living like this—as excess baggage." For a moment she seemed at odds with the whole world, but then she picked up her hammer and beat down vigorously on the tacks. "I still remember the day you arrived on Mount Eyckel, protected by your children."

"But you have children," Maximiliane broke in.

"One of them is dead, and they shot the other one into a cripple."

"You could take him from the hospital."

"I taught him to walk once; I can't do it a second time. And my daughter has written me only twice, once at Christmas and once on Mother's Day. I didn't look after my own parents either. I up and left when I was seventeen. I want to get away from here, and I don't know where to go. I'm making shoes so that others can walk! Your calm makes me nervous, Maximiliane."

One evening at the end of May when Maximiliane returned from working in the fields, there was a young woman waiting for her. She recognized her from a distance, put down her bucket and her basket, set Mirka down in the grass, and opened her arms. It was Anya, the Polish girl who had served as housemaid and nursemaid on Poenichen during the war years. Together with Claude, a French prisoner of war who was serving as gardener, Anya had fled as the front approached.

Beaming, she picked up two of the children at the same time. "How big they've grown," she said, "how handsome." She spoke a mixture of German, French, and Polish. Her first question was about *"Monsieur l'officier."*

"Nie ma?" she asked.

When Maximiliane did not answer, she repeated her question in German. "No more?"

"No," Maximiliane replied. *"Nie ma."*

Anya put down the two children and picked up Mirka. "A new baby," she said. "More beautiful than the others." She sang, *"Stary niedwiec mocno spie,"* a Polish nursery song about a sleeping bear, one she used to sing to them when they had all lived on Poenichen. Joachim, Golo, and Edda joined in the refrain. *"Jak sie zbudzi, to nas zje"*—"When he wakes, he'll eat you up."

Anya stayed overnight. She told Maximiliane and the children that she and Claude had gone to France, to his father's vineyard, but that her love for Poland had turned out to be stronger than her love for Claude. Now she wanted to go home. "Poland is free," she said, adding that she had obtained all the necessary papers. In Marburg she had run into Lenchen Priebe from Poenichen, and from Lenchen she had learned the Mount Eyckel address. *"Lenchen chic. Très chic."* The dress Anya was wearing had been given her by Lenchen, along with some chocolate and cigarettes.

The following morning Anya set out, taking with her Maximiliane's longing for the East. "Off to Lodz," Anya cried as she ran down the mountain, "to Lodz."

At the beginning of June, when the old Baltic uncle, Simon August, suffered a heart attack, Maximiliane assumed his care. "I'm still not calm enough," he said. "I've been given my notice, but the date hasn't been set yet!" Once, as Maximiliane rose to help him, he gently pressed her back down in the chair. "Stay," he said. "I don't need anything. Everyone wants to do something all the time. Everyone runs around."

Maximiliane sat by his bed during his five-hour death throes. Now and then one of the children came in and stood near her. "Don't be afraid," she said. "He is only going where Grandfather and Great-grandma have already gone. There are a lot more Quindts there than here." In fact she was not entirely certain whether that state was to be preferred.

More and more Eyckel Castle became an old-age home for refugees, and the General continued to apportion the permissible rations of sorrow and joy. Maximiliane's children kept out of her way; there were enough other playgrounds for them. How many things could have been bought for these children without squandering money—things that would have been wasted on Maximiliane, an only child. Since there were no toys for sale, however, the children were left with creative play. They made stilts out of branches, and of course Golo was the first one foolhardy enough to stalk around on them; no admonition to be careful ever reached his ears. An old piece of rope tied to the protruding limb of an apple tree served as a swing. Edda sewed and molded dolls from rags, braiding red plaits for them from cloth Martha had sent. Viktoria promptly pulled the braids off the dolls and tore their clothes; she was a destructive child who wept over what she had destroyed, a child who purposely fell down or jammed her fingers just to make someone feel sorry for her and comfort her. None of the other children was washed and combed as often as she, and none looked as neglected as she, a child to whom everyone slipped a little something.

During the hot summer months the little Quints went shoeless to school in order to save on leather. The village children laughed at them, but Edda put her bare foot down. "At home we have ten pairs of shoes each and a big castle and a hundred horses," she shouted, and the village children shouted back, "Fly away home! Fly away home!"

Edda was ambitious and had an unquenchable thirst for knowledge. No notebooks were as neat as hers. In school her ears grew rosy with effort, as her father's had done. If she could not answer a question at once, her hands balled furiously into fists. She worked arithmetic problems carefully and slowly.

Golo, on the other hand, remained distracted, never taking school seriously. He was in the same grade as Edda and sat right next to her. He considered it a matter of supreme indifference whether a word had one *t* or two, two *e*'s or *ie*; he never did learn to spell. Nor was he ever seen reading a book; the aversion he had displayed as a toddler remained with him. Though he could calculate quickly, he always rounded off. Worst of all, he was often late to class or was kept after recess when he was involved in one of his black-market deals. Often he did not show his face in school for days on end. "If he keeps on this way, he'll never amount to anything," said Fräulein Schramm, but even as she spoke she ran her hand through his curls—a temptation hardly any woman could resist. "I'd certainly like to know where you're going to end up one of these days," Herr Fuss declared.

Joachim accomplished rather more than was required in school. Without being asked, he searched for words that would rhyme or started each line with words beginning with specific letters. He used up too much paper and too many pencils. When the teacher dictated an exercise, he listened carelessly, and though he never made a spelling error, the words he put down were different; he improved on the given text. In one composition, "The Road I Take to School," he wrote, "In winter it is still dark when we walk to school. At such times the bears snore in the bushes." When the last sentence was read out loud by Herr Fuss, the children roared with laughter and Joachim blushed. Edda came to his defense. "It's absolutely true!" Golo also affirmed that in the dark you could hear the bears.

"Maybe where you Quints come from they still have bears."

A new wave of laughter broke over Joachim's head.

Maximiliane did not interfere with her children's formal education. Nor, during the crucial formative years, did she ever say, "Elbows off the table" or "Wash your hands before dinner." Most of the time there was no water anyway, and sometimes there was not even a table. Soap and towels were too scarce to be wasted on pedagogy. For a long time the Quints' meals were such that Maximiliane sat her children in a row on the table or on a wall, like little birds on a wire, and spoon-fed them in turn, achieving—and this was what she cared about—a high degree of justice and efficiency.

On the whole the children spent two happy years on Mount Eyckel. Thanks to potato water, mare's milk, and mushrooms, they were better nourished than the local children. At the end of the long, hot summer of 1947—when fields were dry, food rations had been cut even further, and only tomatoes and tobacco grew to

ripeness in the warm castle gardens—the Quints were
healthy and tanned. Maximiliane had become slender
from working in the fields in the heat. For simplicity
she wore her hair tied with a ribbon at the nape of her
neck, a style the General stigmatized as "childish," just
as she had criticized the visit of the Polish girl, which
had aroused her lasting displeasure.

Now that even Mirka had learned to walk, Maximiliane had no intention of spending another winter
with the children within the cold, damp walls of the
castle. They would move to Holstein to join the remnants of the Quindt wagon train. She wrote of her plans
to Martha Riepe. As the first sign of the impending
departure, she sent Golo to Farmer Wengel with the
stolen handcart. "Tell him we won't be needing it anymore."

What kind of people were these, stealing handcarts
and returning handcarts, laughing when there was
nothing to laugh about?

"Come, we'll have a great big fire," she told the
children in late September. She burned all they had
accumulated in two years, and she must have tossed
in whatever came to hand; she always had had a soft
spot for ritual solstice fires. Edda tried to salvage this
and that, pulling half-charred toys from the fire. Whatever she could still use that could be packed up, Maximiliane mailed off to Kirchbraken.

The bedrolls were roped up once more, giving the
children to understand that departure was imminent.
Anxious and idle, Joachim sat beside the bundles and
asked what was to become of the white aunts and of
old Aunt Maximiliane.

"Don't bring up all the aunts now, Mose," Maximiliane begged him. "We can't worry about them. Our
life has to go on." Banal but true.

Excited, Golo ran through the halls announcing,
"It's starting again!" Edda, forever finding more things

that had to be taken along, packed and repacked her bundle. And as always before major events, Viktoria ran a temperature. Without help from anyone, Mirka donned the bedouin tunic Viktoria had outgrown, which reached down to her toes; an independent child, observant, silent, friendly, and exotic. Her membership in the family was visible only in her "saucer eyes," though they turned out paler than Golo's and even than her mother's.

"Come on," Maximiliane said at last. "Don't look back."

She did not possess the requisite permits allowing her to move to Holstein. What complicated errands would procure them? She put her faith in the effectiveness of her five children. "Come" had been the word she most frequently used during her years of dealing with the children. Later she would say, "Run."

The Quint's second attempt to reach Holstein also miscarried. This time they got no farther than Marburg on the Lahn, and this time the cause was not Golo but Viktoria. It turned out that her fever was not a travel fever but was caused by measles. Her temperature rose to 102 degrees, and red patches appeared on the delicate skin of her face. It was too late for precautions; the other children had already been infected.

Each of them went through the kind of measles suited to their individual temperaments. Joachim's case was careful and thorough and long-lasting, Edda's normal, Golo's virulent but short, Mirka's barely noticeable. Five children with the measles in a strange city; no antibiotics, no protection against infection. Joachim with a stubborn case of conjunctivitis, so that every morning his oozing, closed eyes had to be washed out with camomile tea; Viktoria with vomiting and cramps and with a loud, barking cough that no one would have expected from such a fragile little girl—and all this in a barracks camp, the overnight shelter of Christian Emergency Aid, where the Quints had found refuge.

After the children had been admitted to the university hospital, Maximiliane went to look for Lenchen Priebe. She took the outbreak of measles as an intervention by fate: she was stuck in Marburg. The countless packages she had mailed ahead would get to Holstein without her.

She never made a third attempt to join her remaining possessions, though she would probably have felt more at ease in the Holstein countryside with its lakes and leafy forests, its tree-lined avenues and softly rolling fields, than she did in a university town with steep, narrow alleys and tiny squares.

It should be reported here also that in the period following Deacon Quint's admonitory sermon, five wedding rings were put in the collection plate. Thereupon the deacon preached on the parable of the five wedding rings, which was not to be found in any Bible.

8

All evil is repaid in this world; but so are all good deeds. Old Quindt had once extended his protection to Dorchen Priebe, the sixteen-year-old housemaid on Poenichen, after young Franz von Jadow, Maximiliane's uncle, made her pregnant. After his discharge from the army in the First World War, Franz had frequently visited Poenichen, but later he paid no attention to the child and disappeared somewhere in North America. Though Quindt fired Dorchen, he found her a job as a maid in Dramburg and took responsibility for the child. The baby had been christened Helene, but she was always called Lenchen. Two years younger than Maximiliane, she, along with several other village children, was allowed to play with the child of the manor.

Lenchen had changed beyond all recognition, and Maximiliane walked right past her although she was looking for her. But she herself was recognized. Lenchen turned around and grabbed her arm. "Maxe! You're surprised, aren't you?"

Maximiliane was indeed surprised. She was looking at the very model of a "German Fräulein." Lenchen's straight, straw-colored Pomeranian hair was fluffed up and dyed platinum; her lips were brick-red, as was her duffle coat. In addition, she wore nylon stockings and stiletto-heel shoes. But beneath the varnish still dwelt good-natured Lenchen Priebe, even now ready to laugh and ready to help.

Since leaving Pomerania, Lenchen Priebe had learned more than Maximiliane. She understood the art of survival, was skilled in barter as well as in dealings with housing bureaus and rationing offices, knew exactly where the night freight trains carrying coal slowed down enough for you to jump up and fill your shopping bag. She lived on the Rotenberg, still a good address. Most of the houses had been confiscated for use by officers of the American occupation army, but the house where Lenchen lived sported an Off Limits sign because it was owned by an "uninvolved upholder of civilization," one Professor Heynold, who specialized in art history and had a significant collection of modern paintings that had heretofore been condemned as "degenerate."

Lenchen took Maximiliane home with her. She lived on the ground floor in a large room with a connecting door to the owner's parlor, the only room that could be heated.

"Don't call me Lenchen," she said after locking the door. "Call me Helen. Lenchen tells everybody where I come from. I use my father's name now, too—von Jadow."

She opened a drawer where she kept her treasures—several packages of coffee beans, cookies, stockings, Chesterfield cigarettes.

"Just tell me what you want. You can have anything, everything. After all, we're cousins."

Her speech was punctuated by *okay*s and *all right*s. Regretfully she sent Maximiliane away; she was expecting her friend—she said "my boyfriend"—but before Maximiliane left, Lenchen filled her pockets with chocolate and chewing gum for the children.

"I'll get you out of there," she said on the doorstep. "I make the rules in this house, and if I tell them you're my cousin, a real baroness, it will work. Let them make a little more room for us here—they didn't lose anything in the war. The two of us, after all, lost everything." And her "everything" encompassed in equal measure the Quindt estate and the cottage of her grandfather Priebe, a dairyman and subsequent local party leader.

Slightly embarrassed, Maximiliane pointed to the connecting door. "Don't the owners object?"

Lenchen Priebe laughed. "They don't hear or see a thing! But they eat, all the same! The professor is a heavy smoker, and I stop the wife's mouth with a can of corned beef. I couldn't care less what they say about me. Okay? At first I thought Bob would marry me and take me home with him, but the thought never crossed his mind! His unit was transferred. His last night here, he brought Jimmy—'a friend of a friend.' First I cried, but Jimmy came from Texas too. My current friend is called Abraham—that's right, just like in the Bible. One or another of them will take me over there. Other girls manage it, and anything they can do I can do better. American women don't seem to be such hot stuff. By the way, if you need a friend, just let me know. Abraham will bring one along, and we'll have a party here."

"I have five children!"

"Okay, but you don't have a man. By the way, Abraham is black, just so that you know. Don't make a fuss when you meet him. He's a first-rate boy. Leave the kids where they are for now; the Yanks are deathly afraid of catching a disease."

Almost unconsciously she fingered the parchment shade of the floor lamp while she spoke. "They say this is human skin. Made in the concentration camps. Did you know that? The Yanks think that's terribly interesting, and they'll pay as much as two cartons of cigarettes for one."

Maximiliane clutched her throat, that was all. But

never again would she be able to look at a parchment lampshade without a feeling of horror.

Two days later Frau Heynold invited Maximiliane to tea. They drank a thin rose-hip brew, and a tray of sweet rolls was offered. Before Maximiliane had uttered even one complete sentence, her hostess raised both hands to interrupt.

"Please don't tell me anything about your terrible flight. So much misery makes me absolutely ill. You did own a manorial estate in the East, isn't that correct?"

And Maximiliane told the woman what she wanted to hear—game hunts and skating parties.

"Your husband is missing in action?"

"Yes, since the final days of the war."

"Your little girl is ill, your cousin told me?"

"Yes," Maximiliane answered, "but it won't be long before they'll let me take her home from the hospital."

According to the regulations of the High Commission, only close family members of previous residents were allowed to move to such cities as Marburg, undamaged and overcrowded. But Maximiliane succeeded in advancing as far as the residence officer, and in the faultless English she had learned from Miss Gledhill in boarding school she expressed her desire for shelter in the residential area of Marburg. Perhaps the officer was captivated by her beautiful eyes or impressed by the fact that her mother had emigrated to the United States, but in any case the Quints were granted "temporary immigration permits without claim to housing."

They were allowed to take up temporary residence in Professor Heynold's house. "As a favor to your cousin," the professor said to Maximiliane. And he added, "Before they quarter total strangers on us. This way at least you know who you're sharing your roof with."

It had been agreed that Maximiliane was to devote three hours a day to cleaning the house in exchange for her room. For the first time in her life she was given a key to the front door; on Poenichen the dogs had provided security, on Mount Eyckel their widely known poverty had safeguarded them against burglaries. Now she was handed not only the front-door key but also a key to her room and a key to the bathroom—a whole ring of keys.

One by one Maximiliane brought the children home from the hospital, in order of their recovery. First came little Mirka. "An adorable child," said Frau Heynold, and as always, Mirka declared, "Thank you," curtsying deeply. You couldn't have asked for a better child to have around the house.

When Maximiliane arrived with the next child, the lady of the house proved somewhat less friendly; with the third, she was outraged.

"You can't just waltz in here with one child after another!"

"They were born one after another, after all." Maximiliane remained serene.

From then on she was no longer regarded as a baroness from the East and treated accordingly. To her hosts she became just another one of those refugees with their exorbitant demands, shamelessly exploiting the good nature of the local residents. And of course the Heynolds had had no idea that she was the wife of a "militarist and Nazi." Then again, every few weeks she was transformed into the daughter of an emigrant, the recipient of a CARE package from the United States. And even Maximiliane had her token Jew, her stepfather, whom she could bring into the picture as required. The Germans' re-education proceeded under unfavorable circumstances. "Potato pancakes and applesauce" was the slogan expressing their immediate goals in life.

Every few days Lenchen Priebe, alias Helene or

Helen von Jadow, was forced to soften the atmosphere in the house with powdered milk or coffee beans.

The Quints occupied a room facing a hill, somewhat dark but spacious and completely furnished—"over-furnished," according to Maximiliane. Plush and mahogany. The lady of the house responded testily to the second water stain that appeared on the desk top. "I had assumed that you knew how to treat valuable furniture and would not set wet glasses down on it," she said to Maximiliane in the children's presence. When she criticized the "wet circles" on a third occasion, Edda suggested, "We could use square glasses."

The lady of the house, taken aback, was permanently offended by this rude little girl. Maximiliane found herself forced to admonish the children with "Watch what you're doing" and "Don't do that" and "Keep quiet." But she could not watch five children all at the same time; Golo alone would have required two guardians.

After these experiences Maximiliane retained an aversion to polished furniture for the rest of her life. From then on she chose her domiciles according to whether the furniture was meant to be used or she was meant to be its curator.

As agreed, she cleaned house for three hours a day, doing her work neither grudgingly nor clumsily. Since there was no floor wax to be had, and since in the last year of the war Frau Heynold had obtained great quantities of brown shoe polish at a good price, Maximiliane waxed the stairs with shoe polish. Meanwhile, other people were polishing their shoes with floor wax. The structure of the market system was in a decided state of disarray.

The last child to come home from the hospital was Viktoria, still ailing and unfortunately still coughing. It also turned out that the little girl no longer owned a pair of shoes. Maximiliane summoned Golo, who confessed to trading the shoes for cigarettes and the cigarettes for lard. "I had no way of knowing she'd get well!"

At night, when the children were asleep, Maximiliane sat on the polished stairs outside her room and read by the light of the dim hall bulb; not Faulkner and Kafka yet, but from the local library, Cronin and Maugham. She no longer had access to rich offerings of apples and poems, as on Poenichen; both were in short supply, and she was hungry for both. She could not afford to be choosy, but one day her lap did finally hold the poems of Stefan George. When she got to "Hymn to a Young Leader from the First World War," she did not even have a windfall apple. "But you, do not imitate the uncaring crowd / That yesterday was hailed and today condemned to the rubbish heap. . . ."

One day she opened a novel by Daphne du Maurier—*Rebecca*, also borrowed from the town library—but she did not get past the first sentence: "Last night I dreamt I went to Manderley again." Clutching her knees with both arms, she laid down her head and sorrowed for Poenichen as Iphigenia had sorrowed for Mycenae.

Abraham Wolf from the state of Ohio found her in this condition and sat down by her side. "What do you need?" he asked, and he listed all the glories of the American PX. Maximiliane shook her head. Suddenly his teeth flashed in the darkness, and he beamed with understanding. "All you need is love!" He was putting his arm around her when Helene appeared on the landing.

In consideration of Abraham, the Quint children had changed the game "Who's afraid of the Big Bad Wolf?" to "Who's afraid of Frau Heynold?" Maximiliane, called on the carpet by the lady in question, promised to make them stop, but Edda soon found a variant with a milder reference to a certain party. "Please may I take one giant step, Frau Heynold?"

Once again Frau Heynold's wrath was aroused. "You must insist that your children respect adults."

"But surely not fear them," Maximiliane answered.

"I'd like to know who raised you, Frau Quint."

"A whole row of governesses."

Once more it was necessary to sweeten the lady's disposition with a large jar of peanut butter from Lenchen Priebe's private stock. In this house Maximiliane bit all her nails to the quick. Joachim and Viktoria copied her. The maternal power to mold was unusually strong.

Every evening young and old were out and about, hungry and cold, letting themselves be persuaded of the wisdom of new, humane ideas. They gathered in churches, schools, and lecture halls. There were concerts in the Philippinum—Béla Bartók and Stravinsky; to get a ticket you had to hand over a piece of pressed coal. Every seat in the university's large auditorium was filled nightly for required lectures in civics—"The Bases of Present-Day German Existence."

Maximiliane could have heard Martin Niemöller speak on German collective guilt in the university chapel; Ortega y Gasset also traveled through the three western zones to instruct the Germans about their past wrongs and their future tasks. But there were the five children, whom she could not leave home alone. Besides, recalling Old Quindt or her mother, she could not easily believe in collective guilt—more likely, collective shame.

When Maximiliane did leave the children home alone—regularly each week—she went to the movies without first bothering to find out the name of the film. Helen Priebe, who was charged with watching the children on these occasions, was none too particular about her job. It was understandable, therefore, that one such evening a fire, though only a small one, should break out in the room while Golo was fooling around with a lighter. Since Joachim had been able to put it out quickly with water from a saucepan, Frau Heynold's distress at the hole in the plush upholstery of the sofa seemed out of all proportion.

"Where do you run off to at night anyway?"

Maximiliane looked at her questioner and said with disarming candor, "I go out to have a good cry."

Where else but in the darkness of a movie house could the mother of small children cry undisturbed? Each time she came out of the movies, her face was wet with tears.

The children, exploiters one and all, needed her and never let her forget it. Maximiliane was exhausted, and she was on the verge of freezing to death unless she could find warmth somewhere soon. Yet at this very time a provider of warmth was about to enter her life.

Besides spiritual and physical warmth, of course, it was also a matter of the Quint's bare existence, the fulfillment of their material needs. Since the beginning of the year, war widows and orphans had been receiving a pension of twenty-seven marks a month apiece. It had still not been officially determined, however, that the Quints were in fact war widows and orphans. Maximiliane did not know her way around the jungle of laws and regulations promulgated at short intervals by the occupation powers and interpreted by German agencies. But it was child's play for her to lead an official—who up to the moment when she appeared at his desk thought he knew *his* way around—deeper into the jungle.

"But—" she said as soon as the official had made himself familiar with her case. She raised the lids that shrouded her damp, shining round eyes and said, "But my father died in World War One." Or, "But my mother was forced to emigrate in 1935 for political reasons."

Did she qualify under the law concerning liberation from National Socialism, or was she to be recompensed under the reparations law?

The Quint case was tabled, but the official saw his chance to provide the young woman and her small children with some immediate practical help—her name would appear on the appropriate lists. "Of course it won't do for the long run, my dear lady."

Maximiliane had not counted on the long run anyway.

She never read the newspaper stories about what the victorious powers had in store for the vanquished; the Morgenthau Plan had been repudiated before she even heard of it. She read only the announcements about ration coupons and bonus allotments, as well as news dealing with refugee questions.

Joachim had made out another list, one enumerating new concepts and phrases beginning with *refugee*. It grew longer daily—"refugee matters," "refugee misery," "refugee temporary homes." He had already amassed forty-four such phrases.

The hostile attitude toward refugees grew worse. "Refugees have all the luck," people said. The refugees had more free time than the locals; they could search the woods for mushrooms, beechnuts, and pinecones, they were allotted a larger number of priority vouchers, and they were given preferential treatment by the housing authorities.

Though Adolf-Hitler-Platz had long since regained its old name, Friedrichsplatz, though swastikas were fading on the walls of the houses, white arrows still pointed to air-raid shelters. Lately new signs had gone up on the buildings of the narrow old town—Death Is So Permanent, and Be Careful—legible at a distance and intended as a warning to the drivers of American cars. Dangerous Corner was among the first English words and phrases impressed on the minds of the young

Quints—especially Joachim, as it would turn out much later. By now he was attending the Philippinum Classical Secondary School; every afternoon from four to six he read to a law student blinded in the war.

In his commerce with the American occupation troops Golo recklessly used his few English words, made the soldiers laugh, and quickly entered into business dealings with them. At the end of the school day he picked up Viktoria, who as a beneficiary of the American free lunch for children was allowed to eat all the soup she wanted and could swallow. You had to have two bowls before you could have dessert. Other children gained up to six pounds during a single month, but Viktoria continued to look undernourished.

Golo generally took her with him to the "town hall," where the American officers' mess was housed. There they stood near the ventilation grills from the kitchen and sniffed the warm, sweet scent of doughnuts. If too much time passed, they moaned audibly, but as soon as the black face under the white cook's hat appeared, they stopped moaning and began to smile. The cook shoved a warm doughnut through the grating, and the two children, hand in hand, wandered on to the railroad station, where the black market thrived in the waiting rooms.

Black-market activities were punishable within the jurisdiction of the American military police and the German police, but they were never stopped. Golo made good use of the adult conviction that it was the children who were suffering most in the present situation. When anyone collared them and asked what business they had there, Viktoria, following Golo's orders, replied in a thin little voice, "We're waiting for our daddy."

"The poor babies," people said, looking at the small, pitiable girl with her face of glass, her sparse hair, her swollen stomach—caused, if truth be told, by Golo's having shoved several coffee cans into her panties.

As a rule, however, Golo hid his booty under a bandage that he had wound around his own left arm. One day, when he was wearing it not on his arm but on his leg, a German policeman called him over for a reckoning. He tore off the bandage, pulling the scab off a fresh wound Golo had acquired when he fell off his bicycle. The two children were taken to the guard room, where the wound was dressed anew and each was given a sourball. At home their mother, noticing the swelling in their cheeks, hooked a practiced finger into their mouths, fished out the candies, and shoved them into Joachim's and Edda's mouths as they sat doing their homework.

Two candies must be made to do for four children.

When the principal business hours of the black market began to shift more and more to the evening and night, and when there were more and more questions about interzone passes and personal ID cards, and when cigarettes were sold by the carton and no longer by the pack, Golo began to specialize in a single product, building up a pool of steady customers. His goods had the added advantage that when there did not happen to be any buyers he could play with them. Sometimes at home he blew the "items" up like balloons; they were not large, nor were they colorful, but if you tied a string to them, they rose into the air a little.

Had Maximiliane Quint been born one year later, she would have been eligible for the so-called Youth Amnesty. Born in 1918, however, she had to undergo the denazification process. A questionnaire with a hundred questions was used to explicate her relations to National Socialism. The Allied Supreme Command had designated five categories of people, ranging from members of the Gestapo to participants in resistance groups, with punishments for the first four categories, damages for the fifth.

Maximiliane set out for the denazification tribunal without a single deposition in her defense. Instead she took along her children, who in this case were more of a liability. A woman who had brought five children into the world under Nazi rule aroused suspicion from the outset. Moreover, she did not properly present her true maternal and paternal relations. She could have asserted that her mother had emigrated for political reasons, that her stepfather was a Jew, and that her grandfather, the administrator of her estate, had been an avowed liberal who, on her wedding day and in front of witnesses, had characterized her husband as a "fool in Hitler." She did nothing of the sort.

Instead, the presiding officer asked her, "You admit, then, that in 1934 you voluntarily joined a Fascist organization?"

And she replied, "Yes, at the age of fifteen."

The man did not look up from his documents. "Your husband wore the golden party insignia?"

"In 1929 he joined the party from conviction. At the time it was one among many legal parties."

The presiding officer raised his eyes to stare at her.

She returned his gaze and continued. "Is he therefore more culpable than someone who joined the party in 1938 to further his career, fully aware of the pogroms and the preparations for war?" For the first and last time she took her husband's side.

She was there to answer questions, not to ask them, she was told; she had forfeited the public prosecutor's sympathy with this one statement. "Not everyone can afford to have opinions," Old Quindt used to say. His granddaughter exhibited courage and defiance on the wrong occasion.

Nonetheless, one of the attending judges, a watchmaker called Ernst Mann, pointed out her difficult situation as a refugee and mother of five children. Without his advocacy she would probably have been subsumed within Category III—minimally incriminated, with mitigating circumstances. Thanks to him she was assigned to Category IV—fellow traveler. And this was consonant with the facts; she had sung along and marched along, first in lockstep and then, during her flight, with the handcart.

Parson Merzin, the onetime minister in Poenichen, would surely have been delighted to write her a convincing affidavit for presentation to the denazification court. True, he did so for anyone who asked him—"We didn't know any better"; "You know us, Pastor"; "All we ever wanted was to do what was right"—often producing depositions against his better judgment and conscience. He even wrote one for former chief inspector Kalinski, who had caused Old Quindt much trouble, and another for the former local party leader, Priebe.

At the age of eighty, Parson Merzin had found a refuge—not a home—with his daughter in Giessen. He was a widower, his wife having been among the thousands of victims of the air raid on Dresden. In his Lutheran garb, a gift from a colleague in the West, he traveled as much as he could in an effort to visit his former congregants—a true shepherd looking for his flock. His Pomeranian congregation had scattered in all directions. Each time he succeeded in finding still another one, he was greeted with the words, "Oh, Pastor, sir!"

And he appeared to the Quint family in Marburg. Joachim, the only one of the children who recognized him, stared at the knitted cap he wore on his bald head and stuttered, "Your wig. . . . You didn't rescue your wig."

"Oh, son," Reverend Merzin replied, "I could barely rescue my head."

He sat at the table, placing his folded hands before

him. Maximiliane took a seat across from him, her hands also on the tabletop.

He counted the children, repeating the names he had given them at baptism. "But there's another one," he noted in astonishment.

"Yes, there's another one. Her name is Mirka," Maximiliane said.

They fell silent again.

"Sometimes in June I used to pull a pike from the lake." Reverend Merzin voiced one of his many thoughts. "Blaskorken. Do you remember Blaskorken the foreman and his hunting signals? Once I fished for pike with him."

"Are you hungry?" Maximiliane asked, and without waiting for an answer, she opened a can of corned beef and cut a thick slice off the loaf of bread. The children watched as the old man broke the crust from the bread and pushed small morsels into his mouth.

"Us Pomeranians," he said as he chewed, "have always sat together like this when we visited, never talking much. Only Old Quindt—he had a thing or two to say. Do you sometimes talk to the children about Him?"

His musings had run on, and he was no longer referring to Quindt. Maximiliane had followed his train of thought. She shook her head but decided to say something after all. "Sometimes I talk to Him about the children."

The old parson looked at her attentively, then nodded. "That's possible, too."

He had baptized her, he had married her, he had given her a few words of advice along life's way, and now she was returning one of those words to him.

He asked about Lenchen Priebe, who was not at home, and he was given some hints about her current situation. He shook his head. "And we had such high hopes of the peace to come! 'Only those who pray can still succeed'—that was one of the sayings we whispered to each other secretly during the war. Once I preached on it. A lot of people believed it, but even those who prayed didn't succeed. In Pomerania we've never been any good at praying. 'Go with God, Merzin,' your grandfather used to say to me. Do you need a defense deposition for the denazification tribunal?"

"I've already been classified. Nowadays I'm a fellow traveler. First I was only a refugee. My grandfather thought I was a runaway."

"My deposition probably wouldn't have helped you anyway. The tribunals figured out a long time ago that I write them only out of Christian charity—but after all, most of the people in question have already been damaged and punished enough. I bet it's no different here in Marburg than it is in Giessen, where until recently the professors who taught wrong doctrines for twelve years were sweeping the streets—a mopping-up operation intended for both the streets and the street cleaners."

In looking around the room he had realized that there was no place for him to sleep. With his handkerchief he wiped at a spot on his black coat. "Did you ever hear from Blaskorken?"

Maximiliane shook her head.

"You were just a baby at the time." He took his leave, saying to her what everyone said: "You'll make it, you'll see."

At the front door, alone with her, he turned back once more. "Your grandfather said one other thing the last time I was on Poenichen. 'If I had a son, Merzin,' he said, 'I'd tell him, Don't abandon Poenichen.' Maybe he was right. Maybe all of us should have stayed. . . ."

He stopped short, tears in his eyes. Maximiliane watched him walk down the garden path.

100

When she returned to her room, she noticed Golo and Viktoria playing with the balloons for the first time. She inquired as to their nature and origins. She was told that they were trading goods, and her eight-year-old son enlightened her about prophylactics and their use in preventing infection and impregnation.

9

Maximiliane had lined her children up by size. She told the surprised visitor, "All of them are mine."

He inspected the children carefully. "I couldn't have done better myself." A sentence characteristic of this man's charm.

Maximiliane took his statement the way it was meant—as praise. She looked pale on this particular day; in the morning she had given blood at the women's infirmary in order to be able to entertain her guest. For 33 cubic centimeters of blood she earned 900 grams' worth of meat coupons, 200 grams worth of cereal coupons, and a bottle of wine.

The visitor conjured some marbles from his pocket, colored glass balls of different sizes. Holding them up to the light, he noted that two of the children had "aggie eyes," just like their mother. A few minutes later he was crouching on the floor with the children, playing marbles with them while Maximiliane prepared the herring he had brought and "threw them into the pan"— an expression that made him look up.

But too many table legs, chair legs, children's legs in twenty square meters of living space—it was impossible to carry on a game. "You have to get out of here," the visitor told Maximiliane. "Just leave it to me."

He had connections, especially to herrings by the barrel. In the trading chain that started with herring from Travemünde (British Zone of Occupation) and ended at suitcases, briefcases, electric light bulbs, and kitchenware (American Zone of Occupation), he was the first link. At its other end a stocking factory in Zwickau (Russian Zone of Occupation) illegally delivered its goods to the western zones.

The man was keenly aware that the black-market period was coming to an end. Unnoticed by the public, the economy was already deep in production geared toward the day of currency reform, which was still being kept secret. It was necessary to think of the future, and he did; his connection with herring he considered the most substantial of his insubstantial ties. At the end of a victorious war the heroes prosper; after a lost war it is the wartime profiteers who thrive. He watched Maximiliane as she deftly grabbed the herring by the tail and turned them, her freshly washed hair tied at the nape of her neck, her face rosy from the heat. A pleasant sight, bright with promise.

It was easier than he had expected to win her over to his proposition.

"Well, I could try," she said.

Inside an hour the idea of a fried-fish stand had ripened into details, and only two weeks later Maximiliane found herself in a public-market stall, frying herring on the grill of a little stove fired by wood. Roasted fresh herring and marinated grilled herring. Golo and Edda, standing on crates behind the roughly carpentered table, helped with sales. The supply, though limited, was not controlled by coupons.

Mother and children took on the pervasive scent of fish. Sometimes, when the weather was good, Joachim and Viktoria did their homework near the fish stall, and Mirka patiently sat alongside on a crate. The earnings were modest, but before long they would be paid in hard currency, the other partner in the business promised them. "Just leave it to me."

Then he disappeared to take care of replenishing their supplies.

In Mecklenburg they had a saying, "Why buy a cow when the milk's so cheap?" Maximiliane came from Pomerania, where she had not been instructed in such folk wisdom, and she may also have thought that this new man could really become a father to her children. She had been raised on patriarchal principles. The children quickly grew fond of him; he was always full of jokes, was generous with presents, never said, "Don't do that," never raised his voice, much less his hand, to any of them. Only Joachim retired to a corner of the room whenever the man came to visit.

His total dissimilarity to Viktor Quint must have told in his favor. At the first available opportunity, when both Maximiliane's arms happened to be free and she was not holding one of the children by the hand, he put his arms around her. Only half a head taller than she, he did not tower over her like Viktor, and she could lean against him, which she had never been able to do before.

He looked at her and said, "Just look at your eyes! They roll around like aggies." He was from the Rhineland.

It turned out that Maximiliane was quite resourceful. If there was no way to be alone with him, they would just have to go places where you could touch in public. She, the mother of five children, went dancing. What a backlog to make up for! During those few hours she was granted what she had had to go without for years—music, dancing, being in love. She dipped from one pleasure into the next. Bebop, swing, and the Lambeth Walk—it appeared that she was as jazz-crazy as her mother, Vera, had been in the 1920s.

"And to think someone like you grew up in Pomerania," her new partner teased.

"In the south of Pomerania," she retorted.

104

"And to think someone like you has five kids, and not a one of them mine." Then he added, "Your gorgeous teeth! They need something to bite into." On his next visit he brought along a roast big enough for six.

Joachim was the first to realize what was going on. "But you just washed your hair yesterday, Mama," he said, and Maximiliane hugged him. Any caresses she received she passed on to her children.

As far as this man was concerned, Maximiliane relied entirely on first impressions, and these spoke in his favor. His clothes came from American stores: tight-fitting trousers, a lumberjack shirt with toggles, low-cut leather shoes, short nylon socks that allowed glimpses of his bare legs. He was full-grown, well-nourished, and good-natured, and he had a rare quality—male charm.

Later they said, "You should have noticed something," but Maximiliane simply had not noticed anything. She still did not have much experience of life, and her instincts failed her time and again in her relations with men. This time, too, she became the executive organ for some man's plans.

"Let's make nails with heads," he said.

He spoke a language different from hers, and she listened to him in wonder. He really did mean it as a proposal of marriage. He was intent on pointing out to her the advantages of marriage, and he observed that she offered no resistance. To her it was a matter of course that they should marry. She did not bother to listen when he spoke of securing their livelihood, raised questions of residence, and talked of safeguarding her claims on her eastern estates.

But we must deal justly with this man: Maximiliane made it easy for him. He told her a great deal about his eventful life, and his stories were full of contradictions, perhaps intentionally; perhaps he wanted to give her a chance to question him about them. But she was not

105

a suspicious person. Besides, most of the time she fell asleep even as he talked. She was constantly overtired, like every mother of small children; at night she had to get up repeatedly to put one of the children on the potty or comfort another who had woken up weeping from a bad dream.

"What's your name?"

Similar words had been used to question Lohengrin. This man, after reflecting briefly, asked, "How do you like Martin?"

Maximiliane turned her trusting eyes on him. "It's a good name. Martin! Like the saint who shared his cloak."

He was surprised. It seemed highly impractical to share a cloak; that way each person had only half a cloak, and both would be cold. He opened his trenchcoat, pulled Maximiliane inside it, and explained, "This is the best way of sharing a coat. From now on it will be big enough for two." So he even interpreted the stories of the saints in such a way as to make himself look good!

Maximiliane laughed, leaning against the warm, strong, man's body.

She liked to listen when he talked, but his stories reached her like soothing noises. Was his mother a member of the Stinnes family, cast out when she became pregnant? Had his father been a French occupation soldier in the Rhineland? Had he gone to school in Greifswald, and was that why he was familiar with Pomerania?

"I'm an unfinished lawyer." So he said more than once. It is only certain that he was as familiar with the relevant paragraphs of the civil code as with the regulations of the military governments—in every zone of occupation.

Martin had no long-range goals or ideals; he was easygoing and always intent on making each moment

106

pleasant for himself. If he spoiled Maximiliane and the children, it was for the selfish reason that their well-being enhanced his. Maximiliane did not know many men, and there were certainly none like him beyond the Oder and the Neisse. There was not a shred of the Prussian about him. He was a materialist, and that was one of his virtues. He sacrificed his ideals to no one.

Presumably he too had fallen in love with the far-away country of Poenichen, which still held an enor-mous attraction, and about which Maximiliane often talked. An estate of ten thousand acres, subject to no currency devaluation, with a manor and all its furniture and equipment. What claims could be brought to bear there!

"You need someone to look out for your interests. Just leave it to me."

The newspapers were already mentioning the "equalization of burdens"; credits were assigned pri-marily to refugees, and assistance was granted to them. For this reason the fried-fish stand was entered in the records under Maximiliane's name. The *Marburger Presse* had already run a story on "the woman from the East," daughter of a Pomeranian country squire, who had so bravely—"in an exemplary fashion," the newspaper put it—managed to save herself and her children. The ac-companying photo showed Edda and Golo standing behind the counter, Joachim reading off to one side, and Mirka leaning idly against the table; Viktoria was represented by nothing more than one spindly arm. Joachim preserved the clipping in his box.

Valentin was the man's last name; at least, that was what he called himself. A Latin-Roman name. "Doesn't it suit me, though?" he inquired, and it was true; his classically chiseled features had a look of Roman hand-someness, though his hairline was perhaps a mite too low.

"There must have been a Roman among my ancestors," he said. "It happens more often than you'd think in the Rhineland—centuries of occupation, that has its consequences."

His visits were like stage appearances. One evening he put a knife between his teeth, slunk around a piece of furniture, and sang the song of Mack the Knife; not exactly suitable for little children. After he finished, Joachim retired to his corner, his expression anxious and cool. Viktoria was in tears, but Golo and Edda enjoyed the performance immensely. He sang right in Maximiliane's face, "And Macheath spends like a sailor. Did our boy do something rash?"

Maximiliane, more used to sentimental verse, at best to Rilke and not at all to Bert Brecht, was astonished by the fact that such songs even existed and that such plays were performed on the stage, but she did not interfere. She had never made a distinction as to what the children were and were not allowed to hear. But now and again she did send them outside for an hour. "Go out and play."

The only one of her relatives whom she informed of her intention to marry was her cousin Marie-Louise. "I am marrying for love, and only for love." By which she meant that the man was neither rich nor her social equal. Marie-Louise wrote back, "My mother would say, 'In five hundred years no Quindt has ever married for love.' I, on the other hand, say, 'It's about time to start.' "

Everything about the wedding was just a little too hasty and improvised, but "Others marry in haste because they are expecting a baby, and we already have five of them," Martin Valentin said. "We"—a two-letter word irresistible to most women.

Martin even knew how to get the proper marriage certificates. "If we wait until your first husband is legally declared dead, we'll be old and gray, and that would be such a pity." He ran both hands through his thick, dark hair. "What we need is two witnesses to swear that they saw him dead. He did die—you know as much—so we're not doing him any injury, and we're doing ourselves some good. You just have to know your way around. But how would a Pomeranian princess know her way around the legal jungle? Just leave it to me."

Maximiliane left it to him, and he took care of everything to both their satisfaction. The banns were posted, and at the same time Martin Valentin procured for his new family an immigration permit with a claim to residential quarters, according to the guidelines of the Control Commission. He was considered a resident of Marburg since at the end of the war he had been in a Marburg infirmary with jaundice; he had been discharged from the prisoner-of-war camp Cappel and had subsequently been given a job in the American army's ration depot in Marburg. Six square meters per head, thirty-six square meters altogether, not counting bathroom, hall, stairways, and kitchen, unless they exceeded an area of ten square yards. A temporary home on a hillside. The address, however, was less highly regarded.

During Maximiliane's first wedding dinner, which had taken place on Poenichen in 1938, Uncle Max from Königsberg remarked about the bride, "That's all baby fat. Wait until she's thirty!" Now, marrying for a second time, Maximiliane was almost thirty years old, and all her baby fat was gone.

Frau Görke was given written orders to sew a second wedding gown, for which a sheet was dyed and patterned by hand. Frau Görke had still not forgotten the measurements of her Pomeranian client, though now she always subtracted five centimeters from the chest, waist, and hip measurements. In this particular

109

case she cautiously inquired whether something was on the way again.

The question could honestly be answered in the negative. Their first "encounter"—to use Maximiliane's word—had come very close to her still girlishly romantic ideas. The branches of a beech, thickly covered with leaves, hung close to the ground, creating a sort of green bower. The ground was not exactly mossy, but at least it was not a maze of roots. Maximiliane inhaled deeply and said, "I'm very susceptible," an expression that sent the man into gales of hilarity.

"I thought as much," he said, "and I'm prepared."

"May heaven protect us," he was wont to say regularly later, whenever he used a protective device; without prophylactics, Maximiliane would in all probability have been pregnant again very soon. She should have been grateful to her new husband for preventing such an event. He was in love with his Pomeranian child of nature; there could be no doubt that he was captivated by her mixture of innocence and sensuality.

Municipal Inspector Baum performed the civil ceremony. Maximiliane wore the amber jewelry that had been Viktor's gift to her, "the gold of the Baltic"—not in his memory but to honor the day. Lenchen Priebe and Samuel Wixton, her friend from Ohio, acted as witnesses. Just as confidently as she had before, Maximiliane said "I do" a second time. A church wedding was never considered, nor were the children to be adopted; they were to keep their name. "You should go on using Quint as a middle name too, if only for the business," the man told Maximiliane. "Preferably with the *d*."

At the time of the wedding he was hard up, as was the case now and again. In the market outside the city hall he bought a bunch of sweet william; Maximiliane filled the Courland christening bowl with the flowers and placed it at the center of the table. It was more like

110

a child's birthday party than a wedding feast. Black Samuel Wixton and Lenchen Priebe—Helen von Jadow once more—were their only guests; there were no toasts, no elaborate courses. But at this wedding, in contrast to the earlier one, there was a great deal of laughter.

Maximiliane informed only her mother that the second wedding had actually taken place. This marriage was her private affair, unlike the first, which had been entered into for the sake of carrying on the Quindt line.

"Today your fried-fish business is nothing but an open-air stand," the new husband said on his wedding day. "But in six months you'll have a roof over your head. Just leave it to me." At the proper time—after the currency reform—the horses and wagons that were still stabled in Holstein would be sold and the proceeds used to build up their livelihood further.

In the period that followed, he was on the road a great deal. His black-market inventory had to be kept at a minimum so that he would not be stuck with goods that could not be disposed of after the currency reform.

"Stay out of it," Old Quindt used to tell his wife. Viktor had told Maximiliane the same thing. And when she asked her second husband, "Where do the herring come from, anyway?" he answered, "From the water, I presume." But Martin Valentin laughed as he spoke, adding, "I look after the *wherefrom,* and you take care of the *whereto.* You feed the hungry—in the city of Saint Elizabeth! Herring instead of roses!"

He nuzzled her hair and sniffed the scent of herring. "And later on you'll be eating smoked pike from your lake on Poenichen again."

In accordance with her Pomeranian nature, Maximiliane continued to stay out of it.

At night the slightest noise would startle her husband out of his sleep. He would flail around or grope with his hands and grab hold of Maximiliane. When she

111

awoke and asked, "What are you looking for?" he would fall back on the pillow and reply, "My gun" or "My hand grenade," laughing out loud. He still slept like a soldier, alert, pursued by nightmares, until his hands came to rest on the peaceful terrain of the woman's body.

When he was there, the children were not allowed to crawl into their mother's bed. "Now your mother belongs to me for a little while," their new father announced. The children adjusted, especially as he was not often at home. Once the new husband came into their lives, only Joachim turned his head away whenever his mother tried to kiss him on the lips. She made no attempt to change this situation, not even later on. She kissed his cheek instead.

Each time before leaving, Martin used a borrowed vacuum cleaner to turn back the gas meter. Given the meager gas allowance, Maximiliane would not have been able to make do otherwise, and any excess usage would have caused the meter to be sealed off. This man was truly indispensable to the family. When he returned, he usually brought warmth in the form of pressed coal briquettes, and Maximiliane shared warmth with him in other ways.

Two days before the currency reform was introduced, a letter from Martha Riepe arrived. It opened with the sentence "A horse needs more than three times as much acreage for his food as does a human being"— a reproach unfairly leveled against Maximiliane. Anyway, Martha Riepe had sold the horses and wagons for a handsome cash sum. Martin Valentin beat his fist against his forehead several times, but immediately thereafter he burst into his booming laugh, which infected the children.

"Well, that's all right too," he said. No ill feelings. There were never any ill feelings in this marriage. "Then we'll just do something else," he said. "Who knows, it might turn out to be for the best. You have to make do with things as they are and adapt. There'll still be enough for a roof over your herrings."

When he left, Maximiliane always refrained from asking, "When will you be back?" and he never sent her so much as a postcard from the road. One day he would simply ring the doorbell, his pockets bulging with surprises for the children, and for Maximiliane the assurance that the herring catch had been successful.

On the day of the currency reform, in June 1948, it took Maximiliane four hours in the pouring rain to reach the exchange station. The line of patient people stretched for two hundred meters—the length of the linden-lined avenue in Poenichen, which she still used as a standard measurement. A premium of forty marks per person, multiplied by five; her husband was on the road again.

If you had a hundred Reichmarks, you got ten German marks for them; if you had a hundred thousand Reichmarks, they gave you ten thousand, in blocked bank accounts. The relationship of poor to rich diminished to a ratio of 10 to 1, but on this single day absolute equality prevailed.

"Watch it start now," her husband said on his return. "Free market and free prices. Our new, free people will need apartments, cars, streets, hospitals, clothes. They lack everything, from clothespins to school notebooks. Now there will be a great wave of reconstruction. We ought to have some kind of manufacturing enterprise, not just a retail operation—even if it's, let's say, screws. The world is going to be astonished at the Germans' rebuilding energy."

The world was indeed astonished. The war survivors turned into consumers. The hour of birth of the new capitalism and materialism had arrived: restoration, reestablishment of the old conditions. A nation decided in favor of consumption. Only Maximiliane, the only child, who had never had anyone with whom to play at buying and selling, who had been born into a family where nothing was acquired because everything was already at hand, remained shut out from the joy of acquisition, from the "economic miracle." Her purse filled with the necessary money; she walked through the stores, where soon enough everything, or at least a great deal, was again for sale; she looked at the objects, even fingered them, but then she put them back. She could not decide one way or the other, and generally she came home with empty hands.

"I meant to buy us a table," she said.

"Where is it?" the children asked.

"There were so many different ones," Maximiliane answered.

Sometimes she even said, "We don't need that," a statement she had used on their flight—for example whenever Golo swiped something she did not consider essential. Her attitude ran counter to every attempt at prosperity and expansion.

Now and again she looked around the apartment as if to assess whether each piece of furniture could be carried by one person. At those times the children involuntarily clutched their little possessions. "Mama's got her flight look again," they would say in later years. She did not acquire a pet or a houseplant. Once more, acquisition was not worthwhile. In her life she was always on call.

When the first questionnaires arrived in accordance with the Immediate Aid Law for Future Equalization of Burdens, her husband filled them out. Maximiliane's handwriting would have been too large to fit in the spaces. While he wrote, she told him about those Quindt valuables—she called them "treasures"; there were still times when her narratives sounded like fairy tales—that had been buried in the grounds next to the manor house because they could not be taken along.

114

He turned her vague reports into precise information, never appearing as an injured party himself. Instead he said once or twice, "All I did was profit! I'm a war profiteer!" and "You're the best deal I ever made."

She also showed him a yellowed newspaper clipping of a woman at the pillory flanked by two Jews who had obviously been abused.

"That's my mother." She did not explain—or perhaps for the moment she had forgotten—that the woman only looked like her mother.

"That piece of paper is worth its weight in gold," he said. "You're entitled to restitution. Just leave it to me."

The following day he took off again, kissing his "Pomeranian princess" good-bye as he set off for his herring catch. "My Pomeranian princess"—he often called her that, and he treated her like one. Her first husband had thought of her as a Pomeranian goose and had dealt with her accordingly.

By now Martin had seen to it that the fish-fry business moved indoors, into a storefront.

The marriage lasted two years. Then Maximiliane received a summons. A covering letter explained the circumstances.

She brought the children with her to the legal proceedings. When someone tried to send them from the room, she said, "Surely you don't intend to say anything my children should not hear?"

Then she answered "No" to every question put to her.

"No children issued from this relationship?" The word *marriage* was avoided.

"No."

"Do you feel that you have been injured?"

"No."

"Will you bring charges against this man?"

"No."

A blush was her answer to the question "Didn't you miss him during his frequent absences?"

The official leafed through the documents. "It is stated here that his wife Eva, in Lemgo, British Zone of Occupation, regularly did his laundry. Surely you must have wondered why he never brought home any soiled clothing?"

"I am not accustomed to paying attention to a man's soiled laundry," said Maximiliane, summing up in one retort the centuries-old privileges of her rank.

"You never made any inquiries?"

"No."

Only once did she answer a question directly with a complete sentence: "Time will tell." The official looked at her searchingly, but Maximiliane kept her lids lowered, and the meaning of her statement remained obscure.

The marriage was annulled, and it was not charged against her account. She was and remained a Quindt, as her grandfather had promised the eleven-year-old Maximiliane when the notice of her mother's remarriage arrived at Poenichen.

No one ever doubted that the death certificate for Viktor Quint, her first husband, was genuine.

When Maximiliane had finished with this errand, she lined the children up and told them, "Now let's hurry up and forget him." The children were able to follow her suggestion. She herself could not. Every fiber of her being missed this man.

She never saw him again and never learned the details of his apprehension. In his attempt to reach Poenichen, now called Peniczyn, he had got as far as Stettin, or Szczecin, in the Polish-occupied territory. When a frisking turned up a variety of passports issued in all four occupation zones of Germany, he was handed over to the American authorities.

116

A swindler, a bigamist, he left neither a photograph nor a letter with Maximiliane. But she owed him an apartment of her own, almost her own house—a make-shift home in a makeshift homeland. And a fish-fry kitchen under a solid roof, just as this strange man had promised. She stood on her own two feet and did not become a social-welfare case, like so many other refugee women with small children. Besides, he probably did not plan it, but he had turned her into Viktor Quint's widow, thereby entitling her to a pension—though its terms were not yet clear.

She brought out her old quilted camouflage jacket and wore it through the winter months.

The time of fresh herring was over. Maximiliane began to grill sausages. Edda placed them on paper plates and added mustard and rolls. Golo manned the cash register. A family business, open only after school hours.

Maximiliane resumed her custom of going to the movies once a week.

10

A saying attributed to Mother-in-Law Quint from Breslau, herself a war widow, ran: "I've raised five children, I've forgotten how to laugh." The statement had come to Maximiliane's ears and had had its effect. The latest Quint war widow and her children continued to laugh.

For at least three of the children Maximiliane was the right kind of mother. On the other hand, she could not meet the demands Joachim and Viktoria made on her, although she took more pains with them than with the others. Both were cut out to be only children, or at most to share with only one other. They required discussions and explanations, but Maximiliane believed neither in the necessity nor in the efficacy of discussions.

When eleven-year-old Edda placed a memory album in front of her mother during Easter vacation, Maximiliane asked the same question old Baroness Quindt had asked when Maximiliane handed her a memory album: "Do people still do that?" She was told that it was not a memory album but an autograph book.

Cities may be destroyed, countries lost, but autograph books survive any catastrophe. Maximiliane must have thought something of the sort as she held the book and leafed through its pages. She looked at drawings and at stickers lovingly applied to the pages, and she read the contribution of Edda's friend Cornelia Stier:

"May three angels walk beside you, Giving you surcease, All along life's bumpy highway: Love and Joy and Peace." It was not reasonable to suppose that the angels of love and joy and peace would do their job. Edda's angels would have to help her with being competent, with success, with good health. Three hand-drawn yellow angels floated around the verse. Maximiliane was reminded of her own school days.

Now she too was being hurried. Edda was urging her, "Write something, go ahead."

Maximiliane looked thoughtfully at her husband's stray child. "What on earth do you want me to write?" she asked before filling the first page with her large handwriting: "Do what you say, and think what you say"—a variation on Goethe, though she was unaware of it. A small statement but a large thought, the result of her own long reflections, another Quindt-essence, incomprehensible to an eleven-year-old. And for a signature she used the old formula she had read in her grandmother's memory album: "Your mother, Maximiliane Irene von Quindt on Poenichen."

Edda read the inscription and was not pleased. She sulked. "Why don't you write Marburg? Everyone writes Marburg."

"We come from Poenichen, and we belong on Poenichen," Maximiliane insisted.

Edda, who had inherited her father's temper, turned bright red. "But I don't want to come from Poenichen! I don't want to be a refugee all my life! And I don't want to live in a makeshift home all my life, either."

"It's only temporary," her mother said, but even as she spoke the word *temporary*, she felt offended herself. A temporary government in a temporary capital. What temporizing for her ambitious child.

"The other kids' parents have real jobs," said Edda, "not a sausage shop."

"But we have what we need, Edda."

Apparently Edda needed more. The gap between what their mother needed and what her children needed was widening. For Maximiliane, everything was only temporary. "It'll pass, you'll see." She did not buy hardbound books but only cheap paperback novels, which she passed on when she had finished them. To acquire real books, you must have a real abode. She never changed her mind about paperback books; pocket books belonged in your pocket, not in the bookcase. She never wanted to have to leave anything behind again—not a book, not a house.

In so far as she could in their cramped quarters, Maximiliane avoided saying, "Don't do that" or "Stand up straight." But in passing she made little improvements, raising Joachim's head when he bent too far over his books, removing Mirka's hand from where it should not be, pushing back Viktoria's shoulder blades. These were gentle gestures, declarations of tenderness rather than pedantic efforts. The children performed the cruder corrections on each other, sometimes with raised voices.

Visitors to the temporary home on the hillside looked around the kitchen and asked, "Don't you even have a scale? Don't you have an egg timer?" And on their next visit they brought a scale or a timer, quite unaware that Maximiliane neither needed nor used such devices. Gradually the house filled with "objects" that made Maximiliane feel crowded. Already she sometimes glanced over the whole ménage as if she were ready to go, to leave it all behind. Then she took a deep breath, as if gasping for air, and opened the top buttons of her blouse, annoying Edda more each time.

Every inch the children grew and every pound they gained made the apartment seem more cluttered. The constant admonitions—"Move over," "Make room for me"—caused Maximiliane to enlarge the temporary home in a temporary way without bothering to procure the required building permit. An additional room at the back, and at the front a kind of roofed porch one step up, supported by two wooden posts; it had space enough for a bench and table long enough for all of them. The gallery of the mansion on Poenichen, with its five white columns, may have served as a model. The result was in part reminiscent of Poenichen but at the same time underlined the differences between then and now. The crude wood planking was covered by the rugs from Poenichen, which had to be tucked under on all four sides. The stuffed pillows where the 160 napkins had been stored served as seating; they would come to hold symbolic value for Maximiliane: visible ballast; unnecessary objects.

When the Quints' remaining possessions had arrived on a truck from Holstein and the boxes were piled up in front of the house, Joachim said, "We can be glad that we still have what we still have"—a statement that stuck in Maximiliane's memory.

Since the low walls of the temporary home were not suitable for hanging large-scale ancestral portraits, Maximiliane left them rolled up. Then one day she had a letter from her Königsberg cousin. Marie-Louise had finished her apprenticeship in pottery and for the last two years had been studying design at the Düsseldorf Academy with her mother's money but without her approval. She wrote, "You still have the family portraits, don't you? Such things are in great demand here. People want to be rich but not newly rich, so they need ancestors. Unfortunately we did not salvage ours. I can put you in touch with a serious buyer."

Maximiliane wrote back that she was interested in Marie-Louise's proposition, that the pictures were nothing but dead capital, and that she could certainly use the money. Thereupon Marie-Louise invited Maximiliane to come to Düsseldorf for a visit. "Though I can't ask you to stay with me," she added. "I'm living with a friend, a high-up official. He is married."

A long postscript concluded the letter. "You won't believe the news of my sister Roswitha. A few years ago she converted to Catholicism, and now she has entered an order—the Benedictines. Something must have confused her utterly. It must have to do with the concentration-camp trials, where she was an interpreter. Of course Mother sees it as a sign of cowardice and weakness. Roswitha told us that she intends to live by the rules of Saint Benedict, in the 'beneficial alternation of prayer and work,' as she puts it. Some past Quindt killed a Polish bishop, they say. Did anyone ever tell you that?"

No one had ever told Maximiliane. Her grandfather must have considered that chapter not worth mentioning, let alone exalting. She thought hard and long about her cousin Roswitha and came to the conclusion that her transformation was not only possible but even necessary in a representational sense—one Quindt had to take it on herself for all the others. But she did not pass her understanding on to Cousin Marie-Louise. Nor was she able to make the trip to Düsseldorf at once, since she could not find anyone to look after the sausage shop and take care of the children in her absence.

For a while she forgot all about going to Düsseldorf, especially as she received other letters that claimed her attention more urgently. From Berlin came news that her grandmother Jadow, suffering from a chronic urinary-tract infection, had been installed in her doctor's private old-age home. Maximiliane had not concerned herself much with this grandmother aside from sending her ration coupons for years on end, more to assuage her conscience than from real affection. Then there was a letter from Maximiliane's mother that for the first time raised the possibility of an invitation to California. Naturally no one was more excited by the expectation than Golo.

One warm June day Maximiliane finally did set out for Düsseldorf, taking along the ancestral portraits. Her elegant cousin began by giving her the once-over. "No one here dresses like you do, but don't worry—it suits you somehow. Even the scent of smoked and grilled food that clings to your clothes and hair is genuine. You can afford to wear it."

The "serious buyer" for the Quindt ancestors turned out to be a certain Herr Wasser, nonferrous metals, with offices in Hilden. When they were introduced, he raised Maximiliane's hand to his lips. With a gentle tug she lowered her hand and thereby his head to the appropriate level. Herr Wasser raised his eyes and looked at her questioningly. She smiled in encouragement.

They went to a café. Herr Wasser had chosen it, and Marie-Louise von Quindt complimented him on his good taste. She explained that both paintings were by the same artist, Leo Baron von König, born 1871 in Brandenburg, died 1944. "A late impressionist. And by the way, the same artist's portrait of his mother and father hangs in the art gallery here."

"Really, my dear lady, it isn't necessary for the artist to be a member of the nobility as well," Herr Wasser said playfully. He liked the pictures. He was already referring to twelve-year-old Achim von Quindt, Maximiliane's father—portrayed in a light-blue velvet waistcoat, with his brown hunting dog by his side—as "the kid." He did not notice the faulty leg articulation of the trotter bearing Maximiliane's grandfather, Joachim von Quindt, as a young man; but he did notice that neither painting was signed. "Are they really genuine?" he asked.

"You can't prove the genuineness of your newly

acquired ancestors either," Maximiliane retorted, for the first time taking part in the negotiations.

Herr Wasser laughed heartily. He liked the answer as much as he liked everything else about this woman. Straightforward, not at all snooty. In that same spirit— "speaking his mind"—he continued the conversation. He had spent years dirtying his hands, but his wife no longer wanted to be reminded of the fact. "I started out as a junk dealer, but now we call it 'nonferrous metals.' I don't care much about 'ancestors'; I'm perfectly satisfied with the grandfather I've got. But not my wife! She's ashamed. The only time she isn't ashamed is when she's spending my money."

Would the two ladies join him for dinner? he inquired. "A good piece of business should be celebrated in a good restaurant—a little 'family' feast. I'm in a generous mood today."

As he sank down into the plush restaurant chair, he observed, "I can just manage to fit. In the regional Diet chamber they have to replace all the armchairs because the representatives can't fit into the old ones anymore. That's how good the meals are in the social economy. Those gentlemen ought to be forced to go on a diet!"

Herr Wasser opened his napkin in his lap and, reaching for his knife and fork, said, "Those who eat good food get more enjoyment out of life." It was plain that he was speaking of a lifelong pleasure.

The good mood lasted until Herr Wasser asked about the newly acquired ancestors' precise provenance—"By blood, I mean"—and learned that their native soil was Pomerania.

They had finished dessert, *poire Hélène,* and Herr Wasser was clumsily wiping his hands on his napkin. He said, "When I eat is the only time my hands get dirty anymore." Then—"without mincing words"—he gave forth with his deep-rooted opinions on the refugee

124

question. "Pomerania! Eastern territories! The Oder-Neisse Line! Expulsion and all that, I have to tell you it gets on my nerves. The fact is, pure and simple, that we lost the war."

"But not you," Maximiliane corrected him. "*We* lost it, along with our homes."

"You refugees act as if you'd had exclusive tenancy of your 'homes,' " Herr Wasser shot back.

"We were not tenants. We were the owners," Maximiliane corrected once more.

But Herr Wasser, quite in accord with his appearance, remained stiff-necked and thick-skulled. "All you ever talk about is your homeland."

"Don't you suppose," Maximiliane countered, not at all flustered, "that we'd rather have it to walk on than to talk about?"

For the first time Maximiliane entered the ring fully equipped, with the charm of a Pomeranian but with the temperament of her Berlin mother and of that mysterious Polish ancestor. And when Herr Wasser noted patronizingly, "Home, that lives in your heart. You don't have to walk through it every day," she answered firmly and aggressively, "If the Rhinelanders had been expelled, would you be just as willing to give up the Rhineland as you are Pomerania?"

Herr Wasser tried to inject a note of compromise. "Let's not spoil our evening, dear lady. We have to live with the realities. Now we're all doing well again, and with the money from the paintings you'll soon get back on your feet. The bartered grandfather! You ever hear of it?"

Marie-Louise also tried to change the subject and reached for her glass. "Have a drink, Maximiliane. We can't change anything."

"But I am swallowing," Maximiliane said. "Can't you see that I'm swallowing it all?"

Herr Wasser ordered champagne. He was willing

to spend a pretty penny to comfort her. "Your eyes, dear lady, could make a wagonload of nonferrous metal melt."

When they finished their meal, he said, "Let's not put an early end to a perfect evening," inviting the two ladies to the theater. *Mother Courage*. When the play was over, Maximiliane summed up her opinion: "The cart was the best thing."

Herr Wasser agreed with her; he had been reminded of his father's junk barrow, Maximiliane of the handcart during their flight. He laughed heartily and then suggested a walk through the Old Town. Marie-Louise was their guide, Herr Wasser their purse. They went to the Cafe Csikos, ate goulash soup, and slaked their thirst with slivovitz. The owner, a green, white, and red scarf tied carelessly around his throat, came to their table several times, the second time bowing to the ladies and assuring them that they already looked "much better." Maximiliane, who was not used to alcohol, was soon in high spirits. She asked for a "double" of slivovitz because in Pomerania they always drank doubles, at least the men did.

They made a last stop at Papa's Studio, and then Herr Wasser walked the two ladies to the Karlsplatz, where Marie-Louise had parked her car. He offered to see Maximiliane to her hotel. On the walk he took her arm—"We're relatives now, in a manner of speaking"— and when Maximiliane did not object, he told her that his marriage was not a happy one. His wife had lost her roots; the social rise had gone to her head.

Once again Maximiliane paid no attention to the words, hearing only the voice, and she remembered Martin Valentin. Somewhere nearby a locust tree was in bloom; the scent reached her and did its work. It is to be feared that Maximiliane, unused to night life and removed from the protection of her children for the first time in years, would have given in to Herr Wasser's unmistakable suggestion—money is seductive, too—had they not turned into Bolkerstrasse, where her eyes fell on a dimly lit shopwindow. For a moment she was taken aback; she looked again. What she saw was like a signal.

A table in the antique shop displayed a chess set, and she immediately recognized the figures her grandfather and Christian Blaskorken had used when they played by torchlight. There was no doubt; as a child she had spent hours staring at the board and the men while they were at their game. And in a fraction of a second it was all recreated before her eyes: the summer evenings at Lake Poenichen; Frederick the Great in profile, wearing his tricorn, the 159 centimeters of his living form reduced to six centimeters of ivory; Christian Blaskorken, who had come from the war and sought and found the simple life on Poenichen—sheep throwing lambs, fish spawning, and Maximiliane's governesses—pastoral dalliance on the grounds. His blond-haired arms glowed with fish scales—the fish smell, the fish-fry shop. At the age of twelve she had fallen in love with him "forever," and for a week she had secretly—but running no risk—lived under his roof. When old Quindt discovered the idyll, he sent his foreman packing on the ten-o'clock train.

Maximiliane ran both hands through her hair and, prey to memories, pressed her forehead against the display window.

"What's the matter? Do you feel ill?"

"Yes," Maximiliane answered. "Leave me now." And she shoved him aside with such vigor that he obeyed.

Once more Christian Blaskorken had preserved her innocence—or, in this instance, her virtue.

The following morning Maximiliane was waiting for the antique dealer when he arrived to open the shop.

Pointing to the chess set, she inquired where he had got it. Documents quickly revealed the seller—a Herr Blaskorken from Bonn.

The antique dealer looked the inquirer over. She did not seem wealthy. "Are you seriously interested in the chess set? It's not exactly cheap."

"It has great value to me," replied Maximiliane.

"Unfortunately there's no box to store the pieces."

"I know."

Antique stores are emporiums of destinies. Their proprietors are case-hardened; they inquire into histories but do not listen to them. Maximiliane pulled the scrap dealer's check from her pocket. The antique dealer telephoned the bank as a precaution, to make certain the check was covered. He paid her the meager difference in cash.

Three hours later she was on a train to Bonn, a cardboard box containing Frederick the Great and his court and peasants on her lap.

Twenty-five years were wiped away when he stood before her, framed by his apartment door. No sign of surprise in his pale eyes, no sign of recognition. He gave the woman a questioning look. She spoke her magic words, one after the other: Poenichen! Quindt! Hunting horn! Chess set!

Not until he heard the words *chess set* was Herr Blaskorken's attention engaged. He had been forced to part with it, he said; money problems. Besides, he wasn't much of a chess player. The way he lived here— he gestured at the modestly furnished rooms—valuables, mementos, that was all over.

Maximiliane's head refused to believe what her eyes were seeing. The man standing before her was not Christian Blaskorken, he only looked like him. This was not a man who rowed a boat while standing up; this was just another Blaskorken after another lost war.

128

"I knew your father," she finally said, adding in explanation, "I was only a little girl at the time."

His son gave her the relevant facts about his father: fallen near the end of the war, he wasn't sure exactly where, sometime during the retreat skirmishes in the East; at the end he had been a battalion commander. "I didn't know him. He walked out on my mother and me, so I didn't lose much when I lost him."

Back home, Maximiliane unpacked the box. "Look at that," she said.

"What are we supposed to do with it?" Edda asked, answering her own question with one of her mother's phrases. "We don't need that. How much did you pay for it?"

"A lot of money," Maximiliane answered, "and it's worth a lot to me. It's a piece of Poenichen. I know that we don't even have proper beds, but since we don't plan to stay here anyway, temporary beds are good enough. We can take the chess set with us wherever we go. Your grandfather used it. He and Blaskorken, the foreman who—"

"—could row standing up." Viktoria completed the sentence.

"Now both of them are dead," Maximiliane said. "But these ivory men . . ." She stopped and looked at Joachim, who was holding the queen.

"You're referring to the symbolic nature of the figures, Mama?"

"Mose," she said loudly. "Mose, I don't mean any symbols, I'm talking about Poenichen." But the unusual phrase her son had used made her aware that he had taken a leap in his growth and gone way past her: "symbolic nature."

The children were very patient with their mother, all except Edda, and even she was mollified when one day a car called for her after school. Though when her mother got out of the car barefoot, she said in her father's voice, "Put your shoes on, Mama."

It was by no means a small car. A big family required a big car. Without telling the children, Maximiliane had bought it with the profits from the sale of her grandmother's diamond necklace, to surprise them. She never referred to the car as anything but "the wagon"—in which, if necessary, they could stow quite a bit. But the car did serve the purpose of raising the Quints in public esteem and showing their gradual social rise. A temporary home and a large car were not a good fit, however, and there were unfortunately some residents of Marburg who said, "Live like gypsies, they do, rushing out and buying a Mercedes the minute they get their check from the government."

From that time on, the portraits of the two barons Joachim and Achim von Quindt on Poenichen in Pomerania, newly framed in gold, adorned the hall of the Wassers' bungalow.

11

"Now in the name of God let the good Condor fly—
undo the ropes." It was done, and caught and cozened by the
thousand invisible tentacles of air, the huge orb trembled and
wavered for an instant. Then, gently rising, it lifted the basket
from the motherly lap of earth, and gaining speed with every
breath, it finally shot up swift as an arrow, perpendicularly
into the morning stream of light. At that moment the rays of
the sun flashed on its curvature and in the rigging, so that
Cornelia was frightened and thought the whole balloon was
bursting into flame; for the glowing rays cut the lines of the
ropes out of the indigo-blue sky, and the balloon radiated like
a gigantic sun. The earth, falling away, was still entirely black
and impenetrable, losing itself in darkness.

Maximiliane was reading "The Condor," by Adalbert Stifter. In the margin a stranger's hand had placed
two heavy exclamation marks next to the sentence
"Woman cannot endure the sky"—spoken by old Col-
oman just before he interrupted the awesome, glittering
balloon trip to take the unconscious lady back to earth.
This one sentence—"Woman cannot endure the sky"—
turned into a generalization by the author and his unknown reader, was the reason Maximiliane invited her
children to accompany her to a ballooning meet.

They were sitting on the meadow among the other
spectators, watching the preparations at the prescribed
distance of thirty meters. Five balloons were to go up

simultaneously. The presence of fire engines and ambulances indicated the danger inherent in the attempt. Sandbags filled with fine-grained sand hung inside the willow baskets. The balloons, filled with gas until they were as plump and yellow as the sun standing over the meadow, were restrained by ropes. The valves were checked one final time, and the baskets were attached. Then those passengers who had tickets were asked to climb on.

"But not you," objected Viktoria when Maximiliane moved out of the ranks of spectators.

Maximiliane pulled her ticket from her purse and waved it. "I can't always stop to ask your permission."

Together with three others she boarded the basket of the *Zephyr* and gave her weight: 128 pounds. In all, six hundred pounds of human ballast. The rest was sand.

"Loosen the ropes!" They did not add, "in the name of God." The heavy basket slowly left the ground, climbing at a rate of several meters per second. The spectators stood on the meadow waving, but Maximiliane did not wave back, nor did she try to make out her children's heads among all the others. She saw three horses in a paddock, growing ever smaller. She held tight to the basket's rim, leaning out as if on a balcony. Until now she had always lived close to the ground. A train crossed a bridge; she could see but not hear it. The balloon's shadow made a dark smudge across a field of maize. Her ears heard none of her fellow passengers' voices, neither the anxious nor the excited outcries. She was experiencing ascension.

When the balloon dove into the shade of a cumulus cloud, the gas cooled and they lost altitude. "Hold on," ordered the pilot, and emptied a sandbag. The balloon rose again, driven westward by a gentle breeze. At that instant Maximiliane understood—and it is because of this understanding that the balloon trip is here described in detail—that it is necessary to get rid of ballast to rise. She was always able to apply metaphors and similes to herself.

When the balloon broke through the two-thousand-meter barrier, the two passengers who were making their maiden flight were baptized with sand and champagne. Maximiliane allowed both to trickle down her face; she was in a state of bliss and never said a word throughout the flight. The world became smaller, easier to survey, less important. The *Zephyr* did not rise to the height of Mont Blanc, as had the *Condor*.

After two hours, when they had covered a distance of not quite eighty kilometers, they began to prepare for landing. The vents were opened, and *like a giant falcon, the* Condor *plummeted a hundred fathoms straight down through the air and then slowly, steadily sank.*

After the landing the balloon's ripcord was unfastened, and the empty shell collapsed on the meadow. Helpers came running. Voices. Laughter. Maximiliane let herself drop to the ground, heavy as never before. She looked pale and exhausted. Then one of the cars that had been brought for the purpose drove her back to the starting place, where her children were waiting for her, impatient and full of reproaches.

"It costs a hundred and fifty marks for a ride. We asked," Edda noted.

"Did you take out any insurance?"

"We had to sit around for three hours!"

Maximiliane looked from one child to another and said, "Be quiet. Or I'll go up again."

A threat the children answered with laughter.

Four weeks after the balloon flight, in October, word came that Baroness Maximiliane Hedwig von Quindt, Maximiliane's godmother, had fallen down the stairs and had died three days later, at the age of ninety. Maximiliane decided to take Mirka along to the funeral and show Eyckel Castle to the girl, who had no memory of her birthplace.

So, after a long separation, the Quindt family was reunited once more. Among the mourners was the General, who had come, as she put it, "from a sense of duty." Herr Brandes, owner of a brewery in nearby Bamberg, came with his wife; they were the parents of Ingo Brandes, who had died in the war. To Maximiliane's regret and the General's disapproval, Anna Hieronimi did not show up. The white aunts had both died in quick succession the previous winter; they left a large box of hand-embroidered linen doilies, but the time for "frivolities" had still not come.

Little Mirka, now seven years old, claimed everyone's interest.

"The child is seven already?"

"How time flies!"

"Remember that time, the Christmas of 1945? But let's not talk about it."

No one wanted to remember, for the events had not yet shriveled into anecdotage. Life went on, more quickly than before. If you looked back, you lost your hold on it. So they talked about Mirka.

"A pretty little girl, somehow foreign-looking. Where does she get it from?"

"From her father, presumably." Maximiliane's answer was wholly truthful.

"All these war orphans, forced to grow up without a father!" No one had a very clear memory of what Viktor Quint had looked like.

"But you'll make it, Maximiliane, you'll see. The children are through the worst of it."

The funeral service was held in the small chapel. They had to stand throughout, since the chairs had been put to other uses—mostly as wood for the fireplaces.

Twittering and chirping, sparrows darted through the cool vaulting. During the service, conducted by the aging Eckard Quint—by now ordained as a minister in the Bavarian church—Herr Brandes searched the room with his eyes; his wife repeatedly nudged him, urging him to pay attention. The Reverend Quint gave a short sketch of the deceased's life, in a few sentences summing up nine decades, two world wars, and two inflations. He mentioned briefly the Quindt family reunion of 1936 and dwelt at greater length on those postwar years when a number of Quindts from the East had found refuge here on Mount Eyckel, and when a child had first seen the light of the world. Once again the funeral guests' attention was directed to Mirka.

Before asking them to sing the hymn "Jesus, Still Lead On," the Reverend Quint spoke briefly about the composer of the lyrics, Count Nikolaus von Zinzendorf, allegedly related to the Quindts by marriage, and he alluded to the first line, "Jesus, still lead on, till our rest be won." His son Anselm, no longer a jazz trumpeter in American officers' messes but a medical student in his last year at the university, accompanied the singing.

After the interment the inheritance was discussed in the presence of the notary. The deceased's 1918 will named her godchild, Maximiliane, as sole heir. There was no superseding instrument, and the old will was not contested. No one begrudged the heiress her questionable legacy. Even before the discussion was over, Maximiliane had decided to transfer the hereditary title to Mirka. The rooms that had been rebuilt into a youth hostel were still used as an old-age home for refugees, but the death of the last eleven residents during the coming eleven years was a virtual certainty. There were no new admissions.

Herr Brandes asked Maximiliane for a private interview. He had looked over the ruins, he said, and they could still be made to serve as a storage facility for beer; the cellar spaces were in a passable state. Though he was not in a position to pay rent, he could see to it that "neither rats nor rabble make their nests in the old ruins."

"If I may give you some advice as a relative and a businessman, you'll accept my offer. The building continues to remain in the family. My proposal is in consideration of my wife—or rather, of our only son, Ingo, who loved Eyckel Castle. I do have to insist on an option to buy, but you'll hardly find anyone else to take the place off your hands anyhow."

"It's fine with me, Herr Brandes," Maximiliane replied. "I don't care what your reasons are. As for any future plans, you'll have to come to an agreement with Mirka."

"It looks like there'll be plenty of time for that." Herr Brandes glanced carelessly at the child, who was standing on her left leg, supporting her right foot on her left knee—a position she assumed when she was bored.

The Quindt family members, preoccupied with structuring and restructuring their means of livelihood, took their departure speedily and with relief, the General "from a sense of duty."

Maximiliane paid a few visits in the village. As she drove past Wengel's place, the farmer was standing at the barn door holding his handcart. She stopped and waved him over. He examined the car. "That shows you where our money goes." Thereupon she decided to forgo a reunion with Seifried, the farmer for whom she used to work.

On the trip back, Maximiliane made a detour to Stuttgart to visit Friederike von Kalck, who had opened a vegetarian restaurant. Though they had been planning to get together for a long time, this particular moment was badly chosen; the business was being remodeled and expanded to include more kitchen space and another large dining room. Nevertheless the restaurant

136

remained open since the owners could not afford to lose the income.

Friederike, who was once more calling herself "von Kalck on Perchen," did manage to find a half-hour to sit down with her onetime neighbor from Pomerania. By now she was fifty, hurried and skinny, but no longer dependent on her father and brother. "I run this show," she said, and Maximiliane believed her at once.

"On Perchen it was considered a privilege if I was allowed so much as to lead the horses or drive the car. If Father hadn't lost his arm in the war, they'd never have let me on the coachman's box. It's your governess, Fräulein Gering, whom I have to thank for all you see here. She turned me into a devout vegetarian. By now my menu covers two pages. Pomeranian dumpling soup, fruited tapioca pudding the way we make it in Pomerania. Twice a week we have 'blood pudding,' but without the blood. And all kinds of homemade noodles, like the Bavarians make. One has to adapt. Organically grown raw vegetables and fruit. I get all my fruit and vegetables from the country. Three times a week I take the truck out myself to shop."

She rose abruptly, returned just as quickly, and placed a cardboard box on the table. She took from it another box, its front made of glass, and opened it. "The keys to Perchen. Thirty-seven of them. I single-handedly locked every door myself before we left—cellars and attics and wardrobes and chests. I had this case specially made for them. I shall hang it up in the new dining room, flowers to both sides of it. And one day I and my key ring will return to Perchen." She raised her chin, and her long neck grew even longer, as if the keys restored to her all the power on Perchen.

"The Ideal!" she added. The Ideal played a major role in her restaurant; with every paycheck to every employee, with every corn croquette, every beet salad, she dished out a helping of the attitudes she had learned from Fräulein Gering.

"Can you ever get away from here?" Maximiliane asked.

"Not right now, no, but that's because of the renovation. At other times the business can get on without me for a couple of days."

"Don't you want to go back to Perchen?"

"I built the business up here. I can't just drop it. A hundred and fifty meals each lunchtime. There's no such thing as a day off. You have no idea how hard it is to hold the clientele in line now that you can buy meat without coupons again."

"Try whipping them with a leek." Maximiliane was laughing.

But Friederike von Kalck was much too earnest about vegetarianism; she equated biology with morality. "You and your fish-fry shop," she said in irritation.

"Sausages," Maximiliane corrected her.

"Don't you have any ambition? A Quindt behind a sausage counter! What would your grandfather say?"

"Perhaps he'd say that now others are having their turn instead of always us."

"You don't mean to tell me that you're a socialist?"

"No, I don't think so."

"But you talk like Rosa Luxemburg."

They fell silent. Friederike von Kalck observed Mirka, who was sitting quietly and appeared distracted. "You didn't have her in Poenichen, did you?"

"She's a posthumous child."

"Somebody told me you'd married again."

"That was an error." This answer, too, could claim to be the truth.

"I'm glad I don't have five children to raise."

Maximiliane had no response to this declaration, but she could see no signs of gladness in the emaciated face. The two women continued to sit in silence. What

138

did they talk about in the old days, Maximiliane wondered. About personal things? About the prospects for the harvest? "We always just sat together"—perhaps Parson Merzin's statement was true.

"Should I have offered you something?" Friederike von Kalck finally inquired. "It's not serving time; the kitchen is closed."

But the question came too late in any case. Maximiliane had already risen to say good-bye.

The women wished each other all the best. Mirka curtsied and said, "Thank you."

On the way to the parking lot Maximiliane and Mirka passed a dancing school. Mirka stopped to examine the photographs displayed outside. Noting the sign that read "Dancing School," she asked, "Don't they have to sit at desks and write in this school? Are they allowed to dance all the time?"

"Is that what you'd like to do?" Maximiliane was curious.

Mirka nodded, never taking her eyes off the showcase. This child, who always did as she was told, who never got dirty, who never had to be reminded—for the first time she was expressing an independent idea.

As they moved on, Maximiliane began to notice that Mirka was not walking as she had in the past. She was placing one foot closely in front of the other, at the same time swiveling her hips and observing her steps in the reflections from shopwindows. Mirka came to a stop in the middle of the sidewalk, bent down, reached for her right foot with her left hand, raised it effortlessly to shoulder height, and took a few little jumps forward. She was imitating one of the poses she had seen minutes before in the photographs.

The passersby were amused and astonished as they watched the little girl. Her mother's eyes were opened: she became aware of signs of future beauty in Mirka. Every vertebra along the slender, elongated back was visible through the faded blue-and-white-checked dress that Frau Görke had sewn during the last year of the war for Edda to grow into.

To produce this child, legitimate and illegitimate ancestors had given of their best: the eyes of the Polish lieutenant; the long, curled lashes of her grandmother Vera; the flat cheekbones and sallow skin of the Kirghiz; the healthy hair of a Pomeranian blond, and with it the taciturnity of Great-grandmother Sophie Charlotte, which Old Quindt had characterized as a "passionate secretiveness." At the moment this trait evidenced itself in little Mirka as the simple condition of being too lazy to talk, but it would later make her seem "shrouded in mystery."

Not long after Mirka had entered school, her first-grade teacher, Fräulein von Kloden, asked Maximiliane to come in for a conference. "What is the matter with the child?" the teacher asked. "She never opens her mouth." Maximiliane supposed that the most obvious reason for this profound silence was that Mirka had nothing to say.

The detour to Stuttgart led almost immediately to Mirka's future career. She was enrolled in the Gideon Dancing Academy in Marburg, and after only a few weeks she was chosen for private training. Her achievements in public school went downhill proportionally. "All your brains are in your legs," said Fräulein von Kloden, prompting Mirka to smile, flash her pretty teeth, and keep her mouth shut.

In the meantime Maximiliane had legally transferred to Mirka the right to inherit Eyckel Castle and had made a lease containing first option to buy with Brandes, the brewery owner from Bamberg. But this first inheritance was not the last. Over the years other family members thought of the young widow from Pomerania who had responsibility for five young children, and they expressed these thoughts in their wills. Thus Maximiliane, who had lost her huge inheritance in Poenichen—though at the time this fact had not yet been clarified—by and by became the recipient of numerous minuscule legacies. In each case she carefully considered which of her children was most suited to the particular gift.

When Louisa Larsson, another of Old Quindt's sisters, died in Uppsala, one of her granddaughters, Britta Lundquist, informed Maximiliane that a small estate near "Grandma's beach in Dalarna" had been left to her: four acres of forest, a share in a small lake, and three more or less tumbledown wooden shacks; no one had visited the property in five years. In this case Maximiliane's choice was Joachim, for no other reason than that he looked "sort of Swedish": tall, slender, blond, and blue-eyed.

It turned out that Maximiliane could not raise the huge inheritance tax of eleven thousand kronor. The matter rested for a time, negotiations were drawn out over several years, but eventually, when Joachim was already of age, there was a happy ending for the heir.

In the autumn of 1954 the District Court of Pankow, Russian Zone of Occupation, sent Maximiliane a registered letter to inform her that a certain Karl Preissing, retired, had willed his possessions to her. It had taken several months to determine her present address; the testator had been deceased since the previous November. Maximiliane Quint was requested to come to Berlin to settle the claim on the estate.

"I'm traveling to my inheritance," Maximiliane announced. She took Edda on the trip with her and left the sausage shop in the care of Lenchen Priebe.

During their long exodus from the East, Edda seemed to have lost her last memories of her real mother, Hilde Preissing; nor did any of the other children appear to remember that when she was three,

Edda had been delivered to Poenichen by her mother—
a "cuckoo's egg," as Old Quindt called her. Edda was
the only one of the children who liked to boast of her
noble ancestry.

At the East German district court the officer in
charge of inheritances, a Herr Kuhn, asked first about
the degree of her relationship to the deceased, Karl
Preissing.

Maximiliane looked at Edda and hesitated. Was this
the right moment to tell the child that Preissing was her
grandfather and that his only daughter, who had died
young, was her mother? She decided on the equally
truthful information that Herr Preissing had taken her
and her four children into his home for several months
when they reached Berlin after the end of the war. She
avoided the words *flight, expulsion,* and *Russians*.

"And after that he left you everything he had? All
his savings?" Herr Kuhn asked.

Maximiliane gave him a smile intended to exculpate
both the testator and herself, replying that Herr Preissing had taken the children to his heart and that they
had taken the place of his own family after his wife and
daughter died.

"Basically total strangers, then," said Herr Kuhn.

"But we called him Grandpa." Edda set matters to
rights. "Grandpa Preissing with the plug in his ear."

This last remark aroused the evident disapproval
of the official, which is why Maximiliane saw herself
forced to defend her child. "Herr Preissing was somewhat hard of hearing. Besides, I have no intention of
accepting the legacy."

Edda showed signs of outrage but did not speak.

"I wish to have it transferred to my daughter
Edda," Maximiliane continued. "That is why I brought
her along."

Edda uttered a cry of pleasure. She was now the

142

owner of a savings book that represented 12,504 Ost-
mark deposited in a blocked account; intra-German
banking was not yet regulated.

Then there was the matter of coming to terms with
the current residents of Herr Preissing's apartment.
Eventually they declared themselves willing to keep and
continue using the furniture in exchange for a price that
was minimal but was to be paid in Western currency.
It was still possible to travel almost unchecked from one
sector of Berlin to the other.

The lesson that possession is a burden had passed
Edda by without a trace. Among the Quindts the need
for possessions, abundantly satisfied over the centuries,
had also been blunted by an excess of responsibility; at
any rate, it had not been handed down to Maximiliane.
But among her children, and especially in Edda, it surfaced again.

Three months later, when Grandmother Jadow
died in the Charlottenburg old-age home and Viktoria
was asked to come along to the funeral, Edda concluded
that Viktoria was the chosen legatee. Her rage at her
mother was unbridled. "It's not fair! Grandmother Jadow had a big apartment and lots of jewelry, and all I
got was what Grandpa Preissing had!"

"No one said it was fair, Edda," Maximiliane answered. "Nor was it fair that for more than thirty years
Grandmother Jadow collected a good-sized pension,
while Grandpa Preissing had nothing but a tiny annuity.
The world is not fair. All the same, I try to be as fair as
I can. Don't you see that Tora's needs are greater than
yours? She can't make it on her own."

It was unlikely that Edda heard the praise contained
in her mother's words.

A closet in Grandmother Jadow's apartment dis-
closed paper bags filled with pudding powder from
1947, dried beets and dried potatoes from the time of

the Berlin airlift. When she died, she weighed barely forty kilograms; even in the old-age home she had eaten less and less by the month and had hoarded food for fear of starving to death. Since her daughter had no wish to see Berlin ever again and had paid no attention to her mother over the years, Grandmother Jadow had left all her worldly goods to Maximiliane. There would be enough to underwrite Viktoria's long education.

On the day of the funeral Maximiliane took the interurban railway to Pankow; she was already dressed in her mourning outfit. She went to the savings bank and withdrew from Edda's account the largest amount allowed by law. Then she went to a florist and ordered a wreath for which she had to wait a considerable time: fir branches studded with chrysanthemums. Hiding in a doorway, she managed to conceal the banknotes among the twigs and flowers.

In deep mourning, the wreath on her lap, she then took the interurban railroad in the opposite direction. Travelers' pockets and bags were searched at Friedrichstrasse station, but the East German policewoman responsible for the car in which Maximiliane was traveling respected her mourning and refused to glance into her purse or wallet.

The funeral service had already begun when Maximiliane arrived at the cemetery, but she was present when the coffin was lowered. She could look after the disturbed Viktoria, she could thank the few mourners who attended, and she could place her wreath with the others.

Viktoria was complaining. "Let's get out of here."

"In a minute."

Maximiliane waited until she was unobserved to pull the banknotes out of the wreath. In an exchange office at the zoo station she traded the Eastern money for Western currency at a ratio of 4 to 1. The plan for the money transfer had been hatched by Lenchen Priebe.

The last of the legacies yielded an oak table with many leaves, at present in Strassburg. But in this instance Maximiliane was only one among many heirs.

All that was missing now was a suitable inheritance for Golo.

12

During the war there was an armaments factory hidden in the woods not far from Marburg, near Allendorf. When the war was almost over, the munitions dump was blown up by American army engineers. Later the secluded spot was used by the Americans as a dumping ground for captured weapons and mines, which the Germans were made to deactivate. Because of the high price of brass, tons of arms traveled from this depot along the sinister paths of the black market to surface as scrap. The illegal trade was as dangerous as it was profitable.

Every few weeks the Marburg newspaper, naming precise locations, advised the parents of growing children that armaments were still to be found in the area, imperiling children's lives and limbs. Golo, with his sure nose for danger, felt that these details were meant specifically for him. Even during their flight, at the age of five, he had more than once acquired hand grenades and grenade launchers, and his mother had had to disarm him. Lately he had repeatedly run across treasures in the mud of the riverbed, not far from the signs warning of danger from unexploded munitions.

By now he was in his second year of high school. He had been excused from physical education after two accidents during gym class; it seemed the only way to protect him and his fellow students. The gym teacher had ordered him to spend the period sitting at the edge of the gymnasium, which as a rule he did not do. Instead he roamed. He had appropriated the wasteland where the synagogue stood until it was destroyed. The people of Marburg tended to avoid the place. It was there that Golo had set up a small underground arsenal.

Golo had little aptitude for formal schooling, and his sense of right and wrong was no more developed than his spelling skills. Once, during a field trip to Nuremberg's Germanic Museum, he swiped fifty marks from one of the other students and used it to treat the whole class to ice cream. It was not until the boy's generosity impressed Dr. Spohr, the teacher, that the victim noticed the loss of his pocket money. Called to account, Golo explained, "I am only educating the boy in the communal spirit. Freedom! Equality! Brotherhood! Humanity's ideals!"

"We are concerned purely with ideals that are to be striven for, Golo," Dr. Spohr countered. "I'd appreciate it if you'd leave it to others to translate them into reality." Confronted with those beaming saucer eyes, the teacher made his lecture a gentle one.

Since Dr. Spohr had no illusions about his influence on Golo, he asked for a conference with the boy's mother.

But like all mothers, Maximiliane stood up for her son.

"It would have been better if the other boy had bought the ice cream himself. The blame lies with the boy's parents, who gave their child fifty marks to take on a school trip. My son acts from an innate sense of justice. He acted foolishly as far as school is concerned, but we all know that he's not clever."

Maximiliane smiled, her eyes trusting as they looked at the teacher. Dr. Spohr recognized the student's traits in the mother and shrugged his shoulders.

"I have made sure you know what happened. We won't be lodging a criminal charge."

Golo was never punished; he punished himself. He would never manage to get further than secondary school anyway, and he would achieve that result only with Joachim's help. He was not seriously worried about his minimal scholastic prospects. "I'm going to live in America anyhow," he explained, both at home and in school.

"You're better suited to live over there, that's for sure," said his teachers, probably aware that they would miss the unruly, cheerful boy.

"When in blazes are we going to go?" he asked each time a letter from California arrived, for each letter spoke about the trip to America. More than a year before, Dr. Green had offered to pay their expenses. He too had something to make restitution for, he had scribbled in the margin—"By comparison, I managed to get through those twelve years without damage." He had begun to receive regular payments from the restitution funds.

But Maximiliane kept on postponing the trip. Her two natures were in conflict, Pomeranian calm clashing with the restlessness of her Berlin mother, who had spent her pregnancy riding horses and rocking energetically in a rocking chair—activities that must have had some effect on the child thus jostled in her mother's womb.

Finally Golo used his own means to hasten their departure.

Some time earlier he had dug two bazookas from his arsenal and stowed them under the damask napkins in one of the crates. He was only waiting for a suitable time to take them apart at his leisure. The opportunity arose one afternoon in May. His mother was at the sausage shop as always, and so was Edda, who worked there at odd times—lately for pay. Joachim was tutoring

148

another student in Greek. Mirka was at dancing school. Only Viktoria was home, but she was outside working out with her hula hoop, keeping it in motion with hips, knees, and shoulders, speeding it up, slowing it down, and growing visibly thinner from the exercise. She turned and twisted in her cage like one possessed, oblivious to all else. She too was no threat to his solitude; the day before, she had managed a record two and a half hours in which the hoop never touched the ground.

Undisturbed, Golo sat at the kitchen table taking apart his highly explosive find.

The detonation occurred shortly after five o'clock. The police made a note of the time and included it in their report to the newspaper. Parts of the interior of the building were destroyed, and the windows were blasted from their frames; a meter-wide hole gaped in the roof. Miraculously, Golo himself was almost untouched. The only damage he suffered was the loss of the two smallest fingers of his left hand, which were so mutilated that they had to be amputated in the emergency room. Though Viktoria was unhurt, she went into shock; she was still screaming when the police car brought Maximiliane to the hospital.

The following night Maximiliane slept especially long and deeply—she always did after any eventful and exciting day.

What was it Joachim had said? "We can be glad that we still have what we still have." The photograph illustrating the detailed report in the next day's newspaper was intended to serve as one more warning to the parents of growing children. The destroyed temporary home of a noble widow from the East, blessed— so the report said—with many children but now deprived of her modest possessions. Nor did the paper omit a reference to the "lamentable fate of unsupervised latchkey children."

As a consequence of this story, several citizens of

Marburg searched their attics for spare household goods, delivering them to the temporary home on the hillside—a process Maximiliane had to stand by and watch helplessly. What others could spare, she could spare as well. A later photograph was published to show readers the self-sacrificing spirit of their fellow residents. It portrayed the Quints surrounded by lamps, sewing tables, and coffee grinders. In the picture Maximiliane was holding her blouse closed at the throat. In reality she was about to unbutton it, a well-known gesture: she felt stifled.

She took the explosion as a sign from fate. Once more she had become too heavy, once more ballast must be jettisoned. "Who can tell what good will come of it?" Anna Riepe used to say.

Very soon she made the necessary applications for passports and visas. She went to the American consulate in Frankfurt to stress the urgency of the trip by showing the newspaper pictures and the invitation from her Jewish stepfather and her mother the emigrant. Then she made inquiries at the various shipping lines and finally dispatched a telegram to San Diego: "We're on our way." Every family member had to be examined for infectious diseases, and they all had to have shots. The inoculation immediately provoked Viktoria's usual fever, indicating to the doctor the possibility of some contagious disease and thus almost jeopardizing the scheduled departure.

Lenchen Priebe was appointed to run the sausage shop—which the Quints still referred to as the "fish-fry stand." Lenchen had resumed her former name and once more looked like a girl—though an aging one—from Pomerania. She had put on weight from worry, had stopped dyeing her hair, and was wearing out her American wardrobe. Since the occupation forces spent on the average no more than three and a half months in Marburg, there was not time enough to form lasting relationships. And when the troops left for good, Helen von Jadow's dream of America ended. Since she had no training in any trade, she had to find temporary jobs as a waitress in restaurants, in the university dining halls, and at the buffet of the railroad-station restaurant. Life seemed to have meant her only for temporary work; during the Quints' absence, she was to be the temporary manager of the sausage shop.

Once more Maximiliane said, "Come" to her children. She still held them on a tight rein—tighter than she realized, and tighter than was good for them. On the second day of their long vacation they embarked on the passenger-carrying freighter *La Colombe* in Rotterdam.

Before leaving, Maximiliane had the temporary home on the hillside temporarily fixed.

13

If Maximiliane's travel reports were to be believed, several Americans were lined up at the dock calling in unison, "Can I help you?"

While they were still on the high seas, one of the other passengers, a Mr. Jack Freedom of Texas, dissuaded her from her mother's recommendation to cross the continent in a Greyhound bus. "Get a car," he advised. For six people it paid to buy an automobile. Mr. Freedom had a friend who had a friend whose friend Mr. Smith had a used-car dealership in Brooklyn. The car these three Americans helped Maximiliane buy for a hundred dollars was a roomy Rambler, sturdy, canary-yellow, with 180,000 miles on the odometer. All three men assured her that they envied her. They too had always wanted to drive from coast to coast.

Maximiliane had not read Steinbeck or Faulkner or Hemingway. Her image of America had not been prejudiced by literary fantasies of the Wild West. The continent took her unprepared; she was a female Columbus.

But of course she possessed a map. Joachim, who took care of all documents needed for the car and the trip, had conscientiously seen to this as well. Every morning in a drugstore or diner, while the children were still eating their breakfasts, she spread her map out on the table, and immediately several long-distance travelers bent their heads over it to discuss her day's route with her. They sketched the most scenic, the best, or the quickest stretches of highway, occasionally got into arguments among themselves, and wrote along the edges of the map the addresses of friends who would be delighted by a visit from the entire Quint clan, since they had done army service in Germany.

Finally Maximiliane let them point her in the right direction—"Have a good trip"—and off she went, headed westward. Every morning she really did set out for the West, but as a rule she soon found herself on a highway, the yellow Rambler wedged between two lines of trucks, preventing any execution of the carefully laid plan for the day.

Whenever she ran out of gas, she took the nearest exit ramp, asked where she was, had them fill up the tank, bought popcorn, Coca-Cola, and french fries with ketchup. The smell of ham and eggs mingled with the odor of oil and gasoline and reminded the Quints of the fish-fry stand. The radiator was refilled. Mirka and Viktoria scoured the trash cans for comics, from which Viktoria was learning English. The few times she raised her eyes from her magazines, she did so only to say, "Remember to drive on the right, Mama." Mirka simply looked at the pictures.

Now and again, for no apparent reason, Maximiliane would stop by the side of the road and make all the children get out. "Look around. You'll never be here again."

No sooner had everyone emerged from the car than another driver was already stopping, his window rolled down, and a head popping out. "Can I help you?"

If the question was answered in the negative, he was likely to drive on. Often, however, he had a further question. "Where are you from?" Maximiliane had to give a lot of thought to her answer to make it truthful and complete. While she might have omitted Dramburg

County, she would surely have gone back beyond the Oder and the Neisse. But the stranger would point knowingly to the New York license plate of the Rambler. He himself had been born in the Bronx or had grown up on Long Island, he would tell her before driving off with a "So long." Maximiliane embraced a maple tree in Appalachia, betraying Pomerania to the state of Virginia.

Each day the weather grew warmer. They were driving deeper into the South. It must have been in Tennessee that they first decided to set out at dawn to get the best of the day's coolness. When they rented a motel room at noon, they hung the Do Not Disturb sign on the door and slept below whirring fan blades. The motel owners were always willing to put additional cots in the room for the "kids." Hot dusk, drawn blinds, screen windows. Viktoria was the only one who suffered from the heat.

Edda was in charge of the travel funds. By now she was a teenager of fifteen with a ponytail, her forehead and nose brightly sprinkled with freckles; she had been proud of them ever since a waitress in a diner told her that she looked like Doris Day. Edda was the only one willing and able to translate gallons into liters, Fahrenheit into centigrade, and miles into kilometers, but especially to compare dollar amounts with German prices. During the day she filled a notebook with newly learned words, and each night she made Golo quiz her on them. When she had saved up some money, she treated the whole family to ice cream.

Several times a day Golo offered to relieve his mother at the wheel along the straight stretches. Always she told him, "Later." She was not a naysayer. She glanced at his mutilated hand. Would he ever be able to handle a steering wheel?

Just before the approach to the bridge in Memphis Maximiliane once again became trapped between two

154

trailer trucks, and they crossed the Mississippi without catching a glimpse of it. Joachim, who had studied the map, called her attention to the omission. She took the next exit ramp to return to the city, finding herself on a street leading directly to the black slums. Rush-hour traffic; the street blocked by cars, trucks, and pedestrians. They were surrounded. Viktoria complained of thirst, Edda carped that no river was worth a detour, Joachim and Golo agreed with her, and even Mirka was heard to speak: "I've got to go."

"Fine," Maximiliane said, overcome by irritation. "We'll stop here. We'll look for someplace to eat." And she drove the car up on a sidewalk between a couple of overflowing garbage cans.

"But not here!" Viktoria protested. "Not in the slums!"

"At least lock the car this time. You always forget," Edda reminded her.

"If I always forget, I'll forget this time too." Maximiliane slammed the door and started walking away.

They were the only customers in the coffee shop. Two white-haired black women waited on them. They polished the glasses for a long time before pouring the tepid juice, and then they wiped the tabletop once more. The fan purred; it was hot and sticky in the dusky room. Golo's attention was riveted on the jukebox, and he was about to get up when Maximiliane urged them all to hurry. Before they had a chance to pay, a bead curtain at the back of the room was pushed aside and a black man stepped out, making no bones about his disapproval of the whites. In effect he was chasing them from the premises—though without taking a step toward them.

Maximiliane did not move. "Stay where you are," she said to the children.

Another black man appeared, then a third. All three stood there menacingly. "I'm afraid," Mirka said.

At the moment when the three started to move toward them, Joachim rose to his full height, seeming more light-skinned and blond than usual. He went up to the men in silence, his hands balled into fists. He held them at bay and gestured to the family to get out. Eighteen years old by now and six feet tall, the "little man" of long ago, fearful and brave, backed by the white race, the lordly lineage of the Quindts, and his race-conscious father, Viktor Quint.

Back on the street, Maximiliane said, "Let's just forget all about it." Behind her, the door opened once more as the money Edda had left on the table was thrown at them. It rolled across the pavement. Hastily the children gathered it up again.

All four tires of the car had been slashed. None of the luggage was missing.

"Get behind the wheel, Mama," Joachim ordered. "We'll push."

In the afternoon heat they had to use all their strength to move the car several hundred yards through the bustle of traffic to a garage. The owner, a white man, took one glance at the tires and one at the tourists and said, "Forget it."

While the tires were being replaced or, to the extent possible, patched, the Quints took a cruise down the Mississippi on the paddle steamer *Memphis Queen*. A band was playing in the saloon. Joachim and Viktoria were still talking excitedly about the incident with the three blacks; Golo and Edda were standing at a machine shooting lions and elephants. Mirka, who was using the stair rail as a barre, aroused the attention of several passengers.

Alone, Maximiliane leaned against the railing. The riverbanks dissolved in the dusk, the lamps of the saloon turned into shimmering pools of light on the black water. The jazz trumpet rose clearly above the band. Hunting signals and hymns. "Gonna take my heart back home." And now, "Old Man River." Flooded by memories, she shivered and felt chilled with loneliness.

"Have a drink," said a man's voice at her elbow.

Maximiliane glanced sideways and saw the pale-skinned face of a man.

"Lovesick?" he asked.

Maximiliane shook her head.

"Seasick?" He pointed to the water, churned up by the paddles.

Again Maximiliane shook her head.

"Homesick?"

Maximiliane did not answer. "Where are you from?" he continued.

"Germany? Really?" He had, he told her, seen army service in Frankfurt, and he could still speak a few words of German. They managed a short conversation at the railing. His name was Pete Simpson, and he owned a ranch in Montana. Maximiliane gave him a thorough going-over; he had handsome, regular features and was tall and sturdily built. She was attracted to him—but his name was Peter. All her life Maximiliane had had an aversion to the name Peter.

Simpson talked about his ranch, making her see it: the wide-open prairie, cut off to the west by the snow-covered Rockies. Each of his barns held eighty head of cattle. He could move the walls apart to drive through with the tractor, shoving the dung in a ditch on his trip in one direction, mechanically spreading the chaff on the return trip; he didn't even have to get down. He did the work alone, without ranch hands. "Once over, and it's done." When he took a vacation, as he was doing now, a neighbor who lived a mere seventy miles away came over and took care of the chores.

Maximiliane thought about Poenichen, where there were dairymen and milkers and stablemen, and she was impressed by so much streamlining. It was as if, after a long time, she could once more sniff the aroma of swill.

She was sorry that Joachim was not there to hear the conversation. She was still hoping that one day he would develop an interest in the land. Now he cared only for landscape—vistas and hummingbirds instead of cattle and cornfields. As he filled his notebook with verses, she observed him with a feeling of disappointed expectations. How much he could have learned in the United States toward his later career as heir and manager of Poenichen! She never relinquished her hopes for a return. They were fueled by proclamations from the minister in charge of expellee affairs and from the various associations of displaced persons. Accordingly, she still clung to the prospect that Joachim's interests would change. "He'll outgrow it," Old Quindt used to say confidently, himself having had to give up his desire to become a travel writer in favor of Poenichen.

A woman came toward them. Mr. Simpson drew away from Maximiliane slightly and called, "Hello." Then Maximiliane watched as Mr. and Mrs. Simpson moved away arm in arm. The ranch in Montana was walking away from her. In its place Golo joined her, taking her hand. "Come on, there's going to be dancing."

The era of rock 'n' roll had begun: new sounds. They danced the Twist. For a moment Maximiliane watched from the edge of the dance floor; then she took Golo's arm. "Come on, we can do that." She had learned to bend and gyrate while working in the fields and in the sausage shop.

Oklahoma! Cornfields, cotton fields, dark-skinned men and women picking the white cotton blossoms. Meadows with cows grazing next to the steel skeletons of oil rigs. Then Texas! Endless dry steppes, here and there a herd of cattle, and along the barbed-wire fences metal signs exhorting the motorists: Enjoy Beef Every Day. In Amarillo, Maximiliane bought plate-sized steaks for everyone, and they grilled them at the next rest stop. Viktoria refused to eat the meat. Thinking of Enjoy Beef Every Day, she struggled to hold back the tears.

After the meal they sank down in the shade of a huge tree. Maximiliane examined the juicy green leaves and the bark. "What kind of tree do you think it is?" she asked. And when none of the children answered, she wondered, "Where have we smelled this scent before?"

"At Grandmother Jadow's house in Charlottenburg," Golo shouted.

"Right. It must be a camphor tree," Maximiliane agreed. She too stretched out, throwing her arms over her head. Seconds later she was fast asleep, so that the children had to shake her awake when it was time to go.

For miles along the road a big black bird traveled along with them—a blackbird; an equally large blue bird later took its place—a bluebird. When, in New Mexico, a long-legged bird hurried across the highway in front of them, they called it a roadrunner. They discovered and named America.

In Albuquerque the Quints started driving along Route 66. Signposts without town names, nothing but numbers.

Maximiliane stopped and turned to Joachim, who was looking for the corresponding spot on the map. "Here we are," he said. "At the edge of the desert."

Seeing the endless expanse and the signposts, Maximiliane was suddenly reminded of a photograph her husband had sent from Russia; it showed nothing but signposts with the numbers of troop units and no place names, all pointing eastward, deeper into the snowy wastes.

Deep in the heart of America, she told her oldest son about Russia and about Hitler's policies in the East.

"What did Father know about the persecution of the Jews and the concentration camps?" Joachim asked.

"I don't know what he knew. I only know what he believed in. He wanted to take his children to settle the Eastern territories. He believed in the superiority of the Germanic race."

"What's wrong?" Golo inquired after a while. "Why are we stopping? We're broiling in the car here."

And Maximiliane continued driving westward along roads straight as arrows, ending only at the horizon.

They crossed the desert, on the second day finding themselves in a small sandstorm, which so excited Golo that he could hardly be confined to the car. His America was made up of tornadoes, blizzards, hurricanes, and canyons; in his stories the waterfalls of Tennessee swelled to a Niagara. Edda's America consisted of Automats, escalators, portable radios, and refrigerators; Viktoria's, of black slums and Indian reservations. And Mirka—what captured Mirka's fancy? Herself presumably, when she saw her reflection in shop windows and mountain tarns.

In the Rockies, Maximiliane managed a trick she had brought off once before, on her flight from Pomerania: she made the sun go down three times in one day. This time all she had to do was speed up the car to reach the next peak in time; at each new horizon she stopped, waited for the sunset while enjoying her triumph, and then drove on westward. The other time, in 1945, she had had to struggle up the low hills of Brandenburg, pushing and pulling her handcart.

She had been moving westward for over ten years. Now she traveled at a greater speed—sometimes at an excessive speed—mile after mile through the sparsely settled southwest of North America. The road signs indicated the number of inhabitants.

160

"Be careful," Golo warned her. "They only have forty-seven people here."

Surely this land must have room for a handful of homeless Pomeranians!

They walked through the deserted towns of the gold and silver miners. *High Noon* and *Treasure of the Sierra Madre*. Ghost town, Wild West.

Arizona: nesting places concealed in the hearts of joshua trees tall as elms, birds flying in and out among the finger-long spikes. Cedars. Evergreen oaks. *On the Road*.

And finally California, oasis in the desert, land of dreams. They arrived at the Salton Sea, deep below sea level.

"We'll never be here again," Maximiliane said. And they dove into the salty, warm water.

At the edge of a palmetto grove they rested. Golo was the first to discover the rope ladders hanging from the palms. He leaped, grabbing a bottom rung, and in spite of his two missing fingers, he clambered up to the thick clusters of dates. Joachim helped his sisters to reach the ladders, but he himself sat down under a palm and took notes.

The laughter and shouts of the others wafted down from the treetops. Maximiliane stood and looked upward. At that moment she must have been remembering the palms, planted in buckes, that stood along the Poenichen gallery during the summers and spent the winters in the parlor. And she must also have thought of the pine forest her grandfather had planted. She stood straddle-legged, her hands folded behind her back, the spitting image of Old Quindt. When was the last time she had climbed a tree? Was that all over for her? She ran both hands through her hair, took a running start, jumped, and grasped the bottom rung of one of the rope ladders. Then she braced her feet against the trunk, pulled herself upward, and climbed the unsteady ladder to the top. Her children shouted at her to be careful; she did not hear them.

The hot desert wind whizzed through the car as soon as the doors were opened. Stopping at a gas station, they noted that the thermometer registered 125 degrees. In an orange grove they gathered windfall tangerines; the pale straw hats of the Mexican migrant workers gleamed among the dark green foliage.

They were approaching their goal. Maximiliane had already telephoned to announce their arrival. It was late afternoon when they came to the outskirts of San Diego, but Maximiliane drove around the city, making a sizable detour in spite of Edda's objections. She wanted to reach the very edge of the continent, to see the Pacific. From coast to coast. They arrived in time for the sunset.

"Let's wait until it goes down," she said to the children. He speaks and calls the world from rise of sun to its setting. Another one of those Biblical seeds—one never knows in whose heart they will sprout.

The sun's orb was close to the horizon, and for a time it hung suspended above the water. The children had walked away. Maximiliane recalled that on one other occasion she had said to someone, "Let's stay and wait to the end." That had been in Kolbert, on her honeymoon—her first sunset at the ocean. Before the California sun had finished sinking, she was overcome by sadness. Loneliness, just like that other time. The intoxication of the trip was followed by cold sobriety. She would never again take a trip like this one with her children.

She remained a child of the land, one who loved lakes and reed-studded banks; real boundarie, not this merging of sky and sea. She needed land beneath her feet and before her eyes. She turned around to look eastward, where the mountains lay bathed in the last purple rays of sunlight. She said—to herself or the chil-

162

dren or the world—"What am I doing here? I'm from Poenichen."

They drove through the canyons that wound through San Diego, drove around the bays that thrust into the city, lost their way more than once. The last couple of miles were once again the hardest.

14

Dr. Green's neighbors happened to be away on a world cruise. In their absence he sublet their house for the Quints. Thus, besides the usual living rooms and sleeping quarters, they had the use of bathrooms and showers, television set, telephone, and refrigerator.

On the morning of the second day mother and daughter had a chance to spend some time alone with each other. Dr. Green had taken the "kids"—as he collectively called Maximiliane's children—to the beach in La Jolla. He never saw patients until the afternoon.

The two women sat on the porch, which was cooler at this hour than the garden. Maximiliane sat in the glider, Vera in the rocking chair. "Did I take your seat?" Maximiliane had asked as she tucked her bare feet under her skirt, but Vera, with the hint of a smile, had replied, "I don't like to be rocked by others. I prefer a seat all to myself."

"How did you get along all this time?" Maximiliane began. "All I know is how it came out." Her gesture took in the garden and the section of the Pacific Ocean visible from the porch, along with the slender palms lining the road. "I don't know anything about what it took for you to get here. Quindt always said—no, he only said it a couple of times; they didn't talk a lot about you—he said, 'She is in safety.' I tried so hard to imagine what a country called Safety would look like."

Mrs. Green answered the open-ended question in one sentence. "I had my good time in Berlin, Green is having his good time now, and in between we had bad times." She did not seem ready to give her daughter more information so quickly. The rest followed bit by bit on subsequent mornings.

After their flight from Germany in 1935, the Greens—then still called Grün—had eventually reached the United States, making temporary stops in the Netherlands, Paris, and London. The money Old Quindt had given his former daughter-in-law to make emigration possible was spent on their overseas passage.

Dr. Grün's English was not good enough for him to pass the required medical exams. They moved to New Jersey, where he mowed lawns and trimmed hedges on the estates of the wealthy while his wife earned money from the same families as their cleaning lady. Eventually Dr. Grün managed to get a job as a male nurse in Brooklyn Jewish Hospital. At that time Vera was able to resume her photography, but there was no way she could sell her pictures to the major magazines; the American photographic style of the 1930s and 1940s differed markedly from the Berlin style of the 1920s. Moreover, her existing equipment was inadequate to the task, and buying new equipment was out of the question. She therefore worked for local newspapers, photographing smiling brides and newly graduated college girls.

Thus the couple spent several years in marginal circumstances. Then, during the war, Dr. Grün took his state medical boards in Sacramento and passed. He opened a psychiatric practice in Los Angeles, charging ten dollars an hour. Their apartment was so small that in the afternoons and early evenings, when he saw patients, Vera had to go out. Since the Grüns did not have a car yet, Vera went for long walks, roaming among the highways and freeways of Los Angeles. After they acquired American citizenship, they changed their name to Green. There were no insurmountable problems connected with their German origin and Jewish descent.

Dr. Green had been able to salvage the notes he had made in Berlin for a book to be entitled *Body Language and Nonverbal Communication of the Masses*. He continued to do research in his specialty and was soon recognized as one of the founders of "kinesics," the systematic interpretation of human gestures—a science still not acknowledged by traditional psychology. His first article published in America, "Nonverbal Communication," attracted considerable attention. At present he was working on "the dialects of body language." An hour with him no longer cost ten dollars but twenty, and with a yearly income of thirty thousand dollars, the Greens were ranked among the upper middle class. A house in San Diego three blocks from the ocean, two cars, two television sets.

Dr. Green's consultation room sported an enlargement of a photograph that had once hung in his rooms in Berlin: Sigmund Freud flanked by his pupils Alfred Adler and Daniel Grün. The picture had been taken in 1921 in Bad Gastein. "Vienna School." The photograph contributed more to his standing in the United States than did his diplomas. As the years passed, Green had deviated more and more from Freud's teachings; repressed sexuality and sexual aberrations no longer held any fascination for him. In his looks, on the other hand, he came to resemble the master more and more, even to the graying beard trimmed rather like Freud's. The look in his eyes, however, was skeptical rather than kindly.

In the little anteroom where the patients waited, which he, unbeknownst to them, could observe, the walls bore two framed statements characteristic of his outlook. The one, "Why live when you can be buried for ten dollars?" was ascribed to Sigmund Freud; the

166

other, unattributed and possibly composed by Green himself, read, "Don't try to live forever; you won't succeed." Otherwise the walls were bare. Both statements were shocking for a physician's waiting room, especially in California. Dr. Green was in the habit of noting the effect they had on his patients. It was a test.

Two other pictures were conspicuous in his consultation room. One showed a Jewish father who had died in Auschwitz at the age of eighty-seven. The other portrayed Adolf Hitler in uniform. Dr. Green surrounded himself with images, not of his friends and models, but of his opposites—those who had helped him to grow and whom he did not want to forget.

A few mornings later, mother and daughter once again sat on the porch together. Mrs. Daniel Green had put aside all the allures of Vera Jadow's golden Berlin years along with the long ebony holder through which she used to smoke her Oriental cigarettes. Nevertheless she had not adapted to the general image of the American woman of the 1950s. She wore mainly black, a color unacceptable in California even for mourning. Her hair was still closely shingled, and its graying strands were brushed tight to the skull. She was a woman in her early sixties, her glance less bright, less quick, her once passionately animated features softer. She had given up smoking, no longer drank bourbon, no longer listened to jazz. She had also gotten out of the habit of saying, "I've been there before." She no longer took photographs.

But: "I do my own thing," she said, frequently mixing American slang phrases into her conversation. "Every day I spend several hours in the greenhouse. I grow orchids. They have no scent, and they don't move—they're objects more than they are a form of life. They don't bother anybody. They don't even gesture." This last being a dig at her husband's preoccupations.

She herself never underlined her statements with gestures. Her hands lay motionless in her lap. Without rocking she sat in the rocking chair. "Everything is just fine. That's what counts here. I've attained the goal of every American striving. Relax and enjoy."

She rose, went into the house, and shortly returned with a large book. "A German publisher brought out a facsimile edition of some of the photo series I did in Berlin for a picture magazine. *Unter den Linden at Half-Past Four*. At the time the pictures were interesting from an aesthetic point of view; today they're interesting as history—history of photography as well. But maybe publishing the book was just an act of restitution to a person who was politically persecuted."

Maximiliane opened the book, and the first thing she noticed was the series of photographs her mother had surreptitiously taken at Poenichen—"Images of Pomerania." The potato harvest; Quindt, with his manorial bearing, sitting in the gig, Riepe standing behind him on the coach step; the foreman, Palcke; little Erika Beske. All of them dead now.

"Did *he* ever see these pictures?" Maximiliane spoke of her grandfather as Viktor Quint had spoken of Hitler—in awed tones, as if she were speaking of God. Her mother had no need to ask whom Maximiliane meant, for she too stressed *he*, someone who had twice intervened in her destiny.

"After *he* saw the pictures in the magazine, he advised me to leave Poenichen. He sent me on my way. This is where I ended up."

Mother and daughter cautiously approached the subject of Poenichen. "I used to ride a horse called Mistral there," said the mother, and the daughter countered with, "My horse was called Falada, but my legs turned out to be too short. Until somebody"—she remembered, breathing deeply, the rider at Poenichen Lake—"found out that my legs weren't too short any-

168

more. After Joachim's birth, I grew another five centimeters."

"Do you know that Joachim looks like your father?"

Maximiliane had not known. Mrs. Green continued. "When I married him, he looked like Joachim, my Baron Achim von Quindt from Pomerania—a boy they stuck in a field-gray lieutenant's uniform. And I was a woman already. I was a few years older than he. A widow, a mother—everything moved so fast. I think Green would have liked to have a son, but he couldn't have one with me. If things had been different, we might have separated. But I couldn't abandon a Jew; he was dependent on me. Later he couldn't abandon me, because I had given up everything for him and I was dependent on him. We owe each other a lot."

"I was in a similar situation with Viktor, my first husband. Quindt always said, 'He thinks more of his party membership than he does of Poenichen.' And after the collapse I thought I had to protect him."

"Do you have any idea where his grave is?"

"No, they said he was missing."

"But your father should have a grave," Mrs. Green said after some thought. "The time and place of his heroic death—that's how they referred to it in 1918— were known. Or did Quindt have his body moved later?"

"No. There was a headstone for him on Innicher Hill, but they rarely spoke of him."

"I thought at the time that he'd probably die twice— once in body, and again through silence." Mrs. Green paused, then continued. "A strange man, almost a savage, used to live at your lake in those days."

"Christian Blaskorken."

"I don't think I ever knew his name. I do remember Anna Riepe and her tapioca pudding."

"They say I called her Mama and later on addressed her as Amma."

This conversation brought them much closer to each other, although they had to cross a generation and an ocean.

Soon after their arrival Dr. Green had reached for Maximiliane's hand and examined her nails. "This doesn't fit the picture. I'd like to know why you bite your nails. If you'd like to know too—I've got a free hour tomorrow afternoon. Come to my office. Of course, you won't be staying long enough for a proper analysis, and you're a little too old for it, too. Most of my patients are too old, by the way."

"You're not?" Maximiliane asked. "The analyst's age isn't important?"

Green admitted that he had never thought about it. Maximiliane's frankness cheered him. He began to talk about his patients. "Most of them are driven to see me because of guilt feelings," he said. "It really worries them deeply that they're so well off. The very fact that they have something diminishes its value, so they have to throw it away and replace it with something else. They also have an urge to renew themselves so that they won't be thrown away too. They are waiting to be punished for something for which they have no name. They need someone to absolve them, and that's me. My fee is the indulgence they pay. I represent their god, whom they have lost."

"And what about your own guilt and punishment? And your god?" Maximiliane asked.

"Nobody asks those questions."

"Don't you ask them yourself?"

"I try to avoid them."

Dr. Green had risen. In passing he touched Maximiliane's bare arm. "My wife's daughter, of all people. You've got what she lacks—candor. Did she relinquish all of it to you?"

"Wouldn't it be better to look for what *you* lack?"

"I think I'm holding it in my hands." Dr. Green let go of her arm. He went off to his office.

The following day he aked her to lie on his couch so that he could begin by teaching her a few simple relaxation exercises. He gave her the usual instructions. Maximiliane stretched, extended her limbs, sprawled, and Green was surprised by the offhandedness and ease with which she followed his directions. But when there was no further response, he realized that she had fallen asleep, her bent arm across her eyes to keep out the light.

The underlying cause of her nail-biting was never discovered.

The young Quints—by now called the Quintuplets by the Greens' neighbors and friends—continued to find California "heavenly." No one asked them to turn down the record player—they were captivated by rock 'n' roll—or limit their consumption of water, and Maximiliane grilled steaks instead of sausages. They lived in affluence.

" 'Once I lived as the gods,' " Joachim quoted, and in his notebook he wrote, "The morning is the only thing that doesn't work here. It is hazy, and the damp air presses on the city. Thick clouds of fog shove their way between the ocean and the desert until eventually the strong sun breaks through, brightening and heating noon and afternoon, and at last sinking brilliantly in the Pacific, taking the heat with it."

Maximiliane was a morning person. Her body rhythms did not fit the rhythm of the California day. She rose early, rested and cheerful, and had her best hours in the morning. But as the day passed, she lost her freshness, exhausted herself, aged. By evening, at parties or the like, she was "unproductive," as she put it. She spent almost the entire day in the garden watering hibiscus, gardenias, avocados, and unknown plants. She turned the hose on her own bare legs, then retired for some hours to the neighbors' garden to bask in the sun "barefoot all over," as she referred to nudity. In the afternoons she sat under the lemon tree, which bore blossoms and fruit at the same time, holding a book she never read. She had come in fear that Americans would point a finger at Germans, would be suspicious of Germans, would use the word *German* as a slur. She had still not quite lost her reserve.

If Joachim had not pointed out to Vera Green that August 8 was his mother's birthday, she would most probably have forgotten it. The date was not etched in her memory.

On the eve, the children had already prepared a table of gifts. In the morning Joachim added a notebook written by hand: his first poems, under the overall title *Death Is So Permanent.* After breakfast Maximiliane, holding the notebook, retired to the shelter of the lemon tree. Joachim's handwriting was already fully formed, angular but light and without pressure, leaning to the left. Maximiliane opened to the first page, reached out with one hand, and felt the lack of an apple. She got up again, pulled a few Golden Delicious from the fruit bin in the refrigerator, and returned to consume both apples and poems. The apples were beautiful to look at and to hold; they had no worms and not much scent. With her preference for regular stanza patterns and rhymed lines, she found Joachim's poems as anemic as the flawless apples.

> Tracing the lanes of the highways,
> Hairspray and oil,
> Gasoline and
> French fries . . .

She tried to read between the lines to supply what was missing. "That night I raised the muzzle of my weapon. . . ." She was just reading this line when

Joachim joined her. She pointed to it and questioned him with her eyes. He did not speak. She understood and blushed. And the eighteen-year-old son, smitten by his mother's look of surprise, blushed as well. But then she broke into long and infectious laughter.

"Mose," she said only, leaning her face against his body, and he responded as she expected—he folded his arms around her.

"Please don't tell me that one can't live on poetry, Mama."

"I would never say that, Mose. One can't live without poetry. I always had to live on poetry. No—not always; but often. I gave you poetry with your mother's milk. It's my own fault."

Maximiliane had not yet finished with the preparations for the evening's birthday party when the first guests arrived. She tried to sneak away to the house where they were staying to put on shoes and change her dress, but Dr. Green insisted that she stay as she was, "a child of nature." In English, these words were not really what he meant. To those of his guests who spoke German, he introduced her with the German term *Naturkind*, but for the others he had to cast about for a phrase closer to his image. He pointed to Maximiliane's hair, her tanned arms, her casual clothes, her bare feet.

"Pollyanna," suggested an older American woman, a Miss Schouler, but this too was not what her host had meant.

"Simplicity?" asked a German-speaking guest, a Dr. Severin, who had come from Los Angeles. "Some word with the idea of *simple* in it?"

Dr. Green agreed, turned to Maximiliane, and modified his expression. "Simplicia Simplicissima! How do you like it? Doesn't it suit your adventurous life? Born during the First World War, routed with five small children during the Second, robbed of a father, robbed of a husband." It is doubtful that many of those present understood his allusion to the German picaresque novel of the Thirty Years War, with its devastations and survivals, but at least Dr. Green was pleased with his phrase.

All this time he had been officiating over the production of one of his famous drinks, this time a margarita. Carefully, with a light touch, he moistened the rims of the glasses, dipped them in salt, filled them with crushed ice, measured out the tequila he bought in Mexico, filled the glasses with lime juice and triple sec. He was famous for his "sundowners," drinks to be sipped just as the setting sun touched the Pacific Ocean—an event greeted with a universal "Ah!"

Everyone was eager to toast the birthday girl, Simplicia Simplicissima, but Maximiliane had disappeared, removing herself from the heart of the party to the background of the garden. Instead, the toasts were dedicated to her mother, who was slicing a pâté she had made herself, sliding the portions on plates, and passing them around. At the same time she was cheerfully recounting how, on that famous August 8, 1918, her father-in-law had brought a slice of Poenichen pâté of wild game to her bed—during her confinement!

"The village midwife couldn't even tell the sex of the child! It wasn't until the local doctor arrived—much too late—that it was determined that we had not produced the male heir but merely a girl!"

She mixed German and English, grew animated, and once more resembled that Vera von Jadow who had held her *jour fixe* in the west side of Berlin—witty, effervescent, elegant, and in complete contrast to her daughter, who was unused to party talk and therefore "unproductive."

"The christening dinner was held in the large hall of the manor, with footmen in attendance," Mrs. Green continued. "Portraits of ancestors lining the walls. Oil lamps! They had neither running water nor electric light!

174

When the soup tureen was empty, I placed the baby in it—the centerpiece!"

The guests laughed. On this particular birthday, Mrs. Green was the centerpiece.

"The liquor they served was homemade rose-hip brandy. Everything was homemade. Even the ice was cut in their own lake and kept in the ice cellar. In the winter they drove horse-drawn sleighs."

"Where exactly is Pomerania?" Mr. Bryce inquired. "Is it in Russia?"

Dr. Green explained that it was in the Polish sector of Germany.

"So that makes her a Pole." The guests were as enchanted as they were surprised. Hearing her name shouted out into the garden, Maximiliane returned.

"So that's what a Pole looks like!"

"They say Polish women are beautiful and passionate."

Dr. Severin turned to Maximiliane. "What was the name of the place?"

"Poenichen."

"How big was it? Perhaps I know it?"

"You had to weed the main street several times a year," Maximiliane said, to the general merriment of the German-speaking guests. She added, "Poenichen is my larder."

No one understood her remark, and Mrs. Green felt obligated to explain. "My daughter must mean that spiritually she draws her nourishment from the place." She looked at Maximiliane. "Just as my father-in-law, known as Old Quindt, used to give forth with Quindt-essences, his granddaughter Maximiliane seems occasionally given to maxims."

The guests laughed to the extent that they understood the play on words, and Mrs. Green went on to tell them that the same Old Quindt had been acquainted

175

with the last kaiser and that the family had in its possession a personal letter from Bismarck.

"And I shook hands with Hitler," Maximiliane added.

All eyes turned to her as to one of the Seven Wonders of the World. Miss Schouler noted admiringly that this same small country had now produced another great, strong leader—Adenauer.

Maximiliane's eyes became the next topic of conversation. They were compared to Golo's. Mrs. Green reproduced, almost verbatim, the first toast ever drunk to Maximiliane's health: "We are not christening a princess here. Before God and the law all children are equal."

Even California was receptive to princesses, and the conversation turned to the wedding of the year: the marriage of the Prince of Monaco and the American movie star Grace Kelly, the "country girl." Everyone remembered her by the film for which she had won an Oscar.

No one had noticed until now that Mirka was missing. She had gone next door and wrapped an Indian blanket around herself. Suddenly she materialized on the lawn, illuminated by a candle she was holding in both hands. She was roundly admired, and her appearance was applauded. "A regular little princess!"

Mirka sketched a deep bow, which made her stumble over the blanket and fall to the ground. Disappointed by the failure of her scene, she burst into tears. Maximiliane saw no reason to comfort her vain little daughter, but all the other women rushed out to pick up the darling child and hug her.

Edda made herself useful by looking after the guests, and Viktoria—confusing some of the guests, irritating others—stood silently by, her face expressing boredom, as if it was not worthwhile bothering to listen to such inconsequential drivel.

It came time to drive to the beach. They took several cars. As usual, Dr. Green took the kids in his car. Maximiliane accepted Dr. Severin's invitation to drive with him. On the way he explained to her that he had been living in the United States since the summer of 1945. The Americans had imported him, along with many other scientists. It had been his job to work on developing Hitler's retaliatory weapons, which, as it turned out, had come too late.

"Too late for what?" Maximiliane was curious to know.

"For the fight against Communism, of course." Dr. Severin was astonished at her naive question and changed the subject. "Let's stop talking about politics. Let's talk about Pomerania instead. I spent two years in Peenemünde—though most of it underground."

At that moment a car passed them. Laughing, the Quintuplets stuck their heads out the windows. One of the car doors was half open, Golo just inside it. Maximiliane closed her eyes. When she opened them again, the door was just being slammed.

The kids had brought torches, which they stuck in the sand and lit. Dr. Severin took on the job of getting the fire started, and Maximiliane offered to cook the steaks. The ease with which, squatting in the sand, she turned the pieces of meat, salted them, and laid them on party plates earned her general admiration. Dr. Severin urged her to open a steakhouse.

"Well, I could try," Maximiliane said, thinking about her sausage shop—and about Martin Valentin.

Later Mrs. Green and Maximiliane took a walk along the beach. The party had spread out. Dr. Severin was helping the Quintuplets build a rocket launching pad pointed west, across the ocean. Maximiliane and Mrs. Green stopped near them for a moment. "The East is to the west," Maximiliane noted, but she was the only one surprised by the observation.

Her mother told her something of Dr. Severin's life. "He's been divorced a year; his two boys live with their mother, who went back to Germany. He has a house in Beverly Hills, the best neighborhood, with a large pool and a view of the Pacific. Your children are growing up; they'll be leaving home soon. He seems to like you."

"He likes my steaks," Maximiliane amended, and for the second time in one night she thought of Martin Valentin.

A storm was coming up from the south, lighting the hills like a backdrop. The two women started to retrace their steps. "Are you afraid of storms?" Mrs. Green asked her daughter, who replied by quoting her grandfather: "A Pomeranian fears God and nothing else in the world—except heavy storms, runaway horses, hoof-and-mouth disease, pine moths, and war on two fronts. But nothing else in the world."

Much as they might all wish it, the rain would not fall. But the approaching storm sent the party scurrying back just in case.

Most days Dr. Green drove the children to the beach in the morning, but now and then he went inland with them, and when they were on deserted roads he sometimes turned the steering wheel over to Golo. He showed them Spanish missions, Indian settlements, historic lighthouses, and modern observatories. He took them to department stores in order to study the way each shopped. Once he invited them to a bullfight in nearby Tijuana. Not only had he grown younger and more relaxed during the time he spent with them, he had also made many observations useful in his work on the dialects of body language.

That was why he urged Maximiliane to extend her stay in California. He mentioned how attached he had become to the kids and noted also that his detailed investigation of behavioral changes in adolescents under American living conditions was not yet complete.

178

"I won't deny that my invitation has its selfish motives. From the outset I intended to use your children for some of my private research. I can't use my patients because they are disturbed, and most of them are too old besides. For my purposes I need normal, healthy young people as guinea pigs."

"Their vacation is almost over. We have to get back to Marburg before school starts," Maximiliane objected.

"I'm a doctor. I can give the children medical certificates stating that the long journey and the change in climate weakened their health, so that the return flight would be bad for them." As he spoke, he gestured to the kids, who were lying under the lemon tree, laughing and bursting with health, fit for any advertisement. "You see, I thought you could fly to New York. That would give us almost another week together. Of course I'll pay for it."

They agreed to extend the vacation by three weeks. The only one who objected was Edda; she was afraid of losing a whole year of school. Maximiliane sent airmail letters to the four principals of the schools her children were attending, attaching a medical certificate to each letter. Golo sold the old Rambler, managing to get $180 for it thanks to the new tires.

To make up for the lost school days, the kids were supposed to sharpen their skills in English. All of them had already improved greatly except for Golo; instead, his German had deteriorated, patched with English words and phrases.

For three more weeks the Quints lived the simple life underneath the palms. The night before they were to leave, the adults sat on the porch one last time. The kids were strolling restlessly through the garden. The luggage was packed and ready in the garage, five cellophane-wrapped orchids from Vera Green's hothouse lying on top.

For the final time the sun prepared its magnificent

descent to the Pacific. Dr. Green filled their glasses with a sundowner and invited the kids to join them, but no sooner had they taken their drinks than they wandered off again.

White-haired and wise, Dr. Green leaned back in his wicker chair. One last time he studied the kids, periodically calling Maximiliane's attention to one or another detail of their behavior. He raised his hand to emphasize his meaning, so that his observations had the weight of an Old Testament prophet's pronouncements.

Joachim was walking along the path. Reaching for a chair, he moved it close to a palm and sat down. Then he got up again, turned the chair in another direction, sat down again, propped his feet against the trunk, leaned back, and stared into the distance. He changed his position two more times before he was satisfied.

"He's a sitter," said Dr. Green. "He walks just so he can sit down. He'll settle down early. Only a few spoken languages have apt expressions for this. Body language, on the other hand, is international—though it does have its dialects. Joachim makes himself small so as not to give offense. He tries to keep to the edge of events. You'll never see him at the center. He needs little room, his radius of action is circumscribed, and he gives off few signals. Look at Vera—she too keeps herself under control, and she's been that way for years. She grows smaller and smaller so as to give me no points of contact. Even her body no longer sends me messages. In future she—"

"Is all this necessary, Green?" Vera interrupted.

"No, it's not necessary. You were never generous, Vera. Your daughter is. She lives her life unguarded in every direction. She leaves herself wide open, always. All the same, I think she's invulnerable. If I still lived in my own language, German, I would take my researches into other fields instead of concentrating on body language. But it has to be enough for an emigrant."

At that moment his eyes lighted on Golo, who stood some yards away casually leaning against a tree, his glass in one hand, the other shoved into his back pocket.

"Look at your son Golo, look how he stands," he said to Maximiliane, again raising his hand as if in prophecy. "He gives off the same strong sexual emanations as his mother."

"He's only sixteen years old," she objected, blushing.

"He's *already* sixteen years old!" Dr. Green retorted. "He fits in this country. He needs space. For him all objects become objections at which he takes offense. He does not avoid them but forever bumps into them."

"He broke his collarbone even as he was being born," Maximiliane told him.

"Really? That confirms my observations. He's careless with himself. Two fingers more or less don't matter to him. He takes risks."

"He's just careless—and you let him drive the car."

"You can't pack him away in cotton wool."

"But between cotton wool and a six-lane highway there's got to be someplace where he wouldn't be in so much danger. His personality isn't up to the engine! He overestimates both!"

"I agree with you to the extent that I consider him in graver danger than the others. But fortunately, besides carelessness, he also has great skill and a kind of playful attentiveness. And he's a natural technician. He's almost a master at steering the car. A God-given talent. He's good at everything he puts his hand to, and anything he's not good at he won't be bothered to learn; he loses interest right away. I'd love to watch him develop. Of course I'd also like to influence him."

"Would you be able to do that?" Maximiliane asked.

"A real woman's question. A man wants to step in and prevent trouble, a woman is content with helping and comforting after the harm is done."

Mrs. Green joined the conversation. "Aren't you oversimplifying, Green?"

"It's necessary to oversimplify sex-linked traits before they can be recognized. I'll give you an example to show that such traits really do exist. A test."

He called the kids one after the other. When they came to the porch immediately, he said to Maximiliane, "Astonishing! They come as soon as they're called."

"They don't always. You're a magician."

Dr. Green asked all of them—excluding his wife but including Maximiliane—to take off their sweaters.

"But I haven't got anything on underneath," Viktoria objected.

"You don't really have to take it off, Tora. Just pretend."

All did as they were asked, reaching for their sweaters to pull them over their heads.

"Stop!" Dr. Green ordered. "Hold your positions and look at each other."

Golo and Joachim had grasped their sweaters at the nape of the neck; the girls and their mother, arms crossed, had grabbed theirs by the hems.

"Persons of the male gender," Dr. Green explained, "grasp their sweaters in back at the neckline and pull them over their heads. Females reach for the hem."

Astonishment and laughter.

After the kids had drifted away again, Dr. Green turned back to Maximiliane. "Do you want to leave Golo with us? For a couple of years? For longer?" And he added, turning to his wife, "Presuming you have no objection?"

"You have your reasons, I'm sure, Green."

"And you have your orchids."

"Do you often talk like that to each other?" Maximiliane asked.

"Once in a while." Vera was smiling.

"Think it over, Maximiliane," Dr. Green continued. "I could adopt Golo, and you'd have one less to worry about."

"I wouldn't stop him. He's been saying for years, 'I'm going to live in America.' "

"He can't stay now, because the immigration people wouldn't permit it. You only have a visitor's visa. But he could come back. I'd take care of the formalities."

"Ask him. He's old enough."

Dr. Green shouted into the garden. "Golo! Would you want to stay here with us?"

A shout of joy was the reply. Golo ran up in great leaps. Maximiliane had lost the first of her children. She felt as she had felt at the conception.

A little while later Dr. Green pointed to Edda. "Watch her strut. Body language changes from one generation to the next. Ten years ago it would have been unthinkable for a girl her age to show off her breasts like that. She lacks one dimension, though—imagination. Not a single wasted motion, but not one too few either. She'll make something of herself. She's never going to get the short end of the stick, that's certain. Presumably she'll be overweight one day."

"Because she always eats the fat you cut off the meat?" Maximiliane asked. "Don't forget—she's a postwar child. She was hungry for years and years."

"So were the others. And yet she's the only one with that habit. Edda takes in everything and incorporates it."

Dr. Green spoke with relish, like someone who has been given back his mother tongue. His mother had spoken German to him, his father Polish. To each other his parents had spoken Yiddish.

Heavy wingbeats approached the dark treetops. Dr.

Green gestured into the branches of the cedar, where an old cormorant had settled and remained squatting.

The glow of the storm lantern spilled into the garden, creating a kind of illuminated stage on the lawn. There Viktoria appeared. Her head lowered, apparently looking for something, she crossed the grass several times.

"Like a dog scenting out spoor," commented Dr. Green. "She will always be a searcher. You have to give her a lot of time. She tries out everything, won't accept anything as a given. She denies her femininity, and that is why her back is hunched; she hates her sexuality. No one is supposed to notice that her breasts are developing. In everything she is the exact opposite of her sister Edda. She has rather too much imagination and therefore seems fearful. She is a tentative person. You know what I mean by that term?"

Maximiliane knew. She added, half joking, half serious, "You've cast a kind of horoscope for all my children. Mirka is the only one you've left out."

"Right now a very pretty little object," Dr. Green said. "The question is whether she'll ever be anything more. She doesn't strike me as having a great capacity for growth."

"But she's beautiful," Mrs. Green pointed out. "Can't you two see that she's going to be a beauty?"

"She practices ceaselessly," Maximiliane said.

"If you watch her," Dr. Green answered, "she's always striking a pose. Children used to play a game called Statues. One child took another child by the hand, whirled him around, and suddenly let go; the other had to hold the position in which he fell. Mirka reminds me of that game. She needs an audience. She doesn't act, she reacts. I don't see any genuine artistic talent. Call to her. She'll change her behavior at once."

Maximiliane rose and walked down the steps to the garden, hesitating for a fraction of a second. She moved

184

from one child to another, touching each as if to reassure herself, reestablish a contact that felt interrupted. Then she walked to the farthest corner of the garden, behind the hothouse, where she wrapped her arms around the trunk of the cedar and pressed her face against the bark.

Dr. Green's prophecies were self-fulfilling.

15

On her return from the United States, Maximiliane found a "final notice" from the Office for the Equalization of Burdens requesting her to reply no later than October 1 to the questionnaires required for primary indemnification.

"Let not hope and faith forsake us," they had sung at both her christening and her wedding, and at the time it was said that such was the "Quindt manner." But surely it was not the Quindt manner to make claims against the state. Such expressions as "reparations" and "equalization of burdens" wafted unheard past Maximiliane's ears. She did not believe that reparation was possible, and she even doubted the validity of the crucial Christian demand that one must bear the other's burden. In any case, she believed in a higher justice, though such justice might take its time in providing equalization. "He will wipe away all tears."

After her second, "annulled" husband had filled out several questionnaires for her, she had placed the rest heedlessly in a drawer. She was just as incapable of meeting deadlines as she was of constantly repeating the same information on the various forms.

Twice she had been granted indemnification for lost household goods. A modest sum when measured against the contents of the manor in Poenichen, but considerable when compared to the temporary home—

especially as the amount of the indemnification had been adjusted according to the number of household members. Since then she had received a monthly widow's pension of forty marks, with another ten marks for each child. But now it was a matter of the actual, demonstrable expulsion and material damages, of the great equalization of burdens for which the appropriate laws had gone into effect several years earlier. Since Maximiliane earned the bare necessities—or, as she put it, "whatever we need"—in the sausage shop, she had not made any efforts to obtain further government aid.

Edda, the businesswoman among the Quints, happened to see the notice from the Office for the Equalization of Burdens and urged her mother to do something about it at long last. She was all the more insistent as she had read in the paper that a high percentage of the established losses were being granted indemnification.

"If the damage is assessed at a million marks, the reparations are set at sixty-five thousand marks," she announced.

"I want to go back, Edda, I don't want to be indemnified," Maximiliane objected, but she did begin to study the questionnaire.

She did not even know how to answer the question relating to loss of savings. She assumed that stocks and bonds were as unknown on Poenichen as were bank accounts; every winter her grandfather took the money realized during the summer and invested it in seeds and chemical manure. Nor could she answer the question about the yearly income on Poenichen. Perplexed, she took the blank form to the Office for the Equalization of Burdens and consulted the underling in charge of the letter Q. She had to wait in the hall for two hours along with other expellees and war victims before she finally sat across from a Herr Schultze. Looking at him trustingly, she explained her difficulties; then she allowed him to enlighten her about the purpose of the equalization of burdens.

"It is the recognition of claims on behalf of that segment of the population particularly heavily affected by the war and its consequences, by means of an equalization of burdens, taking into consideration the bases of social justice, economic possibilities, and the help required to reabsorb the victims."

Herr Schultze looked up from his pamphlet, and Maximiliane, having her first opportunity to hear about the beautiful and unattainable ideal of "social justice," continued to look at him trustingly.

Herr Schultze took his job very seriously. Citing various paragraphs of the Law for the Equalization of Burdens by number, he talked about "indemnification for damages" as well as "indemnification for loss of income," and he even mentioned an amendment to the law under discussion.

Maximiliane's trusting look became no less trusting but increasingly dreamy.

"Are you listening to me?" Herr Schultze asked.

"No," Maximiliane replied truthfully, her eyes damp and glowing.

"Tears won't get you anywhere." In this Herr Schultze was mistaken, as he immediately demonstrated by mentioning that he too was a refugee—though he came from Bohemia. "Leitmeritz." To cheer her up he added, "There must be someone who knows more about your estate. Someone who worked there, for example."

Maximiliane gave it some thought. "Martha Riepe," she exclaimed, relieved. "Our estate secretary. She lives in Holstein now."

"Well, now," said Herr Schultze. Then he asked, "What line of work was your late husband in?"

"At the end he was a lieutenant first class."

"Active or reserve?"

Maximiliane thought again and said, "For a reservist he was too active."

Herr Schultze smiled indulgently. "And before he was called up?"

"Department head in the Reich Ministry of Genealogy."

"Then he must have been either a career officer or a civil servant. In either case you would be entitled to a pension."

Maximiliane gave him a look of disbelief. "A regular pension, not just the special one for widows?"

"I'm just assuming. The best thing would be for you to go to Kassel, the district president's office, pension-fund section. You must stand up for your rightful claims, Frau Quint! Refugees like us must become integrated into the economic process."

Herr Schultze gave her back her questionnaire and extended the deadline.

That same day Maximiliane wrote to Martha Riepe to tell her that her help was needed in filling out the forms for the equalization of burdens. She invited Martha to come to Marburg for a few days.

The questionnaire was still in plain sight on the table when Lenchen Priebe stopped by for a quick visit. She had managed the sausage shop all by herself for almost three months.

She sat down at the table and, inspired by the questionnaire, began to talk about equalization. "Too bad Parson Merzin isn't alive anymore," she said. "He gave me a certificate, and he would have done the same for you. A parson visits all the homes, so he knows everything, and everybody believes a preacher. Of course, he hadn't set foot in our cottage for ten years. He made two cows out of the three goats and swore that I'd had my own room in my parents' home, when all the time I slept in the kitchen. I never had a room of my own until I got to Marburg. Still, you'll have enough left over even if you stick to the truth."

Maximiliane considered her own claims, compared them to Lenchen Priebe's, remembered "social justice," and came to a decision. Placing her hand on Lenchen's arm, she asked quickly and sincerely, "Do you want to go into partnership?"

Thus one of the first instances of codetermination and coparticipation came about that night in a temporary home in Marburg, and it withstood the test of time. Lenchen Priebe "ran the whole show," as she put it. She applied for a business-improvement loan. Thanks to the efficiency of Herr Schultze—who was also in charge of names beginning with *P*—it was granted within a very few weeks. She introduced Belgian waffles and Serbian shashlik; both sold as readily as Thuringian sausages. Patriotic loyalty and international longings were assuaged in equal parts. Maximiliane remembered the American predilection for ketchup, and she was not mistaken in supposing that the taste would, like everything else that came from the United States, catch on in West Germany. So, for an additional ten pfennigs, you could pour tomato ketchup on your french fries. A better ventilation system was installed, and the dining area was furnished with easy-to-clean plastic-topped tables and matching stools.

Lenchen Priebe had found her life's work. Her next goal was to add a barbecue so that they could spit chickens in two rows. The famous promise Henry IV of France made to his people—"A chicken in every pot every Sunday"—was transformed into the advertising slogan of a short-order nabob—"A chicken on the spit for every German." Thousands of chickens were raised in processing plants for an early barbecue death. Centuries seemed to have passed since Maximiliane used her own breath to revive rain-drenched chicks on Poenichen. Actually, she did not share Lenchen Priebe's

190

dream of barbecued chickens. When she offered the partnership, her decision had more probably grown out of her need to shed ballast.

Winter came before Martha Riepe arrived. The two women had not seen each other since their common departure from Poenichen, and clearly neither had felt any great need for a reunion. Maximiliane's children had no memory of the former estate secretary.

When, soon after the currency reform, her customers stopped bringing her orders for knitting and started to buy ready-made goods, Martha had gone to work as a secretary with the Holstein farmers' association. But she had never stopped knitting. Dressed in hand-knits from head to toe, she looked more like her roly-poly father, Otto Riepe, than like her statuesque mother, Anna Riepe. She looked, as Edda noted, like a ball of yarn. She had inherited none of the warm-hearted straightforwardness of her parents, whose affections had been focused on Maximiliane, child without father or mother, grandchild of the gentry.

Privileges became tangible in the reversals of Martha's fortunes. "I live a whole lot better than this," she noted on entering the temporary home, not without satisfaction. And then she said, "Let's bury the whole thing, Frau Quint," summing up in the words *the whole thing* all the problems that had ever existed between them.

But Maximiliane could not agree. "No, Martha, we won't do that. When you turn things under in the fall, they sprout again in the spring. Those were times when everything fell into disorder, and now we can put it back in order. Our order is called Poenichen. You've known me all my life, so call me by my first name. It's not right for me to say Martha and for you to say Frau Quint. Those distinctions have to stop. Now, tell me everything. What news do you have from Poenichen?"

With all the bookkeeper's joy in narration, Martha

Riepe reported, balancing her accounts at the same time. Debit and credit, dead and alive, East and West. Lives were reduced to bare facts.

Maximiliane had already heard that old Riepe was dead, but she did not know that Martha's brother Willem had become a union organizer in East Berlin; his family lived in the West. Finke the wheelwright had finally been expelled, and only the old Jäckels were still living in Poenichen. "They say a few of the workers' huts have been rebuilt, as well as the farmyard. A communal farm! And those Polacks everywhere!"

"They're Poles who have been resettled from the Ukraine," Maximiliane interrupted, but Martha Riepe ignored the objection and continued.

"The Poles are planning to turn the manor into a fresh-air home for children from Posen—that is, if it can be restored at all. They say it's completely burned out."

During the days that followed, the women bent their heads over the long questionnaires. Several times they came close to quarreling.

"Sixty-three horses," Martha Riepe insisted. "Not a head less."

But Maximiliane dissented. "During the war most of the horses were taken away. There were only about thirty."

This correction touched a sore point with Martha Riepe, who took pride in coming from a manorial estate. "Even the von Kalckes on Perchen had thirty horses or more," she countered. "And Perchen was a drop in the bucket compared to Poenichen."

Maximiliane had her way about the thirty horses— an unnecessary victory, since livestock records for Dramburg County had been preserved. When the Homeland Information Office in Lübeck checked the veracity of the answers, the fact that the number of horses had been underestimated lent credence to the rest. It was equally helpful that Martha Riepe, who appended her signature to the questionnaires in her capacity as estate secretary for years on end, had never been a member of the National Socialist Party or any of its organizations. This, of course, was not indicative of her sentiments; to the end of her life she remained convinced that the Germans had never had it so good as under the Third Reich.

Now she was doing the books for Poenichen one last time.

The yearly accounts she used to have to make out at the end of the agricultural year—after June 30, that is—were always the greatest and most satisfying events in her professional life. She had drawn a line under the year; no matter what the debit and credit columns showed, she cared only about balancing the books—and she always managed. She balanced them this time as well. When it came to acreage, yields, and bank involvement, Martha Riepe could rely on her memory.

During the many hours of discussion, Edda sat by and asked permission to type the answers on the duplicate questionnaires. With the money she earned at the sausage shop she had bought herself a secondhand typewriter that disturbed the family with its clatter whenever she practiced.

Before Martha Riepe signed her name to the original, she glanced at the personal information Maximiliane had already filled in. When she read the names and birth dates of the five children, she felt that she could not truthfully sign such a document. "Edda has nothing whatever to do with Poenichen," she declared.

So the moment of truth had arrived, the revelation Maximiliane had gone to such great pains to postpone and avoid. Edda seemed to know at once what was going on. She sat by in silence. Martha Riepe was therefore compelled to go on. "What is true has to stay true."

"Why does it, Martha?" Maximiliane asked. "The value of truth is always overrated."

"Edda has no claim of any kind on the legacy of Poenichen," Martha Riepe reiterated after a further pause. She spoke with deliberation, only to add immediately, "But that's why I've been saving up for ten years—for her." This statement interested neither mother nor daughter.

"Who was my father?" Edda's abrupt question reduced Maximiliane to laughter, arousing her daughter's displeasure.

"Now you see, Martha." It took Maximiliane only a few sentences to sum up the history of Hilde Preissing, her affair with Viktor Quint, and her illegitimate child.

Edda remained motionless, thought hard, and quickly put two and two together: Grandpa Preissing, whose heir she had become, and the meaning of her nickname, Cuckoo.

Maximiliane ended her narrative by saying, "Now let's forget all about it. You too, Martha. We don't want to end up by turning Edda into a legal problem child." And to Edda she said firmly, "You are a Quint, even if there's no *d*. It's the name that matters."

Martha Riepe had done Edda a great disservice, for Edda genuinely cared about being a Quindt with the *d*. She, especially, had always laid great stress on her noble lineage. She forgot—or repressed, which came to the same thing—the revelation very quickly indeed. But her ambition and her energy increased.

With the return of the Questionnaire to Attain the Equalization of Burdens, Maximiliane's life was once again on the record. One day, along with the other records, it would disappear into archives. Later still it would be put through the shredder, and then she would be a private person again, no longer a war widow or a refugee with a Class A identification granting permanent domicile in the territory of the Federal Republic of Germany as of October 1945. She would be a person on

194

the move, someone with a legitimate passport, someone who frequently changed and easily established homes and domiciles. Only her place of birth would remain the same: Poenichen, Dramburg County.

No one required her to give these place names their Polish form—one of the few concessions to her vulnerable sense of connectedness with Pomerania.

16

The trip to America did not remain without its consequences. For months afterward the young Quints continued to say "Hi" in greeting and "See you" instead of "Auf Wiedersehen." They had increased their knowledge of the world and their facility with languages. In February Joachim passed his final high-school exams with a decent average. With some state aid he planned to begin studying philology at the university in the summer term; in the meantime he had a temporary job in a bookstore. Edda left school early with a certificate; she enrolled in business school and went on working in the sausage shop, which was becoming increasingly remunerative.

Golo never did manage to graduate. In view of his scheduled move to the United States, the honor—as he carelessly and euphemistically referred to his lack of promotion—was doubly regrettable; Maximiliane thought that it was essential to finish secondary school. No one seemed to notice how willingly Golo agreed to postpone emigration to the New World.

During the return flight over the Atlantic, he had several times succeeded in visiting the pilot's cabin; his charm worked not only on the stewardesses but on the pilot as well. He was intoxicated by the speed of flight. There was no way he could learn to fly—but motorcycles and cars were within his reach. Twice he had already "borrowed" motor scooters. The third time he was caught but was not charged with theft because, as on the two previous occasions, he returned the scooter to the place he had taken it from. There was no evidence of "permanent appropriation." The police were satisfied to issue a warning, but they did inform his mother. When she called him on the carpet, Golo promised never to "borrow" another motor scooter, explaining his ready acquiescence thusly: "You can't get any speed out of those tired old things anyway."

In March the Quint family—where Martin Valentin had once found a place with relative ease, though only by the day or night—broke up. First there was only a gap: Golo began to come to meals irregularly, or he stayed out very late. As a rule he explained that he had been taking English lessons. Until one day he brought home a girl.

"Here she is," he said, demanding a place at the table for her. Viktoria and Edda reluctantly moved closer together. "Her name's Maleen."

And that was how his plan of moving to the United States came to be abandoned. Golo left it to his mother to write Dr. Green with explanations and a request for postponement.

It was Maximiliane's belief that, to use Old Quindt's phrase, Golo would outgrow it; she also remembered how lightly she herself had fallen in love. At the same time, however, she remembered Dr. Green's warnings. Trusting in the wisdom of books, she went to a bookstore but was told that no new multi-volume encyclopedias were on the market yet; none had gotten as far as the letter S, for sexuality. Since she was not prepared to make do with reference works consisting of only two or three volumes, she sought out an antiquarian book dealer and asked him to search for a "big encyclopedia." If the children had to grow up without a father, they should at least have an encyclopedia, she explained to the dealer, who was more than a little perplexed by her train of thought.

Keeping back only the christening bowl, she traded the entire Courland china service. It was true that the encyclopedia did not include the latest scientific findings, having appeared in the 1920s and early 1930s, but the antiquarian assured her that "the eternal human questions are answered in depth." Compared to the china service, the twenty-volume encyclopedia had the advantage of being unbreakable. Furthermore, it was easier to pack.

Maximiliane put the volumes on the shelves within easy reach, and the children actually did use them to glean the information their mother still owed them—all except Golo, who had never given up his early aversion to books. He was a man of action rather than thought; he had to try everything for himself; he took apart bazookas and old radios. It could therefore be assumed that he was not content with theory in the realm of sex, either.

Maleen Graf was two years older than Golo, had just graduated with honors from high school, and was slated to spend a year in England as an *au pair* girl beginning in May. Under the pretext of giving English lessons to Golo Quint, secondary-school student, she had brought him to her parents' home. Her father, Dr. Graf, assistant medical director of the University Orthopedic Hospital, was building a new house for the family and was occupied with blueprints, workmen, and interiors. Her mother was active in the Nonpartisan Women's Organization and the Red Cross, where she held an honorary office. Thus both of them had little time to pay attention to their only daughter.

Nevertheless, Maleen's parents became aware that what was going on was not the usual sort of tutoring. They forbade their daughter ever to see Golo Quint, secondary-school student, again. It was at this juncture that he brought Maleen to his home. She remained a foreign body at the Quints' table.

It did not take long for Doctor and Frau Graf to find out that Maleen was frequenting the abode of this "rowdy," as they called Golo. Unlike them, Maximiliane had no faith in the efficacy of prohibitions, considering it preferable that the Grafs get to know the young man their daughter was seeing. She invited them to her house. Except for the drawback that he was too young, she saw nothing to militate against her son's prospects. She still lived in the assurance of being "a Quindt."

She baked a Prince Frederick Memorial Cake such as Anna Riepe had brought to the table only on very special occasions. Though she worked without a recipe, relying only on memory, her cake could hold its own against the original. She brought out the large damask napkins with the Quindt crest and filled the christening bowl with primroses she and Mirka had picked the previous day on the walk between the cemetery and the mill. In all, she showed off whatever remained of the old Poenichen splendor.

But these touches only made the deficiencies of the Quints' temporary shelter more glaring. Furthermore, the careless table manners of the young Quints offended Frau Graf's expectations of adolescent behavior. When Edda arrived late and overheated, the smell of the sausage shop still in her clothes, when she sat down at the table without apology and reached for her portion, the social chasm between the Grafs and the Quints widened even further.

After the guests had risen to leave and were looking for their coats among the jackets and hats of the young Quints, Frau Graf drew Maximiliane aside to say in a penetrating whisper, "You will know how to prevent the worst, I'm certain, Frau Quint."

Maximiliane seemed to think the matter over. Frau

Graf continued. "Can you give me your promise? I don't want to have to be more explicit."

"No," Maximiliane replied. "I can make no promises for my son. It's always been my belief that we have to keep an eye on our daughters, not on our sons. They follow their nature."

Her answer was ill designed to reassure Doctor and Frau Graf. On the contrary, it alienated them even more.

Spring was cold and damp and arrived late that year. The magnolias in Universitätsstrasse, whose blooming meant the beginning of spring to everyone in Marburg, were soaked with rain, and in the end they froze. The young lovers had no other refuge than the car. There was no place in the house where they would not have been disturbed. But since it was easy to look into the car from all sides, they had to drive it to a secluded spot.

Maximiliane had only rarely forbidden her children anything; since they had had to grow up crowded into a small space, she did not want to crowd their development further with prohibitions. For this reason she had never before locked "the wagon." The car keys hung within easy reach from a hook in the hall closet. But recalling Dr. Green's words, she did try to prevent what, granted, she had never until now considered "the worst." She began to lock the car and hide the keys. As a result, Golo forced open the car door—his appropriate response to the situation—without trying to conceal his action.

Maximiliane took him to task. "You don't have a license! In six months you can take your driving test. Wait until then. I won't turn the car registration over to you until you have your license."

"You don't need the registration to drive," Golo objected.

"Then I'll have to sell the wagon," Maximiliane

said, seeing no other way out—a threat that would have hit her the hardest. It was only in the car that she was still occasionally able to feel free and unconstrained.

"Then I'll have to break into somebody else's car," Golo answered, took the wheel, and drove off.

This conversation between mother and son was conducted in a factual, almost friendly tone. The circumstances were regrettable but unavoidable—both realized as much.

Judging that it was much better for Golo to use her car than to appropriate someone else's, Maximiliane put the keys back in their old place. The happiness palpably streaming from Golo and Maleen had its predictable effect on her: such a natural phenomenon had to be honored.

When they were together, the two of them never let go of each other. If for some reason their hands had to part, their eyes clung. At the table they sat arm in arm, Golo eating with his right hand, Maleen with her left. Joachim made a point of not looking their way, Edda grinned, Viktoria made fun of them, and Mirka paid no attention whatever; it would be impossible not to criticize Maximiliane for furthering this puppy love. Golo and Maleen were very similar with their brown curls—cheerful, unconcerned, and totally unruly.

To understand the inevitability of events, we must remember Golo's life from the moment of conception— though such ruminations lead into mythic realms barely compassed by reason. First there was that fateful day after Christmas, when Maximiliane and her husband were lost in the car in a Pomeranian snowstorm and immediately thereafter conceived this child in anger— a husband's anger at a woman who had shown herself superior to him. Then the precipitate birth on the second day of the Second World War, when the infant managed to break his collarbone. An additional factor was his father's wish to baptize him with the sinister, ominous name of Golo. At the christening dinner Old Quindt, already grown taciturn, had mentioned German fearlessness, with some reservations as far as Pomeranians were concerned; but Golo feared not even storms, and he had not been raised by his mother to fear God. Fractured arms and legs were the consequence; every new X ray showed old breaks. Finally, the detonation of the bazooka. There had been no lack of warnings.

By now it was the middle of May. The Japanese cherry trees were blooming on the hillside. The pink clusters of petals hung heavy, unscented and sterile as always, but more than in other years they aroused a subterranean unease in Maximiliane. Since moving to the house on the hillside, she had never done more to landscape the large garden than stick sunflower seeds into the ground along the wire fence at the appropriate time of year. In the summer the two-story house disappeared behind the stands of sunflower stalks, but now, in May, the area was still totally bare. A handful of seeds Maximiliane had saved from the previous summer waited in a pot but were not put in the ground this year.

On the afternoon of May 17—for all the rest of their lives that date was never to leave the Quints' minds—Golo and Maleen walked hand in hand across the road and up the hillside. The following day Maleen was supposed to be leaving for England. Neither of them gave any signs of the melancholy of parting. Laughing, they entered the house; laughing, Golo reached for the car keys. He called to his mother, who was sitting on the porch bench, "See you," and Maximiliane called back, "Take care." The words came perilously close to an invitation to take the car.

Maleen rolled down the side window, waving and still laughing. When the engine did not catch at once, Golo said, "Shit." It would be the last word Maximiliane ever heard from her son's lips. Golo made the engine howl, adroitly turned down the narrow drive, stepped on the gas, and roared off toward the highway, amplifying his youthful strength with the strength of the machine.

Maximiliane did not go to the sausage shop that afternoon. Overwhelmed by weariness, she lay down on her bed and fell asleep. Joachim had to shake her hard, and even then she refused to wake up.

She seemed to know already what she could not possibly know. On the straight, tree-lined road between Gisselberg and Wolfshausen, eight kilometers south of Marburg on Federal Highway 3, Golo must have lost control of the car. It swerved at high speed. There were no indications that the brake had been applied. An apple tree was listed as the cause of death.

Golo was dead when he was freed from the wreckage. No one noticed that there had been a passenger until a single shoe was discovered. Maleen had been flung from the car, and aside from a few bruises she was unharmed. But the shock had so disoriented her that she ran across the fields all the way to Gisselberg.

Later Maximiliane asked herself—as the city editor of the Marburg newspaper asked himself and his readers—whether these adolescents had lacked the necessary supervision and guidance during the crucial years. That she had left the car keys hanging in their usual place although she knew that Golo would make illegal use of them was held against her; she was criticized for playing favorites. She refused to explain her reason: that she had thought it better for Golo to use her car than to break into a stranger's and make off with it. She never had had any use for posthumous explanations of past events.

Maximiliane had never understood the meaning of the concept "motivation," nor could Viktoria teach it to her later. Lacking a logical mind, she had only a minimally developed sense for original causes. She relied more heavily on her instincts.

The coroner suggested that the missing fingers on the victim's hand had played a significant part in the causal chain leading to the accident, insofar as their loss had reduced his skill at high speeds. The passenger, Maleen Graf, could not furnish additional details; she had blanked out the whole occurrence.

To the Reverend Bethge, who paid her a condolence call, Maximiliane expressed the conviction that the invention of the internal-combustion engine would have had to be reversed if her son Golo was to have been prevented from driving. At best, she could only stop him from becoming a thief. She seemed relieved that he had not turned into a killer, that he had lost only his own life and no one else's. The Reverend Bethge, who had known the Quint family for years, ever since he had confirmed the three oldest children, found her controlled and brave.

"Many of the old families of the nobility have their own traditions of mourning. Do you have a special wish for the funeral, Frau von Quindt?" he asked.

"To this day no Quindt has ever died a natural death," Maximiliane replied. "It's always been war or the hunt. My grandfather wanted to be the first Quindt to die in his bed, but he shot himself and his wife when my children and I fled. Nowadays traffic accidents seem to have taken the place of hunting accidents."

Then, without transition, she asked a question that had been puzzling her for some time. "What do you call a mother who has lost her child? Isn't there a word for it? Like *widow* or *orphan*?"

The Reverend Bethge gave the matter serious consideration, but he could not come up with a suitable expression. Instead he searched for words of comfort. "You never really put down roots in Marburg, Frau von Quindt. A body that must be returned to the earth gives you a feeling of home. You will come to realize this when you stand at the graveside. Look on this son as a root in foreign soil."

"I am not a tree, Pastor," Maximiliane replied. This understanding, which came to her for the first time just then, was to stand her in good stead in the future.

"Do you have a favorite hymn that we might have at the funeral service?" the minister continued.

Maximiliane gave him the necessary information about the Quindts and Count Zinzendorf and duly reported that Golo's father was buried under the ruins of Berlin and that they did not own a family plot since her own father had died in 1918 in France, at the age of twenty; nor did she know where his grave was. Golo's other grandfather was buried in Breslau—another inaccessible spot.

Golo was interred in the old section of the principal cemetery of Marburg, near the graves of Anton and Katharina Kippenberg, on whose stone could be read the statement—Joachim called it to her attention—"She loved those who were hers, the birds and the poets." This part of the cemetery was planted with evergreens as well as with linden trees, oaks, and birches—tall old trees to whose care Maximiliane entrusted her son. Now, during the interment, they sheltered the assembled mourners from the rain.

Reverend Bethge took as his text one of Lao-tze's sayings instead of a Biblical verse: "The way is more important than the goal." He wanted his eulogy to express a related idea—the aimless roaming of young people in our time. In this particular case one such young person, having achieved excessive speed, had been thrown from his life's way. Then he addressed himself to the facts he had been told by the mother of this young man dead before his time, a mother who had raised her fatherless and homeless children to the best of her ability. He concluded, "Jesus still lead on, till our rest be won." These words, sharp and to the point, contrasted the boy's short life with the long road of death, the road to the goal. To end the funeral, they sang the corresponding hymn. Most of the mourners knew it.

Doctor and Frau Graf did not attend the service, having already left for England with their daughter, Maleen. Their behavior was considered both understandable and inconceivable. The unanimous opinion held that it was better for a fatal accident to befall one of five children than to take the only child in a family.

Two classes from the secondary school, the one preceding Golo's and his current one, attended in a body. His teacher, Herr Spohr, said a few admonitory words at the graveside and in the name of the school administration laid down a wreath.

Maximiliane, surrounded by her four remaining children, stood to one side as if she did not belong there. Seeking and giving support, Joachim had placed his arm around her. She wore the old camouflage jacket the strange German soldier had given her at the boundary brook near Friedland. Lenchen Priebe had dressed herself from head to toe in black—every stitch obtained for the occasion—and was therefore taken by many to be the dead boy's mother. She went up to Maximiliane to ask in displeasure, "Don't you wear mourning?"

"Where should I wear it to?" Maximiliane responded absent-mindedly, an outsider still. If she had had her way, she would have wrapped herself in rags; she had acquired no proper mourning clothes for herself or her children. Most of the mourners at the funeral gave the Quints a wide berth, as if their misfortune were catching. Hardly anyone came up to them to shake hands. Frau Heynold overcame her reserve, walked over to them, and repeated more or less what Reverend Bethge had already said—that you did not really feel at home in a place until someone you loved was in the cemetery there.

While the Quints were walking home, a car stopped beside them. The driver was an insurance agent, himself a refugee from the East, who had several times advised Maximiliane professionally. He offered to drive them home and used the time to suggest that they take out comprehensive insurance on their next car.

On the way through town Maximiliane's glance fell on an old, faded, but still legible inscription on a wall: Death Is So Permanent. She was distracted, and it took her some time to answer the agent. "Except for hail insurance, I consider any kind of insurance immoral. One must take personal responsibility for any damage one inflicts on oneself and others. Only in that way will we live in awe and be heedful."

In consideration of her present circumstances, the agent forbore responding to her arrogant attitude, simply noting that the purchase of a new car would presumably throw her into considerable financial difficulties.

"We can replace what is replaceable; the irreplaceable—there we are powerless." This statement summed up his concern, the core of all his insurance conversations. He stopped his car in front of the Quints' temporary home. "You should do something about getting out of here, Frau von Quindt. This house is not an appropriate domicile for a family of your rank."

In response, Maximiliane looked around. Her eyes traveled from the rugs that had covered the floors of Poenichen manor to the volumes of the encyclopedia on the bookshelves to the place at the dining table that would henceforth remain empty. For a long time she stared out the window to the empty space where "the wagon" used to stand.

It was her "flight look."

17

Maximiliane's political concerns had been misused and exhausted during the twelve years of Hitler's regime. Now, like many others, she insisted on taking a leave-me-out-of-it attitude. The Bloc of Expellees and Those Deprived of Their Rights, a political party founded in the early 1950s in Marburg, had tried to win her over before the federal and local elections, but she voted for the Liberal Democratic party, which saw private property and private initiative as the mainsprings of all human progress. She voted her grandfather's inclinations, but the love of politics that had inspired him and given him wings, at least until the outbreak of Hitler's dictatorship, was not in her genetic makeup. It surfaced in her daughter Viktoria, who as early as age fifteen concerned herself passionately with such political questions as rearmament; in student discussions she demanded for girls some form of national service equivalent to universal compulsory military service for boys.

Corresponding to her lack of interest in public affairs, Maximiliane had never joined the Organization of Pomeranians Living in West Germany. At Martha Riepe's urging, however, Lenchen Priebe had done so.

Pomerania Day, held every other year at Whitsuntide in a different West German city, this year was to take place in Kassel, which was conveniently situated for everyone. Lenchen Priebe compiled a list of all the former inhabitants of Poenichen whose addresses were known, and with Edda's help she wrote to each one. "Meeting in Kassel for Pomerania Day 1958!"

"We can't do without you," Lenchen Priebe said to Maximiliane. "Poenichen without Quindts, there's no such animal. There never has been no such animal."

By now it was clear from looking at Lenchen Priebe that she was part of the so-called economic miracle; she followed the fashions and the times. She had taken driving lessons, gotten her license, and bought a brand-new Volkswagen hot off the assembly line. In this connection she could have done with a reminder of certain words spoken by Old Quindt. At the time, it is true, it had still been a matter of a handcart, in which little Maximiliane sat while others pulled her—Walter Beske, now a lumberjack in Canada, and Klaus Klukas, dead near Minsk—galloping along the linden avenue in Poenichen. Lenchen Priebe rode at the back of the cart, braking with bare feet. Quindt, who was observing the scene in the company of Maximiliane's governess of the moment, said something to the effect that there would always be those who sat in the cart and those who did the pulling. "What matters is that the cart goes forward." The governess objected that he was looking at the matter too abstractly and that he'd be surprised one day. Quindt, who had long since gotten beyond being easily surprised, merely replied with a shrug that someday there would presumably be others sitting in the cart and others pulling it.

So now Lenchen Priebe, still a little excited, sat behind the steering wheel and gave the Quints a ride to Kassel in her car. "A hundred thousand Pomeranians will be coming," she said.

Not quite a hundred thousand Pomeranians came, but eighty thousand did show up—though some said it was only sixty thousand; the dying off of the older generation was beginning to make itself felt. And there were those who chose to stay away—among them many who had had some success and many who had had none. Most of the onetime estate owners shunned the event, especially those who belonged to the nobility, notwithstanding the example set by a member of the Bismarck family who had elected himself spokesman for the expelled Pomeranians. Three hundred buses could be counted. But already a thousand private cars sat in the parking lots, including Lenchen Priebe's black VW; thirteen years earlier, she had fled Pomerania in horse-drawn and hand-pulled carts.

Women carried placards through the streets displaying photographs, army post-office numbers, and vital dates of husbands and sons who were still missing. Airplanes trailed huge letters that waved in the spring breeze as they arranged themselves into a promise and announced to all, POMERANIA LIVES.

Whitsun weather; a spring spirit prevailed at the religious service, which was conducted by a minister who had been expelled from Pomerania and who felt lucky for this chance to speak to Pomeranian neighbors as he had once done as a minister at the venerable Nicolaikirche in Greifswald. He was standing in a reconstructed church that almost two hundred years earlier had been built in this war-ravaged city by Huguenots persecuted for their faith. . . .

When he combined the phrases *soil of home* and *holy soil* to unite the gathering materially and spiritually, Maximiliane was reminded of the herbal showers and mudpacks Fräulein Gering had administered to the Quindts. *Mens sana in corpore sano*. Her thoughts wandered to the governess's vegetarian diet and on to the vegetarian restaurant where Friederike von Kalck still displayed the keys of Perchen behind glass; she could not get away this time either, as her brother, Jürgen von Kalck, reported when Maximiliane bumped into him in

210

the parking lot. For himself he said that after his release from the American prisoner-of-war camp, where he acquired firsthand experience of the value of tobacco, he had started a career as a businessman by toting a vendor's tray around ruined Frankfurt. By now he owned a chain of cigar stores.

He had recognized Maximiliane by her "saucer eyes" and greeted her jovially with, "Well, well, the little Quindt girl from Poenichen!" Then he had looked at the young Quints, remarking with a laugh, "Four of them! I remember my sister informing me of the latest head count at appropriate intervals while I was at the front. Children are a kind of achievement in themselves." This last remark was clearly a reference to the difference between their standards of living.

"We made do with one son. He is already in charge of a store. Friederike works herself sick in the name of health." He placed his hands where his waist used to be. "As we can see, most people are more likely to spend their money for pleasure. My wife went to Sylt for a week, and I'd planned to join her over the long weekend. So I thought to myself, on the way I'll look in on the doings here. I might see an acquaintance or two. And now I've already seen one."

Patronizingly he put his hand on Maximiliane's shoulder and looked at his watch. "Two hours. Then I have to push on. I must get to Sylt before dark."

"Is that what your wife told you?" Maximiliane asked. When Herr von Kalck looked at her in perplexity, she amplified. "That you have to be home before dark?"

Herr von Kalck laughed heartily. "Your grandfather was given to that kind of remark. Is it true, by the way, that he shot himself?"

"Yes."

Herr von Kalck continued, "Probably the best thing. He wouldn't have been able to start from scratch in the West."

"Perhaps all of us should have stayed, Herr von Kalck. They can expel thousands, but they could not have expelled millions of people."

"You don't mean to say you're still homesick?"

"Yes, I am."

"In that case you're making life hard for your children."

Maximiliane looked for them. They were walking along the rows of parked cars with Lenchen Priebe, looking at the license plates and makes of cars; among them were some small vans pragmatically fitted out with sleeping accommodations for this holiday trip. She pointed out Lenchen. "There's Lenchen Priebe. She brought us here in her car."

"Priebe? Wasn't that the name of the local farmers' leader on Poenichen?"

"He was her grandfather."

"And you're on friendly terms with her?"

"Why not?"

"Just like Old Quindt! No discrimination! The coachman for a friend!" Once more he looked at his watch. "I have an appointment with young Picht from the Juchenow estate. Well, young—he must be in his mid-fifties himself by now. He deals in linens. Twice a year he goes from one estate to the next, Holstein and Münster, calling on those members of the nobility who didn't leave. They order all their linen supplies from him. They say he's doing very well for himself. He's treated very fairly because they remember his rank. And he saves the overhead on shops and storage, which has a lot of advantages. It costs me seven and a half a month just for one of my stores. All the same, traveling's not my kind of thing. Well, maybe we'll run into each other again." He put out his hand. "One side or the other of the Oder-Neisse line."

He laughed, turned back twice, waved, and disappeared in the direction of the town hall.

212

Recalling this encounter, Maximiliane could not bring herself back in touch with the sermon. She stared at the empty nave, the large traditional arrangement of green birch twigs, the crucifix. She could no longer collect her visions or her thoughts. Joachim, sitting next to her, had to give her a gentle shove before she rose along with the others for the closing hymn.

The minister had chosen wisely; the melody was a familiar one, and the words—reminiscent of divine permanence in a shifting world—suited the occasion. He read the first stanza of the hymn and added, "Our Pomerania was not blessed with poets, but Ernst Moritz Arndt contributed a few verses to the new hymnal. This one, which we will sing in unison, was set to music by Heinrich Schütz. His name is closely linked with the city of Kassel, which is hosting our reunion. One supplies the words, the other the music; it is only together that they produce a song—a symbol for the coexistence of East and West."

"We'll just move our pillows a little closer together," Maximiliane's old school friend Isabella had said over the telephone. "Then you can stay with us."

In boarding school Maximiliane had for several years shared a room with Bella, as she was called. She had not seen her since, and they had written each other only rarely. Bella's husband, a Herr von Fredell, had been transferred to Kassel some years before. He held an executive position with the National Association for the Care of German War Graves, and his entire office had been moved. When the Quints arrived, he was not at home but had sent his apologies; he was certain there would be plenty of time for them to get to know each other.

The two "old girls" from the Hermannswerder Boarding School hugged each other upon their reunion.

At the same time, their voices artificially deepened, they said in unison, "But my dear child!"

The first half-hour was passed in exclamations.

"Our housemother!"

"Our solstice fires at the tip of the island!"

"Our secret moonlight boat rides!"

"Our ensigns, who rode into the hall on hobby-horses!"

"I danced and danced with you. . . ."

"Our excursions into town, when your grandfather came to Berlin!"

Both women grew younger, and their faces became girlish again. Between the exclamations, peals of laughter.

When they stopped for a moment, Joachim, standing nearby with the Fredell's two sons, asked, "Did you laugh all the time?"

The women looked at each other in astonishment. Maximiliane undertook to answer. "Yes. I think we laughed all the time."

"The Jute burial mound! We called it a Jew burial mound." Bella stirred up another memory.

Joachim returned to the subject of laughter. "Right in the middle of the Third Reich?" His question expressed interest rather than reproach, but a dark shadow began to spread over the women's hilarity.

"Well, not quite all the time, Mose."

Frau von Fredell stood up. "I'm going to check on our dinner. Excuse me." She turned back to Maximiliane. "Did you ever hear anything about the island? They say the bells from the garrison church are now hanging in the forest chapel at Nikolskoe. 'Be true and honest, all the days of your life.' We always have been, haven't we? The Prussian virtues! We were well trained for bad times. To make a virtue of necessity!" She broke off and went to the door. "I can see it coming, the day when our sons and daughters will have to be nourished on our memories."

She stood leaning against the door frame, tiny and black-haired, descended from a Huguenot family, daughter of a civil servant, wife of a civil servant. She looked at Maximiliane."You were able to stretch out. I was always hemmed in. There's something generous about you—or something careless. It's almost the same thing. I'm so tidy—everything here is so tidy."

Her gaze traveled from Maximiliane to the young Quints out on the balcony. "Edda is the most like you."

"You think so?"

"In her bearing, the way she moves." And Frau von Fredell went off to the kitchen.

Maximiliane joined the others on the balcony.

"You can see Hercules," Viktoria noticed.

Maximiliane's eyes focused on the mountain chain. "Was he already standing there in 1945?" she asked the older of the Fredell boys.

"I think so."

"All I remember is emergency shelters and emergency cots, emergency doctors and emergency offices," said Maximiliane.

Before the rally in the stadium, the Quints decided to spend the afternoon revisiting all the places they could recall.

The railroad station had been rebuilt, the entrance to the air-raid shelter had disappeared, but it was still a terminal, and they could make out the place at the barrier where the black soldier with the submachine gun had fired a shot over the heads of the refugees and shouted, "Get back."

"This must be where Golo broke his leg."

The view still extended far across the town from the railroad station, but new houses and apartment complexes were quickly rising on what had been a field of rubble. The emergency shelter on the square was gone as well.

"This is where Golo traded the flints for the cans of dog food," Joachim said. " 'For army dogs only.' "

Edda could not remember anything but the cocoa. Viktoria had no memories at all but wanted to hear more of what Edda called "those old stories."

Though Maximiliane could not recall the name of the doctor who set and cast Golo's broken ankle, she still knew the lesson she had learned from him: that in order to survive one must trim one's sails to the wind— a lesson she did not pass on to her children.

They strolled through the town; flags everywhere, groups of people. They walked through the blooming Rose Garden along leafy paths to the lake.

"That other time the park was pocked with bomb craters full of scummy water—do you remember? You floated sticks in them."

They rested on a bench. The willow branches hung deep into the water, the clouds were reflected in the lake. Wild ducks and swans. Edda threw them bread crumbs.

"There were five of us then, too. But we were already talking about 'Mirko.' " Maximiliane reached for her youngest daughter's arm and pulled her closer."Now we talk about Golo."

"Usually you always say, 'Now let's forget all about it,' " Edda objected.

Maximiliane did not answer, thoughtfully contemplating this daughter who was not her daughter.

Blushing, Edda avoided Maximiliane's eyes.

More and more people were moving past them on their way to the stadium. Maximiliane rose. "It's about time. Come."

Only rarely had the children resisted the maternal "Come." This time Edda said, "Do we have to? We could wait for you here."

"You don't have to," Maximiliane answered, stressing the *you*.

"We'll all go—all of us. That's why we came to Kassel, after all," Joachim decided.

Edda turned around, angry and self-willed. "But I didn't—" She never finished the sentence.

Mirka had already walked ahead a few steps and was waiting for the others. An older man stopped and looked at her carefully. Leaning on his cane, he pointed to her face with his other hand. "Don't I know those eyes? Where are you from?"

"Marburg." Mirka stepped aside to let him pass.

Maximiliane joined them. One glance was enough. "Herr Kressmann!"

"The little Quindt girl! What was your first name again?"

"Maximiliane."

"Right, Maximiliane. Or must I call you by your last name now?"

"Of course not."

"I recognized you in your daughter. You must have been about her age when you were in my school. In fairness to a very young man—you weren't very well suited to school. I advised your grandfather to send you to boarding school. By the way, you haven't changed one bit."

"That would be too bad if it's true," Maximiliane said. "In any case, I've multiplied," she added, indicating her children.

"All these uprooted people," Herr Kressmann noted.

"We are not trees, Herr Kressmann," Maximiliane countered. "If God had wanted us to stay put, he would have given us roots instead of legs."

Then her eyes came to rest on his artificial leg and his cane. Her smile begged his forgiveness. "In nature

217

everything that is meant to flourish has to be transplanted. It's called *stimulation*. You taught me biology."

"Not old trees! You should have learned that too." Herr Kressmann gave himself a push on his false leg and started to move away. "The people from Arnwald are meeting at the New Mill Inn. If you join us, don't talk to the people about your trees, or you'll stimulate them." He laughed at his own joke, waved his cane, and walked on.

"What kind of opinions have you got all of a sudden?" Joachim asked his mother when they were alone again.

"Only two opinions. One for myself, and one for others." Maximiliane laughed with tears in her eyes. "I never could stand him. But perhaps you really do have legs, instead of roots like me."

"Your roots are in Poenichen, ours are in you," Joachim said as if reciting a line of poetry.

Maximiliane looked at her son, then at each of her daughters. She repeated, "Come." Edda was still in mid-sentence, but Maximiliane took her by the arm and implored her, "Don't say it," adding the old baby nickname, "Cuckoo," which she used to signify "I remember." She pulled out her handkerchief, and with deliberate gentleness she wiped some of the artificial color from Edda's lips; Edda did not object.

The Quints were among the last to arrive at the rally. They found only standing room in the upper tiers of the stadium, where there was no shade. Blinded by sunlight, they saw little and heard less.

Thirty thousand Pomeranians were assembled: flags and banners and clusters of people in peasant costume. Various bands were entertaining the crowd and establishing the mood with folk songs. Above their heads the placards seeking information waved again; the airplane was still circling overhead with its announcement that Pomerania lived.

218

Words of welcome, greetings read out from absent well-wishers, a message also from the federal chancellor that made mention of the reunification presently being "striven for." The crowd expressed appreciation by clapping vigorously. Few noticed that "claims" had shriveled to "strivings." Instead of claims, only efforts.

"A Pomeranian is as loyal in winter as he is in summer." The federal minister for expellees purposely adapted an old saying. He rejected the Oder-Neisse Line as a boundary, and over loudspeaker and radio he pronounced the unity of all expellees in their resolution to return home. "All help for expellees remains patchwork until the cause of our deprivation is removed and they and their children are enabled to return to their ancestral homes. An American saying can hold true for us as well: 'No question is ever settled until it's settled right.' "

Many of the participants took these words more as a comfort than as a promise, and the minister rushed off to Silesia Day to tell that audience the same thing in different words.

Now the principal speaker took the podium and repeated what an old woman had said to him as he was about to begin his address: "All I can say is, Why?" A question answered by the audience with a long volley of applause. The speaker continued by praising the Pomeranian virtues of loyalty and patience, which were proverbial. Summoning up the few great names, he said in extenuation that fame had never been planted thickly in Pomerania. Then again, he added, people in general were not planted thickly there; the only time Pomeranians were tightly crowded was at Pomerania Day. But it had been Ernst Moritz Arndt, a great Pomeranian if not the greatest of them all, who had said of their native land during a dark hour, "Let it be all of Germany."

Then he spoke of the fact that the expellees had had a large share in the economic miracle of the Federal

Republic of Germany, of which the whole world was speaking with admiration and envy. "Like a mighty stream we people from the East have flowed into the West. And here permit me an analogy. The ancient Egyptians dammed the Nile so that its waters would make the deserts fruitful. We expellees found a land laid waste by war. We have fertilized it and made it fruitful with our sweat."

He ended his speech by exhorting his listeners to cling to their resolve to return home peacefully.

Another government official, also in a hurry because he was expected at Silesia Day, addressed the crowd with a terse but admonitory question: "Does the Greater German Fatherland, and with it your lost home, continue to live in you forever and aye?" A question that could not be answered with applause. The crowd remained silent.

No less was expected of the Pomeranians that day than faith in a miracle. But faith in miracles had never been the way of Pomeranians. They listened, were satisfied with the words, clapped their approval, and wanted only one thing—to turn their temporary livings into permanent ways of life. They did not turn into "dynamite" whose explosive powers might have endangered the young, unsecured federal republic, but into fuel, into "fertilizer." A fact future historians were to marvel at. At the end of the war these people, expellees from their homes, had been living in the wrong part of Germany. That was their misfortune, and in time it was to become their fault and flaw in the minds of the West Germans.

At the conclusion of the rally a costumed group sang the Pomeranian anthem; then, accompanied by a band from the federal frontier police, the crowd sang in chorus the third stanza of the German national anthem. "Unity and Justice and Freedom . . ."

Maximiliane, who had formerly sung this song with

220

upraised arm, and then only its first stanza, held her arms crossed behind her back; she could not sing along since she was as unfamiliar with the words as her children were.

Viktoria managed to come away from the rally with a vicious sunburn.

The Poenichen contingent did not have much time left for the local reunion at the Meadow Jug Inn. Most of them were in a hurry to get to the big party in the town hall.

Lenchen Priebe's opinion that they could not manage without the Quindts turned out to be in error. The joy of reunion was mixed with embarrassment. The friendly-patriarchal relationship between the manor house and the villagers had been abolished, and no new relationship had developed to replace it.

An occasional searching look was directed at the oldest Quint, who sat to one side, tall, friendly, and unconcerned. Would he have become their "gentry"? Would he eventually become their gentry still? They looked away quickly and thought of something else. The people of Poenichen would probably have been pleased if the Quints had made their way in the world somehow, though they had no clear idea of what this *somehow* should have been.

Martha Riepe had seen to it that the menu featured sausage and sauerkraut and mashed peas, a dish in high favor in Pomerania during the winters. It tasted better when it was homemade, everyone whispered covertly. The innkeeper's wife, who was from Dramburg, sat down with the customers, and they reminisced about pickled cucumbers, sour game stew, and smoked goose. The way to a patriot's heart was also through his stomach. Pech, the railroad stationmaster, reported that you could buy the local brew in the West again. Nowadays he had a job in Neumünster behind the ticket counter, no longer master of a station but much better paid than he used to be.

The innkeeper's wife treated everyone to a brandy. Bruno Slewenka, the last to drive the Quindts' coach, sixteen years old in those days and now the holder of a gas-station franchise in Wiesbaden, followed with a round of doubles.

The atmosphere lightened. People wanted to know what had become of old man Priebe. Lenchen explained that her grandfather was living in an old-age home, no longer able to move freely—"except backwards." Gradually they fell back into the dialect. "Our baroness," the widow Griesemann said. It seems that when they'd used up their corned beef, they went for a pike in the lake once in a while. Was it possible to talk about such things with the "gentry" sitting right there? Their glances brushed past the young Quints—who, unable to follow the heavy dialect, were bored—and came to rest on Maximiliane, who returned their looks in friendship.

Someone, speaking in a low voice, said that "our Baron" wouldn't allow himself to be seen in the local inn, except at election time. Hermann Reumecke got up and put a coin in the jukebox. He had owned the only inn in Poenichen, and now he and his wife worked in a laundry in Hagen. Their boss had loaned them his van for the trip to Kassel—the same van Hermann Reumecke used to deliver the laundry.

"Bells of home, you bring me greetings" sounded from the jukebox—a song often played in the old days on the all-request radio program, now revived at the band concerts, according to Martha Riepe. Someone else said that the church in Poenichen had been destroyed down to the foundation, and everyone remembered that one of the two bells had been melted down during the war. . . .

News and rumors. Walter Beske was said to have

been an invalid ever since he had had an accident while cutting tall timber. Four years ago! And in a strange country! Erika Beske had become a nurse, had registered with an Icelandic agency in Lübeck, and was now married in the capital of Iceland, Finke the teacher reported. And Hermann Meier, the second son of the distiller, was now working for the Klein-Malchower family as their sole trained distiller; they made a brandy whose label showed the old count and praised Klein-Malchower as a "brandy for the nobility." They'd even had an article in the Pomeranian newsletter. The widow had built up the business in Soest; the count himself hadn't survived his flight by much. Finke, himself in his sixties by now, had the most news.

Births, weddings, deaths. Maximiliane did not recognize all the names. The wall between manor and village must have been higher than she had realized. She knew the village only from horseback and from the coachman's block, at best from her bicycle seat, raised a little.

During those two hours in the Meadow Jug Inn in Kassel, Maximiliane grasped what her mother had understood forty years earlier: differences in rank. Even then Vera's camera had observed Poenichen and the Quindts objectively and critically. Maximiliane saw the photographs in her mind's eye—Old Quindt ensconced in the coach, the inspector standing in the fields, the farm workers (women) kneeling. Now she saw through her mother's eyes and recognized the fact Old Quindt referred to as "the differences."

Richer by a new insight, she left sooner than the others. Besides, she was nurturing the seed of a plan which must still be brought to fruition; it concerned Edda's future life and that of Lenchen Priebe, both of whom Maximiliane had been carefully watching. On her way out she inquired of Herr Pech whether he had heard from his sister again and learned that the former

Poenichen housekeeper was living in Mecklenburg, working as cook in the canteen of a cooperative. He gave Maximiliane the address.

Maximiliane could not feel that she belonged and was safe among people with a common fate. She had lived "on," not "in" Poenichen. Cozy immersion in the mass, shared spiritual intoxication were denied her. She would have gone home disappointed had it not been for the night's loyalty parade outside the town hall. She attended without her family but with her friend Bella.

Hundreds of young Pomeranians marched silently through the town. This time Maximiliane was in the front row as the flags and pennants drew past, and she remembered the years when she had marched through the streets of Potsdam behind the swastika. She became aware of linkages and experienced one of the great lessons in the school of life.

Promptly at ten o'clock the Frontier Police Band played taps. A shiver ran through Maximiliane and spread to Bella, who pressed her arm. She turned her tearstained face to her friend and cried until she laughed.

The women walked home arm in arm. For a long time they sat in the kitchen with Bella's husband. The young Quints had already spread out their sleeping bags in the living room.

"I need to get out of Marburg," Maximiliane announced. "Three of us can't work in the sausage shop, and it's not good for Joachim to live with so many women. But where can I go? I'm not trained for anything."

Herr von Fredell picked up her hand and kissed it. "Achieved so much yet trained for nothing?" he asked amiably. "You have your diploma?"

"A kitchen diploma," both women replied in unison, laughing and thinking of their domestic-science degrees.

Herr von Fredell reached for Maximiliane's hand again and bent over it—outdated displays of etiquette in a kitchen conforming to the social residential building code. "You were orphaned by the First World War, you were widowed by the Second World War, you come from the eastern reaches of Germany, you are of noble descent. You seem predestined for a position in the National Association for the Care of German War Graves."

18

When Herr Schröder, the head of the depart-
introduced the new employee to the general secretary
of the National Association for the Care of German War
Graves, the latter took one look at her personal file and
immediately recognized her as "an emissary from the
German East."

He addressed a few personal and encouraging
words to her concerning both the offices—temporarily
housed in various commercial buildings throughout the
town—and the salary—modest compared to others but
well within the pay scale established by law. He went
on to speak of the idealism that must inspire the workers
at the National Association; he mentioned the organization's aims and tasks; and in conclusion he said cheerfully and benevolently, "I trust you know better than
to believe we keep busy planting heather on heroes'
graves. You must banish all visions of birch crosses
topped with the helmets of unknown soldiers at the
forest's edge, my dear lady." This was the last time
Maximiliane was addressed as "my dear lady." From
now on she was simply one of a hundred and fifty
clerks.

In parting, the general secretary said in almost the
same words what Herr von Fredell had already told her:
Concern with the dead is a highly satisfying and fulfilling activity, especially for a woman, a war orphan,

and a war widow. She would be helping to provide dignified burials in one of the consolidated cemeteries for the victims of two wars, many of whom were still scattered in isolated graves or were not yet identified. These new cemeteries would assure them of a permanent resting place.

Once again Maximiliane was surprised that even her superior knew exactly what was right for her. She herself was not always so certain.

The selection of suitable apartments, which required a deposit of no more than thirty thousand marks—as much as Maximiliane had raised by selling one of her grandmother's pieces of jewelry—was limited. She chose a place in one of the new high-rises. It was the view that decided her. She had the same initial experience as all her subsequent visitors: you entered the apartment, crossed to the window, and exclaimed at the beauty spread out below. Some meant the town, others the wooded mountain chain.

Maximiliane considered the new apartment another temporary domicile, another place not worth furnishing properly. Since she had sold the ancestors' portraits, the walls remained bare. Like the Marburg house, this dwelling became filled against her will with objects brought by relatives and co-workers. She still compared whatever she owned with what she had carried in her handcart during the flight, while other people had long since begun concentrating on what was lacking in their new lives. The few acquisitions she did make were not even useful.

No sooner had they moved in than she brought home a phonograph record, which she showed to her daughters. It was an old pop song, redolent with homesickness, sweet and sentimental. She sang the tune for them and explained how she and their father had danced to the song in a basement bar in Berlin the last time they were together. All the while she was spinning the platter between her hands, seeing on its black, grooved surface the old man who had played the piano, seeing the radio and the waiter listening intently to reports on the air situation, seeing the ruined hotel, the bunker, the flightlike return to Poenichen—

"But we don't have a record player," said Edda.

The only memory Maximiliane carried away from her meeting with the general secretary was the idea of "permanent right to a resting place for the dead." This idea impressed her so deeply that it occurred in every letter she wrote informing her family and friends about her latest doings; her constant inner turmoil made permanent rest seem attractive. Her co-workers, almost all of them "formers"—former journalists, former actors, former officers, former bank clerks—seemed convinced of the virtue of their task, and this she liked; what she liked less was that they talked about it constantly.

When Herr Schröder familiarized Maximiliane with her responsibilities, the central graves registration for France, he expressed regret that in spite of Herr von Fredell's recommendation he could not offer her a more exalted position. Instead, he could merely give her a job—but the job allowed for advancement. It was simply a matter of learning the ropes; she would have to pay particular attention to absorbing the ultimate aims of the National Association. And the work on the graves-registration file was of the utmost importance, requiring precision and an ability to connect disparate facts; it even required devotion. Every single entry, each date, each place name, no matter how minor, concerned a human destiny.

But Maximiliane was not one of those women who build a job into a position. She did not even fully fulfill her current task. On the other hand, it did not fulfill her either. Under her grandfather's guidance she had learned self-control as a little girl, and this skill now saved her from being controlled by others. Promptly at seven-thirty she showed up at her office, never used the office phone for personal calls, never took more than the prescribed half-hour for lunch, gave no cause for criticism, and never did nore than she was told to do.

She had never looked on work as a virtue.

Her office was located in a commercial building where the National Association had rented two floors. A long corridor flanked on both sides by small squares of offices. "Like a cow barn," Maximiliane reported to her children, more in praise than in condemnation. The room in which she worked held four desks pushed together into a block, accessible from three sides. The two adjacent windows looked out on the fire wall of a ruin that had not yet been rebuilt.

Maximiliane laid no claim to space on the windowsill, already overcrowded with potted plants; she did not use the office coffee maker to brew herself a morning cup, and therefore she did not offer to take her turn in making Herr Schröder's coffee. She freely recognized the seniority rights of her co-workers, most of whom were younger than she. If she raised her head, she saw a blank wall studded with vacation postcards from various co-workers: views of Ruhpolding, Grömitz, Alassio, and Majorca.

Sometimes her eyes met those of Frau Hoffmann, who responded with an encouraging smile, causing Maximiliane to smile in return. She tried hard to reduce her handwriting to the height and width of the lines on the forms, and she was just as careful to adapt the motions of her arms and legs to the dimensions of the room. It was harder for her to make do with the amount of air allotted to her. Because Frau Hoffmann, the oldest person in the room, suffered from neuralgia, the windows could not be opened, let alone the door.

The work of those assigned to keeping the central graves-registration files was divided by sectors. Maximiliane was responsible for soldiers who died in Ain Department, within the area of the Dagneux Consolidated Cemetery. She filled in forms that were sent to apprise families that a husband, father, son, or brother was being transferred to Dagneux. She entered surnames, first names, birth dates, and army rank; she indicated the number, row, and section of the new grave. Her written notification was accompanied by an illustrated prospectus with a precise map of the cemetery where, when the transfers were completed, nineteen thousand war dead from twenty-one departments of France would have their permanent resting place, according to an agreement between the French and German governments.

The prospectus was still largely made up of promises that would have to be realized in the years to come. When the work was completed, it said, anyone would be able to see what the vision of the designers of this war sepulchre had been—to provide those buried here with a permanent grave on a handful of native soil, to incorporate the cemetery into its surrounding landscape, to leave the dead soldiers' families with a feeling of satisfaction and comfort, and to send all visitors on their way with an urgent exhortation to peace.

Most of the graves in the Dagneux Cemetery held the bodies of those who had died in the battles that took place along the French Riviera in August 1944, after the Allied invasion. Until now Maximiliane had not been aware of this particular phase of the war. As far as she knew, the only landing had taken place in June 1944 in Normandy, when her husband had been so seriously wounded under such strange circumstances. These two Allied invasions were her undoing, for she remained unable to distinguish between them. She lacked logical thought processes and had never had a sense for the objective, irrefutable aspects of history. When she read the words *Neufville, September 1944* on a file, she did not realize that the reference was not to Neufville in Normandy but to a place of the same name in the south of France. Asked to bring order out of chaos, she created chaos. Some time passed before the disorder wrought by the new clerk came to anyone's attention.

She was then briefly put to work on files dealing with the transfer of bodies, where all she had to do was type onto cards handwritten information about what had been found during the exhumations. Another office cubicle, different faces, but the same flowerpots, the same coffee maker. "1/2 DT," she typed, meaning "Half of dog tag." "Without clothing." "L. thigh, badly healed fracture." She entered height, measurements of thigh and ulna, approximate age, condition of teeth. There were moments when she caught herself lost in thought, chewing her fingernails and staring at schematic diagrams that showed with requisite and admirable precision the condition of upper and lower jaw, skull, and spine.

"You'll get used to it," said Frau Wolf, herself a widow.

Maximiliane did not get used to it. She was repeatedly compelled to seek advice at the Fredell home. Her domestic situation also found a willing and informed consultant in Herr von Fredell. Drafted at the beginning of the war, he had had to abandon his law studies. After the war he got married and was therefore unable to go back to school on his release from the prisoner-of-war camp. Nevertheless he referred to himself as a lawyer, though an "interrupted" one. Whenever he used the expression "interrupted lawyer," she thought of Martin, her Rhinelander.

Herr von Fredell had a great desire to help his wife's friend in legal matters. As far as her claims to a pension went, he believed that she qualified under Article 131, which concerned onetime family members of public servants and also covered refugees and expellees.

Thus Maximiliane, the victim of two world wars, finally made the appropriate application.

A few days later one of her coworkers, a Fräulein Vogel—in charge of the graves registry for the Sailly-sur-la-Lys Cemetery, which primarily held the dead from the First World War—appeared at Maximiliane's desk, placed a dual-language graves list before her, pointed to Number 3412, and asked if it might refer to some relative. "Baron Achim von Quindt, Lieutenant."

Maximiliane read the entry more carefully and realized that it could be no one but her father.

"The cemetery isn't far from Lille," Fräulein Vogel said. "All single graves. Not a group grave in the lot."

"Didn't anyone in your family ever try to find out about his grave?" Frau Wolf asked, exhibiting both a professional and a personal interest.

"No," Maximiliane answered. "As far as I know, my grandfather wanted the body brought home. After we lost the war, that couldn't be done. He had a marker set on—" She broke off, the oaks of Innicher Mountain in her mind's eye. In their shade several generations of Quindts had been interred, with ice-age erratic boulders for headstones.

"Perhaps your husband's body will turn up as well," Frau Wolf said, thinking she was giving comfort. "This is the place where you're most likely to find out. Just don't give up hope. In Berlin, in the process of rebuilding, they're still finding unknown soldiers, and most of the time they can identify them. The main thing is if your husband had any special identifying marks—broken bones, that kind of thing."

Maximiliane looked up from the list of graves to supply the requested information. "He had only one arm. He lost the right one during the Allied invasion in—" This sentence, too, was never completed.

"But that's wonderful. You'll have to tell Herr Degenhardt; he's working on Berlin bodies."

232

Maximiliane pushed back her chair, rose, held on to the edge of the desk. What she had been avoiding so successfully all this time had now happened: her imagination was taking off on its own—foxholes and dredges, the skeleton and jawbone of her husband. The blood rushed from her head, she staggered.

An efficient office is prepared for such contingencies. Frau Wolf rushed up with cologne, Frau Menzel went for the brandy bottle. The flowerpots were pushed aside, and the window thrown open. Herr Schröder was told what was happening and arrived personally to take care of his worker. He asked her if she would prefer to go home and lie down, adding with understanding that it had been his experience that the first shock was always the worst because it brought absolute certainty, but that consolation was soon at hand when the family found out where the grave was located.

Maximiliane's application for a pension had been rejected out of hand. Herr Fredell advised her to appeal the ruling to the top level, the Hessian Ministry of the Interior. The Ministry sent back its ruling: because of Viktor Quint's activity as an SS member in the Reich Genealogic Office, his widow was not entitled to a pension.

Once again Maximiliane had to be comforted by an expert. Herr König, the official in the district president's office to whom her case was assigned, informed her of the final refusal, breaking the news not only gently but also with intimations of bitterness. "Göring's widow gets a pension! And you're not supposed to be entitled! How am I supposed to explain that?"

"I have no wish to be compared with Göring's widow."

"Those gentlemen established a Thousand-Year Reich, and they didn't leave even a little pension for their widows and orphans."

"That's so like those gentlemen," Maximiliane said. "They always kept their minds on higher things." Where she should have made claims, she did not; where she should not have, she did. She never learned to act like other people.

Herr König closed the Quint file once and for all and walked Maximiliane to the door, shaking hands. "You managed to get through the first difficult years. You'll manage in future as well. Soon they will have the machinery in place to pay out the principal indemnity for the equalization of burdens, you won't go away empty-handed there."

Speeding up these claims was another matter Herr von Fredell had taken in hand.

Maximiliane no longer bumped into doorknobs and desk drawers in her office. She adapted, even to such a small cubicle. On her birthday she baked a Prince Frederick Memorial Cake, took it to the office, and earned the appreciation of all her co-workers, with whom she grew ever more popular; her evident inefficiency allayed their fear of a rival besides giving them a sense of superiority. In spite of her origins and her friendship with the department head, she never held herself aloof. She took part in the company outing—a steamboat trip up the Fulda to Hannoversch-Münden. She went from house to house collecting for the war graves, volunteering for the least fruitful and least popular streets; she stood in the November damp and held the white collection box bearing the five black crosses, not at all demanding but rather waiting; she could elicit no more than tiny donations. She contributed homemade straw stars and paper roses to the office Christmas festivities.

The end of the 1950s: Maximiliane was wearing sack dresses in obedience to fashion. The best parts of her body were cruelly concealed, while her knees, thickened by rickets, were exposed. Attempting to wear pointed shoes with pencil-thin heels, she ended by carrying her shoes and walking barefoot. Her body sturdily withstood all fashion's onslaughts. When one of her coworkers asked her to dance at the Christmas party, she took off her shoes right in the middle of the number.

Her partner was a Herr LeBois, descendant of a Huguenot family of Kassel, now one of the "transferrers." After several years of working in the south of France, he was now employed in the home office, though in a different building from Maximiliane's. In spite of her fellow workers' nosiness, their relationship went unnoticed. Maximiliane had inherited a talent for secretiveness from her grandmother, who herself had managed to consign to oblivion her Polish lieutenant and the affair to which Maximiliane's father owed his life. Maximiliane's relationship with Herr LeBois was also so distant from the usual assumptions about how a war widow should behave, especially a mother of adult and adolescent children, that the suspicion never arose.

Lengthy evening walks—no more than that could have been observed. Only Viktoria, gifted with the perceptive faculties of a bloodhound, scented that something was afoot. "Mother has a new boyfriend," she announced when all her sisters and her brother were assembled—a circumstance that transpired frequently; they were all stay-at-homes in spite of the uncomfortable apartment, in spite of their mother's urgent "Run."

Maximiliane neither confirmed nor denied Viktoria's observation, and the others were not much interested.

This "little affair," as it might be called, did not get deep under Maximiliane's skin but was clearly good for it. It remained without consequences and therefore need not claim more space here. The only thing it brought in its train were the evening walks, which Maximiliane continued by herself. Her undiminished grief for Golo kept her from buying another car.

For ten years, whenever she walked in the woods she had kept her eyes on the ground, on the lookout for combustible and edible matter—beechnuts, mushrooms, twigs. Now she raised her eyes, rediscovered the sky. When the first installment of the principal indemnification for the equalization of burdens was granted and paid out with a directive to invest the sum toward securing a living standard in the Federal Republic, Herr von Fredell counseled her to build a house—a suggestion Maximiliane rejected vehemently. She did not want to be indemnified for Poenichen—she wanted Poenichen. One of her rare explosions. She did not absolutely turn down her adviser's suggestion, however, especially when Bella joined in. "There's no such thing as just one home. It's possible to have more than one, even if the others are less imposing. Our sons feel at home here."

Besides, a letter arrived around this time from her uncle, the same General Erwin Max von Quindt whose wife, Elisabeth, had tried so hard on Mount Eyckel to educate the Quints from Poenichen. This Uncle Max had attained an influential position with the Federal Equalization Office in Bad Homburg and urgently advised her to invest her money thoughtfully and with an eye to capital returns. Immediately under his current address his letterhead read, "Formerly Königsberg, Regentenstrasse 12." The general's wife had written a postscript in her own hand—"Have you ever considered having your son Joachim enter on a diplomatic career so that someday he will have a position commensurate with his origins and rank?"

Since at this time Joachim happened to be in Sweden looking after his estate there, Maximiliane neglected to pass on to him his great-aunt Elisabeth's reflections. But he could not have given the suggestion serious

236

thought in any case, since it was entirely foreign to his nature. Instead of the planned two weeks, he spent his entire summer vacation in Sweden, and instead of a letter, he sent his mother a poem—his first love lyric, addressed simultaneously to Sweden and to a Swedish girl. Maximiliane accepted it as a sign that he was definitely lost to Poenichen. Why not, then, acquire a building site? Why not in Kassel? She agreed to Herr von Fredell's suggestion and signed the papers for a razed plot in town.

Ever since her work had consisted of entering information about transfers onto file cards, she frequently dreamed of dentures made of rubber, of thighs with healed fractures, and of charred bones. Because she had never properly learned to type, the work was difficult for her; she paid more attention to the typewriter keyboard than to the names and numbers, making numerous mistakes—for example, mixing up names like Meier and Müller, which occurred so often. She took the long view and was therefore heedless about death sites and grave numbers. To his deep regret, Herr Schröder eventually saw himself compelled to occupy her with still simpler tasks. Neither he nor the personnel director understood that she should have been entrusted with greater rather than with smaller responsibilities. She would have been ideally suited to handling the correspondence with families. Just as at the age of twenty she had gone to the Poenichen villagers to break the news of loved ones killed in battle, she would surely have found the right words now.

Her carelessness and lack of cunning had unexpectedly good results in another matter—that of her property. The value of her land, which she had acquired without much interest or joy, increased immensely in a very short time as construction and the consequent real-estate speculation gathered momentum. Against her will she was once again a woman of means. When a buyer offered three times the original price for the site, Herr von Fredell reached for Maximiliane's hand, bent over it, and said, "A little golden hand!"

He recommended that she reinvest at least part of the sum in lasting goods—oriental rugs, silver, antiques—against the not improbable day when want and depression would recur. Remembering the silver she had buried in the grounds of Poenichen and the rugs that had padded the fleeing wagons, Maximiliane found it hard to believe that in future times of shortage rugs would help; there would never be another train of horse-drawn wagons. By now, too, she had secretly begun to pursue another plan, one she had forged at the Pomerania Day celebrations. This plan grew at the same pace as a new high-rise apartment house that was going up outside her window, shutting off the view and constricting her more and more.

Almost daily Maximiliane continued to furnish refutation of the view that an orphaned and widowed refugee woman of the nobility was particularly suited for the work of the National Association for the Care of German War Graves. She was immune from firing, however, because all government offices had a legal obligation to employ a specified proportion of people victimized by the war. Finally, after a confidential discussion with Herr von Fredell, who was still considered responsible for Maximiliane, it was decided of necessity to keep her busy with still simpler office work. For the final months of her employment she addressed envelopes for letters acknowledging the conscientious execution of requests for photographs and the care of graves.

Her fellow workers watched her inexorable fall with some empathy. This time, too, Frau Wolf had words of comfort. "At least you know that when you get home there's someone there waiting for you." In fact, most of the time it was Maximiliane who waited for her daughters to come home; only rarely were they waiting for her.

Both Viktoria and Mirka had finished school, Viktoria with an advanced diploma, Mirka with a certificate. Viktoria was attending the university in Göttingen, studying the two fields in which she had the least preparation—psychology and sociology. Mirka, for her part, concentrated on the only area where she had any talent—dance. She had her first engagement as a trainee with the ballet company of the Kassel municipal theater. In her spare time she sewed her own clothes, displaying a great deal of imagination and good taste. She augmented her allowance by modeling the smaller sizes at fashion shows held by the local department stores. Secretly she entered beauty contests.

Early in September, before university classes resumed, all the Quints were together again. Maximiliane took advantage of the occasion to invite the Fredells to supper.

Poenichen tablecloth and Poenichen damask napkins. The christening bowl filled with rowans. For the first time Maximiliane herself prepared a Poenichen pâté of wild game. She arranged the slices on a flat plate and served toast and red wine with it. Since she did not have a recipe, she had had to rely on her memory and, where that failed, on ingenuity. Like Anna Riepe, she had used the old measurements: a handful, a pinch, a shot. . . .

The pâté was universally admired. Herr von Fredell allowed himself a single criticism: he pointed out that a dry white wine, perhaps a Chablis, would have been a more suitable accompaniment.

"You're wonderful at this sort of thing," Frau von Fredell told Maximiliane. "You're simply not suited for files full of unknown soldiers. I'd love to trade places with you. I'm sure my husband would have no objection."

239

Maximiliane looked at her friend, her friend looked at her husband, her husband looked at Maximiliane. An equilateral triangle of looks. No encounters actually took place; they were probably studiously avoided.

"You're not a career woman. You have more talent for marriage," Frau von Fredell continued.

"More talent maybe," Maximiliane conceded, "but not much experience. In a way I've never been married. I was always only a widow. 'A natural-born widow,' somebody once called me. It always embarrassed me. You keep on living year after year while the other person is quite dead. Sometimes I've felt like a murderess. There was always an empty place at my side. Other widows fill it with words, by talking about their 'late husband,' their 'fallen husband.' I could never do that. I wasn't a good widow to him."

Joachim raised his glass and looked at her. "But you are a good mother."

Maximiliane had never overcome her tendency to blush at a compliment. After looking at her children in turn, she concluded, "I suppose I'm a maternal animal."

When the pâté was finished and had been adequately praised, Maximiliane held the empty platter in both hands and announced to the assembled company that she had decided to put this concoction on the market under the name of Poenichen Pâté of Wild Game. "We'll have to change the ingredients—a third game, two thirds pork—but otherwise we'll use the original recipe. The pâté will be put up in small earthenware crocks bearing a label with that statement Bismarck wrote to my great-grandfather." She held up the letter and read from it: " 'My wife begs yours for the recipe for the Poenichen game pâté. Ever yours, Bk.' In facsimile, with a picture of Old Quindt alongside."

"What are you planning to do? Set up a meat-processing plant?"

240

Every word came from a different throat; the Fredells were as dismayed as the young Quints.

"Not me—Edda," Maximiliane explained, handing the letter from Bismarck around the table. "She's shown more family feeling than all the others, and she has a good head for business. She spent years working in our sausage shop. Besides, she's the only one of us who has strong feelings about money. You can tell more about people by their attitude to money than by their attitude to God. Joachim has plans of his own that can't go hand in hand with the production of pâté, Viktoria wants to redistribute the world's wealth, and Mirka has never lived on Poenichen."

One after another she looked at her children. Her reasons had been chosen at random, but the others were too surprised to realize it.

Maximiliane sketched her plan succinctly. "They say that the most game is in Holstein, so the business should be established in Holstein. There are only a few months when you can shoot hare, so the rest of the time we'll have to depend on venison. Crocks of two different sizes—two hundred grams and five hundred grams. You reach the expellees' hearts through their stomachs. Most of the Pomeranians have not become wealthy again, and most of them weren't wealthy in the first place—so, no pistachios and truffles; nuts and cultivated mushrooms instead. You have to advertise to the right audience; the Pomeranian newsletter would be best. One of the descendants of the von Quinten from Lübeck is supposed to be a specialist in raising pigs; he can be our supplier. We'll have to acquire a fallow farm near him. Herr Picht, our Poenichen neighbor from the Juchenow estate, will be our representative to the nobility who did not leave; they can't make their own pâté on the estates anymore because they lack the staff.

Martha Riepe can take over the bookkeeping. And don't forget that Edda wept because she was so hungry."

She looked at Edda, remembered Dr. Green's warning, and added, "But you have to be careful not to get fat."

She leaned back. She had just made the longest speech of her life.

19

That particular descendant of the von Quinten was named Marten. He was in his early thirties, had reddish-blond hair, and was unmarried. He owned a farm a few kilometers from Eutin in the hilly region of Holstein, twenty kilometers as the crow flies to the Baltic, eighty kilometers to the North Sea. His farm, called Erikshof after an earlier Danish owner, had been bought as an investment in 1921 by Marten's grandfather, August von Quinten. When the situation became more difficult after the war and during the postwar years, which favored agriculture, Albert von Quinten, Marten's father, had made the farm over to his son—at just the right time, in his own opinion; precipitately, in the opinion of his neighbors.

Marten von Quinten spent several hours a day at his desk figuring out ways to make the farm profitable—an activity that made the farm even more unprofitable. His most recent calculations revealed that his operation could support no more than two and a half workers, a figure that included himself as a full-time laborer—a self-deception. He was a cheerful and openhanded person, though at times a little arrogant.

Martha Riepe would have called Erikshof, with its two hundred acres, a "drop in the bucket"; but in terms of Holstein it was a sizable property that Marten von Quinten, when he had been drinking—which was frequently—called an "experimental farm." In the wake of governmental recommendations for specialization, he had first concentrated on dairy farming. But when the steady downpour of governmental milk subsidies began to let up, he had sent his cows to slaughter, spent the proceeds on young bullocks, and changed over to cattle raising.

This conversion, also supported by public monies, had not improved the farm's profitability, because with all his ingenuity Marten von Quinten lacked persistence and therefore did not wait long enough to see results. For a short time he entertained the thought of selling a few acres to a building developer or setting up a campsite near the little lake that was part of the property. The administration of the farmers' association in Lübeck was already muttering that Quinten wouldn't hesitate to start a vineyard if wine making had government supports in Holstein. About a year earlier he had decided to use low-interest loans to go in for pig breeding.

Taking the advice of the farmers' association, he had joined with two neighbors in a cartel. One of them, Fenz, was responsible for the actual breeding. He produced three, instead of the customary two, litters a year and sold the piglets to his neighbor Harmsen. Harmsen, in turn, reared the animals until each weighed about twenty kilos and then sold them to Marten von Quinten, on whose land they were supposed to grow to about a hundred kilos.

Other farmers had arrived at the same decision at about the same time, so that Marten von Quinten, whose first act every morning was to glance at the stock reports in the Lübeck newspaper, saw difficulties in disposing of the first batch of pigs even before they were ready for market. The price of pigs had fallen; his profitability calculations were already in error. By then the farm was mortgaged to the hilt, and Herr von Quinten had reason to be even more worried than he was.

His mother and father, Albert and Eva-Marie von Quinten, had renovated one of the former farm cottages after the refugees who once occupied it had left. This was to be their retirement home. They meant to give their son free rein and to stand by with advice if not with much action.

When he received the letter announcing Maximiliane's visit, Marten von Quinten went to ask his mother who this woman might be. After some reflection, she decided that it must be someone from the Pomeranian or East Prussian line of the von Quindts. "Whichever it is, she must have fled. But there's nothing more to fear from the refugees."

Since they were expecting the delivery of eighty piglets on that particular morning, the farm was in a considerable uproar, especially as the thermometer of the unit that controlled the temperature in the barn stubbornly refused to budge from minus-two degrees centigrade, though the outdoor temperature stood at twenty-six. Herr von Quinten was personally occupied with the repairs. The drinking-water mechanism wasn't functioning properly either.

Thus Maximiliane's arrival passed unnoticed. She parked her newly acquired little Citroen in the farmyard between a diesel-powered Mercedes and a manure cart, got out, and took a deep breath of the mingled odor of pig manure, linden blossoms, and diesel oil. Two shaggy dachshunds barked at her before retiring to their sunny spot at the top of a broad flight of stairs leading to the front door. The farmhouse was a roomy, comfortable brick building, though the white paint on the woodwork was peeling.

Hands on hips, Maximiliane stood still for a long time, looking around carefully. No one responded to either her knocking or her shouts. She walked around the farmhouse and glanced at the rear lawn, which was in the process of turning into a meadow. A couple of old rhododendron bushes merging with a fruit orchard gone to seed were the only signs of cultivation. She crossed the spacious farmyard, thought she heard voices, and followed the sound. When she came to a barn that resembled a factory, she opened the first door she came to.

Once inside, she decided to leave the door open so as to be able to see better in the half-light. At the same moment a hundred pigs broke out into hysterical squealing. Maximiliane, unaware that it was she who had caused the uproar, called to a man who was raising his arms imploringly on the far side of the stalls, "Your pigs are hungry," as she had learned to do on Poenichen. But the sentence was drowned out by squeals. The man's gestures seemed to convey that he wanted to tell her something. She left the shed, closing the door behind her, and walked around the building in search of the door behind which she believed she would find this excitable person. For a second time she brought into the shed a hearty breath of fresh air as well as light and noise, so that the ear-shattering squealing of a hundred pigs started up again.

Someone grabbed her arm with no attempts at gentleness and led her back outside. She had had her first encounter with Marten von Quinten, lord of the manor.

Maximiliane learned that pigs are enormously nervous and sensitive animals, susceptible to every change in temperature, every noise, every breath of air. The estate owner remained in front of the barn door for a second, listening until the animals quieted down. Only then did he pay any attention to his visitor. He led her into the house, wiped his sturdy red hands on his corduroy pants, fetched the brandy bottle from the gun cabinet, filled two glasses, and welcomed his Pomeranian cousin. It might be a while before the truck with the piglets arrived, he explained; they could wait in front of the house. And as they sat there Maximiliane experienced everything she had done without for so long, from the scent of blooming linden trees and the odor of the barns to the shaggy dachshunds and the conversation about farming.

"Did you know," Herr von Quinten asked, gulping his brandy even as they talked, "that a milk cow drinks more than fifty liters of water a day?"

Maximiliane had not known. No one had ever measured the amount the cows took from Lake Poenichen every day. She shook her head, and Herr von Quinten figured out for her that sixty cows required three thousand liters of water daily, and since a cubic meter of water cost—

He interrupted himself before he could complete the multiplication. "Let's forget all that. Now I raise pigs; they drink less because they don't produce milk and don't have to be milked. Pigs are more intelligent than you'd think, by the way. They take care of their own drinking arrangements. But why am I telling you all this?"

"Because I like to hear it," Maximiliane said, turning her full gaze on him.

Herr von Quinten, who was enjoying not his first but his fourth drink of the day, was heard to say ten minutes into their first meeting, "Too bad you're not twenty years younger." After a more careful look, he corrected himself. "Ten years would be enough."

Maximiliane looked around, breathed deeply, and repeated, "Too bad."

Understanding seemed to grow quickly between the two of them—and all the more as Maximiliane never quite realized that it was easy for her companion to arrive at the same quick understanding with other women. For his part, he did not realize that her "Too bad" referred to the farm alone.

Next Herr von Quinten spoke of drainage and fencing. Maximiliane had heretofore believed that on these subjects she was able to keep up her end of the conversation. But he talked of the "operation" rather than the "farm," and he said "electrified fence" rather than "pickets" and "silos" rather than "ricks." Not a single horse in the barn, no chickens scratching on a compost heap; the pigs were fed carbohydrates, phosphates, and proteins, the swill ran down the drains. "Once over, and it's done"—even in Holstein. But unlike Mr. Simpson from Montana—and this marked a clear distinction between a German and an American—Marten von Quinten allowed his visitor to share in his vicissitudes. Whatever he undertook, he told her, somebody else, other farmers, tried the same thing at the same time; he had trouble selling his product.

"Each of us spoils the market for the others; there's not enough demand. My pigs don't get to the consumer but to a slaughterhouse."

Thus he himself paved the way for the topic Maximiliane had planned to broach to her pig-rearing cousin. Though their exact degree of relationship was impossible to determine, each felt justified in addressing the other by first name.

Until this discussion on his own front steps, Herr von Quinten had been all too eager to follow the lead of the farmers' association, the regional agricultural chamber, and the market reports. From now on he put his entire faith in Maximiliane's inspiration. She was faced with persuading not a cautious or suspicious business associate but a reckless one.

When the piglets had been unloaded, Herr von Quinten took Maximiliane to one of the farm cottages that Pomeranian refugees had abandoned five years before but that he had been unable to sell because it stood too close to the road. By now the thatched roof had been replaced with an aluminum one. There was running water and electricity, though the house was not yet connected to the local sewer line. Five sufficiently large rooms were available, and there was space for subsequent expansion. They would certainly be able to agree on a suitable rent.

After looking over the future production facilities, they walked to the edge of the woods. Herr von Quinten wore binoculars around his neck, and he instinctively placed them at his eyes, showing Maximiliane where game could be found in June. Fallow deer, still flourishing in Holstein. Too bad, though, that he didn't have a proper wife to prepare the hunt meal—but his mother assumed the office by default, and he had hired a girl from town to help out. Maximiliane could tell from the tone of the last remark that the girl's assignments went beyond the usual housework.

So they stood at the edge of the woods and looked at the handsome old trees, most of them beeches reseeded in the 1880s. Valuable timber, but no market for it, as Marten von Quinten explained.

When he stopped at one of the hedges that divided the fields into large, irregular rectangles, a swarm of black thrushes rose from the thickets of whitethorn and blackthorn, elder and hazelnut. These hedges, he explained, broke the force of the east and west winds, but they also retarded the progress of agriculture in Holstein. Without them nothing would stop the wind from sweeping across the land, people said. But it was his opinion that without them the fields could be cultivated far more efficiently. And to the objection that the hedges furnished nesting places for birds that destroyed pests— well, as far as he was concerned, he preferred relying on chemistry when it came to getting rid of vermin and weeds.

The hedges made it impossible for Maximiliane to imagine that she was in Pomerania. Still, a field of rye spread out before her, not as extensive as on Poenichen, but large enough to allow comparison; puffs of noontime clouds hovered, and the corn was in flower—almost like Pomerania. It was the *almost* that grieved Maximiliane. No more cornflowers, no wild poppies, no camomile in the blue-green field rippled gently by a breeze from the east. But at the edge of the paved path the weeds flourished all the more luxuriantly, as did the hedge mustard. For the first time in years Maximiliane caught herself humming one of the old songs—a woman of over forty!

When she placed her arms around the trunk of a beech, Herr von Quinten gave her a thoughtful look.

At this first visit her daughter Edda's name went unspoken. The discussion was limited to a detailed consideration of the money from the equalization of burdens and of the Poenichen Pâté of Wild Game.

At the dinner in Kassel Herr von Fredell had stated, "Your way of conducting inheritance claims, my dear Maximiliane, is going to keep the lawyers busy for weeks. I'm going to have to bow out of this one; your affairs are too complicated for an interrupted lawyer."

His assumption was validated only in part, since a lawyer who was a friend of the Lübeck Quintens, a Dr. Jonas, successfully took the responsibility in a number of instances. Several affidavits also made her case easier.

Viktoria, whose university education had been secured by the legacy from the Charlottenburg grandmother, signed a waiver. Her addition of a statement disparaging "the possession-crazed bourgeoisie" unfortunately rendered the document invalid, but after repeated intercessions she agreed to sign a second waiver, this time without embellishment and therefore legally binding.

At this time Mirka was already earning so much from photographic modeling that she refused her share of the inheritance, dramatizing her gesture with a breathtakingly lovely sweep of her long, limber arms.

250

Nevertheless, a clause providing for "emergencies," though these were not more narrowly defined, gave her some rights to the profits of the future company.

Joachim, the firstborn, who was now calling himself Mose Quint, was still writing poetry and was beginning to be published. He had retired to "the Swedish forests," as he put it. He sent a letter in which well-chosen phrases announced that he had no interest whatever in questions of family legalities. Handsome as they were, his sentences were worthless from a legal standpoint. Propriety was achieved only when he signed a declaration composed for him. Joachim continued to enjoy sole and undisputed claim to the estate in Poenichen, now Peniczyn, near Kalisz/Pomorski. True, at the most recent Pomerania Day the federal chancellor had no longer spoken of "efforts," as he had in Kassel, but only of "hopes for a peaceful return to the homeland." Barely perceptible shifts in emphasis. Desires shriveled down to the idea 54"just being able to take a trip there."

On Maximiliane's second visit to Erikshof, planned to last several weeks, Edda came along. With her, it was not a matter of carefully stringing details together; all that was necessary was to let matters take their course, which was done by all.

Only once did Maximiliane have to say "Cuckoo" in warning tones to her daughter, who blushed in reply. Herr von Quinten wanted to know what the word meant. Maximiliane answered, "Just wait for spring; then she becomes as freckled as a cuckoo's egg." And as she spoke, she realized for the first time that Marten's face was freckled the year round; even their freckles matched.

"I can't wait until spring," he declared, and Edda blushed again.

They spent their time in the older Quinten's reed-thatched home, discussing building loans and equalization-of-burden payments: a percentage of the assessed value of the farm had to be paid every three months for years on end. "A considerable financial burden for the Erikshof," old Herr von Quinten said—a remark in which Maximiliane scented reproach. In this conversation, equalization payers and equalization beneficiaries confronted each other. But when the old man stressed the fact that upon marriage with someone expelled from the East the assessment would be forgiven, it was proven anew that the interests of both parties dovetailed in the most fortunate way.

The discussion moved on to the details of preserving pâté in the best way; to the tried and true method of keeping it in glass jars and the difficulties of shipping such jars; to the advantages and drawbacks of aluminum cans; to the costly china crocks; but especially to recipes.

Frau von Quinten suggested that the smoked bacon be rendered first. The question of whether to use sherry or port wine was left open for the present; Maximiliane thought she remembered that on Poenichen they had used home-distilled potato brandy, which Frau von Quinten, born and bred in Lübeck, considered barbaric. Someone who had married into the Quinten family owned a liquor business in Lübeck; they would be able to arrive at some sort of deal with him.

For the sake of truth, Maximiliane should have used this opportunity to make a confession. Frau Pech, the last housekeeper on Poenichen, who now supervised the works kitchen on the Klara Zetkin Collective, had indeed replied to Maximiliane's inquiry. But she claimed to be unable to remember the recipes used exclusively by the Prussian estate owners—which was as much as to say that she was unwilling to recall them.

Maximiliane had found recipes for pâtés in four cookbooks and designed a fifth based on them. When she spoke of it, she did indicate the principal ingredients; but she maintained a modicum of secrecy, reinforcing the myth of the Poenichen pâté of game.

Eva-Marie von Quinten, Marten's mother, a good ten years older than Maximiliane, ten centimeters taller and ten kilograms heavier—more than a match for her, therefore, in many ways—did not deliver her final judgment on Edda until the latter was walking down the garden path with Marten and could be observed from the rear. As she had all her life dealt with female staff, with good results, she now dealt with Edda: she inspected her behind.

"You can always tell a woman by her behind. If they have small, quick bottoms, they don't last long. And those with a broad, soft behind do too much sitting; you can't get rid of them." Edda's behind was adequate to her future mother-in-law's requirements: not too small and not too broad; firm and vigorous.

The wedding took place even before the Poenichen pâté went into production, but preparations had been going on apace. The first jars of Poenichen Pâté of Wild Game would be ready for the market in time for Christmas. The labels were already printed: to the left Bismarck's letter in facsimile, old Baron Quindt on the right.

When Edda wrote her mother for her birth certificate, Maximiliane decided to conveniently lose both the birth certificate and the certificate of adoption—both taken to safety by Martha Riepe along with the other documents from Poenichen. Since the bureau of vital statistics for Poenichen/Peniczyn no longer existed—that is, had been destroyed in the aftermath of the war—legal status was conferred on the affidavit Maximiliane had sworn to after their flight, which averred that "to the best of my recollection I gave birth to a child of the female sex on March 5, 1939."

At the wedding dinner Marten von Quinten discoursed at length on the "to the best of his knowledge female sex" of his wife, and Maximiliane exchanged a look and a smile with Edda. She had succeeded in turning the legal problem child into a legally impeccable wife. Edda achieved what had been her firm goal from the moment she learned her true heritage; she became a member of the nobility—and of a rank higher than was ever held by any Quindt on Poenichen.

Her dowry included a dozen damask napkins from Poenichen, embroidered with the family crest. The guests marveled as they unfolded them on their laps. The crest of the Poenichen Quindts was compared with that of the Lübeck Quinten. Both had the same five leaves in the lower half, but the upper half of the Quindts' showed three geese in single file with outstretched necks. Pomeranian geese! Stubble geese! Smoked goose! Smoked breast and sour stew! They remembered only too well. The crest of the Lübeck branch, on the other hand, showed only one skinny bird, presumably a wagtail, a pippit with a long, jerky tail, called "field thrush" in the East, and common in Holstein.

"Whatever became of Eyckel Castle?" The man who had been so young at the family reunion and was now so old, Herr von Quinten, Marten's father, leaned across the table to address Maximiliane. "I have such clear memories of the family reunion. Who would have thought at the time, more than a quarter of a century ago, that one day we'd be so closely related. I must admit that I don't have any recollection of you. You must have been a mere schoolgirl."

"I was sixteen."

"I do remember the Labor Service leader, and of course the ancestral old lady. You must have been her heir?"

Maximiliane told him the story, omitting this point and that. "At first I rented Eyckel Castle to Herr Brandes from Bamberg—his wife was a Quint, without the *d*, before her marriage. He donated the beer for the family reunion. He needed storage space. Then last year he bought the castle. The buildings were so damaged by that time that they had to be boarded up for safety, and he couldn't use them even for storage. He didn't want the place as a gift because of the gift tax, but he was prepared to rid me of it—that is, to rid Mirka of it; I had transferred the title to her—and assume responsibility for the old ruin." She and her youngest daughter exchanged a look and a smile, but none of those present realized their deeper meaning. "He paid the minimum. Four percent of the assessed value."

"What a pity that no namesake lives on the old family property anymore. Well, that's life."

Thus Herr von Quinten had given himself his cue. He tapped his glass and rose to his feet to make the required speech. Compared to Old Quindt on Poenichen, Quinten could hold his own in eagerness but not in ability. He assured the wedding guests—the majority of them Quintens from Lübeck and a few neighboring estate owners, with only the immediate Quint family, the bride's mother, her sisters, and her brother—that the bride came from a good stable. What might be objectionable in the father, a Silesian Quint, was more than compensated for by the Pomeranian Quindts.

"As far as the father of the bride, a war victim, is concerned," he continued, "I stick to the Latin saying *De mortui nil nisi bene*—'Nothing but good about the dead.' I will, however, dare to claim that Viktor Quint would have been revered as a hero if—well, if we had won the war. This statement should not lead anyone to conclude that I vote the Holstein Nationalist ticket."

The neighbors nevertheless drew this conclusion.

He turned to Maximiliane to praise her as the mother of the bride. "Whenever you, my dear Maximiliane, enter a room, we all feel as if it were growing warmer." This remark was genuine, original, and worthy of applause.

He raised his glass and said, "United Forever," meaning the bridal pair and not Schleswig-Holstein. This toast was less original but was also considered worthy of applause.

It was not necessary to check the bride's behind. Determination could be clearly read in her face; she was marrying this man for good. "United Forever" was a substitute for "Until death do us part"; there had been no religious ceremony.

Young Quinten replied by thanking his parents for having been content with two children, so that he had to share only with his sister, Liselotte, and not with three sisters—although he considered himself fortunate to have acquired two sisters-in-law. His eyes dwelt particularly on Mirka, who was the central attraction of the party and was photographed more frequently than the bride. Then his glance passed on to Viktoria, whose audible silence attested to the fact that she was doing her duty by her presence but who expressed her disapproval of the whole performance by wearing a gray, shapeless sweater, refusing alcoholic drinks, and eating only vegetables.

Young Quinten pointed his upraised glass in her direction. "And perhaps Cinderella is gracing our table? Could it be that I married the wrong sister? Do I have to inspect her feet?" The laughter was at Viktoria's expense. She neither sought nor needed her mother's consoling glance.

Next Quinten toasted his new brother-in-law. "The first artist in the long line of the Quintens, as far as I know. I'd be pleased if before the night is out he could recite something of his own." He continued by saying that though he had not yet had the good fortune of reading any of his brother-in-law's efforts, it was clear that at the table of a Holstein farmer one did not have to dine on words alone.

At that moment the main course was brought in. Quinten concluded his speech, tarrying only to urge his neighbors to chase stags and does his way in future. "We will soon find a use for them in the game-pâté factory."

He sat down and, as host, reached for the carving set to perform, more in goodwill than with skill, the traditional hunting ritual of single-handedly carving the two haunches of venison.

Edda took the utensils from him. "Leave it to me."

Maximiliane recognized the seductive sentence and remembered her second wedding, the christening bowl filled with sweet william, apple tart and cocoa served because of the children. . . .

Marten willingly handed the tools over to his wife, leaned back in his chair, and watched with pleasure. This would be his principal activity from now on.

Edda carved quickly and deftly. She was admired and praised. "Where did she learn to do that?" All eyes turned to the mother of the bride.

"She comes from Pomerania." Since this answer did not seem to suffice, Maximiliane added, "She's good at everything."

This explanation once more smoothed her daughter's way. In her view—which she kept to herself—in any marriage only one of the partners could flourish; in this case it was not yet clear which it would be.

The main topic of conversation during the wedding dinner was the future manufacture of Poenichen game pâté. "Bone and skin the game, sprinkle it with cognac or sherry, cover it, and keep it cold," said Frau von Quinten at the head of the table, while at the foot Frau Fenz proposed, "You don't have to use truffles, capers will do it."

"But pistachios!" Frau Harmsen added.

Viktoria listened reluctantly. The idea of manufacturing pâté while the majority of humanity was starving was unbearable to her.

In connection with the game pâté, Joachim told the story of the canned meat "for army dogs only" that his brother, Golo, had gotten in exchange for some flints in 1945 in the Kassel railroad terminal. He reminisced about how greedily they had devoured it.

The conversation switched to Golo. The Quints explained to the others that he had had a fatal automobile accident. Edda mentioned that just recently another young man, probably also speeding, had crashed into a tree on the same road three trees farther on, and that the trees were going to be cut down.

Everyone talked about the handsome old trees along the roads of Holstein.

"These highways tempt people to drive too fast," Frau Fenz said, and her husband added, "Our oldest son, Hasso, just bought a heavy motorcycle. It cost almost as much as a Volkswagen."

"Sometimes it can cost a life," Maximiliane remarked. After a brief pause she added an explanation, speaking with cheerful melancholy. "Most of the time the motor is stronger than the character."

The difference between a Pomeranian wedding of the 1930s and a Holstein wedding of the 1960s seemed to Maximiliane smaller than she had expected. It was as if it had been only yesterday that she sat next to Viktor and laid her hand on his arm—"Let it go." She had not been able, then or later, to prevent anything— not the confrontations between Viktor and her grandfather, not the outbreak of war, not the division of Germany, not the restoration of the old conditions.

Viktoria's look now seemed to charge her with all of it. She would have to see to Viktoria's future next. . . .

258

She sighed audibly, reached for her throat and the buttons, met Edda's look, and lowered her hand.

She was exhausted. The separation from this child, too, had tired her. Unnoticed, she left the party, got into her car, and drove to her hotel to sleep.

No one expressed it, but it is probable that everyone entertained the same expectation: they would be meeting again soon, even before the usual time, for another celebration on the Erikshof—though the party would be smaller then.

20

At his birth in May 1938, Joachim measured fifty-two centimeters, was slender and blond, and had blue eyes, thus fulfilling all the demands his father made of him. According to his descent and the provisions of the entail, he was destined to be the sole heir of Poenichen. For seven years he was raised in preparation for this future. A breast-fed baby, he was nursed by his mother long and amply, aside from one paternal intervention lasting several days. In an effort to control the infant's nourishment, Viktor had brought to Poenichen a book titled *The German Mother and Her Firstborn Child*. For as long as he was on the premises, he was adamant that its instructions be followed precisely.

According to this authority, a newborn baby was not to consume more than 160 grams of milk at each of five daily nursings. Joachim was therefore taken from his mother's breast several times during each feeding to be placed on the kitchen scale; then back to the breast, then onto the scale again, just as long as it took to reach the prescribed weight increase: a procedure that strained Maximiliane's patience along with that of the baby, but that came to an end with the father's departure. The scale was returned to the kitchen, the book was put on the shelf. By the time the other babies came along, their father had forgotten the instructions for the German mother in favor of more significant historical events.

This episode in a childhood otherwise so carefree must be reported, since it may well be the cause of the fact that Joachim became an anxiety-ridden little boy who needed closeness and comforting. During the months of their flight from Pomerania and for a long time after, he anxiously clutched in his sleep the "little box" in which he kept his treasures. All his life he was pursued by a particular nightmare: he heard the neighing of horses or the sound of an engine fading into the distance; he jumped up, looked for shoes, shirt, books, writing materials; he hastily packed everything into a suitcase, a cardboard box, or a knapsack; but he was always too late, never able to catch up with the departing wagon train. He was left behind, alone.

Instead of replying with a speech at Joachim's christening dinner, Old Quindt countered the baby's father with a toast: "The Quindts were always good at talking, drinking, and shooting, but they were just as good at doing without. Let us drink to the hope that at the right time this child will be good at it too. It's only a matter of doing, and doing without."

In large measure Joachim Quint did without talking as well as without drinking and shooting.

As to shooting. When compulsory military service was reintroduced twelve years after the end of the Second World War, he was among the first age group to be drafted. It must be remembered that when he was five years old he had been given tin soldiers to play with—an officer and five men, three of them on horseback; judging by the uniforms, they were from the Seven Years War, veterans even then, their paint peeled off. His grandfather, who had lost his life on the western front at the age of nineteen, had been the last to play with them. Joachim had lined a small crate with cotton, bedded the officer, his men, and their horses in it, and covered them carefully, explaining, "All must sleep now."

He voiced a similarly innocent view in a discussion with an officer of the new federal armed forces, a Captain Freese, who was recruiting for future officers among the graduating students of the Marburg secondary schools. Joachim inquired how it was possible to persuade a soldier to run in the direction of fire when the innate instinct of self-preservation would counsel flight; was it that the power of an officer or noncommissioned officer was so great that he was more feared than the enemy? With enormous patience the captain replied that he, Joachim Quint, was wording his questions incorrectly, a criticism already leveled against his mother when she was in school—clearly an inherited failing. In an effort at clarification, Joachim added that he took a special interest in such questions because his father, both his grandfathers, and three of his great-grandfathers had fallen in battle.

Over the next few years letters from the district induction center arrived regularly every six months, addressed to Joachim Quint at his mother's home. Since a notation on the envelope prohibited forwarding such letters abroad, Maximiliane tossed them in a drawer. Joachim's temporary deferment eventually turned into a permanent discharge. He was the first descendant of the Quindt line who did not rush to the colors.

What Joachim finally decided to do had not been provided for in Qld Quindt's toast, though it can be presumed that the old man himself was responsible for planting the seed in the young one: writing—or, more precisely, writing poetry. If conditions had permitted, the forebear would have liked to write travel literature on the model of Alexander von Humboldt, but managing Poenichen allowed time at most for some trips abroad and the reading of a few books. His literary bent had been passed down to Maximiliane; she had nourished both the unborn and the newborn baby with poetry.

262

The first sounds of which Joachim was aware as a child came from the potted palms in the forecourt of the Poenichen estate, where his cradle had been placed—sounds with a certain poetic quality. The reeds of Lake Poenichen also blended in as he lay in his wicker basket while his mother and a young lieutenant bent their heads over a volume of Rilke's poems; one or another line often reached his ear. No wonder, then, that this bent, first suppressed and later nurtured, should have to burst through—not a volcanic eruption; rather, a quiet extrusion.

Maximiliane, child of nature, had given birth to a poet who wrote lyrical apostrophes to nature. Old Quindt would probably have said, "He'll grow out of it." Maximiliane had also been convinced that the time would come when her son would devote himself to agricultural studies so as to be able to manage Poenichen one day. Granted, she herself was not quite clear what this "one day" would be like.

When eventually she did ask the question she had promised never to ask—"Can one live on poetry, then?"—he had answered, not without arrogance, "It's not a question of whether one can. One must."

At that, she had nodded.

When this conversation took place, Joachim was about twenty years old. His chest was still as narrow and hairless as his grandfather's had been; all his life a boy, refined, not at all a Pomeranian. But he had been born with a noble air; he was the "little lord," the very image of the old-fashioned local idea of a poet.

By now he topped his mother by more than ten centimeters. Maximiliane, who had read her way up to more modern poetry, saw in her son's constructions what she saw in him; narrow-chestedness. Nevertheless, her statement "It's better that he use his conflicts to make poetry than to make ulcers or gallstones" tended less to be approval of Mose Quint's verse than

263

a definition of Maximiliane's nature; she had preserved an astonishing critical faculty toward her children's achievements. Mother love did not blind her; rather, it made her more clear-sighted. "He lives like a poet," she said to others, and she was prepared for the sake of her favorite son to regard a poetic way of life as a kind of poetry.

He published his first volume of poetry himself. Entitled *Dangerous Corner*, it had originally been scheduled to appear as *Death Is So Permanent*. It was dedicated to his brother, Golo. Without a contribution from his grandmother Vera, he would have been unable to bear the printing costs. The title page gave the author's name as Mose Quint; a pet name had become a pseudonym.

While he was at the university, he met a Swedish student who was studying German literature in Marburg, as he was. There had always been a close though often inimical relationship between Pomerania and Sweden: several Swedish invasions of Pomerania, as well as conquests of Swedish territory by Erich of Pomerania. Joachim spent several years trying to conquer one single Swede. He followed her transformations with surprise, fear, and joy. Stina Bonde came from Stockholm, where her father was co-owner of a respected publishing house, Bonde-Förlag.

It was clearly an ideal solution for a poet to marry the daughter of a publisher, but Joachim was not interested in ideal solutions. He held back time and again. He was still looking around, as he had done as a child. For years he tortured himself with his legacy: the son of a National Socialist! To get rid of his father, he ended up by leaving his fatherland—at least that was what he said in a poem entitled "Poem for the Fatherland."

Even before the summer semester ended, Stina Bonde took off for home, her only explanation being that it was midsummer in Sweden. Several days later

Joachim followed her. He wrote his mother that he had to look after the inherited Larsson land.

There were some communication problems between Stina and Joachim, although she spoke excellent German and after a time he spoke some Swedish. True, the deeper subtleties of the language, which Joachim cared about, frequently remained concealed from Stina, as well as unimportant to her. The spiritual closeness Joachim yearned for did not come about. He tried to achieve it by way of physical closeness, saying in his poetic way, "You carry my seed away in you and do not know where," which made Stina laugh. When on another occasion he said that every woman must feel a little bit pregnant after every encounter with a man, she was already on her way to the bathroom and pointed out only that there was no such thing as "a little bit pregnant." She remained cool, was almost cold in contrast to Joachim's mother. Stina returned to the bedroom fully dressed, a cigarette between her lips, while Joachim still lay in bed thinking.

"Nobody could tell from looking at you," he said.

"I should hope not," she replied.

The transcendent remained a mystery to her, at least in winter.

That conversation took place in Stina's apartment in Stockholm. After Joachim had stayed with the Bondes in their suburban house—over Christmas, no less—without an engagement being announced, Ole P. Bonde decided to allow his daughter to lead an independent life. She made use of her newfound freedom. Her kitchen was like a laboratory where she calibrated meals according to their caloric content and ease of preparation, took prepared foods from the freezer, was constantly on the move between the telephone and the garbage disposal. In the mornings, while it was still dark, she wrapped herself in bear fur, fur hat, and fur boots and drove to her office, where she translated Russian and German books into Swedish for her father: a chilled, enlightened woman before whom Joachim retreated.

Then the first tepid rays of the April sun, which Joachim was not even aware of, made her shed her pelts. The dreamy look returned to her eyes; she threw a pair of jeans into the car and drove off to Dalarna with Joachim.

Her father came from the same region. He had been raised on a farm that now belonged to strangers. He had sold Bondehus in Järna because the place and its archaic customs made his wife shun it like the plague. As a child Stina had spent her vacations with her father's father, her beloved "Farfar"; since his death she had not gone back to Dalarna. But after Joachim told her that he had inherited a piece of land with several buildings not far from Lake Siljan, they went there several times and began to make the buildings, which had stood empty a long time, habitable again little by little.

Each time they crossed the Dala River, Stina said, "North of the Dala there are no more oaks" and "This is where the blue mountains start." She rolled down the window and placed her hand on the car roof; Joachim, whom she called "Jokke," turned up his coat collar. Under the birches that were just beginning to sprout their first leaves, a white sheet of blooming anemones spread out.

Stina turned into the grassy path that led to Larsgårda. Stopping at the wooden gate, she got out, slammed the car door, ran to the red-painted house, unlocked the door, pushed open the white-painted shutters, and let winter out.

She took possession of Larsgårda. She slipped into the wooden clogs that still stood by the stairs from the previous summer, or she went barefoot. She pulled her sweater off as soon as a warming breeze touched her, she leaned against the wooden wall that turned warm quickly, she stretched, she sprawled; no sound of a human voice could reach her. She was transformed.

Early in the morning she took a pail to the neighbor, Anders Nilsson, and returned with milk still warm from the cow, drawn by hand. She poured the milk into an earthenware jug, poke the fire, added birch logs, and pushed the electric hot plate aside. She washed her hair under the pump although there was running water, and she let the wind dry it. Her steps grew longer; Joachim could barely keep up with her. Suddenly she slowed, pulled on another sweater, and jumped into the lake, which was still chill with winter. In the summer she swam all the way across it, climbed ashore at some spot or other, returned at some time or other, her hands full of cloudberries she had picked in the bog. She held them out to Joachim, who was still lying among the reeds along the bank.

Their first summer in Dalarna she took him to Bondehus. He was submerged in a stranger's childhood, having lost his own. Stina showed him everything she meant by her phrase "the building blocks of childhood"—the rocky wooden bridge, where as a little girl she had watched the raftsmen; the place where they set up the maypole on midsummer's eve; the spot where Farfar sat to fish.

"A true Darkarlar," she told him. "Three days before he died he lay down on his bed, though he wasn't ill. He sang a song none of us had ever heard. He went very gradually. On the last day he was only able to hum. He smiled without opening his eyes, and he knew exactly who was sitting by him—my brother Olaf or my father or me. I was twelve years old. *Kulla,* he called me, *min kulla*—'my girl.' He just went away, waving as if he were far off. He lived in peace. He died in peace."

Stina leaned against a hayrack where newly mown grass was drying, spreading its scent. She pulled out a wilted flower. "We call these priests' collars," she said. Joachim made a note of the name; he was still collecting words.

That same day he said to Stina, "I love you."

"You love Dalarna," said Stina. They loved the same thing.

Visitors began to arrive even before midsummer—Stina's brother Olaf and his friends; a couple of young Larsson descendants from Uppsala. The small wooden houses and sheds belonging to Larsgårda became filled with life. Some of the visitors brought their guitars. In the pale nights they sat along the lakeshore, the men fishing and making a fire, the women cooking the fish. They sang and laughed and ran through the woods, in and out among the whitely shimmering birch trunks. During the day they swam in the lake and picked flowers on the meadows; if a young woman picked seven different kinds of blossoms and put them under her pillow on Midsummer Night, she would dream of her future husband. The girls devoutly counted off the petals, and during the brief darkness they disappeared into one of the barns with their companion of the moment. No one ever learned who appeared in their dreams. None paid any attention to the others, none to himself.

Joachim too roamed restlessly among the trunks of the birches and pines, but he caught none of the girls. He sat alone under the overhang of the wooden verandah waiting for the sun to rise over the mountains, where it had disappeared for two hours.

One morning all the guests got back into their fully automatic cars and returned to the 1960s.

When the last car had turned onto the road to Mora, Stina dropped the arm with which she had been waving, turned to Joachim, and said, bemused, "Jokke."

And he began anew his conquest of the Swede. At night they sat at the lakeshore, once more alone. Stina hugged her knees as if she wanted to hold on to herself, but then she put out her hand, clung to Joachim's arm, and spoke the words no poet has ever been able to resist—"Read to me, Jokke."

Through Herr Bonde's good offices, a small German publisher brought out a second volume of Joachim's poetry; the edition remained small, selling only six hundred copies in addition to the ones that were given away. He also wrote a series of impressive essays, "Midsummer in Dalarna" and "Christmas Customs in Dalarna," which were broadcast by several radio stations.

Critics compared him to Oskar Loerke and Wilhelm Lehmann—formidable yardsticks. It was said, in any case, that the name of Mose Quint should not be forgotten. Joachim sent the first copy to his mother, the second to Viktoria; he did not suppose that his other sisters were readers of poetry. When Edda sent him an invitation to the christening of her first son, he returned his regrets. He included a poem with his letter, but it was not suited to recitation at the festive meal: "Be timid, child./Don't let them teach you/Not to fear./Take care. . . ." Joachim considered such lines to constitute "literature engagé."

"I assume," he wrote to Edda, "you will not stop at this one son; you are like our mother in that. You are fruitful by nature. Later on I shall come and look over your bliss of children. Right now I cannot get away, but perhaps you and your husband will visit me in Dalarna. Midsummer is the best time."

He ended almost all his letters with the same invitation. The journey was a long one; he had no need to fear too much company.

It took Maximiliane four days to get to him. He had moved so far away and yet had always been closest to her. He had put a painful strain on the umbilical cord that still connected her to her children.

Every few hours she checked the road map until

eventually she arrived at Lake Siljan. The map did not show the smaller hamlets, so from this point on she had to ask her way. At last someone nodded, said, *"Den tyska skalden,"* and pointed out the road to Larsgårda.

Midsummer was past, the visitors had left. Stina had gone to meet a German television team from Stockholm, since it was easy to miss the turnoff if you did not know the area. After some hesitation, Joachim had agreed to let them make a film about him and Larsgårda.

When Maximiliane's car stopped on the grassy path before the gate, Joachim did not even turn around, so deeply was he absorbed in what he was doing. Wearing a dark apron, the sleeves of his white shirt rolled up, he was using a stick to stir an evil-smelling mixture that was cooking over an open fire in an old tar barrel.

Maximiliane had to call his name twice before he responded. Slowly he pulled the stick from the mash, leaned it against the pot, and wiped his hands on his apron.

"What are you up to?" Maximiliane said in greeting, and bent over the pot. "Have you turned into a charcoal burner?"

He explained. He was making paint so that during the next couple of days he could paint two little wooden shacks—the former smithy and one of the hay barns. He was using an old Bonde family recipe: dissolve ferric sulfate in water, stir in finely ground rye flour, boil for a quarter of an hour.

It did not seem advisable to interrupt the procedure. Maximiliane's first activity upon arrival, therefore, was to help Joachim boil paint. While he stirred, she slowly poured in powdered red dye from Falun, and finally the last ingredient, a ladle of manure. His neighbor, Brolund, used urine instead, Joachim explained; others used salt or tar.

Hardly had they finished—all that was left was for the mess to cool down—than Stina's car turned into the grassy path, followed by a van from which five men emerged. They unloaded their gear, its use clear even to the layman: film equipment.

Maximiliane looked at the men, at the lights, then at her medievally versatile son, who was just about to wipe his hands clumsily on his apron again. She understood the connection.

That evening they made a fire at the lake. Joachim freely poured out aquavit. Stina, wearing the old traditional peasant costume she had borrowed from another neighbor, grilled fish on a rack she had taken from the refrigerator shelf.

After they ate, in the long dusk made even brighter by spotlights and cables, she sang the song of Dalarna, handing Joachim the guitar so he could accompany her. She sang in Swedish before translating the words into German, her accent adding to the general delight. "God bless the men who live there, by the river, on the mountains, in the dale. . . ." Following the director's suggestion, and with the help of his assistant, the cameraman pointed his lens at the lake, at the mountains, and at Joachim before turning to the "modern woman from Stockholm who for a few weeks every year at midsummer puts on the old hand-woven, hand-dyed Dalarna costume and lives by the old ways." All this time the sound man was managing to record the plop of a jumping fish, the croak of the frogs.

The following morning they filmed Stina as she wound the old grandfather clock, its wood painted in colorful patterns. She was wearing a green apron with red straps over her ankle-length full skirt. Her bare feet were hidden by the crude wooden clogs. Then they ran cables to the room under the slanted roof and set up the floodlights and moved a few pieces of furniture: the room where Joachim Quint worked, where he wrote. At the director's request, he read his latest poem aloud; the manuscript was still lying on the bare desk top.

271

Subsequently he agreed to tie on his apron and for the benefit of the camera paint one wall of the former barn bright red. His mother was responsible for calling the cameraman's attention to the fact that the color came from nearby Falun, with its copper mine. She also remarked that one of her daughters was living in Holstein and manufacturing Poenichen Pâté of Wild Game according to an old family recipe, and that the demand for it had spread not only domestically but also abroad, notably to the home of pâté, France.

The filming took three days. Then the equipment was stowed back in the van, and the crew from the German television network took their leave. Stina left as well; she had things to do in Stockholm.

While she was gone, Maximiliane stayed at Larsgarda. Alone she rowed on the lake or roamed through the pale Swedish nights, wearing her old camouflage jacket, feeding her longing for Poenichen. She began to be plagued by rheumatism because she spent too long sitting on the damp lakeshore. She stayed in bed for a few days while Joachim took care of her. Pushing a table close to her bed, he set up the chess set Maximiliane had brought him as a present. Though they started many a game, they never finished; each time Joachim said, "Tell about Poenichen." And Maximiliane told him about the evenings by Poenichen Lake, when Old Quindt and Inspector Blaskorken played chess on the landing stage by the light of torches while she herself, dripping wet under her father's full-length terry-cloth robe, stood by and watched. "Then, when Old Quindt began to have arthritis—Quindt arthritis—I sat by his bed and took over Blaskorken's side." She stretched, crossed her arms over her head, and enjoyed the luxury of staying in bed and being taken care of.

This time Joachim also asked about his father. He was thinking of writing about him. "I'm going to go looking for clues. I'm sure some people must have notes of some sort."

"Martha Riepe," Maximiliane said. "Maybe his sister Ruth in Munich."

"And what do you know about him?"

"He thought I was a Pomeranian goose. He was right; I never looked beyond Pomerania. Actually I never looked beyond Poenichen."

"I admire his strength."

"He was not strong. He was susceptible to someone who was stronger. He was seduced by power."

"I could call the book *The Long Way Around to Meet My Father*," Joachim said.

It would be ten years from this conversation before he published the book, under a different title—*Approaches to My Father*. The ivory box that had stood on the mantel on Poenichen, in which as a child Maximiliane kept the few testaments to her own father's life, and which Joachim cherished later, served as the starting point for his collection of traces.

Before leaving, Maximiliane asked her son two questions—whether he was considering taking out Swedish citizenship, and whether he wanted to marry Stina—questions that were related in cause and effect. He answered, "I'm still uncertain." If it would have given him Swedish citizenship into the bargain, he would not have hesitated to marry Stina.

"Is she faithful to you, by the way?" Maximiliane asked, remembering Stina's behavior with the television director.

"No," Joachim replied.

"And what do you do about it?"

"I suffer."

"Is that your only contribution to solving the problem?"

"Now and then it helps me write a line or two."

Maximiliane had brought back an erratic rock the size of a baby's head. Now she carried it along the maple-flanked avenue of the cemetery in Marburg. Because it had been a long time since she had visited there, she had to search for Golo's grave, the heavy weight in her arms. Finally she found the Kippenberg grave, read the inscription, stopped to breathe deeply, and then located her son's grave. She laid the rock on it. In the time that had passed since she had been there last, grass had been sown; Golo now lay "under the greensward," no longer under a bed of flowers.

The cemetery custodian surprised her in the act of putting down the stone. He pointed out that it was forbidden to erect a marker without authorization and that she would have to procure a permit. Maximiliane stared first at him, then at the heavy rock. There was too much that cried out for explanation; unable to decide on an answer, she prepared to lift the stone again. But, exhausted, she ended by crouching near it. The attendant tried to explain to her that a verbal request was sufficient, but even verbal requests were too much for her. She rose with difficulty and left.

Six months after her return from Sweden, Maximiliane watched a forty-five-minute television show called "Back on Their High Horses," which addressed itself to the question, "What has become of the descendants of the old nobility from the German East?" The third example: scenes from Dalarna. Joachim Quint, heir to the manorial estate of Baron von Quindt on Poenichen in Pomerania, living in retirement in the Swedish forests, once more on an inherited estate—though its size, no more than forty thousand square miles, was never mentioned. He was shown fishing, mowing the grass with a scythe, and painting a wooden hut. Instead of Pomeranian home-brewed brandy, he enjoyed aquavit, the report claimed, and the commentator went on to explain that his Swedish girl friend was in Stockholm earning the money required for his style of living.

Of the three days of filming, less than five minutes remained; the scene in which Joachim, as Mose Quint, read a poem was considered irrelevant to the topic and was cut. But the program did feature her statement about the Poenichen Pâté of Wild Game, manufactured in Holstein so many years after being praised by Bismarck.

21

Maximiliane did not stay to participate in her downfall at the National Organization for the Care of German War Graves. She handed in her resignation, and for several years she lived, as she put it, "without fixed abode."

When people asked her, "Don't you have to be registered somewhere?" she always answered, "I never stopped being registered in my native village." Pomeranian willfulness.

By this time the words *refugee* and *expellees from the homelands* had almost entirely disappeared from political statements, recurring only on the occasions of the continuing Pomeranian, East Prussian, and Silesian Days and in the newspaper items about them. The only time the words were taken seriously was on résumés and tax forms—purely private concerns. The end of the Cold War was in sight, détente with the East. Maximiliane seemed to be the last of the refugees.

It was often said that the energy of the many millions of willing and unpaid workers, the East Germans who had been expelled from their homes, was one of the causes of the German economic miracle. Not much of the credit could go to Maximiliane. Though she had set up her fish-fry stand even before the currency reform, she had long since made it over to Lenchen Priebe. True, she had won Edda, the most competent of the

Quints, for the German economy. But her own contribution to the pâté factory was limited to the recipe, a few ideas, and the seed money from the equalization-of-burdens payment. Then she retired.

Nor was she a useful member of the consumer society. If you asked her, "What exactly do you live on," she answered, "On whatever I don't spend." Admittedly, one or another small legacy dropped into her lap from time to time to fatten her coffers; Dr. Green had died in California and had remembered her in his will. Instead of "We don't need that," she now said, "I don't need that."

The only child from Poenichen had now become an only woman.

She sublet her apartment in Kassel—furnished—to one of her former co-workers, a Frau Sand; what she needed, and it wasn't much, she tossed into her "wagon."

On the evening before her departure she paid a last visit to the Fredells, who had built a bungalow on a wooded hillside with a view of the Kassel Basin. The oldest of their sons was an officer candidate in the federal army, the other was studying law, both to their father's great satisfaction.

"My sons are making tracks," he said, presumably meaning that they were following in *his* tracks. Every time he said "my sons," his wife looked at him strangely.

They sat in the large living room. Herr von Fredell filled their glasses. "We had hoped—I'm speaking for Bella as well—that you'd settle in Kassel for good."

Maximiliane thanked him with a smile.

Herr von Fredell asked about Viktoria.

"She's started to study political science."

"Where does she get her interest in politics?" Herr von Fredell asked. "It's highly unusual for a girl. If Joachim had gone in for politics, perhaps even gone into the state department, that would have been understandable."

"I assume she got it from my grandfather. Everything is passed on, but not always to the right person."

"Mightn't she have inherited it from her father?" Frau von Fredell proposed.

Maximiliane looked at her friend in surprise. "I never thought of him like that."

"You hardly ever think about him at all."

"At our wedding, my grandfather called him 'a fool in Hitler.' " Maximiliane considered this a sufficient reply. It was not the first time people had obliquely criticized her for not having dealt adequately with National Socialism and its consequences. In earlier years, the thought had invariably put her to sleep, and she had answered, "Later." Later she did think about "Viktor and the consequences." By now she no longer felt the need to think at all.

"I've lived it to the end," she added, turning to her friend. Bella understood. Herr von Fredell looked at her questioningly. But as far as Maximiliane was concerned, her declaration brought the subject to a close. She steered the conversation back to Viktoria. "She's been at the university for almost six years."

"She's got to finish sometime," Herr von Fredell reasoned. "She can't continue going to school forever. What exactly does she have in mind?"

"Whatever she studies, she does it to prove to me that I made a lot of mistakes in bringing her up. Lately she has been including 'society' in her arguments."

"You seem to take it very lightly."

"Perhaps she's 'making tracks'? Has she decided to follow my tracks? I don't know where I'm going either."

This seemed the signal for her departure. She rose. "It's time. I want to get an early start in the morning."

The Fredells walked her to the gate. Herr von Fredell sketched a kiss on the hand; he had adapted his manners to the present day. "Have a wonderful trip." He asked if she was not afraid of the long drive.

"I'll take my time and look around. I haven't seen much of the world."

"I envy you a little bit," Frau von Fredell said, hugging her friend and simultaneously looking at the heavily loaded car and the road stretching away from them.

"I envy *you* a little bit," Maximiliane said in her turn, indicating the spacious house, the autumnal garden, the man of the house at the gate. The two old schoolfriends smiled at each other.

"Now I shall satisfy my grandfather's thwarted longings for travel," said Maximiliane as she got into the car.

"You've profited from Viktoria's psychology courses," Frau von Fredell noted.

"I find that I'm constantly learning." Maximiliane slammed the car door, started the engine, and did not look back. She did not even wave as the Fredells expected her to. It was never her way to look back.

Once more she drove westward—more precisely, southwestward. Her immediate goal was Paris.

A fashion magazine, *Madame*, lay on the back seat. Mirka had sent it to her from Paris. Mirka's picture graced the cover, her sturdy brown hair brushed close to her skull and loose on her back, longer than her skirt. Her odd little face with its flat, prominent cheekbones, without makeup and without expression.

Maximiliane thought about her youngest daughter, who had been written up in a three-page article. She was described as the top model of tomorrow or the day after, a countess from the "high German nobility," born in a romantic castle in the south of Germany, where her mother had laid the little girl on an American sugar sack and followed her contours to cut out the parts for a tunic: "her first encounter with fashion."

Mirka did not seem to have given the writer much information. He characterized her as "silent" and "shrouded in mystery." It was his opinion that she spoke only when she could be sure that her words would be published. He had asked her about her knowledge of languages, essential to any model in top international circles, and she had replied that she was fluent in body language, which was even more important. The writer agreed that her beautiful shoulders and equally beautiful legs had a lot to say—a compliment she had apparently rewarded with one of her rare and therefore "precious" smiles, along with the frank and self-critical remark, "I must have been bow-legged as a child. At night when I went to sleep, my mother used to tie my legs together and swaddle them in a diaper."

Asked if she was good at arithmetic, she grew haughty. "I am never going to have to do arithmetic." Which was followed by the comment, "This young Mirka von Quindt will be good at selling her body."

She was not asked her age, but there was a question about her birth sign. One of the photographs scattered throughout the text showed her in a loden-green hunting outfit. "A Sagittarius with high marksmanship."

"What do you consider the most important invention of our time?"

"Pantyhose. Without it, miniskirts would be unthinkable."

In one of the photographs, she wore a batiste diaper loosely knotted twice around her throat, crest-embroidered. Affectations.

"Where did you get your odd skin-coloring? It's so unusual, one is tempted to call it earth-colored. You can't get that on any beach in the world."

Here, too, Mirka had an answer suitable for publication. "As a baby, I was fed on mare's milk. They say

280

such children grow wild." This remark furnished the caption for still another photograph. When the writer pointed out that Hungarians made yogurt from mare's milk, if he was not mistaken, Mirka answered that yogurt was her principal nourishment; it made her immune. To what, she did not say. Finally she announced that her mother, an officer's widow, had scrimped for years to give her daughter dancing lessons.

"So that's where you learned to control your body so perfectly!" A spontaneous exclamation on the part of the writer, reproduced verbatim.

It was at this point—the mention of "body control"—that Maximiliane's reflections, lasting for hundreds of miles, began. She was probably the only person who knew that there could be no such thing as "perfect control over the body." She remembered an event that had happened about two years earlier. Mirka had called her at the office. "It's urgent, Mama. I need a specific sum of money for a specific purpose."

When no answer was forthcoming—Maximiliane gave a great deal of thought to these two sentences—Mirka continued, "I have to fly to London."

In spite of this information, which for Mirka explained everything, Maximiliane still had no suspicion of what it was all about. About life or death, of course. Mirka, more upset than Maximiliane had ever seen her cool daughter be, went on. "You would have been relieved yourself if you'd had this chance."

Maximiliane understood, not the words, but the tone of voice. The sentence was shouted rather than spoken. She said, "Come."

"Can't we discuss it over the phone?"

"No."

So rarely did Maximiliane demand obedience from her children that she had a credit balance with them. Her "Come" was still valid currency.

She resumed their conversation at the question

Mirka had left unanswered on the phone. "Which one of you did you have in mind? Mose? Yourself? Or Golo by any chance? Shouldn't he have been allowed to live even seventeen years?"

"Don't take everything so literally, Mama."

"If you use words, I'll take them literally."

"But I'm speaking in general."

"There are only individuals—you, for example. Who is the father?"

"One can't really think of him as a father."

Maximiliane waited, and Mirka admitted, "I don't know."

"Cavorting and aborting," Maximiliane said.

"I have to have the money. What about Mount Eyckel?"

This interview had preceded the negotiations with Herr Brandes. As it turned out, their inquiry to him came at an excellent time. We know the rest, at least about Mount Eyckel, from the table talk at the wedding in Holstein.

Maximiliane's thoughts began to wander—from the Abbess Hedwig von Quinten, who was mentioned in a 1342 document as the owner of Mount Eyckel, to her own daughter Mirka, who aborted her baby in London with the help of the money realized from the sale of Eyckel Castle.

It would have been more realistic, Maximiliane thought, if Mirka had named the pill as the most important invention of the present day.

The interview in *Madame* concluded with a question addressed to the readers. "Does the woman of the 1960s and 1970s look like Mirka von Quindt, independent and self-assured, impenetrable and invulnerable, an enemy of the man she wishes to please? Or does today's Eve no longer wish to please?"

Following habit, Maximiliane had driven toward Marburg not on the superhighway but on old Route 3.

282

As she approached the city, she glanced at the familiar sights: the tower of the Elisabethkirche, the ducal castle on the hill, to its left and below it the home of the Heynolds, easy to recognize by its two slate-covered turrets.

She decided against stopping in at the "Grillroom" because Lenchen Priebe was likely to regard an unannounced visit as a way of checking up on her. On the other hand, she would feel slighted if she found out that Maximiliane had not looked her up. The friendship forged during hard times had reverted to a relationship of dependency. Differences had suddenly become noticeable again; to call each other by their first names, as during childhood, did no good. Neither did Maximiliane's assurance, "It's your place now, Lenchen." What remained was the five percent of the profits to be paid yearly, as stipulated by contract. Maximiliane would have been happy to change the agreement, but Lenchen refused to take charity, as she put it.

Nor did she visit Golo's grave. Without stopping, she drove along the Lahn River. But she could see the cemetery along the slope, beautiful in its autumn colors. She had made up her mind to visit a different cemetery. She kept on driving along Route 3, where the trees lining the road had long since been cut down. It was no longer possible to make out the spot where Golo had lost his life.

One glance to the right at the wooded slope and the place under the beeches where what she called her "first encounter" with the Rhinelander had happened. Martin Valentin appeared in her dreams more frequently than in her thoughts.

She remembered a quotation from one of Viktoria's Mother's Day letters, which were always dispatched dutifully: "Raising a child is a matter of example and love." A sentence from Pestalozzi, which modern psychology had adopted and which until now Maximiliane had repressed, just as she had other unerring statements from Viktoria.

Maximiliane had never stinted her children when it came to mother love, but neither had she ever set them a good example in the ordinary sense. Her lack of instinct where men were concerned was close to defenselessness. It must be noted in extenuation that she had married her first husband to save Poenichen from the worst measures of the National Socialist dictatorship. Meant to serve the purpose of allowing her to spend her life on Poenichen, he himself had contributed to the fate that made her leave it. There is an explanation for all subsequent "encounters" as well—and there had been more of them than have been mentioned here. In the past two decades men had been scarce, and since she honored the sixth commandment, her choice was even more limited. She needed warmth; she had found it at least temporarily in the arms of various men and had passed it on to her children, which though not exemplary was a matter of creature comfort and necessity, and therefore the right thing for the children as well.

Maximiliane was approaching Giessen, where she could pick up the superhighway. Her thoughts returned to Mirka, the cellar child, conceived in an air-raid shelter in a place whose name she never knew, somewhere on the other side of the Oder. *"Nyet plakatye"*—"Don't cry." An admonition spoken by a nameless soldier of the Red Army at the crucial moment, taken to heart by Maximiliane and passed on to the child, who rarely cried but also seldom laughed. Today, if only for photographers, she smiled. Mirka, this child of God, who did little harm and wasn't of much use, who beautified the world; an unwanted child, a burden Maximiliane had taken on herself as she took on all burdens, raised as a "posthumous child" for all legal purposes, independent at an early age. Whatever Mirka owned she stuffed into

284

a bag she called "the dog"; always someone turned up who would take care of her, whom she ran away from— or rather, whom she left at her own alluring pace. She did not let herself be captured; she accepted presents, but she was not for sale. She was attached to nothing and no one. Not a dancer but a model.

As it turned out, Dr. Green had been right in this prediction as well.

"Are you going to keep up this mystery about where we're going?" Mirka asked. "Fifty kilometers more, and we're in Lille."

"The place is called Sailly-sur-la-Lys," Maximiliane answered.

"And what business would we have there?"

"We're going to visit a German military cemetery."

"A war-graves junket! I thought you quit your job with the war graves."

"I'll explain when we get there."

Mirka asked no further questions; she had never been given to curiosity. Patient and silent, she sat beside her equally silent mother. No swarm of crows rising from the freshly plowed fields aroused her attention. The landscape grew increasingly monotonous. Maximiliane missed the turnoff to Armentière, and in order to check the map she turned into a field path. From the glove compartment she took a memo pad with the precise sketch of the location of the cemetery, which she had made months ago at her office. "Just off Route Nationale 345, one kilometer from the center of the village. The Lys is a tributary of the Schelde."

She turned off the engine, raised her eyes, and in the distance saw a wooded river basin. Suddenly she listened hard; rolling down the car window, she gripped Mirka's arm. A horn rang out. A *trompe de chasse!*

"Off to the hunt!" she said, excited, sinking back in the seat, her hands firm on the steering wheel. A pack of dogs crossed the path, horsemen close behind them. For a few long moments she succeeded in returning to Poenichen and to the man who used to blow the old French hunting calls.

"All over," she said at last.

"Did you see the photograph in *Madame?*" Mirka asked. "The hunting outfit is from Bogner, exclusive."

Maximiliane started the car and put it in reverse. She did not notice the shallow ditch separating the path from the field. The left rear wheel slipped, the car stuck, and the wheels churned in the wet, clayey soil. Maximiliane had had lots of practice in driving along field paths, so she knew that a few twigs placed under the wheels would allow them to get traction.

"Come with me," she said to Mirka, pointing at the little wood. "We'll get some branches."

"Don't bother, Mama. I've got a better way." Mirka got out of the car, went to the road, and waved. It only took three cars before one stopped. The driver, a man in his fifties, elegant and clearly well-to-do, was immediately willing to serve as horsepower. He pulled the ladies' car from the ditch. On a visiting card he wrote his Paris telephone number. "Do call me sometime," he said to Mirka. She dropped the card in her purse.

"You have to let people help you, Mama," she said when they were alone again. "You always want to do everything yourself."

They reached Sailly-sur-la-Lys just before noon. The streets were empty, and it was raining. Maximiliane parked the car near a church, asked a child the way to the cemetery, and was directed to the local graveyard. Turning back, she asked again, this time adding, *"Pour les soldats."* The child pointed to a distant clump of trees. A few moments later Maximiliane and Mirka stood in the pouring rain in the English military cemetery of the Second World War.

They drove back to the village once more and decided to stop at a café. They ordered *café au lait,* and Maximiliane asked the owner about the cemetery where the German soldiers were buried. "First World War," she stressed.

The owner called to a man who was sitting at the bar sipping red wine, *"Clientèle, Louis."*

Soon Louis Seguin—amputee, invalid, and veteran of the First World War, in charge of maintenance at the German military cemetery—joined them in their car. He was friendly and talkative, and he complained that few people came to visit. He asked about the name; he knew the names of most of the dead. *"Le baron?"*

For twenty years, he explained during the short drive, he had been working at the German military cemetery, and no one had ever come from the family of Baron Quindt. He mowed the grass, he trimmed the hedges. For whom? Of course it had been a long time, and most of the widows were dead themselves, but surely the children were still alive! He counted off the decades on the fingers of his left hand. *"Alors,* 1918, 1928, 1938, 1948, 1958, 1967. *Mon Dieu!* How time flies! Almost fifty years!"

They had arrived at the entrance gate to the cemetery. *"Voilà."*

Maximiliane stopped the car, and they got out. The rain had abated. The custodian pointed his cane at a row of trees; the firewall of a house with a rusty metal sign advertising Cinzano glimmered through branches where black birds crouched. He said, "Poplars," then he said, "Crows," then he pointed to a few linden trees and said their name, then he pointed to a hedge and said, "Whitethorn." Maximiliane was not familiar with the French names, but she recognized the trees and the bushes even though they were bare.

Why hadn't the ladies come during the summer, Monsieur Seguin mourned, or in spring? When the hedge was in bloom and the iris blossoms stood tall?

He fetched the graves-registration list from the righthand sandstone pillar next to the gate, but he put it back at once. In this instance he had no need of a list! His head held the numbers and names of almost every grave. *"Monsieur le Baron* is number 3412."

He pointed across the rows of graves and addressed Mirka, who stood by unimpressed. "A whole city! Young men, all of them! *Monsieur le baron* has a corner plot, a good location."

He hobbled on ahead through the grass; there were no paths. At the tall cross in the center, which towered over the cemetery, he stopped and pointed at the inscription: "Here rest the German soldiers." On the other side the same in French: "Ici reposent des soldats allemands." He told them the number of inhabitants in his city of the dead—5,496. But each had a grave of his own, he said. In his cemetery there were no mass graves. Each one had a little cross, all of them alike.

He hurried on, came to a sudden stop, took off his cap, and pointed to a cross. *"Ici."*

As he had said, it was number 3412. Baron Achim von Quindt. Lieutenant. His unit and the date of death. November 6, 1918. His birth date was not given.

Lowering his voice, the custodian asked, *"Le père?"* and pointed to Maximiliane. She nodded. He pointed to Mirka. *"Le grandpère?"* Maximiliane nodded again and said to Mirka, "In Poenichen there is an erratic rock in his memory in the place where the other Quindts are buried."

The custodian retired. He would leave the ladies alone, he said, but first he inquired whether he should provide some decoration for the grave. Maximiliane told him no.

Should they need him, he would be waiting by the car; he had trouble standing for long. Like Rector Kressmann at Pomerania Day in Kassel, he knocked his cane against his wooden leg.

288

"The first Quindt to lie in a row of graves," Maximiliane remarked when she and Mirka were alone. "Until now I always thought Golo was the first." Chewing her nails, she gazed thoughtfully along the line of crosses. Diagonals formed at the intersections, and the metal signs gleamed in the damp.

"Ranks tightly closed," Maximiliane continued with a trace of bitterness and irony. Mirka looked at her, puzzled.

"A line from the Horst Wessel song," Maximiliane explained. When Mirka still did not understand what she meant, she added, "The national anthem of the Third Reich."

Mirka was unable to follow her mother's train of thought; she had never been interested in history. Friendly but indifferent, she asked, "How old was he when he died?"

"I don't even know his birth date. I assume barely more than twenty."

"A twenty-year-old grandfather," Mirka said, amused. "I'm older now than he ever got to be." She did not seem to consider this a cause for grief. "Where is my other grandfather buried?" she asked. Thoughtful now, she added immediately, "My father doesn't have a grave at all."

"And just maybe your father is still alive." Maximiliane hesitated only a fraction of a second before she spoke.

Mirka looked at her in surprise. "What do you mean?"

"I knew your father hardly any better than I knew your grandfather." Maximiliane pointed to the grave. "I saw him three times. He was a soldier in the Soviet army. He was advancing on Berlin, and I was in flight to Berlin. He came from Lake Balkhash, and he looked like all Kirghiz look. It's him you have to thank for your looks and your success."

"Forcible rape?" Mirka might have been talking about the weather.

"It didn't take a lot of force. I was afraid. And besides, I had four babies."

The hour of truth, its significance barely grasped by Mirka, took place in a German military cemetery. Why? Why did Maximiliane consider it necessary, at this time and in this place, to enlighten Mirka about her antecedents? The explanation of Edda's illegitimate birth had happened against Maximiliane's will, and she had, as best she could, annulled it. Why wasn't she ever consistent? Did she want to destroy the legend Mirka was spreading about her noble descent? Did she want to make her revelation at a fateful spot, her own father as witness, at a place where the pointlessness of xenophobia was just as clear as the pointlessness of class differences? Had she intended to tell her daughter in this place that she descended from the nobility—and by no means the "high nobility," as the article had it—on only one side and that her father was a simple Russian soldier?

"Lake Balkhash?" Mirka broke the silence. "Where is that?"

"In the interior of Asia. In the Kirghiz steppe."

Mirka asked for no other facts. Her mother could not have supplied them if she had.

They started on their way back and soon arrived at the gate. Maximiliane closed it behind her, recognizing the five crosses in the latticework, the emblem of the National Association for the Care of German War Graves, for which she had worked for years. Not until this moment was she able to put an end to that chapter.

When they got into the car, the custodian held the doors for them—first for Mirka and then for Maximiliane. He begged the ladies to pray for his sick wife and poor children. Maximiliane, ignorant of local customs, inquired sympathetically about the nature of the illness.

290

Mirka reached into her pocket and handed over the expected tip.

Their drive back to Paris was accomplished in almost total silence.

It was not difficult for Mirka to trade in one unknown father for another. A Kirghiz fitted nicely into her life. Only a few days after their excursion to Sailly-sur-la-Lys she had her hair cut short so that the Kirghiz shape of her skull could be shown off more openly. She incorporated the unknown Kirghiz into her legend. A German countess her mother, a Kirghiz her father. "He was descended from Genghis Khan," a subsequent article about Mirka von Quindt explained.

Edda was sitting under the dryer in the beauty parlor in Eutin, rapidly leafing through some magazines. She almost didn't recognize her sister Mirka: her hair was short as matchsticks, while in Holstein women were still wearing beehives; her skirts—which in Holstein were still being worn a handsbreadth above the knee—ended at her ankles. And then she read the gossip column: "Her father a Kirghiz, her mother a member of the German high nobility."

Edda's first thought was, How will the Lübeck Quintens take the news? She pushed aside the glorious legend; what remained was the rape. After more than twenty years a taint shadowed the name of the Quindt family. No sympathy, no interest in the exotic. She herself was from Berlin-Pankow. Even the brief marriage between her mother and the shady Herr Valentin, of which her in-laws had since learned, had aroused clear alienation on the part of the Quintens. Edda's second thought was, Then Mirka and I aren't related at all. But this satisfaction was of no use to her because she could share it with no one. She decided against inviting her mother to the christening of the child she was expecting in April.

22

Life often follows literature closely, missing not a single cliché.

Maximiliane had an affair with an artist—or more precisely, with a painter living in Paris. Now, the probability of falling in love with an artist is higher in Paris than anywhere else in the world, especially if you are living in a hotel in the Latin Quarter. Mirka had recommended the place to her mother with the words "You'll be right in the heart of Paris." Having opened the window on the rue de la Huchette and smelled the odors rising from the Chinese, Serbian, and Croatian restaurants, Maximiliane had corrected her daughter. "At the stomach of Paris, you mean. But the stomach isn't far from the heart."

Though her plan to make a few changes in her daughter Mirka had failed, she extended her stay in Paris from the original few days to many months, with a few side trips. The reason was the painter.

The usual course of a woman's life—infant, girl, bride, wife, mother, grandmother, widow—is often disturbed, but in the case of Maximiliane Quint it was turned completely upside down. Maximiliane was a grandmother before she had been a lover. This she became at last, in her fiftieth year. The whole episode did not fit neatly into the pattern of her life; she was already too old to believe in miracles. Her love would have to get along without miracles. Nevertheless, for weeks the departure times of the Metro were determined not by the timetable but by her needs; thunderstorms did not break over Argenteuil, where Maximiliane and the painter happened to be, but over Saint-Denis. . . .

On the morning of November 1, a bright, belated summer day, Maximiliane had set out to tour the Cathedral of Notre-Dame, guidebook in hand and Mirka's advice in her head. Hardly had she crossed the Seine than she was caught up in the stream of churchgoers. She surrendered herself to it and was carried into the half-filled nave.

Already she was in a cheerful mood, hearing the organ, the nuns' antiphonal chant. She knelt like the others, rose like the others, sat down, knelt again, followed the rising and waning ripples that began at the high altar, quivered through the nave, and ended at the portals. Unexpectedly a sideways movement—hands stretching across the pews, reaching out to her—disconcerted her. In Pomerania one did not hold out one's hand to a stranger.

The next human wave carried her outside through the south portal. She walked down the steps to the Seine, faithful to the guidebook's instructions, casting a glance at the fishermen and booksellers, at the Palais de Justice and the Hotel-Dieu.

Paris as it was supposed to be.

Maximiliane returned to the Latin Quarter to lunch at the Jade de Montagne on the boulevard Saint-Michel, as Mirka had recommended. She found an empty seat but had to wait a long time for service. Because of the holiday, the restaurant was crowded. Still in a happy frame of mind, she looked around at leisure, observing the other diners' faces, finally also taking in the paintings on the walls, all of which seemed to have been done by the same artist. She had had little practice in looking at and evaluating paintings; her taste was both unspoiled and untrained. Unable to determine what the pictures were meant to represent, she left her seat, went up to them, and studied them intently until the waiter came to take her order. There were some difficulties in communication, which a man of about forty at a nearby table smoothed over.

When the waiter had gone, the man asked her in German with a slight Rhenish accent that should have made her cautious, "Do you like my pictures?"

No subterfuges this time. This love took the direct path of art.

Maximiliane answered with a question of her own. "Why do you add to the world's ugliness? Why don't you make the world more beautiful?"

The man smiled at her naive question, picked up his chair, and moved it closer to Maximiliane's table. Then he told her that in recent decades the task of art had changed, and he explained his pictures to her: protests against the environment. Since Maximiliane did not know the artists he modeled himself on, such as Bacon and Wunderlich, his pictures had the advantage of originality for her.

"Does the concept 'fantastic realism,' or better yet, 'surrealism,' mean anything to you?" he asked.

Maximiliane raised her shoulders in a gesture of total ignorance.

Before the man could continue with his explications, the waiter brought her soup. Maximiliane reached for her spoon, looked at the man with her still-potent eyes, and said, "The fantastic realism of onion soup."

The man introduced himself; he even handed her his card. *Ossian Schiff, peintre;* a sketch of a stylized sailboat under the name, a Paris address in the same arondissement. He mentioned that the owner of the café, whom he had known for years, took his pictures in payment—ten meals per painting.

"That's how I keep my head above water. On holidays like today, I even enjoy it."

He was not blessed with material goods, he continued; he was the fifth child of a village schoolmaster near Aachen. Given the first name his father had wished on him, he said with a laugh, he had no choice but to become something unusual, such as an artist.

"Only pigs save," he said, waved at the waiter, and ordered another half-liter of red wine, this time paying cash. He turned back to Maximiliane. "The Germans always want to know what something means, the French see only the painting."

Then he changed the subject from art to art dealing. It took Maximiliane a while to understand; then she quickly put a stop to the conversation by saying, "I don't even own a wall where I could hang a picture."

The painter's interest in his companion diminished: a tourist who would be content with buying one or two cheap colored prints of Paris from the bookstalls along the Seine. He turned to the lamb chop on his plate.

But by now Maximiliane's interest had been whetted. For some years her dealings with men had been limited to the dead of two world wars, and now she was sitting across the table from a live one at last. His appearance was quite in keeping with the common image of a Parisian painter: dark-haired, bearded, a little pale, carelessly dressed, but strong and clearly full of vitality.

She herself looked quite healthy at this time. In a fifty-year-old woman, healthy looks replace beauty, though hers was a kind of beauty that had never been striking. The observer only became aware of it after seeing her several times, and then he was impressed. Ossian Schiff, his own paintings before his eyes, was operating with limited perception. Only later would he say, "You are the same inside and out."

At their second meeting, which took place three

days later in the same restaurant and was initiated by Maximiliane, he did not recognize her. This time it was she who pulled her chair over to his table.

"I dreamed about you," she said reproachfully. "You were running through the halls of the Louvre holding a big stamp in your hand, a sulfur-yellow atomic mushroom, and you stamped all the pictures with it. *The Raft of the Medusa.* Even the *Mona Lisa.*"

"What a pity, I should have thought of it myself," said Ossian Schiff. "All those holy pictures must be destroyed." He pulled out a pencil, picked up his paper napkin, and with a few strokes drew Leonardo's *Mona Lisa,* adding an atomic mushroom in the upper lefthand corner.

"The upper left." Maximiliane confirmed the co-incidence of dream and reality.

When they had finished the main course, Ossian Schiff asked her permission to treat her to an ice-cream dessert, the chef's specialty.

"When I was twelve, raspberry ice cream would have been bliss," Maximiliane said. "When you get close to fifty, a hot-water bottle has the same effect."

The painter looked at her quizzically. He wondered whether her remark was simply a reference to the cool-ness of the restaurant. Her next statement—that she would have to be leaving because her car was parked in a no-parking zone—informed him that she owned a car, so she could not be entirely without means. Without money, Paris is only a village—an observation that has been made often enough.

His experiences with young women had been such as to make him cognizant of the advantages—or at least some of the advantages; he was not aware of all of them yet—of an older woman. Probably calculation first; only then affection.

"Would you like to see my studio?" he asked.

296

The question came easily, the answer without hesitation. "If it's warm."

"No woman has ever been cold with me," Ossian Schiff declared, explaining that he lived alone. "As an artist, I'm not in a position to support a wife."

"I have all the support I need," Maximiliane countered.

When they were in the narrow hall of his apartment, Ossian Schiff showed her the studio window, pointing out that it gave a view of the Seine; and when Maximiliane vainly tried to see the river, he added what he always added. "If there weren't three rows of houses between."

His first act was to remove the chain of amber beads from around her neck. "I don't like to see women in chains."

He too wore a chain around his neck, but a capsule dangled from it. "Potassium cyanide," he explained. "A sufficient amount. It makes living easier. This way life is a voluntary act."

He was surprised that his announcement failed in its intended effect. But at the end of the war and in the months just following, Maximiliane had seen many of these lockets holding cyanide, and she had learned that the constant body temperature decomposed the chemicals, rendering them ineffective. She kept her knowledge from him, then and later.

His moods changed rapidly. Maximiliane was a stranger to mood swings. She had been raised by her grandmother according to the rule "A woman never shows her feelings."

Cheerful one moment, the next Ossian Schiff abruptly turned to the window, looked down, and said, "I carry my death date on my back. Everybody can see it except me."

"I can't see it," Maximiliane answered. She took him by the arm, turned him around, and with a look at the wide bed expressed her desire as freely and easily as men have always done. She stood before him a little provocatively, her hands on her hips, her eyes restless, her breasts, which had nurtured four children, prominent.

If in her youth Maximiliane had been instinctively carnal, she was so no longer; she enjoyed lying in a man's arms, but it was no longer compulsive. No more preventive measures either—she no longer needed to fear pregnancy. She had stopped being a breeding ground.

She could still have left the city, and perhaps she should have. Paris and Maximiliane were not suited to each other. All the people talked too much and too fast, so that she understood next to nothing: human sounds, which she absorbed along with all the other sounds of the metropolis. She did not care for the crumbly croissants that seemed to delight all the other tourists—bread that ran away from you! She gathered up the crumbs with her hands and threw them to the pigeons. Croissants made her hungry for coarse black bread. Nor did she ever get used to the sign on the house next to her hotel: "*Ici* . . ." In 1942 a Frenchman had been shot on the spot by the German occupying powers.

At night when she awoke she heard the rumbling of the Metro deep underground, heard the bells of Notre-Dame ring out the hours, drowsily mumbled to herself, "What are you doing here? You come from a village in Pomerania." She fell back asleep and slept out her midnight realizations. Several times a day she took refuge under the three broad chestnut trees in the grounds of Saint Séverin church. There she sat on one of the pillar socles—a peaceful place.

But one night she had a dream. She was leaning over a miniature scale model of Paris, everything easy to recognize: the Seine, the boulevards, Sacré-Coeur, the Madeleine, and the Eiffel Tower. The only person rushing through the canyons of the streets was the man she had come to call Ossian. Tearing up the last plane trees and chestnuts, he threw them aside, raised a rampart of dead wood around the city, sanitized Paris against all nature until it was made up entirely of stone.

Maximiliane awoke in fear and exhaustion. But later she found the three chestnut trees still in place, though bare and sickly. She decided to leave before even these trees were cut down.

That same night the man said, "I need you." And he said, "What dreams you have. You're very creative."

At first Maximiliane must have stimulated him. Later she calmed him. She lived by his side, made few demands, and was content to come second—his work came first. She was one of those women who willingly let themselves be harnessed to a stranger's cart—not in order to be pulled, but in order to pull it.

"You're going to bring me luck," Ossian Schiff said the same night. "You're helping me achieve a breakthrough."

It was high time for an artistic breakthrough. He was already in his forties, too old for an unknown artist—too young, on the other hand, to be Maximiliane's lover.

Mirka, who was then living in Meudon with a photographer old enough to be her father, whispered to her mother the first time she met Schiff, "He's much too young for you, Mama."

Edda, who had found out from Mirka, wrote, "I've already had to tell my family that my sister is the daughter of a Russian soldier. Do you expect me to have to tell them that my mother is living with a painter ten years younger than she is?"

Edda seemed to expect her mother to declare immediate renunciation. Everyone seemed to expect renunciation from a widow with four grown children. These were the same people, Maximiliane noted by the way, who also expected renunciation of the former German eastern provinces in the "matter of eastern policy." Renunciation of something that did not belong to them, had never belonged to them, and therefore was no loss to them.

"Gonna take my heart back home." Ansel Quint, who was a doctor in Thuringia, had learned to play the jazz trumpet by listening to that tune the first winter after the war, on Mount Eyckel. And now a rock band was playing it in Saint-Germain-des-Prés, where Maximiliane and Ossian Schiff sat in a subterranean bar. Maximiliane hummed along, and her eyes began to glow, as always when she remembered. She began to tell stories, first about the castle, then about Poenichen.

Ossian Schiff was an attentive listener. When she stopped, he commanded, "Look at me" or "Go on" and finally "Come."

He handed the waiter some money and pulled Maximiliane up the cellar steps through the streets to his studio. There he said, "Be quiet" and "Sit down." When he was finished with his preparations, he said, "Go on telling me about this place, Poenichen."

He drew a circle on a block of paper and filled it with what he heard; he sketched and laid on watercolors without stopping, without pause. First a child's eyes, brown as beer, dark-rimmed, eyes that had seen nothing. Then he put in blue sprinkles, like lakes. He painted with a magnifying glass, made pictures like miniatures, still lives, medallions. It was not clear which of them was more exhausted in the end, the painter or his model—the Scheherezade.

In the days that followed, he continued to paint new round pictures, always larger, filling the "cherry-saucer-aggie eyes" with whatever they had seen during their first twenty-five years of life: Pomeranian lakes and pine forests, roads, reed-covered shores, flights of cranes, moraines, snowstorms, thaw. Once more Maximiliane made the wagon train trudge through the snowy plains of the East: horses, wagons, people, dogs, like silhouettes; red fire-glow in the sky, first in the east, at the right of the painting, then coloring the whole sky.

Words turned into pictures. Ossian Schiff made them visible, made them invisible again.

In the weeks that followed he painted ever new irises, pictures round as apples. In high spirits he ornamented them with blossoms and stems. He painted eyes enlarged tenfold, a hundredfold. Another time he put ten eyes side by side and in rows, whole sequences of pictures on one sheet, no longer in watercolors but on wood or canvas in acrylics, quick-drying, indelible. "You can do your laundry on them as if they were a washboard," he said to Maximiliane. But without his noticing, she had left.

She had been overcome—it was a morning in March—by a sudden longing for larks. At the Metro stop she bought a ticket to Clichy, got out at the last station, and running rather than walking, followed a paved road past gas stations and repair shops until she came to the first field path—and truly: larks rose, hung on the blue air, and sang. Maximiliane stopped, took a deep breath, unbuttoned her coat, and did not return until it was almost night.

"I went to the country," she told Ossian Schiff, but he did not expect an explanation; he was busy putting golden highlights into the pictures.

The day came when he packed all the paintings into a portfolio and said once again, "Come." They went to see a gallery owner in the rue des Petits-Champs, not far from the Louvre. Schiff had known David Mayer-Laboillet for a long time, but the dealer had not accorded him any recognition. Now he acknowledged the originality of the new pictures. Pop art was just coming into fashion, and here it was, mixed with fantastical surrealism. The pictures could be put in a category; they did not have to be turned back into words. Nothing had to be explained to Monsieur Mayer-Laboillet. He did not need picture stories, just pictures.

The exhibition was to open as early as the beginning of April. When Maximiliane addressed the envelopes for the invitations, she included Mirka, who had just come back from being photographed in Morocco in the upcoming fall fashions: "Fur Under a Desert Sun." Mirka held out the prospect of bringing along two or three wealthy buyers and asked for additional invitations. She also insisted that her mother dress according to the occasion. She made a date to meet her in a fancy shop on the rue de Rivoli.

Holding her shoulders stiffly, pressing her slightly rickety knees together like a twelve-year-old, Maximiliane stood before the mirror; as always, just a little too hefty.

"It's not the fault of the dress," Mirka noted objectively. "Don't look so unhappy."

"I don't just look unhappy, I am unhappy." Maximiliane tried to make room for her shoulders in what Mirka called "the little two-piece."

While Maximiliane was changing, Mirka examined her mother's body coldly, comparing it just as coldly with her own. She drew her conclusions. "You get prettier the more clothes you take off; it's just the opposite with me."

The purchase took several hours. Finally, in the fourth shop, they found an original "Salzburg dirndl" that in Mirka's opinion made Maximiliane look "exotic."

"You'll be the high point of the vernissage, Mama."

As it turned out, neither Ossian Schiff nor his paintings—and especially not Maximiliane—was the center of attention. it was Mirka, who had brought along her own reporter; he was the one who realized at once that Mirka's eyes must have served as the model for the

302

pictures on exhibit. "Doves' eyes," he said several times in conversation, and made a note of the phrase.

Ossian Schiff gave a single glance at Mirka's eyes and decided at once: eyes that had seen nothing worth seeing. Then he had his picture taken with her.

In spite of the generously low-cut dirndl dress, Maximiliane was not perceived as a woman, not even as the constant companion and mate of the painter Ossian Schiff. Instead she was noticed as the first buyer. The second and third pictures were acquired by Henri Villemain, the gentleman who had pulled Maximiliane's car from the ditch on their trip to Sailly-sur-la-Lys, and to whom Mirka had had an invitation sent. He had to get all new furnishings anyway, having just separated from his wife. Besides, he had the necessary means; he owned a metals concern that manufactured cooking utensils and canteens for the French army and lately also for NATO.

Eleven pictures in all were sold. Mayer-Laboillet offered Ossian an exclusive contract. The painting cycle *Les Yeux* brought Ossian Schiff, the German painter resident in France, great renown, especially for the novel shape of the pictures. Only three reviews appeared, but that was because on the same evening twenty-four art exhibits opened in Paris. "Ossian Schiff, a mythic name," *Le Figaro* wrote. "It seems made to measure for its bearer. He paints like a magician or an oracle. He paints the past, but he also paints the future: visions. What looks like a 'return to the bucolic' is transmuted into the visionary-dangerous by bombs hovering menacingly close to the 'idylls.' " Another critic, however, mistook the bombs of the Second World War for sexual symbols and spoke of "unmistakable derivation from the new Viennese school."

On the whole Ossian Schiff could be satisfied with his success, but so could Maximiliane: Poenichen had paid off once more. She put the picture, purchased for six hundred new francs, in the same box where she kept the illustrated books about Pomerania, the collections of Pomeranian folk poetry, and the anecdotal histories of Pomerania—the kind of books that expellees from the East were customarily given as birthday and Christmas presents. Included also were a few issues of the periodical published by the Pomeranian organization of expellees. The paper was always forwarded to her but seldom reached her. She was not suited to the role of a subscriber; subscribers stay put in one place. Maximiliane's Pomeraniana made a respectable collection. She pushed the box back under the bed she had been sharing with Ossian Schiff for months.

That same spring students and later workers marched through the streets of Paris. At first these demonstrations seemed to have no other object than spring itself; they were cheerful, not yet a revolution, the intention to overthrow the world order not yet overt. Maximiliane felt physically and mentally swept along; she sensed something of the great breath of history, a new day, but at the same time she was reminded of the stream of refugees. Ossian Schiff became aware of her restlessness. Unused to money in his pocket, he decided, "We're leaving the city. We'll go someplace else, and there you'll tell me about Paris, and I'll paint whatever is reflected in your eyes."

The first sign that one day he would need other models appeared when he took her to see the Medici graves in Florence and looked at the Michelangelo statues not only with the eyes of an artist but also with the eyes of a man. In front of the allegorical figure of Morning, he said in surprise, "But that's a fifty-year-old woman!" Of the opposite figure of Night he noted the same—with the same surprise.

Maximiliane stood by his side; her body had wrinkles in the same places as Michelangelo's statues. She recognized the age of her own body. Schiff looked at her as if she were a piece of art: scrutinizing, evaluating, appraising, and tender. He forgot the moment; Maximiliane never forgot it.

Now of all times, surrounded by groups of people, many of them German tourists, she said, "I would have liked having a child by someone I loved." In that one sentence she summed up the life of a woman. The wish for a child could not be satisfied by grandchildren, whom Edda regularly bore. She often looked with longing at babies carried in their mothers' arms.

The visit to the Medici graves took place on August 8, 1968, Maximiliane's fiftieth birthday. In the morning they had picked up their mail at the post office. Joachim covered several pages with his mother's "Maxims," which he had collected. "In November I like November" and "Don't waste your character on trivialities" and "I have two opinions about everything"—the last reflecting a Quindt-essence.

Viktoria wrote from Paris, "Now that this is the place where the world is changing, you go away! You refuse yourself! I made the concierge give me the key. It took threats of violence, though. Four of us are living in your apartment."

Mirka reported that there had been a weeks-long strike in M. Villemain's factory and that he was in financial difficulties but continued to be generous to her.

A letter from Anna Hieronimi, who did not write often, had been forwarded. "I make you welcome in the circle of fifty-year-olds. By now it's too late to wish a woman happiness." Two sheets closely covered with her small handwriting reported on canning and preserving. "I lose myself entirely in my garden." Finally a remark that captured Maximiliane's attention: Herr Brandes was having Eyckel Castle rebuilt as a hotel.

A letter from the local schoolmaster was forwarded from her address in Kassel. "I'll never forget the day they said in the village, 'The little baron has arrived.' And that was fifty years ago! I was a child myself in those days. Emma, the daughter of Jäckel the carpenter, has been expatriated from Pomerania with her son, and she is still living in Camp Friedland. The boy can barely say a few sentences in German. Now there aren't any of us left in Poenichen."

Maximiliane could not recall the daughter of Jäckel the carpenter. Martha Riepe had stopped writing long ago. Lenchen Priebe wrote only at Christmas.

No word from Edda. Her silence was eloquent. Ossian Schiff had forgotten her birthday, though he did think of it several days later.

Maximiliane traveled through Europe with him for months that turned into more than a year. Whenever she liked a place, she did not always compare it to Poenichen; on this trip there was no need to embrace trees. She translated into action the realization she had attained during the balloon ascent: that it was necessary to throw out ballast in order to become lighter and rise.

The time of space travel had arrived. Spaceships diverted attention from Earth to the universe. The two travelers, sitting in a hotel in Delphi watching television, saw the first human beings take a first step on the moon. Earth had become a blue, shining planet in one of numerous solar systems—something that could be photographed. In Haifa they saw an astronaut move from one capsule to another, and in Istanbul they saw the capsule land in the Pacific.

Maximiliane seemed not in the least astonished by these epochal events in the universe—it was as if she had always known about them. In the middle of the night she threw open the French windows in their hotel room and leaned out, looking over the Bosporus and saying, "I find myself in the universe." Once more she felt the earth turning with her. But Ossian, her companion, was sleeping.

Standing before the Theseum in Athens, she took a deep breath of recognition: "Pomeranian classicism." One of the models for the manor in Poenichen.

Sometimes they spent months on end in one place. Ossian Schiff painted and drew; Maximiliane provided him with materials and nourishment, and she had the finished paintings sent to Paris to M. Mayer-Laboillet, who responded only rarely and with guarded statements.

When they returned to Paris, it became evident that Ossian Schiff had succeeded in a slight breakthrough but not in a major one. The apple or egg shapes of his pictures, at first greeted as a refreshing novelty, were now regarded as mannered. M. Mayer-Laboillet explained that in the intervening time the art market had become even more shaky; styles changed with every fall and spring fashion, and with the general devaluation of the currency, collectors bought pictures as an investment and looked for more famous names.

The cyanide capsule, which had been removed during all the time they were abroad, reappeared. Ossian Schiff seemed permanently displeased that Maximiliane's daughter and her friends had occupied the studio during his absence and had sold a number of his paintings.

During their absence Paris had changed. The revolution was over and had been enshrined in the history books as the "May revolution." Maximiliane felt exotic in the Latin Quarter: pale-skinned, short-haired, too old by thirty years—but without any desire to be young again. Their hair long, their jackets shaggy, the girls wearing long skirts and sad, soft expressions, the students roamed the streets of the quarter, sat smoking on the rim of the fountain on the Place Saint-Michel; from time to time policemen drove up, checked IDs, and looked for drugs; without resisting, the suspects let themselves be stowed in the police car.

A few times during her stay in Paris Maximiliane fulfilled her duties as mother and daughter. Twice she went to Berlin to look up Viktoria, the foolish daughter who always acted and felt neglected and in whose life the wild sixties were reflected more clearly than in the lives of Maximiliane's other children.

Maximiliane arranged her second trip to Berlin to meet her mother at the airport. It had been a certainty in Vera Green's mind from the first day of her emigration that should she survive her husband, she would spend her final years in the city where she was born and raised, the city of her professional and womanly triumphs. A genuine Berliner. But she had left when she and Berlin were both young; now, after an absence of thirty years, both had aged; Berlin divided, herself widowed.

Maximiliane helped her furnish an apartment in the new Opera Quarter. Vera Green would be able to live on her husband's royalties, which continued to pour in. Besides, she intended to have his books published in German, the language in which they had been written. It became clear at once: Vera Green, née von Jadow, Widow von Quindt, lived up to every imaginable ideal of widowhood. She had been less well suited to the roles of wife and mother, and she had never accepted the role of grandmother. Maximiliane's remark that Viktoria was living in Berlin, in a commune, went unacknowledged.

When Joachim was awarded a major literary prize, Maximiliane traveled to Düsseldorf to take part in the festivities. She sat in the front row beside her son and tried to establish contact with him with her elbow while a string quartet played the slow movement of a Haydn quartet.

The principal speaker devoted a few sentences to Mose Quint, along with the other prize recipients. He mentioned that at the age of seven the poet had left the village of Poenichen in Pomerania, destined heir to a great name and a great property; early in life he had come into a literary legacy, the heritage of Oskar Loerke perhaps, or Wilhelm Lehmann. "Who wants to live without the comfort of trees"—a line from a work by an earlier recipient of the same prize—could be applied to Mose Quint as well. Though he belonged to a new generation, he felt an obligation to the previous one. In this case recognition was being given not to an innovator, a revolutionary, but rather to a walker in the woods who had deserted his Swedish forests only to participate in this hour of celebration. A clear upheaval in generations could be discerned in the fact that the prizewinners, though born in the East, were formed by their experiences in the West.

Toward the end of the ceremony Mose Quint read two of his poems. One was based on a line by Gryphius—"Mortals, mortals, cease your versifying. Tomorrow, ah, tomorrow we must be off." The other was one of his Pomeranian Nursery Songs, which, starting with the line "Ladybug, ladybug, fly away home," was a barely concealed accusation against his father, a National Socialist, but did not spare the mothers for having allied themselves with such men. The uneasiness and the palpable restlessness of the audience were rechanneled by the subsequent spirited third movement of the quartet.

At the end of the ceremony, Maximiliane was congratulated on her talented and promising son. She was expected to say a few appreciative words about the building in which the ceremony took place, the new "House of the German East," but she said only, "Now all of the German East can fit into a single building." A maxim which her son Joachim incorporated in his collection.

When she left the Association for the Care of German War Graves, Maximiliane had not waited to be fired; now she did not wait to be fired from her job as a woman. Even Ossian Schiff began to notice the signs of her restlessness. True, he was not familiar with the look Maximiliane's children called "Mama's flight look"; he had never fled, had never seen a refugee wagon train. He simply believed what men believe so readily— that she did not feel equal; he too had heard of Women's Lib, of women's "self-realization," of the idea that they needed a separate existence, independent of men.

This understanding came to him at a moment when Maximiliane said, "I'll just throw a piece of meat in the pan" and he watched her handling meat and pans. An old scene from her Marburg life repeated itself down to the least detail. Recalling all the small, profitable restaurants in the rue de la Huchette and the rue Saint-Jacques, Ossian Schiff said, "Shouldn't we open a bistro together?"

He said "we," but he meant "you." He must have been thinking of his own tenuous existence as a painter and, mindful of the currency devaluation, of a safe investment. "We could call it Maxime or Chez Maximiliane or just Restaurant Allemande, like the Algerian and Korean and Indonesian restaurants. Sauerbraten and dumplings. Roast goose and cabbage. Potato pancakes and applesauce."

Did he want to be rid of her? Did he want to hold on to her? Presumably he wanted both.

"I've always cooked only for those who are hungry; I don't cook for people who are full up," said Maximiliane in one of those rare moments when the Pomeranian baroness broke through.

"We could get rich."

"What I need can't be bought with money."

He stood at the curb, and this time too she did not look back. She disappeared from his life. A runaway.

310

23

When Viktoria went "underground" in Berlin from time to time, she always informed her mother, leaving a telephone number where she could be reached. Later she joined a nine-member commune consisting of students of both sexes as well as one computer programmer and one female bank trainee.

She spent her nights in a slum district in the cellar of a building marked for demolition, where she mimeographed flyers she would distribute the following day to passersby on the streets or to her fellow students in the corridors of the Free University or in the university dining halls. The content of these flyers was not significantly different from that of the flyers Willem Riepe had long ago covertly dispensed on the Alexanderplatz. Willem Riepe, son of the coachman on Poenichen and brother of Martha, had been arrested by the Gestapo and held in Oranienburg concentration camp for five years. He too had wished to change the world, and it had indeed changed. Viktoria was simply detained for three hours in the station house. Her life was never in danger.

"Get the hell out of here and go home," the desk sergeant said; he thought the twenty-five-year-old woman was a fifteen-year-old girl. She still looked as if she were made of glass—though by now the glass had become a little clouded. This time too she ran a temperature and had diarrhea besides, as always when she was excited. To avoid revealing the commune's address, she had given that of her mother in Kassel. This was how Maximiliane came to know about the incident, and she placed the official letter with the missives from the selective-service bureau concerning Joachim's draft.

By nature weak, Viktoria made herself strong for the oppressed and took up the cudgels against the exploiters and the so-called establishment.

When, on one of the first days she spent in the commune, she "turned on" in the company of more experienced pot smokers, the resulting disorientation was not only to her senses and her understanding, but primarily to her stomach; she threw up for hours. In this case—though in few others—she learned from experience. In future she smoked plain cigarettes instead. The old, battered pocketbook she always carried around with her still held the stuffed animal of indeterminate species that Frau Hieronimi had sewn for her out of rags twenty years earlier and that she had played with as a little girl.

When they founded their commune, the members had marched to the nearby river and in a kind of ritual thrown all the room keys into the water. None would ever be alone, no one would be able to retire with one other person, everything would be done jointly. "Sleep with the same guy twice or more, You walk right in the establishment's door," read the hand-lettered sign in the hall. The motto was completely in harmony with Viktoria's theories, but in reality she slept with no one— more precisely, no one slept with her. She was considered a glass angel, though she was not treated like one. For her part, she had fallen among exploiters. It was she who did the shopping, washed the dishes, bore the expenses for most of their communal existence, and thus paid off the debt of having been born into the upper middle class. Thanks to the legacy from her grandmother, she had her own bank account.

In the course of very few years she had protested against the emergency laws and the oppression of blacks in the United States, and had demonstrated for the Black Power movement, for the integration of foreign laborers into the German Federal Republic, against the Shah's visit to Berlin—in the course of which she had been arrested—against the war in Vietnam, and against hunger in Biafra. She had shouted, "Ho,Ho,Ho Chi Minh" and carried placards through the streets: a member, though a weak one, of the extraparliamentary opposition that wished to change society from the ground up.

When Maximiliane was asked about her daughter, she replied, "Tora demonstrates," as if talking about a career. Old Quindt would surely have said, "She'll grow out of it"—an opinion no halfway intelligent person would dare to hold in the 1960s. In this case there was nothing to grow out of. It was too deep-rooted: aggression growing out of neglect and fear.

Viktoria—or, as she was usually called, Tora—delicate, sickly, always at risk, had been more protected as a child than her brothers and sisters and yet had always felt disadvantaged. Presumably meant to be an only child, she had accidentally landed in a family of many children. A "plug person," as her mother put it; when the children had baths, the times were such that two children at a time had to share the tub, and each time Viktoria ended up sitting on the plug while Edda rested in the more comfortable end. In contrast to her younger sister, Mirka, who always occupied the spotlight, Tora stood at the edge. Nature had endowed her with neither charm nor humor. In summer she was menaced by sunburn, in winter by respiratory infections. Instinctively she tried to submerge herself, and yet at the same time she had no talent for any kind of shared living. Her head was rebellious, her body submissive.

That year hundreds of students went to the Frankfurt Book Fair; they marched through the exhibition hall, and they invaded the public lectures to call for the politicization of literature and life. Viktoria had a private demonstration. She walked corridors that were decked with huge blowups of women's bodily parts. On her back and flat chest she wore signs reading, "A woman's body is not a bulletin board"—forced by her message to make a bulletin board of her own body. She aroused more laughter than agreement; a single camera was turned on her—"a fringe apparition in the maelstrom of the fair."

She was in her late twenties when she proclaimed, "Never trust anyone over thirty." She managed to be caught up in every new trend, and often also in turbulence. When it became fashionable to go topless, she appeared as a witness in a trial in criminal court with her chest bared, her hair stringy, her skin too pale, her shoulders hunched. For many years she refused to wear a bra—not for convenience but as a protest. She would presumably have been an easy victim for the feminists if a different trend had not snatched her up first.

For some months she worked as a saleswoman in a department store while living with a student, Udo Ziegler from Ulm, who was studying literature. Both wore their hair equally long, shared their jeans and sweaters, and lived in total community, though once again it was Viktoria who washed the jeans for both of them—granted, not too often. Those changes in society that had not been achieved by force were now—and this trend too came from the United States—to be brought about by gentleness. "Make love, not war." Soon Viktoria was fired from her job for agitating.

She carried the banners "My womb is my own" and "We don't talk about the pill, we take it" to protest against Paragraph 218 of the German Basic Law at a time when no one took the least interest in her womb. She had few occasions to use women's hard-won sexual freedom.

Since every generation is quick to blame the previous one for the deplorable state of the world, Viktoria accused her mother, this time not by letter but face to face.

They met in the bar of the Zoo Railroad Station. Viktoria had refused to go to a bourgeois restaurant. Maximiliane remembered her pleasure when she met her grandfather at the Café Kempinski on his visits to Berlin and he allowed her to bring two of her friends from boarding school. It was difficult, if not impossible, to give Viktoria pleasure.

"Wouldn't you like to take a shower in my hotel?" Maximiliane suggested.

"White men used water and soap to convert the Indians, and in the end they destroyed them" was Viktoria's response.

With one look at her daughter's ragged coat, Maximiliane said, "As long as there is so much real poverty in the world, isn't it arrogance to act poor when you're not? You have money for a new coat."

"Can't you understand that this is my way of expressing solidarity with the oppressed?" Viktoria asked in reply, attaching to her reproach all the complaints she had so long suppressed: against her upbringing, against the lack of sexual enlightenment, even against her "feudal" background.

Then, without transition, she turned the conversation to a topic she was just working up into a paper. She asked about her mother's "prenatal disposition," using a vocabulary that made her mother blush. Maximiliane answered Viktoria, though with a completely incomprehensible sentence: "Just before, Adolf Hitler's eyes rested on me." But then she broke off without telling her daughter that she considered Hitler the real begetter—at least the cause of conception. The course of events seemed too complicated to explain.

"Where were you at the time?" Viktoria asked.

"In Berlin. At the Reich Sports Field. A mass demonstration."

"I thought I was born on Poenichen."

"You were. But your origins are in Berlin."

"Are you talking about my conception?"

"Yes."

"But that goes counter to every theory."

"But not to the facts." Maximiliane kept on viewing Hitler's piercing look as the cause of all the difficulties this foolish daughter made for herself and others.

"During your birth, by the way, the radio broadcast a special bulletin," she added. "German U-boats sank thirty-eight thousand enemy gross tons, and then—"

"Surely none of that matters," Viktoria interrupted.

"If the light of day is so important, the first sounds the newborn infant hears might be just as important."

"How long did you nurse me?" Viktoria asked next.

Maximiliane thought hard, finally remembered, and admitted, "Not long. You're a bottle baby."

"You see." Viktoria was triumphant.

"My milk stopped." Maximiliane felt a need to apologize. She even added, "Instead you were bathed in tears. You're an April child."

But the mother's tears could not move the daughter.

As a rule Maximiliane tried to make spiritual rather than physical contact with her children. But now she put her hand on Viktoria's head and twisted a strand of her hair around her finger. Viktoria thought that her mother was criticizing the length of her hair; annoyed, she pulled away.

Maximiliane remembered the old woman from Pasewalk who had taken Viktoria on her lap in the

316

emergency shelter—which of many shelters it was, she no longer knew—and had said, "Hair can tell you a lot about a person," as if this child would let people twist her around their little finger, just like her silky curls. She further recalled the memorable Christmas Eve on Mount Eyckel, the first postwar Christmas, when Viktoria had placed her hand on the red-hot top of the stove to call attention to herself; and she recalled Dr. Green, who had compared Viktoria to a dog sniffing out spoor.

She voiced none of her memories, nor did she say that six weeks before Viktoria's birth her father's girl friend had placed a three-year-old child in the family's nest like a cuckoo's egg. By now she had also forgotten the significant conversation—caused by physical exhaustion and emotional tumult—that had taken place a few hours after Viktoria was born. At the time she had, as happened only rarely, expressed an independent idea, first to her husband, who was spending a short furlough in Poenichen before assignment to Russia, then to her grandfather: "Somewhere someone is dying; his soul is freed and seeks new shelter. Whose soul may have taken refuge in this child?" An idea and a question that one of them could not understand, the other could not answer.

A mere few months after this meeting Viktoria would be studying transmigration of souls, first as an academic discipline, then as an ideology incorporating "metempsychosis," and she would later turn to Buddhism. But now, unenlightened, she was still meeting with her mother in the Zoo Railroad Station.

At the time she belonged to a group that called itself Red Morning. Most of her friends had joined the "establishment" by now, hoping for civil-service status, striving for lifetime security. A new, left-wing middle class was forming. Viktoria alone had remained behind, looking like a tired, old baby.

317

"From now on," she announced to her mother, "I'll be working in a day-care center. Right at the source."

"For a while I worked at the source too," Maximiliane answered.

Viktoria looked up. "You?"

"On my knees. On Seifried's farm. Field work. I was given vegetables and potatoes in return. And later I scrubbed floors and stairs. Don't you remember Professor Heynold and his wife in Marburg? In exchange, we were given room and board."

"But you were never a wage slave, you were always one of the privileged! The worst thing is, you're satisfied with everything. You're never aware of your situation. You spent years and years in a university town—you could have done so much there to find your consciousness!"

"Perhaps I would have found myself and lost you?" Her answer came in the inflections of a question, cheerful and even. "I spent my time standing in the corridors of offices," she continued, "to get a residence permit, to get food coupons and shoe coupons. Later I stood behind a counter where I grilled and sold fish. Besides, twice a week I had to cut six people's fingernails and toenails." With a look at Viktoria's bitten nails and her own, she added quickly, smiling, "Insofar as it was necessary."

For a moment something like complicity was in the air. But the daughter did not return her mother's smile after all; she seemed to have taken a vow never under any circumstances to smile. She went on talking about women's self-realization in general and her mother's in particular. When Maximiliane responded by talking about self-satisfaction instead of self-realization, Viktoria was sharp in correcting her.

"It's more or less the same thing," Maximiliane insisted. "I always tried just to scrape through. I tried

318

to bring up five children without a father or grandparents." She broke off, and after a short pause she added, "I only managed with four of them."

At last Viktoria seemed to have achieved her objective: to penetrate to the place where her mother's composure and patience came to an end. Tears filled Maximiliane's eyes.

Inexorable, Viktoria continued the conversation. "Helping and nurturing—are they to be women's task forever?"

"As long as it's necessary. Everyone has to do what is necessary. Are women to start breaking and smashing too?"

The railroad police were just in the midst of their customary patrol, asking people—mostly juveniles—for identification and tickets. Since Viktoria was with her mother, she was not approached, which she clearly felt to be an insult.

Maximiliane rose. "I have to go." She pushed a hundred-mark note toward her daughter. Viktoria reluctantly accepted it.

"Where is it you have to be?" she asked.

"The movies," Maximiliane answered.

After this meeting Maximiliane did not hear from Viktoria for a long time, but she learned from a letter from her cousin Marie-Louise that they had accidentally bumped into each other in Düsseldorf.

"Pure hippie! She's fallen under the spell of that sixteen-year-old guru and gone completely to seed, but she seems a lot happier. Of course I offered her all sorts of help—she's a Quindt, after all. A good thing my mother didn't live to see the day! Viktoria pressed a pamphlet about 'transcendental meditation' into my hand and advised me to read Hermann Hesse. I've heard nothing from my sister Roswitha in the convent. If it's true that no news is good news, she must be just fine. By the way, I have my own interior-decorating shop in the Euro-Center arcade now. I'm sure you'll be glad to know that I was able to buy back the ancestral pictures from the scrap dealer; the antique business's good times are over. I was able to prove to him that the painter couldn't have been Leo von König. Besides, he needs money more than he needs ancestors. I was able to find two handsome art-nouveau frames. I've got them hanging in my studio. The main thing is to keep them in the family. They're von Quindts, never forget. You married out of the family, my dear."

Maximiliane did not answer the letter; she had no expectation of ever being able to make her cousin understand her.

Another long time passed without any word of Viktoria, either directly or indirectly, until a postcard arrived from Katmandu. "I am on the way I have learned is the right one. Here in the hills of Nepal we experience hours of forgetfulness and complete bliss."

Who was included in this "we" Maximiliane learned only later. It was an Iranian student named Fatima Taleghni.

Visiting her friend Isabella von Fredell when she returned to Kassel to give up her apartment for good, Maximiliane commented, "It seems that Tora read too much Hermann Hesse. Instead of merely reading *Siddhartha*, she takes off for India. Writers don't seem to realize what their books can do. Do you remember when we were studying Asia in school? Katmandu and Nepal and Tibet—what did they have to do with me? I didn't even bother to listen."

Then she looked around the room and noticed the large globe. She commented, "You own a globe now."

"Lit up from inside, too," Frau von Fredell said. "The physical world for me, the political world for my husband. The old role divisions."

"Lately Bella has become a little rebellious," Herr

von Fredell offered in explanation. He rose and turned on the light inside the globe.

"You care more for oceans and mountains, I presume."

The globe began to glow. Maximiliane gave it a push.

Herr von Fredell pointed out that she was turning the earth in the wrong direction. Maximiliane stopped short, putting her hands on the globe to arrest the world in its course. "If I want to visit my family, a map is no longer good enough; I need a globe. I have to plan my itinerary by longitude and latitude."

She laid a finger on Dalarna, where Joachim had found "the lifestyle suited to my artistic existence." She traced the meridian, stopping at Holstein, where Edda's ambitious plans had found long-lasting fulfillment in the manufacture of Poenichen game pâté and the establishment of a new generation of Quints. She turned the globe searching for the Bahamas, where Mirka was vacationing with M. Villemain; she had given up her modeling career before achieving top rank. Then Maximiliane's finger pointed to California, where Dr. Green's grave was located. She turned the earth more swiftly, then stopped it, seeking Katmandu. She wavered, overcome by memories, and she encircled the globe with her arms as if she wanted to seek its support.

Her friend asked, "Are you ill? Would you like some brandy?"

"Don't you ever feel the world turning under your feet?" Maximiliane countered.

Herr von Fredell said, "It will pass. I see such feelings in my wife. It's the years." He enunciated his words meaningfully but with the proper discretion.

"When I was thirteen, the deaconesses at my boarding school sounded the same way when they said, 'My dear child, your days are coming.' And when I got married, our midwife in Poenichen talked about 'weeks,' and now it has become 'years.' Women's delicate times. Perhaps something in us really does have to change? But biologically."

Maximiliane removed her arms from the globe, casting one last glance at it, and placed her finger on the spot that marked Berlin. "I forgot Berlin, where my mother lives."

"And Mount Eyckel," Herr von Fredell added, "where all of you are rooted, as it were. By the way, we've heard some talk that the castle is being renovated into a hotel. And you sold it for a pittance. How could you sign such a contract, my dear friend?"

"I'm sure it's an act of divine injustice. Or should I contest the agreement retroactively?"

"Of course not. That would be insane."

"I always signed everything, like Hindenburg. I admit my reasons weren't always entirely objective. There were also ideals involved—or rather, irrational things, things not always subject to reason."

"Ideals! The irrational! And you're surprised that your daughter has gone to India. She'll have finished sowing her wild oats one day, though. You'll see."

"Unfortunately she doesn't have any oats to sow," Maximiliane objected. "She's spending her substance." Then she turned back to her old school friend. "Can you imagine that I might have become a hippie if I'd been born at the right time?"

"I can imagine it only too easily," Frau von Fredell answered.

"Me too," Maximiliane said. "But I am rooted, and my children are not. I am rooted in Poenichen."

"Your children are rooted in you." Frau von Fredell spoke with finality.

Three months later Viktoria came home: "cured," as it was expressed by Edda, with whom she spent a few days; "canonized in a secular sense," in the words of Joachim, with whom she had sought refuge in order to have some quiet in which to do her work.

322

Little by little Maximiliane received more detailed news. On her return trip from India, Viktoria was arrested for drug dealing at the hippies' gathering place outside the Blue Mosque in Istanbul. Because she was confused with another German national who had a similar last name, she languished in jail for almost six weeks before the error was discovered.

The first long letter Viktoria wrote her mother gave glimpses, though only by allusion, of her future plans. "It is necessary to forge links between the despairing and destructive earnestness of the socialists and the irresponsible egotism of the flower children, who use drugs to flee from an inhuman reality into a dream world. 'Simply because something does not yet exist does not mean that it is either wrong or senseless,' says Herbert Marcuse. Two movements are spreading over the world at the present time: one leads to possessions, the other away from them. I believe, as the Stoics already taught us, that the happy life can only come through renunciation. Let us only remember Socrates, who lived in total poverty free from all desire, or Diogenes and his pupil Crates of Thebes, who lived like a beggar with his rich wife, or the barefoot orders and the mendicants. The link leads to the hippies. We harbor a yearning for wholeness, for completion, even after the old sex roles are abolished. This yearning must not be allowed to end in the resignation of one group and the radicalization of the other. An amalgam of saints and revolutionaries might be able to save the world, Ignazio Silone said. Ritualistic radicals. . . ."

Eighteen months later Viktoria submitted her doctoral dissertation. It was titled "On the Concept of the Good Life in Zeno, Considered in Light of Contemporary Psychology, with Special Consideration of Student Revolts in the Western World During the 1960s."

24

Before the official opening—to which, as usual, representatives of the district, the town, the unions, and the building trades had been invited—the Mount Eyckel Hotel was to host a Quin(d)t family reunion. The idea originated with Frau Brandes, the second wife of Brandes the brewery owner, with whom he had lived for several years even before the death of his first wife. Thus, the plan for a family reunion owed just as little to a Quindt as did the restructuring of the castle into a hotel.

The second Frau Brandes was thirty years younger than her husband, and more high-spirited; she was also—why else would she have wanted to marry him?—concerned with security. The brewery Herr Brandes had acquired by marriage forty years earlier would revert to his late wife's family on his death. The new wife had studied architecture for a couple of years; she was, in her husband's words, a "half-hatched architect."

Here on Mount Eyckel an architect's dream had been turned into reality. In fact, however, an experienced contractor and various housing boards had determined its ultimate shape. And since Eyckel Castle had been designated a national landmark, the district conservator had also imposed a number of restrictions, especially concerning the front elevation; the guidebooks particularly pointed to the "polymorphic facade of Eyckel Castle." But the Landmark Office had raised no objections to restructuring the castle grounds—on the contrary, it welcomed the enterprise, which would mean that the crumbling masonry had a chance to survive.

To the extent that Herr Brandes remembered the family reunion of 1936, he passed his memories on to his wife so that they could serve to inspire the arrangements for the second such event. A weekend in May was picked; the month was particularly flattering to Franconia, as it was to all German highland locations. The invitations were mailed out; in some cases the current address was followed by "Formerly Giessmannsdorf in Silesia" or "Formerly Königsberg in East Prussia."

Maximiliane received several invitations, along with a request to pass them on to those Quindts and Quints whose addresses she knew. She sent four of them to her children, writing "Come" in her large handwriting on the back of the envelope, signing the note with *M*, which she always used to stand for "Mama," "Mother," or "Maximiliane." She sent another invitation to Vera Green; after all, for a brief period she too had been a Quindt.

This time there were again some who refused to attend the reunion—a few because they had no burning desire to contribute to Brandes's success. But the line of those who set out to satisfy their curiosity and their need for a change of atmosphere was still long enough. The reunion also attracted a number of representatives of the next generation and the generation after that, descendants of the late senate president Ferdinand von Quindt and of Mathilde von Ansatz-Zinzenich, who had coined the phrase "Rich people like us simply don't know what it is not to have money."

There was no need to fear disturbances on the part of the younger Quindts, not even Viktoria, who had by now received her Ph.D. and who, coming from Cologne, was one of the first to arrive. The motto of this family reunion was, once again, "To participate means to agree." The proceedings were less "Germanic" than they had been in 1936; there would be no national anthems, no flags. The "great historical upheavals" mentioned at the previous reunion by a speaker quoting Hitler had since taken place. One of the current guests, a Herr von Larisch, did recall the other occasion but contented himself with showing a few slides of that celebration, "on the whole quite a successful one, when we met in all innocence."

Nor was there a religious service this time; there were no longer any parsons or deacons among the Quindts. No one composed poems for the occasion; no exhibition of family escutcheons, documents, and genealogical tables was arranged, because none of the participants were interested. The "blood of the Quindts" also went unmentioned. Hereditary factors were of no concern to anyone, the theories of a former day having been politically perverted and rendered useless. There was no consecration of the flags, no torchlight, not even homemade pea soup with sausages cooked in the stewpot; no dormitories of mattresses, no voluntary labor, no bliss induced by dripping-and-jam sandwiches.

Those who had not seen Eyckel Castle since the first postwar years hardly recognized the place. All the walls except those of the so-called Dower House had been repaired; the timbering had been replaced; the garden, where once they had kept rabbits and chickens and raised potatoes and tobacco, had been laid out in exemplary fashion by Frau Brandes, who had consulted slides of old prints owned by the Germanic Museum. Soon all the long-stemmed roses and rose arbors would be in bloom. The lilacs and elder bushes along the walls had been incorporated into the design. Stone benches beneath the chestnut trees alternated with comfortable gliders. The guest rooms were furnished in a rustic style, the doors marked not with numbers but with names—"Dürer Room" "Holbein Room," "Tristan and Isolde Room."

Herr Brandes had personally seen to the room assignments. Though the difference between rich and poor was not as great as in the old days, it was still a consideration. It was evident even in the parking lot, where Maximiliane's little Citroen stood cheek by jowl with the Mercedes 300 of Dr. Olaf Schmitz, whose wife was a Quindt by birth and who was the managing partner of AKO Plastics, Inc., formerly AKO Dynamite.

Without having read Bert Brecht, Herr Brandes shared the poet's view that the rich belong among themselves, as do the poor. Whereas in 1936 a distinction was made between the ennobled Quindts and the commoners, now they were divided according to property. Since not all the guests could be quartered in the new hotel, some had to stay in the village, at the Hart. Among these were Frau Hieronimi, with her son and daughter-in-law, and the two widows of retirement age, Frau von Mechlowski from Gera and the widow of Deacon Quint, who lived in Gotha with her son Anselm; both had arrived from East Germany and were treated to a glass of wine or a cup of coffee by all their relations; they were grateful for every kindness and embarrassingly undemanding.

Maximiliane was assigned one of the best rooms—the tower room. It was not her wealth that entitled her to it; rather, it had something to do with Herr Brandes's plans. He personally led her to the room and gave her an expectant look. "Well?" he asked at last. "You're speechless, right?"

Maximiliane looked at the double bed and replied, "Ever since I grew up, I've preferred sleeping in a single bed with another person to sleeping alone next to an empty bed." A remark that bewildered Herr Brandes but strengthened his intentions.

"There are too many widows among the Quindts," he noted regretfully.

"You shouldn't apologize for that state of affairs. Others are to blame."

"I'd like to talk to you about something, by the way."

"Later," Maximiliane said, going to the window. "First I've got to find my way around."

Arriving from Berlin, Vera Green landed at the Nuremberg airport a half-hour after Joachim, who came from Stockholm by way of Frankfurt. Maximiliane went to fetch both of them. Asked about Stina Bonde, Joachim replied, "I waited too long. She married the sales manager of the publishing house. Now and then she thinks about Dalarna, and then she drives out."

Maximiliane put her arm around his shoulders, removing it only when she had to shift gears.

Vera Green, who had been a true Berliner in California, seemed like an intellectual American from San Francisco in Germany. No sooner had she arrived at Eyckel Castle than she went to the bar and asked for bourbon to restore her balance; but it turned out that they were not prepared for American tastes. Herr Brandes added bourbon to his handy shopping list; Vera Green had a glass of champagne instead—it had the same restorative properties—and announced, not in private but to at least ten ears, "It's astonishing. All in all, I was a Quindt by marriage, as you call it, for all of five days. And look at the results! Clearly I've earned Old Quindt's praise—'I think you've done a good job.' What a wonderful increase: five grandchildren and God knows how many great-grandchildren."

She inserted a cigarette into her holder, which was ebony as in the old days. She had readopted her mannerisms: she leaned against the bar; she had on a black velvet pantsuit; she wore her hair—white by now—in the same cut. A leftover from the Roaring Twenties— a "ghost" to some, "amusing" to others.

The photographer who had been hired to take pictures of the reunion for the hotel brochure had found his first subject, but he had to endure various critical remarks from onetime star reporter Vera von Jadow, Widow von Quindt, Widow Green.

When the car of the Holstein Quinten turned into the parking lot, Maximiliane was standing at the gate with Sister Emanuela, formerly her cousin Roswitha. The little Quinten spilled out, all of them more or less reddish-blond, all freckled, the youngest still in a carrier. Edda, who had a tendency to overweight even before she bore children, was opulent, or as Maximiliane noted, "swelled with pride, not just a lot of fat."

Sister Emanuela turned her ageless nun's face to Maximiliane. "You arrived here just the same way that other time. I was standing at the gate then, too."

Maximiliane pointed to the children's father, Marten von Quinten, who was getting out of the car and stretching to his full height and breadth. "I arrived on foot and without a husband. Instead, I was pregnant. It was winter, not May. But you're right, in every other way it's the same."

The two women smiled at one another.

For two days there were constant comparisons of occasions that defied comparison—the family reunion of 1936, the winter of 1945–46, and the days at the beginning of May in the 1970s. People took each other's measure, using make of car, clothing, and jewelry as yardsticks. There was still such a thing as the diamond collar from the estate of Grandmother Sophie Charlotte, and Maximiliane could exhibit it on such an occasion on her still-remarkable throat. Everyone was on display—age, health, and property were compared.

"You gotta know how to let others have," Maximiliane said.

"Where did you pick that expression up?" her mother asked, and the daughter answered, "From someone who came from the Rhineland."

Maximiliane picked up the little Quintens one by one: their hair of equal length, all of them in jeans, no visible gender distinctions, raised according to enlightened and nonauthoritarian principles, now and then scolded by Marten if Edda happened to be out of earshot.

"Planned parenthood," Edda said. "Marten and I share my opinion on that." A slip of the tongue, no more; it was ignored.

"We don't have accidental children," she added. In this sentence Maximiliane recognized Edda's father, remembered the studbook he had kept during her fertile days, and turned to Marten, whom she still held dear. "Free enterprise in the barns. Planned economy in bed."

Marten broke out into his infectious laugh. Edda, in the outraged tone she had become accustomed to using with Maximiliane, said, "Mother!" immediately explaining to her children, "You don't have to say Grandmother, you may call her Maximiliane."

The children were unable to; the name turned out to be too long and complicated for their burgeoning linguistic abilities. Their attempts came out something like "Ane."

Maximiliane picked up the baby—named Joachim to uphold family tradition—rocked him, thought him too heavy for his age, said as much, and offered to change him. Edda threw her a package of paper diapers. Maximiliane undid the baby's pants, threw away the dirty inset, and replaced it with a clean one. That was all there was to it. "Very practical and efficient," she said. It sounded not like praise but like regret.

Edda took the baby from her. "It's not good for an

330

infant to have too much change in the persons he relates to," she said. "And if you think he weighs too much— he's fed entirely on demand. Satisfaction of needs." Abruptly she changed the topic. "We'll have to have a talk with you about the business, Mother."

"Later," Maximiliane answered. "You haven't even unpacked yet."

"We ought to do it right away. Who knows when we'll get another chance to be alone."

Maximiliane dropped to the edge of the bed and pulled the tallest of the little Quintens between her knees. "All right, let's talk about the five-percent clause."

"How did you know what we wanted to talk to you about?"

"You usually talk figures. You did even as a little girl."

Marten von Quinten tried to leave under the pretext of finding a shady spot for the car.

Edda stopped him. "Please stay. I think it's better if you're present." And then, turning to Maximiliane, she began. "We have four children."

"I've figured that out for myself."

Edda's face grew red with suppressed anger at this answer. She bit her narrow lips before continuing. "Let's talk about the business, then. The original recipe is yours, we admit. But by now the composition of our pâté has changed completely. The walnuts tended to go rancid, and there were complaints. We had to start using expensive pistachios. And instead of capers we use truffles now. Have you any idea what a pound of truffles costs? And dry sherry besides! Last year we packed a jar of elderberry jelly spiked with black-currant liqueur in each gift box, without extra charge."

"You sent me a box like that for Christmas," Maximiliane agreed.

"Then you know. It's no longer a matter of Poenichen Pâté of Wild Game. If we keep the name, it's only because it's known by now—and that television program about the East German nobility had something to do with that, no one's going to deny it. But people are used to eating well again. Their demands are constantly increasing. Nowadays it's not enough to advertise in the newsletter of the Pomeranian expellees' organization. We have quite a different clientele." Edda turned to her husband. "You go on."

Marten was reluctant. "This isn't the kind of conversation you have in a bedroom. We should be discussing these things over a glass of brandy."

"Sober," Edda commanded. "Well?"

"Well," Marten repeated, turning to Maximiliane. "You remember my idea of raising red deer in an enclosure. To do that, the entire wooded area had to be fenced in with wire mesh. It gave us a tax deduction, but the expected subsidy from the Chamber of Agriculture didn't materialize. Of course it isn't according to the rules of the hunt, I know, but one day it's sure to be a very nice item in our profit balance. Unfortunately the project earned me my neighbors' scorn and envy."

"And their admiration," Edda added.

"In any case, they won't deliver game to me anymore. Some time will have to pass before we learn whether red deer breed more rapidly with good feeding and optimal living conditions. Once upon a time, after all, the wild boar turned into a domestic pig."

"Presumably that took hundreds of years," Maximiliane objected.

"There's one advantage, at any rate. Fewer fawns are caught in the harvesting combine."

"Does that still happen?" Maximiliane was concerned.

"Please let's not talk about fawns now," Edda interposed. "Let's get around to pâté of turkey. We could fill the warehouses with turkey pâté and rationalize the whole enterprise. Turkey farming is relatively risk-free, and we have the coops. Whatever we do, Mother, we'll have to make a new contract. Your input in the firm is just about zero."

"Old Quindt is right once again. Your father placed a cuckoo's egg in all our nests."

"Mother!"

"I don't understand," Marten said.

"Let Edda explain it to you. She'll know best about that as well, I'm sure."

Half an hour later the Holstein Quintens made a second sensational entrance. In harmony and peace they stepped into the lounge, the three children who could walk preceding them, the baby in his father's arms. They were greeted with admiration: an example of the well-being and vitality of the nuclear family.

Soon thereafter, however, Mirka's arrival, jealously noted by Edda, drew everyone's attention away from the Quintens. Mirka appeared at her husband's side, her year-old son, Philippe, riding her hip as if he were part of her outfit. A pretty, quiet, cheerful baby who had inherited many of his mother's traits, most notably her eyes—"doves' eyes."

Mirka stuck to the bargain she had made with Henri Villemain before their wedding—not a word about rape. Her father Russian, her mother a member of the German nobility—that was enough. In order to forge closer ties with the ennobled Quindts, he had agreed to inspect "the site of birth," and he admitted, "I'm surprised."

M. Villemain, speaking broken German, explained to his brother-in-law Marten von Quinten that he had picked his wife and her mother out of the gutter. Some of the bystanders, among them the Lübeck Quinten, did not understand the joke and thought their own thoughts, especially since they knew that in Paris Maximiliane had lived with a painter and Mirka had been a model, both for photographers and in fashion shows, the one activity as unbecoming to her status as the other. But they did no more than think. The Villemains were said to be rich—defense industry, a castlelike villa in Muedon, a vacation home in Antibes. And if you refused to be impressed by riches, you could at least be impressed by Mirka's exotic beauty.

The weather did its part to make the festivities a success. Though a gusty wind was blowing, the welcome to the participants could take place outdoors as planned. The ladies, depending on age, rank, and wealth, mantled their shivering shoulders in crocheted stoles or mink. Since the official opening of the hotel was not for two days, they were among themselves, Quindts among Quinten. The photographer plied his trade without causing too much of a disturbance.

As he said, Herr Brandes fully intended to keep his address free of figures about the cost of the renovation and restoration so as not to rob his guests of speech or appetite. He himself, he admitted readily, had thought it impossible for such a splendid hotel to rise from the old masonry.

"It is to my wife's credit"—as he spoke, he placed his aging hand on a very young shoulder—"that today we can once more speak of Eyckel Castle and not merely of 'Eyckel ruins.' My role was secondary. In French there is a subtle distinction between *meriter* and *gagner*— I took care of the latter, the earning. Furthermore, the idea of inaugurating the Mount Eyckel Hotel with a family reunion, on the other hand, is again to my wife's credit. All the Quindts from far and near are to have something like a homestead here."

Until now there had only been the past for Eyckel Castle, he continued. Now it had been given a future. Regrettably he was not able to give an authoritative history of Eyckel Castle, all extant documents having been lost in the tumult of the postwar years. "But perhaps the young poet we number among us, who as a child played here in the castle grounds, a genuine Quint von Quindt—with and without the *d*—descended from the Pomeranian and Silesian lines, will one day compose this chronicle. The castle reflects a piece of German history, especially that of our unquiet century. First a chivalric keep during the Middle Ages, then the base from which the Quindts set forth to colonize or Christianize the East—I don't want to trap myself in political snares here; then the slow decay of the castle down to the nineteen thirties, and then its enlargement into a National Socialist youth hostel. During the war a reception camp for bombed-out citizens of Nuremberg, after the war a refugee camp, an old-age home until it became uninhabitable, and finally nothing more than a storehouse for the beer from my brewery; then condemned because of its dilapidated condition, a rats' nest. And today. . . ."

He paused. At a gesture from him, several floodlights lit up the castle facade; at the same time the lamps at the driveway, designed on historical models, were lit up to advertise Brandes beer.

Unfortunately it was not yet dark enough to bring out the full effect, but the reunion participants eagerly directed their gaze on the castle of their forebears.

Herr Brandes let himself be carried away by the greatness of the moment. "If we have left the former Dower House standing in ruins," he said, "the reason is not only—though it is that too—because it is meant to stand as a symbol for the rise and fall of the Quindt family. It is intended at the same time as an emblem for all the poverty, want, and destitution remaining anywhere in the world. It is meant to convey that as part of the increasing democratization of the world, Eyckel Castle is now accessible to the general public. Some, especially the younger people among us, might object that the hotel will prove too expensive for most people.

I'd like to say in reply that these youngsters will grow older, and one day they too will be able to afford it. Furthermore"—Herr Brandes raised his voice—"provisions have been made for one of the rooms to be always available free of charge to any Quindt—whether an 'original' one or a Quindt by marriage. This stipulation had been contractually secured for the next twenty-five years."

His announcement was received with thunderous applause, and Herr Brandes ended his oration with proud satisfaction. "As you have seen for yourselves, the emergency shelters have been turned into cozy guest rooms, not luxury class, but Category A—medieval romanticism combined with modern comforts. A bathroom and a television set in each one."

His punch line, of which he was particularly proud, did not meet with the expected enthusiasm, but there was indulgent applause.

Herr Brandes tied on a leather apron and personally tapped the beer keg standing at the ready. The big drinking bout could begin.

A gentleman of middle years bowed to Maximiliane and handed her a glass. "Max von Quindt."

He turned out to be the grandson of her beloved great-uncle Max from Königsberg. He was a major in the staff cadre of the Federal Armed Forces, worldly, elegant, but with a trace of the cheerful sarcasm that had also marked Uncle Max.

The evening wind had tousled hairdos; the ladies went back inside to consult their mirrors, and the gentlemen pulled combs from their pockets. After apologizing to Maximiliane, Max von Quindt also took out a comb— made of tin, with several missing teeth—which he pulled through his graying hair.

"I never thought I'd use this comb so long," he said, "and certainly not in such surroundings. I made it myself from a piece of tin in the prisoner-of-war camp in Minsk, winter of 1945."

"So it's a talisman." Maximiliane smiled.

"Something like that. It helps me keep tabs on my attitude toward life. The same comb in the pocket of a prisoner's stripes, in my dress uniform, and tonight in my tuxedo." He took Maximiliane's elbow. "Will you entrust yourself to my spiritual and practical guidance?"

Maximiliane looked around searchingly and asked about his wife. In answer he said, "One Quindt is quite enough for her. Sometimes even too much. She couldn't bear a whole collection of Quindts."

In searching for family traditions with which to embellish the reunion, Frau Brandes had found a hymn by Count Zinzendorf, who was said to have been related to the Quindts. "Heart and heart are joined together." Frau Brandes must have considered the words exceedingly appropriate to the occasion. To general astonishment, each person found the printed text at each place setting.

Even this time, then, it was not possible to avoid hymns altogether.. But once again higher significance was put at the service of a lesser occasion. During the past decades the Quin(d)ts had only rarely demonstrated a readiness to support one another. Though most of them might be the issue of a single root, even this truth was questionable, judging from circumstances among the Pomeranian Quindts.

"It's all a matter of blood." The ironic exclamation Old Quindt made to Riepe the coachman after Maximiliane's birth comes to mind. In this instance, after all, we are dealing with the blood of an almost unknown Polish lieutenant, which flowed in Maximiliane's veins instead of Quindt blood. Among the living, there had not for a long time been anyone who knew that her "saucer eyes" came from that very lieutenant, with whom Maximiliane's grandmother had had a brief but fateful love affair in the dunes at Zoppot.

Nevertheless, Maximiliane was a genuine Quindt, a gratification to all those who hold environment to be more significant than heredity. As any half-baked sophomore with even the slightest awareness of the Oedipus complex must realize, in her case it was a matter of a grandfather Oedipus complex. She had never met a man who could measure up to Old Quindt. Instead, she had come to resemble him more and more herself, especially now, at the same age he had been when she was a little girl. Instead of Quindt-essences, Maxims. She was developing into an original.

The band Frau Brandes had hired for the evening had just struck up the theme from *Elvira Madigan*, jazzing up Mozart to a fare-thee-well. A flood of warmth washed over Maximiliane, this once not for biological but for spiritual reasons. The very first notes penetrated down to her toes, only later reaching her brain and releasing memories.

These same strains, not heard since, had been tapped out on her bare toes more than thirty years before by a lieutenant of the artillery. An idyll on the shores of Lake Poenichen shortly before the outbreak of the Second World War. Occasionally real life alone is still daring enough to be sentimental. A fairy tale in which the horse Falada neighed and five paces away her little boy lay in his wicker basket. She turned to see Joachim sitting five paces away from her. She sought out the eyes of the man—thin, blond, distant, and as absent as possible—who occupied his chair.

The heat wave dissipated, the memories receded. How long would it be before her body, aroused by the words and hands of the cavalryman, stirred only to torture her? She was already in the transition stage: from joy by way of terror to pain.

The evening took on a festive air. Flames glowed

338

in the fireplace, candles flickered on the tables. The meal was à la carte, featuring many specialties—game, fowl, trout; nor was there any lack of children's portions and diet plates. Besides the better beers of the Brandes Brewery, Franconian wines were offered.

When dinner was finished—some were still lingering over coffee or brandy, and the children had been put to bed—the current elder of the family was urged to say a few words. It was Klaus von Quindt, an old man from the East Prussian branch, former owner of the Lettow estate situated southeast of Allenstein. He was hard of hearing, like most Quindts of an advanced age. He finally gave in and spoke for all those Quindts who came from the German East—and that was the majority. He refused to remain sitting, supported himself on the arm of his chair, and like all the Quindts, omitted the clumsy phrases of introduction.

"When I went to school in the tradition-laden Frederick College in Königsberg, I memorized a poem. It was written by Adalbert von Chamisso. Barely a one of you will know it or remember it. It is called 'Castle Boncourt.' "

> In dreams I am a child
> And shake my graying locks.

"These lines amused us particularly in those days. I shall try to remember the final stanzas."

> O castle of my fathers,
> Still standing fast in my mind,
> You've vanished from the living world,
> Plowed furrows now we find—

The old gentleman hesitated, thought hard, and raised his hands in helplessness.

It was Maximiliane who helped him out. "Be fruitful, precious acres—"

He nodded at her thankfully and continued

Be fruitful, precious acres,
I bless you, with gentle vow,
And bless him twice, whoever
Guides the plow above me now.

"Not all of us here will be able to achieve the fortitude of Chamisso, who was a French émigré," he said, and he continued without transition.

"Recently I read that each inhabitant of the Federal Republic of Germany counts at least one person among his family who came from the East. The great migration of nations has ground to a halt. Some among us still recall—with great reverence— Simon August von Quindt, who was native to the Baltic region. Twice in his lifetime he was forced to abandon his home, and now he is buried here in the village cemetery. He gave us a demonstration of how a Balt becomes extinct with decency. And those of us who used to be East Prussians and Silesians and Pomeranians will also have to learn to become extinct with decency.

"But I want to voice another thought, one that occurred to me only during the last hour. The Quindts and Quinten, with and without the *d*, have for centuries included officers, civil servants, farmers, even a few businessmen, among them many deserving men. Of those who were expelled from their homes, some never really succeeded in the West. For them, being uprooted became something like dematerialization. It gave them the occasion, as I see it from my present vantage point, the chance for spiritualization in a metaphysical, religious, artistic, or charitable direction.

"I never paid much attention to genealogy, but as far as I know, before the great catastrophe—I shall not fix a date; some think of it as 1945 and others as 1939 or 1933, and some go back to the Versailles Treaty. As far as I know, then, before that time the Quindts counted among their number some liberals—I recall

Joachim von Quindt on Poenichen—but one and all of them were materialists and therefore egotists. As I look around this gathering now, I can see some changes.

"One of us is a Sister of God, having entered a Benedictine convent only a few years after the war. We number among us a writer and therefore an artist, and one of our women has been doing volunteer work with the German Red Cross for decades. After his belated return from a Russian prisoner-of-war camp, my late brother Ferdinand was able to assist in establishing amendments to the laws for the equalization of burdens. The number of such people is sure to be even larger; each one of you may make his own additions. There is even one young Quindt among us who, I am told, has written a dissertation on happiness. In the old days the Quindts did not sufficiently concern themselves with happiness. The Quindts always stuck only to duty. Young people, searching for new paths toward new objectives. Will these roads be accessible to others? No longer to me. I speak for my generation. In our subconscious and in our dreams, our lost home is ever present."

He paused and, before resuming his seat, added as an afterthought, "No one can pass on his dreams."

There was silence—moved or alienated. They had expected his speech to extol the splendid examples of new beginnings, to point with pride to the factory in Holstein or the reconstruction of Eyckel Castle.

Maximiliane rose, went over to her uncle, and kissed him on both cheeks. Only then did the applause break out. It was meant both for the man who was being kissed and for the woman who was kissing him.

People changed places, exchanged happy and sad news. Vera Green reported to a large circle of listeners that her husband's definitive work, entitled *Wordless Speech*, was already in its fourth edition, making it possible for her to live very comfortably. Photographs were passed around, black-and-white, yellowed snapshots of old manors and roomy townhouses, color snaps of bungalows and vacation homes. There were even a few photographs taken at the 1936 family reunion; it was possible to laugh at them now. The uniforms! The hairdos! The arms raised in the Hitler salute! They looked around and noted with satisfaction and pleasure that the Quindts had grown better-looking as well as more prosperous.

Memories also wandered back to the singular Christmas Eve of 1945, which was transfigured into a veritable legend of Bethlehem as old Frau Hieronimi told it. "Somehow or other, it was the essence of Christianity. We shared what little we had. We had a warm drink that tasted wonderful. We ate cookies we had baked together, without everything and with vinegar. Maximiliane's newborn baby slept in a crate beside the stove."

She looked for Mirka, who was leaning against the bar next to her brother-in-law, Marten. The others also looked around, trying to compare what could not bear comparison. The only things that were the same in Eyckel Castle were the candles, and even those were different—in the past they'd had to use Hindenburg lamps, fat stumps set in saucers.

"The chamber pot for the white aunts from Mecklenburg!"

"I wonder where all their valuable embroidery ended up."

"It would fetch a lot now—real linen, every stitch by hand."

"Frivolities from Mecklenburg."

"And Bing Crosby was singing 'White Christmas' on the radio."

Joachim moved closer to the table and shared one of his memories. "On Easter Sunday Mother took all of us to the village. She carried Mirka in a cloth sling across her back to keep her hands free. We went to a farmer's house, I don't remember his name; she did field work for him. We went in through the front door without knocking, straight to the kitchen, where they were all at dinner. A roasted pascal lamb was on the table. We stood there lined up in a row, and Mother said, 'For Easter I wanted my children to at least be able to fill their eyes.' We stood and stared; the farmer stared back. Then he got up and angrily clenched his hands on the tabletop. Viktoria started to cry, and Mother told us, 'Come. But never forget.' And to the people at the table she said, 'Not you either.' "

The memories had shriveled into anecdotes. Many of them were cause for laughter, and some of the laughter still masked fear.

Joachim was urged to put all these stories on paper some time. Over and over one or another person said, "If I only had the time, I could write a couple of novels." There must have been more frustrated writers sitting cheek by jowl at this family reunion than on any other occasion before or since.

Sister Emanuela held long discussions with Viktoria about the difference between compassion and the sense of community, about "true happiness" and "metaphysical unease" during an age that believed in progress.

M. Villemain talked with Max von Quindt, the major in the high command, with Mirka serving as the required interpreter. "For me," Major von Quindt said with great determination, "there is only one just war— the war against war." The triple repetition of the word *war* dismayed the Frenchman.

Conversation at other tables also touched on war, especially on the postwar period, on the collection of used paper and cigarette butts, on abstemiousness and thrift. Meanwhile the speakers drank after-dinner coffee, champagne, and French cognac as they put out half-smoked cigarettes.

"Sacrifice," said Dr. Olaf Schmitz, who had been born in Breslau. "Where did sacrifice get us? We sacrificed Alsace-Lorraine, we sacrificed our colonies, we sacrificed the South Tyrol, Upper Silesia, the Polish Corridor, Danzig and Memel—and all for the sake of peace. Those sacrifices earned us nothing; they appeased neither us nor Europe. Can anyone still seriously believe that the sacrifice of the eastern territories will guarantee us peace?"

Old Klaus von Quindt suggested that they ought to think in terms of longer time spans. "Perhaps one day the partition of Germany will have the ssssaaame result as the partition of Poland?"

"But all Europe admired the Polish national spirit. Today they admire the national spirit of the Palestinians. Why is it that the Germans are not at least credited with a feeling of patriotism? Why do they laugh at us when we speak of our German homeland?"

Before the question could be answered, a waiter stepped up and requested the gentlemen to change places. At that, they changed the topic as well.

Some of the tables were pushed aside to open the floor for dancing. The band alternated golden oldies with tops of the pops—something suitable for every generation. Maximiliane danced with her son and both her sons-in-law. As they were dancing, M. Villemain tried hard to make conversation, but she told him, "I always prefer dancing with men to talking with them, especially when I'm not good at their language. It's easier to communicate with one's legs. With a single exception."

M. Villemain gave her a questioning look.

"Old Quindt on Poenichen. My grandfather. You never met him. Hardly anyone here ever met him."

344

The hour grew late. Several of the participants had already retired, and the band was packing up its instruments.

Sister Emanuela asked for the floor. "Not for my words," she said, smiling, "but for the word of God." She recited an evening prayer that, she explained, was used in Protestant churches just as much as in the Catholic faith. "Abide with us, Lord, for evening will come, and the day is drawing to a close. Abide with us in the evening of the day, in the evening of life, in the evening of the world. Abide with us when we are overcome by the night of affliction and fear, the night of doubt and temptation, the night of bitter death."

Her prayer was followed by an audible silence, partly expressing emotion, partly embarrassment. The situation was unusual: a prayer in a room where they had just finished dancing.

M. Villemain, standing at the back, thought the prayer was just one more speech and applauded. The spell was broken and dissolved in laughter.

Maximiliane embraced her cousin. "It's been a long time since anyone prayed for me."

25

No screech owl woke Maximiliane; but the morning sun touched her face, and her eyelids were not proof against the light. She rose, pulled on her coat, and left the hotel in bare feet.

She walked through a morning damp with dew, turning into the path that led to the woods. She had gone that way so often in the old days: the sheepfold over there, where the juniper grew; the meadow where Farmer Wengel's horses used to graze, now surrounded by an electrified fence, a respectable pasture. The field path had turned into a paved commercial road, but a single step to the side was enough to let her feet touch sorrel, plantain weed, and camomile. The paths ran from one Eden to the next. The apple trees were in bloom, the whitethorn was in bloom, and in the valley the Pegnitz River glistened under the sun's rays, denying the pollution.

In the confusion of birdcalls, the chaffinches won out. Maximiliane strayed off the road, wandered through the previous year's dead foliage and the moldering leaves of the year before that, spied some beechnuts lying on the ground, picked one up, put it between her teeth, felt a great deal and thought hardly at all, and turned back when the village church bell rang out seven o'clock.

She walked back to the hotel. Its new black-and-white half-timbering glowed from afar. The refurbished weathervane indicated that the wind was blowing from the southwest; in the afternoon there would probably be a thunderstorm.

In the breakfast room opening off the hotel's entrance hall she met her daughter Edda. The younger woman, wearing a light-blue floor-length dressing gown and carrying Baby Joachim in her arms, was placing brochures for Poenichen Pâté of Wild Game on the breakfast tables.

Instead of a greeting, Edda said, "You shouldn't dress that way, Mother. You can't walk around here in bare feet."

"I once had a governess who made me run barefoot around the flower beds in front of the manor every single morning."

"I have four children, I work, and I have no household help to speak of."

"You're comparing times that can't be compared. You should compare the conditions of your life now with how it was when we lived here."

"But at least you didn't have a husband who made constant demands on you."

"That's a subject I can't talk about."

Maximiliane ran both hands through her hair, shook it as the wind shakes a tree, and picked up the latest pâté-of-game brochure. She did not read it, however.

Lightfooted, Joachim ran down the stairs. He gave his mother's shoulder a brief touch, easy and without pressure, like all his gestures. Looking at Edda, he noted with a smile, "I see that I'm too late. I wondered whether to put an announcement of my new book of poems on the tables." He pulled a folded sheet from his pocket and handed it to his mother. She put aside the other brochure and picked up his flyer. "Auxiliary

Phrases," she read. Under the title a poem was reproduced in facsimile.

Joachim sat down next to her. "I'm sure people need pâté more than they need poems," he said.

"People need both," Maximiliane replied. "In times of need, poems are even better than pâté. The body needs to be nourished daily; it digests everything, eliminates everything, and so has to keep on eating. And the spirit needs poems. Because it always forgets, the spirit also has to be fed daily."

"What are you talking about anyway?"

"About the five-percent partnership in the Poenichen Pâté of Wild Game. Old Quindt as a trademark. Poenichen for sale by the quarter-pound. I was born with open hands, that's what Schmaltz the midwife kept on saying. That's why I never amounted to anything."

Maximiliane held her hands out to her son, palms upward, cupped. Joachim held his hands against hers, as always balled into fists. "You can hold more in open hands than you can in fists," he remarked.

"Green's 'wordless language,' " Maximiliane said.

The early risers could be heard coming down to breakfast. The smell of coffee wafted through the door leading to the kitchen.

Unnoticed, Viktoria had come downstairs. She too sat down by her mother and read through both leaflets.

"Have you got something to pass out also?" Maximiliane asked her after Joachim had walked away.

"I've got all kinds of pamphlets and leaflets in my bag."

"What sort of children have I put into the world?" Maximiliane wondered. "Reformers, every last one of them, wanting to change the world. Joachim wants to change it with poetry, you with slogans, Edda with pâté. Mirka is the only one who just wants to brighten it."

"Last night down here, and then up in my room,

348

I realized a couple of things," Viktoria said. "I've gone up a dead-end street."

"Even dead ends are open to the sky," Maximiliane answered, never questioning what dead end Viktoria was referring to this time.

When Viktoria looked at her in surprise, she added, "I've only just learned that myself. It's one of Mose's 'auxiliary phrases.' "

After breakfast people set out for excursions in the surrounding countryside. Some drove to Gössweinstein and Bamberg, others walked to the nearby stalactite cave. This time they did not go in groups, as they had at the earlier family reunion, but in twos and threes, holding private conversations. Nor was there any singing or picking of wildflowers. There was no lecture in the cave, since no one who was knowledgeable about the locality was present.

Maximiliane's children decided to go to the village to revisit the sites where they had played, where they had been caught stealing apples, where they had gone to school.

"Aren't you coming?" Joachim asked his mother.

"Run," she said, as she had said so often in the past. She stood a long time watching her children move down the mountain. She had never missed Golo as much as she did this very moment.

"All this is your accomplishment," said Vera Green, who had come to stand beside her.

And Maximiliane replied, "My husband always saw women as breeding grounds."

"How are you fixed for money anyway?" Vera asked her daughter soon after, as they sat in one of the gliders.

An hour later her Uncle Klaus asked the same question; he was seriously concerned for her future. The next to ask was her cousin Marie-Louise, who found fault with Maximiliane's "outward appearance." The last to ask was Frau Hieronimi.

She replied either, "I'm looking for a five-percent partnership" or, "I could use a little legacy."

Whereupon the remark was sure to follow "You're not so young anymore, you know" or "But you need a fixed place to live" or "Don't you care anything about security?"

"I let other people worry about that," Maximiliane said.

"You're not one of the lilies of the field." Marie-Louise von Quindt put considerable sharpness into her remark.

"That's too bad," Maximiliane countered.

Her attitude about life, and the words she used to express it, were received by some as "lovable," by others as "imprudent," and by Frau Hieronimi as "headstrong."

The last to approach her with a concerned look was Herr Brandes. Maximiliane anticipated his question. "I can see that you're worried about my future."

"Indeed I am. And I mean it sincerely."

Herr Brandes took Maximiliane's arm and pulled her to one side so that, as he put it, they would have "an atmosphere of quiet and mutual trust" in which to discuss something that was to both their advantage.

"Why don't we go to the bar? No one will disturb us there at this hour."

At the bar he personally uncorked a bottle of Pommery. "I'm sure in Paris you got used to French champagne."

"I got used to Paris, not to champagne," Maximiliane answered.

Herr Brandes filled the glasses and came straight to the point. "One thing is missing in this hotel—everyone noticed it last night and this morning. It's an ambience, a human touch. My wife can build structures, she can furnish them, but she cannot make them livable. She can't fill a thing with life. To put it more specifically: you belong to the most renowned line of the Quindts. More presence than activity. An appropriate salary. An appropriate apartment."

He paused and waited. When Maximiliane said nothing, he made a great production of cleaning his glasses and poured out more champagne. "I don't see a reaction. Aren't you tempted by the ancestral seat? More beautiful than ever, so they all tell me. I hung a few old etchings in the salon, maybe you noticed. And a copy of the Quindt family escutcheon, the lavish Renaissance version. For comparison. Please—if you think we ought to, we'll talk about a share in the profits. You're not entirely unfamiliar with the restaurant business. I could justify it to my manager and to my wife. After all, before the currency reform you managed to get a little food shop going. The pâté factory in Holstein is all due to you as well. You are experienced in the ways of the world, and you've seen a thing or two. In the more modest hotels, where I presume you've had to stay until now, there's generally more to be learned than in the good ones. The eastern estate also taught you from childhood how to treat the help. Hardly anyone nowadays has that skill. Presumably you also know languages, and that's even more important with the help than with the customers."

Maximiliane listened, let Herr Brandes have his say, and waited.

"Do I have to explain what assets you would bring to me?"

"I was not entirely clear about my assets," Maximiliane countered.

"I have an extremely competent manager. But the guests' well-being depends on someone not quite so competent. If I may be allowed a little indiscretion here—"

Maximiliane finished the sentence for him. "I'm not exactly young anymore."

"Quite right. Fifty, I'd guess."

"Almost fifty-five."

"So you don't have too many choices left. The situation in the hotel business is not so good as all that. What I can offer you here is a lifetime job, a permanent position."

"In that case I can't take it." Maximiliane gave her answer without hesitating.

"Try to figure out a woman!" Herr Brandes refilled their glasses. "Did I understand what you said? You'll do it on a temporary basis? To start with, until the hotel is launched? Fine. Every house has to be warmed by use, my wife always used to say. My first wife, I mean."

Maximiliane drained her glass in one gulp and said what she always said in similar situations. "Well, I could try."

"How could you agree to go to work for a man like Brandes! After all, we owned Mount Eyckel for centuries!" Edda was outraged.

Maximiliane assumed an expression suggesting that she might at any moment give the warning cry of "Cuckoo." Before she could do so, Edda clarified the situation. "Don't forget, I'm a von Quinten now. And Herr Brandes is nothing but a common brewer."

"Perhaps we live in an age of brewers." Maximiliane was unmoved. "The Quindts were on top long enough. Now let it be someone else's turn. Lenchen Priebe, for example, or you, or Herr Brandes. He's very efficient. The big beer industries are in trouble, but he keeps his business within proper bounds. He has a good eye for the appropriate scale. And when he talked about democratization, that's what he meant. I don't know whether you say what you mean and do what you say. I don't know to this day."

Any other mother would have let it go at that, but Maximiliane had an emotional reason to add to the practical ones she had just offered. "Herr Brandes had a son—an only son. He was a fighter pilot who was shot down. He was my first love—I was sixteen years old. I met him here, on Mount Eyckel, and I spent two days with him—and I slept through most of them."

In the afternoon there was a short, refreshing spring thunderstorm. After it ended, the Quin(d)ts took their departure, one after another. Maximiliane alone remained. The following day she took part in the hotel's official opening, and a week later she started her job, which was inadequately described to the labor office as "hostess." From now on she lived in a hotel, which satisfied her need for a home.

A short time later, Viktoria was hired as company psychologist by AKO Plastics.

26

If one or another of the hotel's guests learned that Maximiliane von Quindt came from Pomerania, he was likely to tell what he considered an apt anecdote, preferably to a large audience, perhaps the one that went, "When the King of Prussia made a state visit to Pomerania, going to even the remotest sections, the local paper reported, *'Hail, King, to you* is sounded far and near, and the most thunder echoes from the rear.' "

Maximiliane was not quick enough to prevent such pleasantries, so she only replied truthfully, "I've heard it all before."

"Is that right?" said the person in question, and the resulting laughter was at his expense rather than that of the Pomeranian baroness. In any case, it was once again possible to laugh at distant Pomerania.

Only twenty thousand Pomeranians attended the 1976 Pomerania Day in Kiel. The speakers said that they were searching for a larger homeland where Pomerania could be one province among many. By now Pomerania had become a utopia.

The protests, branded as revisionist by the Polish government, against the "Renunciation of the German Home Areas in the East" had ceased. The expellees had kept to their charter of August 1950, forswearing revenge and retribution, tirelessly participating in the rebuilding of Germany, and in all this losing sight of the

354

third article: the creation of a united Europe, its people free from fear and compulsion. But others had had the same experience. The love of home of the expellees from the East was cultivated in museums and institutions where the German cultural tradition was preserved and catalogued.

Now and then the letters Maximiliane received contained newspaper clippings with the notation "This will interest you." Articles on trips to the former German eastern territories—Silesia, Pomerania—generally subtitled "Nostalgia Tourism." Maximiliane put the clippings, unread, with her Pomeraniana. She never unpacked the box.

One day she received a travel diary in the form of a round-robin letter from Martha Riepe. Together with twenty other compatriots from Dramburg County, among them four from Poenichen, Martha had undertaken a bus tour to their old home. Lenchen Priebe had also gone along, no longer under the name of Priebe but as Frau Schnabel. A year before, she had married a widowed fellow Pomeranian from Stolp who was now in charge of the business side of her restaurant, by this time a favorite student hangout. As a wedding present Maximiliane had cancelled her five-percent share in the profits. Lenchen Schnabel, née Priebe, conceived von Jadow, sent a postcard from the Hotel Skanpol in Kolobrzeg, formerly Kolberg—"Greetings from our old home"—with a number of signatures Maximiliane managed with some effort to decipher.

She did not read Martha Riepe's report, placing it unopened in the box. Martha Riepe's opinions were of no use to her.

So that when, one fine day, she got on a chartered train with a tourist group to travel to Pomerania, she was much more poorly informed than all the other pilgrims. She went alone; she had invited none of her children to join her, nor had she told anyone about her plans. It was a night train; the tour guide would collect their tickets and passports, and the following morning they would wake up in Pomerania.

Their expectations turned out to be in error. They were not allowed to sleep through the two border crossings. The border was where passports had to be presented in person, according to the new, contemporary dispensation.

She stood in the corridor like most of the travelers. The train crossed the German-German frontier near Oebisfelde, and then it crossed the German-Polish border. Stettin, now Szczecin. The Oder, now Odra. Thirty years ago she had set out in the opposite direction, crossing the river with her children in a small boat and using one of Grandmother Sophia Charlotte's brooches to pay the ferryman. This time too it was night, but she was traveling as a tourist in a chartered train, her return-trip ticket in her purse. The train crawled along, slow enough for her slow memory. One of her fellow travelers opened a window. There was a smell of brown coal, a spray of sparks, reviving memories of war and overcrowded freight cars.

In the first light of dawn, she saw a pack of wild boars in a potato field; they were rooting up the seed potatoes, as they always had. Here the potatoes were not blossoming yet; they had already been in bloom in Brandenburg. The first avenues of birch trees, the first sandy paths and hooded crows: the East. The lupines along the embankment kept pace with the journey from West to East.

Then a turnip tract, the outlines of her childhood, a tract of rye, a tract of potatoes. A woman who looked as if she might have been Anna Riepe's sister mentioned that when she had pulled turnips, she could not see to the end of the field; ten hours' work a day. Twice a day the inspector came by, once a day the farmer's one-horse carriage stopped and moved on. When there was

356

a thunderstorm, they lay down flat on the ground; lightning jumped into the overhead lines and sparked along the wires.

Others had other memories.

Two storks stalked through a marshland poking for frogs. Tree-lined roads, an almost forgotten sight. What an enrichment of the landscape. But in the same breath Maximiliane envisioned her son Golo, whose car had shattered against just such a tree.

The morning did not break with sunshine; there was no scarlet dawn. Instead it began to rain. Pomeranian country rain. Curtains of water concealed the view. The train crawled slowly through the railroad stations. The place names had to be translated back into German: Svinvin meant Schivelbein. The woman who looked like Anna Riepe's sister recognized the house where she had lived. One glance showed her everything. The window frames needed painting, the garden fence should be repaired. Nothing but lettuce and runner beans in the garden, not a single flower. And just look at those curtains!

Worn out by the sleepless night and shivering with cold, the travelers to Pomerania stood in little clumps outside the Koszalin railroad station, waiting.

The man standing next to Maximiliane turned up his coat collar. Laughing, he said, "The Pomeranian climate is bearable only to pigs, the old nobility, and the pine moth."

Maximiliane did not return his laugh, but she looked at the man intently.

"Don't misunderstand me," he said. "You're clearly not a pine moth, so you must belong to the old nobility."

This time they both laughed, and Maximiliane confirmed his belief that she was not choosy about the weather.

She was not choosy about hotels either, such as the Skanpol in Kolobrzeg, A rating, a hotel that had played host to Lenchen Priebe along with all the other visitors to Pomerania. Maximiliane gave no thought to ratings; it did not matter to her where she slept. She had shared a sleeping bag with Ossian Schiff, she had lain under olives and oaks. She never expected elevators and running water to be working all the time. Herself in the hotel business for years, she overlooked the difficulties. And should the sink stop up so that the water could not run off, she did not view this as the triumph of one economic system over another. It was not her way to divide the world up according to ideologies and outlooks, according to above and below, right and left, East and West. She refused to recognize such distinctions. From time immemorial Pomerania had resisted technological progress with natural obstacles like thunder and lightning, snowstorms, and weeds: floods, burst pipes, broken telephone poles.

Her grandfather had repeatedly claimed that one of the Quindt ancestors was a municipal official in Poland. Besides, some drops of Polish blood ran in her veins. The sound of Polish was familiar to her: the words used by the farmhands on Poenichen, the words used by Anya, who had looked after the children during the war years and who had become her, Maximiliane's, confidante—a woman of her own age. Her grandfather, to whom she owed her most significant lessons in geography and history, used to say, *"Po morye*—it's a Wendish phrase meaning 'before the sea,' " *Po morye*— Pomerania. And now Pomorze. Consonant shifts.

Maximiliane laid aside the brochure, written in German, that had been handed them as they checked into the hotel. In this way she was spared reading in black and white that this had been Polish land from the beginning, Germanized only temporarily and returned to the mother country in 1945.

When she entered the dining room that night, she was shown to a table where the man with whom she had exchanged a few words in the morning was already seated. He too was traveling alone.

"Should I introduce myself?" he asked. "Or do you happen to know my voice already? Wilm Lüppers. Radio actor. Specialty, local dialects; subspecialty, Pomeranian; subsubspecialty, a Pomeranian farmer."

Maximiliane nodded in recognition and looked him over. "You do look like a Pomeranian farmer."

"I don't just look like one, I was supposed to be one. Like my father and his father before him. Now I'm playing the part of a lifetime. Our farm is situated between Treptow and Deep, two hundred and fifty acres. Grain fields and grazing land. Almost unchanged, except that everything's a little older—the trees, the buildings.

"This is my second trip. They're expecting me. I'm allowed to look around our farm, and they even let me take pictures. They entertain me. The farmer's wife kills a chicken for me. My mother was just the same when we had visitors. The woman's name is Maria, and my mother's name was Marie; she was called Mariechen. The man who's working the farm now is called Jurek Barbag. Thirty years ago, when he was a little boy, they resettled him from his home in East Poland to the place they'd expelled us from. Our 'destinies' bear a remarkable resemblance.

"Sometimes I fantasize that one of these days the Goths are going to claim the areas east of the Oder. After all, they lived here once, even before the Poles. You just have to turn the wheel of history back far enough. Imagine if at their departure the Pomeranians had had a leader like Alaric and had established the realm of the Pomeranians in the West. Let's say in the Rhineland."

"How could I imagine all of that?" Maximiliane said. "I'm having enough trouble coming to terms with what I can see."

"Tomorrow morning I'll make sure that Jurek Bar-bag puts his rubber boots in exactly the same spot next to the front door where my father used to put his boots. Would that convince you?"

Maximiliane nodded.

"In the kitchen, next to the stove, little Jurek rides my old hobbyhorse. Its mane is thinning, and it's lost its tail."

"If little Jurek rode the hobbyhorse last year, he won't be riding it this year," Maximiliane corrected him.

"You're right. Little Maria will be riding it now. I brought Jurek some Lego blocks. Western culture. Also chewing gum, of course. For his father I've got an electric drill so he can do his own repairs. The play we intend to perform for a couple of days is called *Détente*. We're not enemies—but we're not friends either. We're strangers to each other. But we have a lot of common concerns—for example, neither of us wants war. . . . If I'm allowed to interrupt myself, what kind are you?"

"A Quindt. From Poenichen, Dramburg County."

"Consequently guilty of the Germanization of the old homeland." Herr Lüppers shook his head in mock disapproval. "Ah, those Junkers from east of the Elbe! Prototypical capitalist exploiters!" He beckoned to the waiter and ordered two glasses of vodka. Vodka was one of his means of communication.

"You won't find much," he continued. "The larger the original property, the greater the destruction. Divine justice—the great equalizer. Insofar as the mansions are still standing, they're used to house kolkhoz directors instead of estate owners. Not much has changed in the overall arrangements. And where the manor houses were destroyed or razed, the stones have been shipped to Warsaw and Danzig to reconstruct castles and patrician homes."

When the vodka was placed before them—half-

360

filled tumblers—Herr Lüppers grasped his glass. *"Na zdrovie."*

"A double," Maximiliane noted, looking at the contents. She added, "Poenichen has always been my larder."

"Have you hired a driver to take you there yet? I need mine tomorrow. He speaks German. His grandmother was German. Taxi number seventeen. But you could have him the day after." Herr Lüppers rose. "I want to spend a couple of minutes with the Treptow contingent at the next table," he said. "I just want to listen a little, form my own opinion."

"By now I have two opinions about everything," Maximiliane replied.

That night Herr Lüppers succeeded in making Maximiliane laugh. Together they ate Polish dishes but Pomeranian ones as well. Borsht but also dumpling soup. He went with her to the landing stage by the lake when she wanted to watch the sunset. They passed wooden pavilions where cod and plaice were grilled and eaten. Maximiliane was vividly reminded of the smell of her fish-fry stand. But the owner shrugged his shoulders. He had run out. *"Nïe ma,"* he said.

"Nïe ma," Herr Lüppers repeated. The Polish answer to their German question. "No more. *Il n'y a plus.*"

"What brings you here a second time?" Maximiliane inquired as they walked on.

"Curiosity. I observe my fellow countrymen vacationing in places where they used to have to work. Property is the best medicine for homesickness. In the West they have a house, a garden, and a car. Why should they want to come back here? West German television is thinking of doing a special about a Pomeranian farmer who pays a visit to his old home. If the project goes through, I'll get a bigger or smaller part in it; how many actors can do Pomeranian dialect, after all? And this farmer meets a woman of the Pomeranian nobility who is afraid to see for herself what she has known all along. Should I go to Poenichen with you?"

"No. Perhaps I'll go tomorrow."

The following morning she walked along the row of waiting cars for hire and watched the German tourists get in to drive to Stolp, to Falkenberg, or to Treptow. She herself remained in Kolobrzeg to look for the old Kolberg. She looked for traces, for the boardinghouse where she and Viktor spent the first days of their marriage, and she could not find them. Instead, from the leveled wasteland where once the Old Town had stood rose the colossus of the Marienkirche. It was visible for miles, though that other time she had not noticed it at all. Her memories had been leveled along with the houses. At the place where the Persante River ran into the sea, she stood for a long while staring into the water—water that had flowed through Poenichen Lake. Did this have to suffice her: everything in a state of flux?

She walked along the beach, past sand castles, beach baskets, and blown-up dugouts, seaweed clinging to their rusted iron bars. She passed the "family baths" where she and Viktor had danced in the evenings and where people were dancing once again. At intervals she told herself, "That's all right," or she nodded in assent.

Encountering barriers and warning signs that denoted a military base and forbade further access, she came to a stop, stunned, and turned back. She sat among the dunes for a long time, but she did not look out to sea; instead she stared inland, more sky than ground before her eyes. She walked along the rush-covered banks of the Persante, where yellow iris bloomed among the reeds and multicolored dragonflies whirred. She heard and saw an oriole, whose call she had forgotten.

Each day she extended her reconnaissance, conquering the land from the coast on inward, finding her-

362

self on sandy paths leading to open birch woods, on swampy subsoil where marsh grasses grew in bushy clumps. She passed farms where dogs barked and herds of geese barred her way.

She nodded. Everything was right.

At night, in the dining room, when Herr Lüppers asked about her day's adventures, she said that she had seen two wagtails. With one voice, they remembered the local name for the bird. At the end of dinner Herr Lüppers raised a finger in admonition and said, "The larder. Don't forget your larder."

But the next morning Maximiliane did not set out for Poenichen either. It was Corpus Christi Day. She followed the stream of churchgoers and stood in the nave of the Marienkirche, in the forest of birch trunks that scaffolded the powerful vault. Swallows and sparrows flew in and out among the beams. The congregation knelt, made the sign of the cross, sang, and prayed. Maximiliane understood nothing but "Hosanna" and "Amen," but these exclamations also merited her nods. Pomerania had become a Christian country once more. Jet fighters rising from the nearby military airfield thundered across the sky, headed for the Baltic.

In the dining room Maximiliane heard people talking about "back home" in Leverkusen and Gelsenkirchen, no longer in Maldewin and Bütow and Rügenwalde. They mentioned buying souvenirs—vodka, amber necklaces—and swimming at the beach; you only get one vacation a year, after all. Now they'd had their chance to see it all again, and back home they'd have the photographs developed and send prints. They wrote down the measurements for curtains—unless they still remembered them from the old days.

"The West Germans are right to envy us our 'homeland,' " Herr Lüppers said. "First we travel to our homeland, then we go home. We have both. Next year

I'll bring my wife—and the kids too. They can pitch a
tent in the meadow. My wife and I will help with the
harvest and sleep in my parents' beds, under the same
picture: Jesus walking in the cornfield. Before setting
out in the mornings, I need two vodkas; when I get
back at night, I have to have four."

He gave Maximiliane a searching look. "Like a
horse," he said, emptying his glass. "You shy like a
horse."

It wouldn't have taken much for Maximiliane to
return to West Germany without having seen Poenichen
at all.

But on the last morning she brought herself to hire
a car. The driver could not speak a word of German,
but what she needed were a car and a driver, not someone to entertain her. She was not talkative at the best
of times. Presumably one day she would grow as taciturn as Old Quindt and his wife, Sophie Charlotte, had
been in their old age.

A Pomeranian summer day. A light blue sky with
large white clouds on the horizon. The land even vaster,
endless. Cornflowers were in bloom. Their familiar
scent penetrated the open car window. The scarecrows
were wearing out the farmers' Sunday clothes. Quiet
streets and roads, sometimes a bus or a truck. The farther south they drove, the more fields visible at a glance
became tracts too large to survey. The Pomeranian
sandy soil started here. No longer farming country but
kolkhoz economy. Narrow paths led from the road to
what had once been small manor houses and were
now—Herr Lüppen's report had been correct—the kolkhoz administrative offices. Maximiliane nodded.

The church spire of Dramburg came into view. The
driver pointed in the appropriate direction, but Maximiliane had already recognized it. She made the driver
understand that he was not to go by the road that by-

364

passed the town but was to drive through it. When they crossed the old marketplace, she glanced at the brick church and nodded. She made him drive around the square and recognized the inn where her grandfather had had Riepe meet him and drive him home after he had finished his business in the county seat. She also recognized the butcher shop in the main street whose overzealous owner had once displayed a blood sausage artfully shaped into a swastika. The name over the door now read Josef Labuda; the shop sold textiles. Everywhere there were unplastered new structures. The devastation was still visible. This was a small town ravaged by war, its wounds not yet healed.

The street signs bore the name Piła; the driver pronounced it "Piva" and added, "Schneidemühl," making Maximiliane nod. Then they came to Kalisz/Pomoski, and there, only five kilometers from Poenichen, Maximiliane lost her sense of direction. She was unable to show the driver the turn in the road. For the first time she said Peniczyn instead of Poenichen. The driver had to stop and ask twice before he was given the right directions. The information came from the lips of a soldier in a Soviet uniform. Turning to Maximiliane, the driver explained, *"Rosja."* She nodded once more. In the soldier's face she recognized an Asiatic.

What could Maximiliane have expected? The linden-lined avenue with the manor house standing at its apex, a picturesque ruin? The telephone poles? The greenhouse?

They had already passed the outbuildings, now clearly part of the kolkhoz. The village street had begun. They were driving along the estate grounds, which were no longer separated from the street by a wall but by an impenetrable thicket.

"Stoj," Maximiliane told the driver.

He parked the car in the shade of an ash tree that Maximiliane recognized. She tapped his shoulder, pointed to her watch, and indicated a span of two hours. He nodded, and Maximiliane got out, ready to hunt for Poenichen.

It was noon. Somewhere the frogs were croaking. There was no other sound. No human being far and wide.

Maximiliane pushed through the thicket of trees, shrubbery, and weeds. She could no longer make out the path of the former linden avenue. Nothing recognizable was left. Nor could she see any part of the former manor house. Destruction was total and irreversible. Thirty years had sufficed.

A horse was grazing in a clearing.

Maximiliane followed a trampled path, the kind children make, and came to a copper beech. She recognized the tree in whose shade she had played when she was little. Once, when they were ready to leave on their exodus, Golo had hidden among its branches. She walked on, and unexpectedly she was at the edge of the grounds proper, where the locusts had always bloomed and were blooming still.

She had not found the manor, not even its ruins. But she would not give up. She thought of Delphi and Olympia, where the ruins had been preserved for over two thousand years. Exploring a different beaten trail, she went back through the thicket.

In the end it was not her eyes but her foot that found the manor, discovered the broken pedestal of a column. Maximiliane stopped to look at the stone. No longer white but graying and moss-covered, it was nevertheless recognizable as part of the verandah. Not far away she found another piece of pillar, then a third: the only remnants of the large building. Obviously Poenichen too had served as a quarry, its valuable stones used to rebuild Warsaw or Danzig. What remained was a rise in the ground, covered by soil that

366

had long since been overgrown with greenery, maple and yew, linden and cedar, native and alien.

The quiet of noon was abruptly broken by the bark of a tank cannon. Further reports followed regularly at brief intervals.

In the dusky thicket, sitting on one of the pillar stumps, Maximiliane made her own belated ratification of the Polish agreements. She shed not a single tear. She ran both her hands through her hair and shook it; it was shot through with gray. She chewed her finger-nails as she looked around. The juniper was in bloom, as were the wild briar roses. Grass had grown over everything. "You've always got to keep the totality in view," Old Quindt had said long ago.

Maximiliane rose and walked back slowly, wandering down the village street. Weeds grew between the paving stones as they had of old, the sandy strip beside the road was as rutted by wagon wheels as it had always been. The row of one-story houses of the Beskes, the Klukas, the Schmaltzes, just as before.

Sitting on benches next to the front doors, as before, old dark women sat and watched little children. The bigger ones were playing where she herself had played with Klaus Klukas, Walter Beske, and Lenchen Priebe, at the edge of the village common in the hazel bushes, where Polish ducks and Pomeranian geese peacefully nattered side by side and stuck their beaks into the mud.

An old woman was sitting outside the house where Schmaltz the midwife used to sit. Maximiliane walked up to her and, without speaking, pointed to the empty place beside her. The woman nodded, moving a little to one side and wiping the bench with her skirt. Maximiliane smiled at her, sat down, and said, *"Dobre dzien"* and *"Proshe."* She counted the children, who were moving closer out of curiosity—she could count up to three in Polish. Round-headed, blond children, no different from the old days. She pointed to herself and held up the five fingers of her right hand, then turned down one of them. The old woman nodded; she understood—five children, but one of them was dead.

Maximiliane took from her purse the things she had brought with her—coffee and chewing gum, crayons and chocolate. She was used to taking gifts to the farm-hands' cottages.

"Janusz?" she asked, pointing to the children. "Urek? Josef? Antek?" She pulled one of the children—two-year-old Zosia—on her lap and played with her the game Anya used to play with Golo and Edda on Poen-ichen. She even remembered the words to the song about the sleeping bear who must not be woken. She sang, *"Jak sie zbudzi, to nas zje"*—"When he wakes, he'll eat you up."

The children did not know the game, nor were they accustomed to being sung to. But Zosia seemed to enjoy both. Maximiliane had to sing the song twice. She laughed at the child until the little girl laughed back; she conquered a Polish child's heart. A bloodless con-quest had to begin somewhere. And a fourth of the blood in her veins was Polish.

The old woman got up, gesturing to Maximiliane to wait, and went into the cottage. She returned with a bottle and a glass. *"Samachorka,"* she said, and *"Dobre,"* pointing to herself and then to the bottle. It was home brew. She poured the glass three-quarters full, as was the custom in Poland. Maximiliane said, *"Na zdrowie"* and drank—swallowing it all.

"Palac?" the old woman asked, pointing in the di-rection where the estate had been. Maximiliane nodded. With her open palm the old woman wiped away every-thing that was already invisible and said, *"Nïe ma."* When she had come here—Maximiliane could under-stand this much—everything was already destroyed. The woman pointed to the distance, toward the east. Maximiliane nodded. The she said good-bye, *"Do vid-*

368

zenia," but she knew that in spite of the words, which meant "Until we meet again," she would never return. She had not embraced a tree.

She went along the village street until a barrier and a sign barred her way. The military area started here. She turned into a field path. On one side a tract of potatoes, on the other a wide, melancholy field of maize. Blooming camomile, corncockle, and wild poppies. The wind ruffled the stalks. Maximiliane stopped and was reminded of the way Rector Kressmann, when teaching physics, had explained the wave theory by using the example of a grainfield bowing in the wind. The larks, used to firing practice from the tank artillery, hung suspended in air, trilling.

As she stood there, Maximiliane recalled a line from a song learned by heart at age fifteen and preserved for this moment by her independent memory. "You shall remain, our land, even as we perish"—one of the prophetic songs of the Nazi movement, now come true. In her way she felt what the philosopher in his way meant when he had written about the gentle power of field paths, which would outlast the gigantic force of the atomic age.

Baron Joachim von Quindt, fifty years old at the time, speaking on the occasion of his only granddaughter's christening, had said, "The main thing is to be Pomeranian, and that's always proved to be the stronger. In the long run the Goths, the Wends, and the Swedes, all of whom settled here at one time or another, turned into good Pomeranians."

Had he been right in trusting the shaping power of the Pomeranian earth? At her wedding he had said, literally, "The soil couldn't care less who walks on it. The main thing is that it's cultivated properly." The opinions of an independent liberal thinker who never had to translate his views into action and who preferred not to leave Poenichen alive, who in talking to his coachman and friend Riepe voiced as early as 1918 the conviction that the Quindts would reach the end of the line one of these days, as would the German Empire and Prussia.

It was only from a distance that Maximiliane saw Poenichen Forest, which Old Quindt had had restocked shortly after the First World War—a "forest of peace," as he had called it—and next to it Poenichen Heath. The heath later became a troop-training area for the German army, used for artillery practice; now it was an unsurveyable military terrain used by the fighting forces of the Warsaw Pact, where Soviet and Polish tanks did their firing as did tanks on heaths in the German Democratic Republic. Simply as an exercise, just to keep in practice, to maintain the military stalemate between East and West. . . .

A shiver ran down Maximiliane's spine; she shuddered in the bright, warm summer day.

The road to Poenichen Lake was barred, as was the way to Innichen Mountain, where, among erratic rocks and old oaks, lay the graves of her ancestors. Slowly she walked back; sentimental ditties were in the air, but she was not singing. If she had been asked about her impressions at this moment, she might have said that she felt "ordinary." She had felt equally undefined thirty years ago during their flight, her compassion for the human race not to be expressed in words.

At the gate leading to Peniczyn Kolkhoz, she stopped and looked around. The old stables and barns, maintained for centuries, had been kept. Three fodder silos had been added, as well as a two-story residence for the workers. The smell of swill tea wafted over from the compost heap.

A man who had been watching her now approached. He looked like all inspectors look. In broken German he asked, "What want?"

370

Maximiliane shook her head. *"Nïe."* She did not want anything.

By means of gestures and a few words, she learned from him that Peniczyn Kolkhoz had been run for a long time by a manager who was not the man to whom Otto Riepe, acting on his master's instructions, had handed the drainage plans. Since then, the job had changed hands three times. The present manager owed the visitor nothing; he had never heard the name Quindt.

No one who hated her; no one who loved her. When she got back home, people would ask her whether she had found out about the buried silver, and she would have to tell them truthfully that she had not given a thought to the Quindts' fixed assets.

She recalled her own defiant reply to Rector Kressmann at the Pomerania Day in Kassel, when he had spoken of all the "uprooted people." It proved its truth to her now. People did not have roots like trees. Everything must be transplanted in order to flourish. The same biological laws applied to human beings: the strong, young growths flourished; the sickly, old ones wasted away. "Dying out" was what her East Prussian uncle Klaus had called it on the occasion of consecrating the Mount Eyckel Hotel.

When she returned, she would transform her temporary employment into a permanent job.

Two hours for Peniczyn; then Maximiliane returned to the car.

The driver stopped once more at the town marker. In his experience all these Germans wanted to cast a last look at their old home and snap one last photograph. But Maximiliane shook her head. She had no desire to look back.

At her request they took a different route, past the detour leading to the former Perchen estate of the von

Kalcks. They drove through the Pomeranian flatlands along roads where the treetops touched overhead; at both sides of the roads, on the far side of the ditches, young maples and linden trees grew in expectation of future road widening. Maximiliane, catching sight of them, nodded.

Near one of the lakes—they were already beyond Tempelburg—she asked the driver to make one last stop. She got out, walked to the edge, and took off her shoes. Then she waded some distance through the shallow, sun-warmed water, startling a heron. Still carrying her shoes, she returned to the car.

"*Dobre*," she said. All is well.

By the time they arrived in Kolberg, night was beginning to fall. The car stopped outside the Hotel Skanpol. The driver, so taciturn up to now, suddenly grew chatty, pointed his finger at the odometer, and pointed next to his watch. He wrote the numeral 100 on a scrap of paper: to be paid in German marks. He practiced practical socialism. If the object of his journey had been a village hut, he would have charged only half as much. But someone who had once lived in a *palac* had the means to pay double. Maximiliane, aware of his calculations, gave him a glancing look, nodded in agreement, and even smiled as she handed him the money.

Herr Lüppers was waiting in the lounge for her return. He asked, "How were things in the larder?"

"It's empty," Maximiliane answered, pushing past him on the way to the elevator. She did not come down to dinner but lay on her bed and slept, and even the jet fighters could not wake her.

The following morning she stood on the railroad platform in Kaszalin among the other tourists on their way home—all the former refugees and expellees who had built new homes in the West.

Now she too would be able to settle down.